CW00524273

www.zackargyle.com

Cover illustration by Ömer Burak Önal

Cover design by Zack Argyle

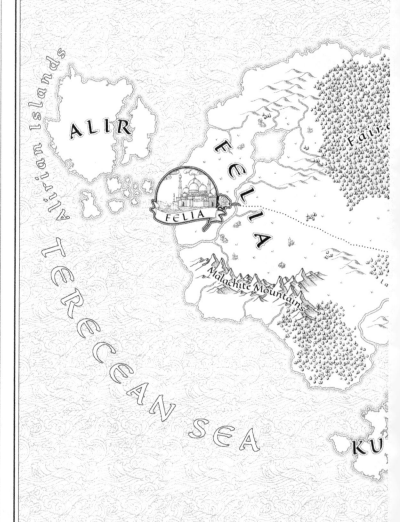

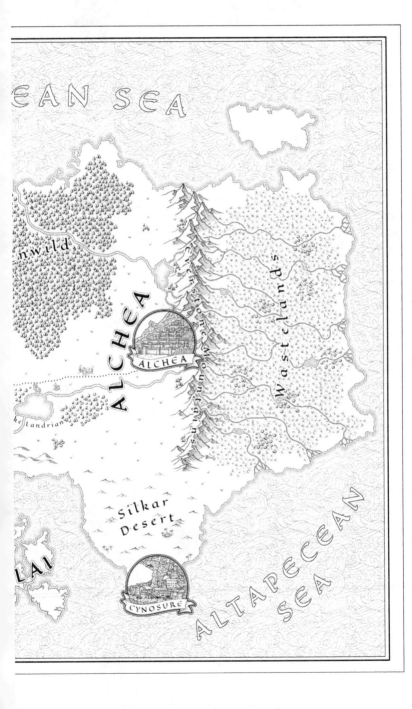

STONES OF LIGHT

ZACK ARGYLE

THE STORY UNTIL NOW

While expecting their first child, Chrys Valerian and his wife, Iriel, attended the Rite of Revelation for their friends Luther and Emory. When the child is revealed to be an achromat (brown eyes), he is blinded and taken to be a priest of the Order of Alchaeus. Outside the Temple, Iriel almost loses their child but is saved by a stranger who also gives Chrys a thread-dead obsidian dagger.

Chrys goes on to investigate the Bloodthieves, where he rescues a young girl named Laurel, who runs away back to her home in the Fairenwild. When she returns to Zedalum, she loses her position as a Messenger, and also loses her best friend, a chromawolf named Asher, as he returns to his pack in the wild.

Eventually, Chrys discovers the truth of the Blood-thieves, that they are headed by an Amber threadweaver named Alabella, and fellow high general, Jurius, is working for her. Chrys' son, Aydin, is born and they take him in for his own Rite of Revelation, where they learn that, not only is he an Amber threadweaver, but Father Xalan is a Zeda spy. They run away to the Fairenwild where Chrys, Iriel, and

Aydin narrowly escape Jurius with the help of a pack of hungry chromawolves and Laurel, while Father Xalan is captured.

Laurel brings Chrys and his family to Zedalum, where they meet the Elders and learn about Amber threadweavers and the coreseal. Shortly after, Chrys' mother, Willow, arrives and shares the truth: Chrys was born in Zedalum. They soon realize that Father Xalan is really Pandan, Willow's brother and Chrys' uncle. They devise a plan to rescue him. Laurel and Willow recruit Chrys' old crew (Luther, Laz, and Reina) to break out Pandan from Endin Keep's prison.

At the same time, far to the south in Cynosure, Alverax Blightwood wakes up in a pit of bones. He soon discovers that he is an Obsidian threadweaver and decides to use his new power to get revenge on Jelium (an Amber threadweaver) for killing his father. The plan backfires and he narrowly escapes. He decides to leave Cynosure and head north. The leader of the caravan betrays him and hands him over to Alabella, who takes him into the Bloodthieves.

While Laurel, Willow, and the crew try to break out Pandan, they come face to face with High General Henna. She chases them through the keep, and Willow leads the group to Jurius' room. When he emerges, a fight ensues, and Jurius kills Pandan. Then Laurel kills Jurius, and in his final moments, he turns the dagger around and stabs Laurel in the heart.

Alverax joins Alabella and a small army of Bloodthieves into the Fairenwild, where they set fire to the forest. The people of Zedalum abandon their treetop homes, dropping down onto the Wonderstone so they can flee. The Bloodthieves attack the unarmed Zeda people, and Alverax watches in horror.

When Chrys brings down Iriel and Aydin, the child's Amber powers lash out and bind Iriel and the baby to the Wonderstone, crushing them. Chrys, in an attempt to save them, finally gives into the Apogee and shows amazing powers as he slaughters dozens. He seeks out Alabella but is bound by Amber threads while she flees.

Alverax rushes forward when he sees a woman and child dying and uses all of his power to *break* the threads of the wonderstone. The earth shakes.

In the end, Laurel is still alive, but she has lost her ability to threadweave and is in the care of Alabella. Alverax is alive, heading west toward Felia with the Zeda people. And Chrys—still controlled by the Apogee—abandons his family and heads east.

The epilogue concludes with an odd woman exiting a holy cave in the Wastelands, looking for her brother.

CHAPTER 1

I T WAS a curious feeling to be trapped in his own mind. Helpless. Powerless. Looking on as each step rebelled against him. Life had become a dream, and he feared he would never awaken.

Chrys Valerian, a Sapphire threadweaver and former high general, had become a slave in his own mind. The Apogee was in control.

A week had passed since the coreseal had shattered. The accompanying quakes had wreaked havoc across Alchea, causing unstable buildings to collapse, stone roads to crack, and avalanches from the mountains to come crashing down with fury. The Apogee seemed to care about none of it. Nor did he care if he was seen. He wanted only to reach his destination. As they ascended the Everstone mountains, Chrys thought it may have something to do with the thread-dead obsidian that Henna had found.

"Mmmm."

The Apogee reached into his pocket and pulled out a pocket watch. Chrys groaned inside at the reminder of his son who had received the gift from Great Lord Malachus. It was the only physical reminder he had left of his family, and the Apogee, annoyed at its mere existence, tossed it on the ground with disregard. It landed along the well-worn mountain trail, and the last Chrys saw of it was a shimmer in the corner of his eye.

He felt his mind slacken into deep despair. He'd lost so much—his wife most of all. The memory of his own eyes meeting hers in the Fairenwild—so pleading, so hopeful— just before he turned and walked away. She would never forgive him. He was the husband that deserted his wife. The father that abandoned his son. The friend that forsook. The man that slaughtered. Even if he could regain control, there was no returning to how life was before.

His boots trudged through a tangle of weeds as they made their way through a familiar mountain pass. The last time he'd walked this ground was when he'd returned from a massacre. It felt fitting. The first time he'd let the dark part of himself take control was just beyond the peaks of these mountains, and now he returned with the darkness once again in control.

The Apogee continued onward, following a dim set of boot prints toward Ripshire Valley, the site of the slaughter. Beyond that was the unknown. The Wastelands. Home to the small, inhuman people that fought savagely to defend their mountain border.

He wondered where Iriel might be. If their son, Aydin, was safe. He'd left them in the Fairenwild, in the midst of flames and bloodshed, with nowhere to go. He would never forgive himself for that. What is a man if he cannot protect those he loves?

The sun had begun its descent but, at such an altitude, it seemed to drag on for an eternity. Fresh footprints appeared. They passed a soiled patch of dirt. Chrys had a guess at who they may find ahead. For their sake, he hoped that he was wrong, that it was a lone hiker. Or even a small group of climbers. However unlikely, he hoped, because he knew the grim alternative.

"Mmmm," the Apogee whispered as he inspected the footprints.

His feet trampled forward, following tracks of pressed grass until they rounded a small peak. Alchean soldiers huddled around a fire in the entrance of a large cave. The same cave from which the obsidian had come. High General Henna's soldiers were still exploring its deep tunnels.

One of the soldiers looked over and saw them. There did not seem to be any official lookout on duty, just those nearest the fire. "Hello!" he shouted through the wind.

Chrys felt his hand raise into the air, a spurious white flag. The Apogee smiled in return as they approached the camp. Half of the soldiers were asleep in the cave, safe from the wind and latent rain, tucked beneath piles of wool blankets. Those around the fire stayed seated, unafraid of the stranger approaching. Blankets pulled tight around their shoulders as they shared sips from a warm broth.

"Finally. We've been waiting to hear from the general for a week."

The soldiers all stared at him as he drew near. One gestured next to himself on the log they were using as a bench. "The wind is freezing out there. Come on in."

The Apogee cocked his head to the side. "I think I will."

He opened himself to threadlight, watching as his veins lit a bright, cerulean blue and warmth flooded through him. Hundreds of thin lines of incandescent light illuminated before him, connecting him to the world. His veins, like rivers of glacial water, flowed blue beneath his wind-bitten skin. By the time the soldiers noticed, it was too late.

3

Chrys felt something stir within him, a cold storm seething in his chest. Then, it moved, reaching out, searching, grasping, inviting, until, finally, it delved into the depths of the closest guard's very soul. Energy flowed through the connection, and the guard brought his own blade to his chest. That same man looked down in shock as he slid the sword between his own ribs.

The Apogee moved forward with a cold intensity. He grabbed the soldier's blade off the ground and dragged it across the dirt as he entered the cave. Those awake, stumbled back. Those asleep awoke to death.

Chrys felt anger swelling within the Apogee as he moved through the camp, and in that anger, he felt the barrier that bound him weaken.

Please, they are innocent, Chrys begged.

The Apogee snarled. *There can be no mercy.*

The remaining soldiers stared at the Apogee from within the cave, knowing well that there was little they could do against a threadweaver. Little did they know, the Apogee was much more than that now.

One brave soldier stepped forward. The others stood cautiously behind him. "General Valerian. You don't have to do this. I was there during the War. I saw the aftermath, and I saw the regret in your eyes. Please, we've done nothing."

Chrys recognized the man. Henry, perhaps? He, along with many others, had descended the mountain to observe the massacre in Ripshire Valley. He knew what the Apogee was capable of.

In that still moment between deaths, Chrys threw all of his will against the barrier in his mind. His hope and anger joined together in a massive wave, crashing against the wall, trying to regain control.

But the wall held firm, and the Apogee clenched his teeth. "You will pay for that."

His mind reached out to Henry; a bridge formed between them. Then, something flowed from Chrys *into* the soldier. Henry screamed, clutching his skull with both hands as he fell to his knees. Somewhere, even deeper in the recesses of his own mind, Chrys felt something odd, the vibration of a plucked string.

"Kill yourself," the Apogee demanded.

Henry brought a blade to his neck and pulled.

Curses erupted throughout the line of soldiers as his body fell to the dirt.

"I need two of you," the Apogee said. He pointed to the only female soldier, a sharp-faced woman with shoulder-length dark hair pulled back in a tail. "You will be one. Come here. Of the rest of you, I will take the strongest. Choose amongst yourselves, or I will choose for you."

He tossed the sword forward at their feet and, for a moment, the soldiers stood in silence, staring.

Chrys needed to help. With every ounce of his bound soul, he wanted to protect them. To save them from himself. From the dark part of his soul that had taken control.

The dark-haired woman ran forward just as a man with red hair turned to his neighbor and rammed a knife through his gut. The others gasped in shock, not knowing what they should do. The same red-haired man attacked another, and, with surprising speed, the soldiers turned on each other. One man tried to grab the sword off the ground but was brought down with a savage strike to his spine. Teeth bit into necks. Fingers jammed into eyes. Blades ripped through cartilage.

Not all fought—some tried to hold onto their honor—but it ended the same, nonetheless.

Chrys felt his hope flutter away.

When the brawl ended, dead men lay bleeding out on the rocky floor. The red-haired man was the only soldier left standing, despite a cut down his cheek that would surely scar. His build and hair reminded Chrys of Laz but, where Laz was carefree and naive, this man had the look of a feral beast that found himself just where he'd always wanted to be.

"You're not Chrys, are you?"

"Do not use that name," the Apogee growled. He eyed the woman. "We will come to know each other quite intimately. But first, tell me your names."

"I'm Velan." The red-haired man brought a fist to his chest.

The woman held back tears, but Chrys could see the fear in her eyes. Still, bravely, she replied, "Autelle."

"Good. You may call me Relek. You cannot yet understand, but you have been chosen. You will be gods among men." He gestured to the corpses littering the cave. "Burn the bodies. We do not want an army coming over the pass before we are ready for them."

Velan nodded and got to work.

Autelle joined in with tears in her eyes. Together, they stacked the bodies into a pyre, stuffed it with moss and mushrooms, and let it burn.

"Mmmm," the Apogee said, watching. "Let us go. She will be waiting."

CHAPTER 2

LAUREL'S DREAM of living in the grounder city was not what she'd imagined. All of the wonder and splendor lay overshadowed by a new reality: she was thread-dead. She could still feel the knife piercing her skin, splitting between her ribs and driving deep into her heart. Pain. Surprise. Shock. Pressure building, surging, crescendoing until something broke inside of her. Shattered glass.

She should have been happy that she was alive, but it hardly felt like living. The world had lost its color. The wind had ceased to blow. She was a spec of sand on a gray beach waiting for the waters to rise.

And yet, in the aftermath of the storm that broke her, there was still one sliver of hope.

Alabella.

The Amber-eyed woman who led the Bloodthieves claimed that she could make Laurel a threadweaver again. Laurel knew there had to be a catch—some stipulation within the generosity—but did it matter? Could the cost possibly outweigh the reward?

She wasn't stupid; she knew who she was dealing with.

These were the same people that had kidnapped her and tried to have Chrys murdered—the same people that Jurius had worked for. To their defense, they hadn't harmed her, and Chrys' baby *was* strange. If there was anyone that understood what it meant to have Amber eyes, it was Alabella.

The truth was that as soon as she had her threadweaving back, she'd head straight for Zedalum. Her grandfather was probably fighting the elders to let him leave the Fairenwild to search for her. Her biggest hope was that Chrys' mother, Willow, had explained everything to them. They would have to understand.

She missed the Fairenwild, the scents, the hypnotic flight of the skyflies overhead, and Asher. She wanted nothing more than to tackle him and squeeze him with all her might. But those all could wait; they weren't going anywhere. When she was fixed, Zedalum and Asher and her family would all be waiting there for her.

Carefully, Laurel lifted herself from the bed. She moved to the large mirror beside the armoire. In its reflection, she inspected the stitches over her left breast. The skin seemed to be healing well but, as she looked up, the heart beneath the wound broke yet again. Staring back at her was the ghost of who she was. Her cheeks seemed more gaunt, her frame more thin, and those eyes. Still the sight of them was enough to drive her mind to madness. So insignificant. So colorless.

In death, she'd lost the blue radiance of a Sapphire. If being thread-dead wasn't punishment enough, achromatic eyes were the final falling autumn leaf.

She glanced to the door; no one was there. No one ever was, but it didn't stop her from checking. Her shaky hand reached out and opened the chest beside her bed. It was temporary—at least that's what she told herself, as she pulled out a small vial of red liquid. Alabella had called it a *transfuser*. Where she came from—a city called Cynosure—it was common for threadweavers to sell their blood. What the people of Alchea called a Bloodthief, the people of Cynosure called an apothecary.

She downed the vial in a single drink. Luke-warm iron slid down her throat, and the magic diffused into her blood-stream. Her veins simmered with Emerald threadlight. She'd have preferred Sapphire, but she didn't have the luxury of being selective.

The transfusers barely tempered the withdrawal and, though she was only supposed to take one with each meal, she found herself sneaking them more and more. What did they expect? She was stuck in a room all day, alone, with nothing but the inescapable craving of threadlight to accompany her. After a week, the part that disgusted her was not the fact that she was doing it, but that she'd grown fond of the taste.

She looked down at the chest and stared at the vials. The threadlight that infused the blood kept it from spoiling, so the blood in front of her would be good as long as it was available. But at the pace she was using it up, she worried it wouldn't last as long as it was supposed to.

The morning sun gleamed through her window, reflecting rays of glaring light through the glass vial. It was too cold outside to keep the window open, and too cold inside to keep the drapes closed. Regardless, the sun's posi-tion told her it was time for her physical therapy.

Laurel left her room, taking slow, careful steps down the hall until she arrived at a large room. A woman greeted her, thick with long brown hair and hands the size of dinner plates. "Laurel," she said with an energetic smile.

"Gelda," Laurel mumbled.

She hated therapy, but the tightness in her chest had already begun to fade, despite the stitches holding strong. As she approached the chair to sit, she recalled being chastised for wanting to lay down. Gelda claimed that being in a constant upright position would stimulate blood flow and aid in her recovery. So not only was she sleeping in a cold, stone building, but she was forced to sleep upright.

Gelda unlaced Laurel's shirt and inspected the wound. "Stitches look well. Nothing's torn. Thank you for being careful, I know it's hard with the limited mobility."

The next part was Laurel's least favorite; she'd even tried to convince them to let her do it herself. Gelda's wide hands compressed across Laurel's breast, firm and slow. She then rotated her hands and pushed down again. And again. And again. Each compression was agonizing, but necessary, in order to "promote clearing of internal secretions". She could have lived her whole life without learning the word "secretion".

"Do you have any plans for the day?" Gelda asked.

Laurel winced as Gelda's hands pressed against her chest. "It's not like I'm allowed to go anywhere."

"Oh, don't be so dramatic," the large woman said. "You'll be out and about in no time. You're recovering incredibly well. For an achromat that is."

Thanks for the reminder.

Laurel finished the rest of her physical therapy in silence. They took a walk, climbed some stairs, and did breathing exercises that included an absurd task that Gelda called "guided huffing". Breathe in for three. Huff once. Huff twice. Huff a third time. Carefully, of course. Huffing too hard could tear a stitch.

Gale take her and her stupid exercises.

Laurel turned to the doorway and left, making her way back through the hallways to her room. As she approached, she found a strange looking woman waiting for her. The woman's two-toned hair draped over each of her shoulders, one half a dark maroon, and the other a pitch black. The glasses she wore must have been custom made, because the oversized lenses curved along the edges of her brows. Laurel had never seen the style and wondered if the woman had come from somewhere else entirely.

The woman waved and smiled with bright silver teeth on her upper canines.

With the smallest sliver of hope, Laurel looked over her shoulder. There was no one there. She looked back at the strange woman and smiled cautiously in return.

The woman approached with remarkable swiftness. "Achromic eyes," the woman said with a clear voice while staring at Laurel. "Disproves my theory of a secondary mineral source."

Laurel raised an eyebrow and took a step back.

"My apologies. I only just arrived and had the most curious conversation with Lady Alabella concerning your recent traumatic event. She believes we could be of use to one another." She gestured to Laurel's door. "May we sit?"

The last thing Laurel wanted right now was to talk to a stranger. Her chest still hurt from Gelda's compressions, and her feet were so cold on the stone floor that all she wanted was to crawl into her bed. Unfortunately, if Alabella sent her, Laurel had no choice. She needed to play along if she was going to get what she wanted.

"Any friend of Alabella is a friend of mine," Laurel said before stepping forward and opening the door. They entered the room, and the woman took a seat in a chair in the corner. Laurel sat on her bed. "So, who are you?"

The woman laughed. "Forthright, I can appreciate that. My name is Sarla. Sarla Maltess. I'm a scientist, a physicist, an engineer, and most recently a surgeon. I am whatever is needed for the question at hand, and you are an exceptionally unusual question."

"There's nothing exceptional about me anymore." Laurel laid back against the wall.

"You were a threadweaver, no?"

"I *was*," Laurel replied.

"According to the debrief, you *were* a threadweaver. Your chest was punctured by a blade which, theoretically, shattered your theolith. The Alirian general carried you to the hospital where you were stabilized by the attending physician, only possible due to the high volume of threadlight in your veins, and, when you awoke, your novel achromacy manifested. Lady Alabella's people heard your story and she had you extracted. Fortunate for you, her transfusers have tempered the withdrawals, but your cardiovascular system maintains dependency on threadlight.

"How much has Lady Alabella explained to you about the process of ventricular mineral grafting?"

What? From deep in her chest, Laurel felt her heartbeat quicken. The stitches over her scars seemed to stretch in harmony with each pulse. She wanted to crawl into her bed and throw the sheets over her head. *Ventricular mineral grafting*? She didn't understand half of what the woman said, which terrified her.

"I'd like to speak candidly with you. The surgery we are going to attempt has resulted in the death of most who have received it. We recently had our first successful procedure, but we've been unable to reproduce the results. I have a theory that some human systems see threadlight as a virus

12

and reject it. Your body has accepted its presence once before, and I believe it will again."

Light from the rising sun reflected off of the lock from her bedside chest. She raised a hand to cover her eyes.

Sarla smiled a curious smile. "It will be a risk, of course. Fortunately, there is time for you to decide. The surgery will depend both on your own recovery and either awaiting shipment of our last theolith or recovering more from the Fairenwild."

Laurel perked up. "What about the Fairenwild?"

"Infused gemstones can only be found below the surface," Sarla said, as if Laurel should understand. "Lady Alabella believes there is a cache in the Fairenwild."

"What? Why would she think that?"

"She has some old texts that speak of a path to the core in the center of the forest. We are hoping that there will be a surplus found therein."

Laurel's mind raced. The elders were right. A path to the core. The coreseal. The wonderstone. What did it mean? The elders believed that it guarded the world from evil. Alabella believed it led to what...a cave? The last thing she wanted was for the Bloodthieves to find her home. Alabella had already admitted that she knew about the Zeda people. But if the Zeda guards spotted them, who knew what they would do.

"I want to come," Laurel said.

"Where?" Sarla startled. "The Fairenwild? I'm not certain that you're well enough for that type of journey at the present."

"When are you going?" Laurel asked. "I'll be ready."

"We're going tomorrow."

Gale take me.

"I can handle it. Anyway," Laurel said, grasping for an

excuse, "I can guide you there safely. I know the path. I can spot hugweed and treelurks, and even help if the chroma-wolves attack."

Sarla frowned. "I'll talk to Alabella. It could be nice to have a native guiding us."

"How many are going?"

"Tomorrow is no more than an exploration," Sarla explained. Her eyes seemed to be searching Laurel's. "We'll be no more than ten. If we find infused gemstones, we will return with a larger party for extraction."

Ten people. If they were careful, it was possible. And if they were lucky, Alder would be sleeping on guard duty. She was curious how they planned to open the coreseal and, "What exactly *is* an *infused gemstone*?"

Sarla opened her mouth to speak, then stopped. She clenched her jaw and looked up for a moment before leaning forward. "Threadweaving is not a blessing from the Heralds like most believe, nor the Lightfather, nor which-ever deity it is you worship. The truth is more easily explained. Every threadweaver is born with a small sliver of gemstone in their heart called a *theolith*—a mutation of sorts. This gemstone is the source of threadlight that runs through a threadweaver's circulatory system."

Laurel wanted to laugh at the absurdity, but the doctor seemed so serious. "Wait, so you're saying I have a rock in my heart?"

"Had," Sarla said flatly. "The blade shattered your theolith. It then poured its threadlight through you, which saved your life but removed the source. Thus, you are now achromic. Once we've obtained more of these theoliths, or gemstones infused with threadlight, we will insert a small shard into your left ventricle to serve as your new theolith."

Laurel's mind was a whirlwind, racing this way and that,

crashing through memories and tearing apart all that she knew to be true. Was being a threadweaver nothing more than a pebble in your chest? The Zeda people taught that it was a sign of being "chosen" by the Father of All, and that the reason so many Zeda people were threadweavers was because they were a chosen people. Perhaps they were both true?

More importantly, it explained how they planned to fix her. It wasn't safe. It wasn't sure. It was an assumption that her past would allow her to live where others had died. But it was the only trail ahead; there was no other route to take if she wanted to undo what had been done. She couldn't live the rest of her life without threadlight.

"Okay," Laurel began. "Tell me what I need to do."

"Continue your physical therapy. We must wait for your heart to recover. Enough to survive the surgery, but not so long that threadlight becomes viewed as a foreign substance. On that note, it is important that you continue drinking the transfusers. We need your body to think nothing has changed, to decrease the chance of rejection."

Sarla adjusted her glasses and nodded as she stepped out of the room, leaving Laurel once again in silence.

Laurel sat back against the wall. She had a lot to think about, but, more than anything, she needed to prepare. Tomorrow, she was headed to the Fairenwild.

CHAPTER 3

HERALDS SAVE ME.

Empress Chailani of Felia sat atop a rose-colored throne, flanked by an immaculate collection of white drapes that flowed down from the ceiling like rays of threadlight. White roses filled the outskirts of the room, budding along the walkway, up the carpeted stairway, and amassing beneath each of the colossal throne-room windows. The ceiling towered overhead, each step—though muffled on the velvet floor—a choral prelude to their presence.

Alverax walked behind the Zeda Elders, beside the woman he'd saved, Iriel Valerian. His hands shook as he passed a dozen threadweaver guards that stared at him with their chromatic eyes. He tried not to return the gaze, but their dark skin instilled in him an immediate sense of kinship. Of the dozens of Felians in the throne room, only one was not dark skinned, an Alirian man with hair like white marble. Being in Felia felt good, and not just because he'd spent the last weeks trudging through the countryside and smelling like a taractus turd.

As they reached the bottom of the stairs leading to the

throne, the Empress rose to her feet. Her hair danced as thick dreads fell gracefully past her cheek. The gold in her crown matched the gold of her dress and the clasps adorning her hair harmonized flawlessly. White sleeves faded to the same shimmering gold along the curves of her waist. Against her umber skin, each golden accent shone like the sun. And her eyes, blue as the sea itself, froze the room with the simplest gaze.

Two others stood beside her.

Before he realized it, Alverax found himself standing while the rest of his retinue knelt before the Empress. He quickly corrected his mistake, cursing under his breath.

A man with a sultry voice raised his hands and spoke. "Introducing the Lady of Light, the Sun Queen, Empress Chailani Vayse. And with her, the Mistress of Mercy, her sister, the Sun Daughter."

"Please, stand," the Empress commanded. "It is not every day that a people lost to myth come promenading into my city."

Elder Rosemary smiled. "Privacy is a boon only in its broadest application. Empress Chailani, you honor us with your invitation."

The Empress furrowed her brows. "In the City of Sun, we value transparency, so let me be clear. I do not trust you, nor your people. Some believe you to be counterfeits, a guise for mass immigration. Perhaps a constituent of the Bloodthieves to infest our streets. Others do not believe the Bloodthieves would be so forthright. That you are who you claim to be. If the latter are correct, then we will have much to discuss, and perhaps reparations to be made. If they are wrong, then the Heralds will greet every one of your people by the end of the week."

Alverax swallowed hard. What if they were both right? If

they found out that Alverax *had been* a member of the Bloodthieves, it would jeopardize the entire safety of the Zeda people. The last thing he needed was to be responsible for mass genocide.

"Then I pray our story finds its way into honest ears." Elder Rosemary gestured to the women standing beside her. "Please, allow me to introduce the Elders of our people. We do not have a singular shepherd. Instead, five women are called to be the ruling council. Our most senior member is Elder Violet here to my left. Beside her is Elder Ashwa and Elder Ivy. To my right is Elder Rowan. And I am Elder Rosemary. As I presume you've heard, our home was destroyed by the very Bloodthieves you fear. We have come seeking sanctuary."

Empress Chailani nodded as she observed each of the women. She turned to the older man at her left and whispered something Alverax could not hear. While he responded, the young woman to Chailani's right spoke up.

"And who are the others?" she asked.

The Empress turned to the young woman and scowled. "Excuse my sister. She has forgotten her place. However, the question stands. Who are the others you have brought with you?"

If Alverax had felt uncomfortable before, the feeling blossomed as the Elders turned to look at him and the others. He had not wanted to come in the first place, but the Elders insisted that keeping the presence of an Obsidian threadweaver a secret would endanger their people. The Felians valued truth and transparency; their justice for dishonesty was renowned.

Elder Rosemary continued to be the voice of the Elders. They hoped that her calm demeanor would encourage at least a small measure of sympathy from the Felian royals.

She gestured to the only other man in the group. "He is called Dogwood. In Zedalum, he led the training and application of our threadweavers. You should know that the majority of our people are threadweavers, though few are trained to fight. Beside him are Trill and Anise. They are our historians.

"The other two are not of our people. The woman is Iriel Valerian, wife to High General Chrys Valerian of Alchea. The young man is Alverax Blightwood. We have brought them both here in the spirit of transparency, and because we know you would not believe us otherwise." She paused just long enough to regain their full attention. "Alverax is an Obsidian threadweaver, and the child in Iriel's arms is an Amber threadweaver."

The older man standing beside the Empress huffed, then whispered something. He had the brilliant green eyes of an Emerald.

The empress began her descent of the velvet-inlaid steps beneath her. "Stories of Obsidian threadweavers have been passed down among our people for centuries. If what you claim is true, then I, for one, am comforted to know of their reality. It is confirmation of our truths. However, Watchlord Osinan has reminded me that there is one particular line of relevance in the Tome of the Heralds: 'purge Amber lest their chains bind you.'"

Alverax turned to Iriel who clutched her child with a little more fervor. Were they implying that they would murder a child? What did he know of their culture and religion? He knew they worshipped the Heralds, whom they called The Timeless Ones. But that was all. He didn't know *how* they worshipped the Heralds. Human sacrifice? Infanticide? Religion—even true religion—has a tendency to twist itself into nothing more than justification for human turpitude.

"Though it is a less obscure doctrine, it is doctrine none-theless." The empress continued her descent. "It is also our custom to reward candor—of which you have shown much —and for that I make you this promise. I will allow no harm to come to the child. The decision is not, however, invari-able. And so, if our scholars discover reasons to revise it, we will do so. Concerning the Obsidian, in our texts, such threadweavers were seen as the closest allies to the Heralds. Their right hand. Tell me, boy, are you dangerous?"

Alverax froze. The Empress of Felia was addressing *him*. "Umm, I don't think so? Elder Rowan does. Iriel doesn't. That's another story. But, in general, I don't think I am. I've never killed anyone. Directly at least. So, I guess on that count I'm not."

Iriel came to his rescue. "Alverax is brave and strong, but he is not dangerous. He saved my life in the Fairenwild, and that of my son. If anything, he is a hero."

From behind Elder Violet's head, Alverax saw the Empress' sister leaning over so she could see his face. They caught eyes and her head tilted to the side. She was even more beautiful than her sister. In Cynosure, all of the Felians hid the coarseness of their hair by keeping it slicked or dreaded, but the Empress' sister let it explode into a cloud of dark curls, celebrating the texture. Not to mention the smooth skin she flaunted so effortlessly. *Heralds.* He was staring.

"It does not surprise me to hear of heroism coming from a Felian. Although I'd wager only one of your parents was from here. Was it your mother or father?" The Empress asked.

"My father," he replied. "I never knew my mother."

She turned from him, as if his presence had run its course, and turned back to Elder Rosemary. "*Your* paternity is far less clear. You claim to be the people of Zedalum, a secret city deep in the Fairenwild. Osinan, share what we have learned about the Zeda people."

The man to her left stood forward. His long hair flowed back behind him in thick braids, and his gray beard moved as he spoke. "There have long been rumors of a people living in the Fairenwild. Some accounts call them ghosts, others call them spawn of the earth's core. One account claims they are separatists from the days of the Timeless. We do not know the truth, my Empress, but it is *possible* that they are who they claim to be.

"However, it is more likely that they have come to infect our city, cattle bearing a plague. The timing is too coincidental to be ignored. The Bloodthieves arrive, and not a month later a swarm of locusts follow. True or not, their presence is a threat."

Alverax had gotten to know the Elders fairly well over the last week of travel, and he knew that look on Elder Rowan's face. Pure, unadulterated indignation. He honestly wasn't sure how the old woman was still alive. Someone with such a high level of anger must be constantly on the verge of a heart attack. For whatever reason, the bubbling ire creeping out from the corner of her mouth brought Alverax a weird sense of comfort.

Until she spoke.

"Madness!" she shouted. "You threaten our children, you threaten our people, and you threaten our honor. We came in the spirit of honesty, not to be slandered by conjecture and fear-filled guesswork! Come, Rosemary. We will find elsewhere for our people to live."

"Rowan," Elder Rosemary said sternly. "Now is not the time to be unreasonable."

Elder Ashwa spoke for the first time. "We are all on the same side. Our home was destroyed by the Bloodthieves, and we have come to a city under similar threat. Perhaps the Father of All has led us here so that we might help each other."

"As heroic as that may sound to you," Empress Chailani cut in, "we have more than enough strength to protect ourselves. The Bloodthieves are a mosquito. They pose no real threat to us. An army of threadweavers, however. Where you see a chance to help, we see a chance to attack from within."

"If we could prove our pedigree, would you let us stay?" Elder Rosemary asked.

Watchlord Osinan nodded. "Now is not the time to play games. If you have proof, bring it forward."

"We do," Elder Rosemary acknowledged.

"These pagans don't deserve our secrets!" Elder Rowan shouted.

"Guard your tongue!" Osinan's eyes were fire.

The Empress' sister jumped to her feet. "Osinan, stand down! I understand your hesitation but, if what these people claim is true, then they deserve our patience. Test your feet in their waters. Uprooted from their homes. Run out by wicked men. Forced to find shelter in a foreign world with foreign customs. They have every right to be tired, and angry, and impatient. Let us be patient. Careful, yes. Thorough, without a doubt. But let patience be our guiding light."

Bright sunlight filtered down through towering windowpanes. Both parties, humbled by the princess' words, bowed their heads in shame. Alverax stood breathless, staring. The corners of his vision seemed to blur as the world focused on her. There was something about her. She was the first ray of light in the dawn. But, to his heart's lament, she was also a damn princess.

"The Sun Daughter is right." Empress Chailani stepped back and took her seat on the throne. "Elder Rosemary, I apologize for our manners. Please come forward and present your case. We will try our best to be honest truth seekers, but do not expect blind acceptance. The world is shifting, and dangers are rising like the tides. We must protect our people, as you must protect yours.

"The rest of you may leave. We will speak with Elder Rosemary alone."

Alverax and the others were led away by the guards. He looked back over his shoulder and saw Elder Rosemary ascending the dais carrying a chest. While looking behind, he saw Elder Rowan smiling to herself and, in that moment, he understood. The old bat had faked it. Somehow, she'd known that the Empress' sister would come to their aid.

He slowed down and approached Elder Rowan. "How did you know?"

"Know what, boy?"

"How did you know that the sister would defend you?"

Elder Rowan smiled at him for the first time. "You are more observant than I would have given you credit for. The most important lesson in politics is: assess your assets. We asked around and learned who was likely to be in the room. The Empress' sister is known to be empathetic and merciful, a balance to her sister's staunch sovereignty. We knew that they would put on a strong front and, if we could get Jisenna to show us mercy, we would have a better chance at—"

His mind lost track of the Elder's voice, focusing only on

a single word she'd spoken. A name. A symbol. Jisenna. Her name was Jisenna.

Focus, he told himself. *Forget about the girl.*

"—It helps that I am old. Both men and women are more sympathetic to the elderly. So, in short, we didn't know. It was a well-informed wager."

A well-informed wager. Alverax had underestimated her. He'd assumed she'd gotten where she was because people were afraid of her, but there was clearly more to it. It made sense. Not just any old lady could become an Elder. He wanted to know more. How did she get where she was? Was she married? His grandfather was—

"There are a dozen rooms in the east wing you may use to rest," one of the guards said, a tall man with a nose ring and a bald head. He led them down an empty corridor. "The Empress has asked that you stay in your room until the negotiations have concluded."

Elder Rowan nodded and turned back to Alverax, offering the remnant of a smile. "I'm quite certain that you didn't hear a word I just said. If I may offer one suggestion before we part ways—and I hope you are listening now— don't do anything stupid."

With a tone soaked to the core with sarcasm, he replied, "I'll do my best."

They parted ways and Alverax ended up in a large room with an unbelievable view. Out of his window, the Terecean Sea as far as the eye could see, dotted with a large archipelago that formed the start of the Alirian Islands. Dozens of ships traveled between, carrying valuable trade cargo. Down below, at the piers, thousands of people traveled like ants along the streets and boardwalks. Nearly every building in Felia was white. He'd seen similar designs in

Cynosure, inspired by Felian architecture, but these were something else.

If Cynosure was the moon, Felia was the sun, and he basked in its warmth.

———

HE'D SLEPT LONGER than anticipated, but the mattress was a billowing cloud, and he felt nearly weightless on its surface. He smiled and severed his corethread. Threadlight burst apart beneath him, and his body drifted into true weight-lessness. It surprised him how casually he was able to threadweave now. At first, he had to open himself to all threadlight and then filter all of the threads he didn't want to see. Now, he could shift just his corethread into view. It was less awe-inspiring, but much more effective.

Just as he embraced his weightless state, a knock came at his door. He scrambled to sit up but, without the force of gravity pulling him down, he went spiraling up into the air. The ceiling greeted him with a thud. He scratched at the wall, scrambling in a chaotic display of clumsiness, then finally pushed off down to the ground. He grabbed onto the bed's corner post, repositioned himself, and pushed off once again, gliding toward the door in time for a second knock.

Unsure how to open it in his current state, he spoke. "Yes? Hello? Who is it?"

A deep voice replied. "The first stage of negotiations is complete. The Empress has released the room restriction, but we ask that you do not step outside the palace gates."

Alverax smiled. "Great. Thank you."

Now that he was rested and no longer confined to his room, he was ready to explore.

But first he had to awkwardly float in the air for another minute.

When his corethread finally reappeared, he fell to his feet, with more grace than he deserved, and opened the door, stepping out into the broad hallway where he dodged a stream of busy workers. The decor in the Palace of the Sun was unlike anything Alverax had ever seen. Flowers everywhere, lining stairwells and windows, and tied together into immaculate bouquets everywhere he looked. Against the white stone used for the majority of the palace, the red was a striking juxtaposition.

Within the sprawling main entryway, a massive indoor fountain centered the room. Hundreds of potted plants lined its edge. The greenery, draped with white and red linens, connected each plant with the next. He'd never had the chance to step inside Endin Keep, but he had a feeling it didn't share the same elegance as the Palace of the Sun.

The flowing fountain reminded him of a small waterfall back in Cynosure, deep in a cave east of Mercy's Bluff. He and his friends had spent countless nights soaking in the base of the fall, talking and dreaming. Often, they'd dreamed of leaving Cynosure.

For the next hour, Alverax wandered the palace, silently exploring, admiring, and daydreaming. What he'd most wanted to explore was the colossal hippodrome he'd seen on their way to the palace. It was like an elegant, regal version of the Pit in Cynosure, and he imagined himself seated in the stands, cheering on whatever games they played within.

It felt so good. These were his people. His grandparents were Felian, born and raised, but had left to Cynosure for reasons he'd never cared to ask about. Alabella had as well, but he hated thinking about her. He'd never had a mother, and he knew that deep down there was some weird psychological need he'd let her fill, despite her ill-intent. What worried him more was what she was planning to do now that the coreseal had been broken. Was the rest of her plan a lie? Or did she really want everyone to become a threadweaver?

He turned a corner and felt a surge of warm air billowing out from an open doorway. A small sign marked the room as *The Sun Bath*. He appreciated the pun but was more excited about soaking in the warm waters. Steps inside led down to a vast, open space with two separate pools of water, lit only by a few wall lamps. Steam rose up from the farther pool.

Alverax stripped off his clothes and placed them under a bench as he made his way over to the far side of the room. He stepped down into the water, embracing the warmth. The smell of the steam reminded him of stone after a good rainfall. The water had always been comforting to him and, now that he was an Obsidian threadweaver, it felt even more like home. Weightlessness. He'd never made the connection before. His love for water had, in a way, been a precursor.

He let himself slip below the surface of the pool. Back in Cynosure, he was the undefeated champion of breath-holding. A dozen people had tried to dethrone him in the pools not far from Mercy's Bluff—one kid passed out trying—but he always won. He had a vivid memory of his father glaring down at him in disapproval after one such game. Once a giant taractus turd, always a giant taractus turd, and his father was the largest of them all.

As he meditated below the surface of the pool, he opened his eyes and noticed a large grate on the far wall. He wondered where the water came from. But then, as he was floating and enjoying the surrounding warmth, massive hands reached down, grabbed his shoulders, and wrenched him out of the water like a beached whale. Two fit men in black pinned down his naked body to the stone floor.

"Who are you?" the first shouted with a deep voice.

Alverax struggled to respond as his face pressed harder to the floor.

"Answer him!" the other demanded.

"I'm nobody!" Alverax whimpered. "I was just relaxing!"

A woman's voice cut the tension. "Wait. I recognize him." Her bare feet pressed against the floor as she came closer. "Cheth, give him a towel. Innix, release him, but stay close."

His cheek throbbed from the stone and his back still ached from the guard's sharp knee. He wanted to stand up and yell at someone for mistreatment of fine assets, but instead he stayed sprawled out on the floor until Cheth returned with a towel. He wrapped himself and turned around.

Heralds, no.

It can't be.

Princess Jisenna.

The Mistress of Mercy.

The Sun Daughter.

In the Sun Bath.

Don't do anything stupid, Alverax.

After a brief moment, the princess tilted her head to the side.

"Alexander Grant," he said before he could stop himself.

"What?"

"I—" he shut his mouth...finally.

She raised a brow. "Do you know who I am?"

He nodded, afraid to speak.

"If my sister discovered that you were in my bath waiting

28

for me, she would likely consider you an assassin. She could have your entire people imprisoned or executed."

"Well, they're not exactly my people," Alverax blurted out. Without thinking. Again. Because surely thinking would not be helpful given the current situation.

"So, you would be content should they all die?"

"No—" he stumbled. "Of course not. I was just in here relaxing. I swear I didn't know it was your bath. I should go." He shuffled away from the pool toward his clothes beneath the bench.

"Is it true?" she asked.

He turned to her.

"Is it true that you are an Obsidian threadweaver?" Her eyes danced from each of his black eyes, looking for a deeper truth. She stepped closer. "Truth be told, I never believed such a thing was possible."

Alverax let out a laugh. "Neither did I."

"How do you mean?" she said, looking puzzled.

Heralds save me.

The Elders definitely did *not* want him to share his connection to the Bloodthieves. If the empress found out, who knew what they'd do. And as much as he liked to pretend that he was a good liar, he knew it wasn't true. It was the one useful trait he could have inherited from his father. Instead, he got the man's smile.

Jisenna pursed her lips. "It appears I've stumbled upon some secret that perhaps the Zeda elders would not have me know."

Seriously, Heralds. Any time now. "It's not a secret. It's just that I don't even understand it fully."

"Maybe I can help?" Her hair fluttered as she spoke. The closer she came, the more clearly he could see the freckles on her collarbone and the curves of her neck.

He caught himself, quickly shifting his gaze to meet hers once again. "I know it sounds crazy, but I wasn't born a threadweaver. So, unless you know how someone can become a threadweaver, I'm not sure you can help."

Her eyes never left his as she listened. It wasn't until that moment that he realized... her eyes were brown. She was an achromat. But her sister's—Alverax remembered from the throne room—were blue as the sea itself.

"You're serious," she said, brushing her hands over her arms. "I have chills, Alverax. There have been rumors of such things in the past. They say the Heralds gifted powerful threadlight to their most trusted. Those are stories. But you are *real*." She paused, eyes narrowing. "I must ask you—and I will know if you lie to me—are you here to kill me?"

"No," he said defensively.

Her eyes narrowed. "You are not a Bloodthief?"

Heralds. Any question but that. His eyes fell to the surface of the water. His myriad thoughts crashed into each other, a cacophony of waves against a rocky shore. There was no honest way to answer without damning himself and the others. He wasn't, but he had been. Maybe if he just left it at that. Omission.

"I am not," he replied.

Her lips curled into a frown. "But?"

"No *but*. I am not a Bloodthief."

"Then why do your words taste like stale bread?"

He didn't respond.

"Well, if the negotiations continue as they have today, I imagine we will see each other again soon. They will want to study you and dig into the particulars of your conversion. Thank you for the unexpected company. I promise not to disclose of our meeting here. Perhaps someday you will be more forthcoming. For now, I am still in need of a bath. Innix, please show our friend to the exit."

The large man nodded.

"Oh, and Alverax," she said, holding her black and gold shawl with both hands. "Next time we speak, you should tell me about this 'Alexander Grant' character."

She winked and it nearly killed him.

CHAPTER 4

A WEEK HAD PASSED since the Apogee—who called himself Relek—had slaughtered the Alchean soldiers in the Everstone Mountains. Chrys' last vestige of hope, a single spark in the chaotic darkness, was the dream of reuniting with his family, and it faded with each step he took.

The red-haired man, Velan, practically worshipped Relek. Autelle, on the other hand, hadn't spoken a single word since they left the campsite in the mountains. Every night, as Chrys lay dormant within the Apogee's mind, he could hear the sniffling sound of Autelle's tears. If he were able to cry himself, Chrys might have joined her.

As they continued their trek, they entered a swampy forest east of the mountains. Thick vines hung between trees, and most of the ground was submerged by varying levels of water. Strange creatures swung from tree to tree on arms that seemed too long for their bodies. Others hung from branches by their tails, making noises that sounded dangerously close to laughter.

The first night in the swamp, Relek killed one of the creatures and cooked it on an open fire. Skinned and roasting on a flame, the animal had the rough appearance of a small child. Velan ate his worth, but Autelle refused. Chrys thought he heard her whisper the word *cannibal* under her breath at least once.

Chrys didn't know what to think of Relek. He'd assumed that it was some broken piece of his own subconscious, but, with each passing day trapped in his mind, Chrys began to doubt. Relek was something more. He had to be. If he wasn't, none of it made sense.

The worst part was that it had now been weeks since he'd left Iriel and Aydin in the Fairenwild. The truth, though he still refused to accept it, was that he would likely never see them again. Even if he regained control, he was lost in the Wastelands.

What hurt the most was knowing that Iriel would forever see him as the man who'd left her when she needed him most. Part of him wondered if Relek was only in control because Chrys allowed him to be. Because he was too weak to fight. Too defeated to contest. A failure. Nothing but an empty voice in another man's head.

They kept pace for another two days, Relek guiding them past hidden traps and unseen dangers. At one point, a hairy gray creature—like the great apes of western Alir—twice the size of a man, with yellow spikes down its back, sat at the base of a tree, peeling a bright red fruit. Thick tusks wrapped around its jaw like a wild boar. When Velan pointed it out, Relek called it an *ataçan* and instructed them not to make eye contact.

Autelle's mind seemed at the verge of collapse. She'd begun whispering to herself, looking over her shoulder, paranoid about each and every crunching leaf or drip of water. The first time she spoke, she ranted about the entire experience being nothing more than a nightmare. She claimed that she was still in the cave, asleep, with a high temperature, and none of it was real.

If only that were true.

The terrain sloped upward, and Relek paused. "Beyond this ridge is Kai'Melend. The people there will not take well to our arrival. Be calm, and do not act."

Velan nodded and Autelle stared at the ground.

They hiked over a mossy ridge and found themselves looking out over a sprawling jungle city. A massive statue of a beast similar to the one they'd seen previously stood on a raised pedestal in the center. Homes built on low stilted foundations fanned out in tight groups just above the swamp water. Ladders. Rope swings. And hundreds, if not thousands, of wastelanders. Young and old, all with small frames, grey skin, and beady, grey eyes.

A memory of the war flashed in Chrys' mind. He remembered the first wastelander he'd ever seen. So close to human, yet so very different. Large canine teeth glinting in the sun as the enemy screamed their attack. Drooping, pointed earlobes waving as they rushed forward. White hair, like the people of Alir. And the tattoos. Every wastelander had strips of black curling over their arms and necks.

The memory faded, and the swamp returned.

Wastelanders shouted and grabbed weapons as they sprinted toward Chrys' group. One of the massive ataçan creatures leapt down from a platform, hitting the ground with a resounding thud and an explosion of water. It moved forward, using its long arms to pull itself on all fours, until a wastelander with impossibly thick arms leapt atop the beast's shoulders.

Relek stepped forward and raised his arms in the air, crossing his wrists, then bringing the tips of his fingers together, palms out.

The wastelanders hissed.

The warrior atop the ataçan leapt off and strode forward, his thick arms swinging low as he eyed the strangers. In a nasally voice, he spat a smattering of foreign syllables and, somehow, Chrys understood. *This sign is not for your kind.*

Relek released the sign and reached out a hand in invitation. Odd sounds formed from his own tongue. *I have returned to the hive.*

The ataçan beat its chest and released a series of deep grunts. The wastelander stepped back, scowling with its wide, thin lips. *If it is true, say it. Speak his name.*

Deep in his mind, Chrys heard the response, clear as though it were spoken in his own tongue. *I am Relek, the Great Anchor, God of the An'tara, King of the Hive.*

Every wastelander who could hear his voice dropped to their knees, crossing their arms and connecting the tips of their fingers in the same way, prostrating themselves before him.

In that moment, Chrys knew with certainty. The Apogee was not a piece of his imagination. It was not a broken shard of his soul. It was a monster. A wastelander spirit of some kind, worshipped by the pagans of the east.

Relek never told them to rise. He let them bow as he led Velan and Autelle toward the village. In the distance, another figure appeared. She wore more clothing than the rest of the wastelanders, covering almost the entirety of her limbs and torso. Neither she nor Relek spoke until they were close.

Brother, the woman said with a gravelly voice.

Lylax, he replied. *You look well.*

She coughed. *Now is not the time for humor. How you*

managed to live in one of these frail corpses for so long, I will never understand.

It was no easy feat.

It is crippling.

It is, but do not worry. I anticipated your distaste. Relek smiled. *This woman is human. I brought her for you.*

Lylax raised her brow. *She is not gifted.*

My options were few.

It will do.

It is good to see you, Relek said. *Though I am surprised that after so many years you have not returned with an army in tow. I hope you have not grown soft. There is no room for mercy this time.*

Do not worry, brother. I've given instructions to the smartest of the beasts. They will prepare the way for us.

Like most wastelanders, Lylax was a full head shorter than Chrys. She looked up, inspecting Autelle, then pulled out a knife. Tears streaked down Alchean woman's cheeks as Lylax drew close. The wastelander woman cut into her own palm, followed by a clean slice into Autelle's, then placed both palms together. As soon as the hands touched, both women screamed out in pain. Their backs arched. Their heads threw back with force. The wastelander body convulsed wildly, her head shaking back and forth in an unnatural blur of speed. Then, finally, she fell to the ground, swamp water splashing beneath her lifeless corpse.

For a brief moment, Chrys felt a sliver of hope that something had gone wrong, and that Lylax had died. But then Autelle smiled, and the curve of her lip was wrong.

She was no longer Autelle.

Like Relek had done to Chrys, Lylax had done to Autelle.

Another memory from the war flashed in Chrys' mind.

A wastelander, strong, taller than the others, his entire cheek covered with dozens of perfectly circular tattooed dots. There was a certain greed in his smile as he eyed Chrys' Sapphire veins.

That smile.

Relek.

She is stronger than she looks, Autelle said, the words ripping Chrys away from the memory. She waved her hands back and forth, inspecting them.

"My god," Velan said with excitement in his eyes. "I...am I to be a vessel as well?"

Relek turned to face him. "Yes."

"Is there another?" he asked.

"You will be *my* vessel. This man, Chrys, killed many of the wastelanders. I will give him to them as a gift."

Velan's eyes grew wide. He dropped to his knees and tried, poorly, to mimic the sign of worship that the wastelanders had made, but his hands were trembling. "I am ready."

"Come here," Relek commanded. Velan stood and took a step forward, putting out his hand like Autelle had done. Lylax handed Relek the blade and he cut down each of their palms.

Chrys could feel the pain of the blade as he stood watching the exchange. He realized that these might be his final moments. The woman's previous vessel, the wastelander, seemed to be dead in the swamp water. If Chrys did nothing...

He would never see his family again.

Chrys threw his will against the barrier in his mind, one last savage attempt at freedom. Weeks of pent-up anger, fear, and hopelessness came surging down against the barrier like an avalanche, crushing against it, demanding release. He felt the barrier weakening in his mind.

Relek gasped.

Chrys did it again. For his wife and for his son, he beat at the barrier with every scrap of strength he had within him.

"You are too late," Relek whispered.

Chrys felt his body convulse. A raw scream came pouring out of his throat as his back arched in pain. He threw his will one last time against the barrier, but it was already gone.

His body toppled into the swamp water.

CHAPTER 5

THERE WAS a much-needed comfort in returning to her training exercises. Iriel Valerian breathed in as she bent her knees, keeping her core tight, and running her fists through the fighting forms she'd practiced so many times before. Performing them again felt like coming home, and the quiet of the Felian courtyard gave her life.

It wasn't that she didn't like being a mother—it was beautiful, and she already felt herself growing in ways she never would have otherwise—but she just wasn't convinced she was good at it. She'd barely been able to keep Aydin alive, and that was the bare minimum for the job.

The worst part was that he knew. Somehow, the little newborn knew that she was failing and refused to latch for his feedings. The truth of it nearly crushed her, settling in her stomach, in her heart, her mind. Anxiety for her child's wellbeing. Anxiety that she wasn't capable. Anxiety that she was failing. And resentment every time Aydin cried when she just needed one minute alone. Then guilt for her own resentment.

Iriel shook her head and cleared her mind of her child

—she cleared her mind of Chrys and where he might be—and she embraced the kata.

She brought her foot up into the air and stumbled as her muscles reminded themselves of months-long deprivation. But soon enough, she felt the quivering muscles in her stomach steady themselves, and her stance solidified. She couldn't imagine women giving birth without threadlight to speed up the recovery.

She moved onto the next, and the next. Her hands moved like blades through the air, cutting forward, then pausing while her shoulders and forearms tightened.

Her father had paid for her first lessons when she was young. The confidence that came from being an Emerald threadweaver often came at the expense of injury or harm. While Sapphires could *push* weapons and change the flow of a fight without much thought, an Emerald had to be smarter. Since she was young, she'd trained with palm-guards, a technique first developed on the islands of Kulai. A special glove that was worn with metal only on the insides of the hand. When a blade struck toward an Emerald, they could *pull* the weapon to their hand, grasp hold of it with the shielded palm, and disarm or reverse the attack. She missed the feel of the steel against her hand.

Running through the forms gave her the sense of control she needed. Since fleeing Alchea, it felt like she hadn't made a choice for herself. Every decision came down to what Aydin needed. It didn't upset her—frustrated, perhaps—but there was still an overarching sense of pressure that seemed to cloud her. She just needed to be alone, and, stones, no one ever told her how difficult it would be to find alone time as a mother.

She finished up her kata, brow glistening with sweat,

and nodded to the Felian guards posted along the wall-walk, a habit she'd picked up from Chrys.

As she walked slowly through the hallway, she thought of her missing husband. She wished Chrys were there with her. Stones, she just wished she knew that he was okay. She'd seen the look in his eyes, the coldness, that foreign gaze, and she feared what it meant for him. Would he ever return? His mother, Willow, had also yet to return, and, though she knew it was stupidly selfish, Iriel wished Willow were there to help with Aydin.

It seemed silly to feel so lonely. She was surrounded by people, and there were many among the Zeda that she'd grown close to. Like Cara, the burly chromawolf trainer who'd been unable to have children of her own, who had offered to help with Aydin whenever Iriel needed a break, or at least whenever Iriel's guilt of unloading her child on another was less than her need for solitude. At times it felt like Cara was mothering Iriel as much as she was Aydin.

Then there was Alverax, the biggest surprise. Throughout their time traveling from the Fairenwild to Felia, she'd become unexpectedly protective of him. Almost like a younger brother. Sure, he'd saved her life and the life of her child, but, even more than the debt she owed him, she saw in him a young man trying to do what was right.

When she finally arrived back at her room, she pushed open the large, oak door and found Cara seated in the rocking chair with Aydin quietly asleep on her shoulder. She gave Cara a silent wave as she entered.

The broad Zeda woman smiled in return. "Never woke up," she said. "He's a hard sleeper, this one. Doesn't seem to have much of a preference for position either."

"I'm glad he slept for you," Iriel said, taking a seat on the bed. "He's had some rough nights since we arrived in the city. I swear he liked it better out on the road."

"A boy after my own heart," Cara said. "All this stone...it's too stuffy. I don't like it. Nothing quite like the smell of tree bark and a chill breeze to give you life."

Looking out the window, Iriel remembered the cold nights she'd spent traveling from the Fairenwild, fearing for the health of her newborn.

"It gets easier," Cara said.

Iriel turned to her.

"How you're feeling," she continued. "It's more common than you'd think."

"What do you mean?"

Cara smiled. "People focus so much on the physical pain of childbirth that they forget the mental burden is often worse, and longer lasting. I saw the smartest woman I know barricade herself in a room for two days, a few weeks after she gave birth. People thought she'd gone mad. When she finally came out, she was perfectly fine, apologized, and now she's the best mother I know. Point is you have to give your roots room to grow and accept that you're bound to run into a few rocks along the way."

"Is it that obvious?" Iriel asked.

Cara didn't need to respond.

Iriel put her head in her hands. "I just feel so restless. My husband is missing, and I'm stuck here. I want to be out there searching of him, fighting for him. Helping. Doing something. Anything. I was worried about it before, but I thought it would just go away. If anything, it's gotten worse. I'm starting to think that maybe I'm just not made for motherhood."

"Iriel," Cara said with a soft voice. "It's like comparing granite to clay. The clay may take shape more easily, but the granite, once you've chiseled it into place, is so much stronger. For some people, motherhood comes more easily. For others, it takes a hammer and chisel. No one is *made* for motherhood. Motherhood is made for *you*. Some of us aren't so lucky."

Her words cut Iriel to the core. She felt so ungrateful. Here she was complaining to someone about something they'd spent decades craving. Given the circumstances, Iriel had plenty to be grateful for. "I'm sorry. I...shouldn't complain."

"You've been through hell," Cara said. "Complaining is healthy. I just don't want you to be so hard on yourself. A few dark clouds don't make a storm. Just give it a bit of time."

Iriel smiled and moved to lift Aydin from Cara's shoulder. "Thank you...for everything."

"You know I love doing this." Cara helped lift the child so he wouldn't wake. "Reminds me a bit of taking care of my little chromawolf pups. But I never had them this young."

Carefully, Iriel laid the child's head back onto her own shoulder. He seemed to fit perfectly in the crook of her neck.

Cara stood and walked to the door. "I'll chat with the elders and see if they have anything you can help out with. It's good to stay busy when you're feeling down. And don't forget, you're not in this alone."

Iriel mouthed the words "thank you" and settled into the rocking chair.

Despite Cara's calming words, a deep restlessness remained.

She only hoped she could rein it in.

CHAPTER 6

IN THE EARLY MORNING AIR, long before the sun had peaked its grand eye over the horizon, Laurel breathed in the dew and repeated the same lie over and over again.

Everything will be okay.

But she knew better.

The Zeda people would see Alabella's party as they approached the wonderstone and, in no time at all, dozens of armed threadweavers would descend from the trees. They would never let the grounders leave alive, and Laurel would never receive a new theolith. For her own sake—for the sake of the tremble in her left hand that refused to steady itself—she needed to make sure they weren't seen, even if that meant incapacitating the guard stationed on the entrance platform.

Part of her dreaded the idea of returning to Zedalum. She hadn't left things well with her family, and there was a good chance her grandfather would be taken by the next Gale. If she was too late, she could never forgive herself.

While she waited, she felt at the stitches over her breast and was surprised to find very little pain. It still held soreness deep below the surface, but the skin and muscle had recovered well. Sarla had explained to her that drinking the transfusers would accelerate the healing of her chest, but it had its own side-effects. Laurel had to drink extra water to account for the vomiting.

When the others arrived, Laurel was sitting under an apple tree hiding from the moon and a growing mob of storm clouds. Her eyes—heavy with bags and the whites stained red from lack of sleep—opened at the sound of footsteps. Alabella walked along the path accompanied by a thick Alchean man with arms too large for his shirt, carrying a sack over his shoulder.

Up until now, Laurel had only seen Alabella in fanciful dresses, but now she wore a pair of dark trousers and a loose-fitting top. "Laurel," Alabella said. "I heard you were out here waiting."

The man smiled and extended his hand. "Name's Barrick. Nice to meet you."

Laurel rose to her feet and was surprised with how large Barrick's hand was; it seemed to envelope the entirety of her own. "Hello."

"Are you sure you're up for this?" Alabella asked, with the slightest twitch of her brow.

"I'm fine," Laurel quipped. She rubbed at the veins on the back of her left hand while eyeing the bulging Sapphire blue running through Barrick's forearm.

"Just, take it easy," Alabella said. "Every rose begins a bud."

Barrick snorted. "As long as I don't end up with a thorn in my arse."

Alabella ignored him. "The others will be awaiting us at the border. Let's be off."

They traveled many hours before reaching the edge of

the Fairenwild. There, dwarfed by the great feytrees, five people sat in shadow with a large wooden pushcart and a few bags of supplies. It felt odd to be approaching the forest with others. All of her messenger runs had been done alone. Now, not only was she not alone, but she was with a dangerous group of Bloodthief grounders.

The closer they came to the rest of the party, the more quickly Laurel was able to note the colorful eyes of each of them. Together with Barrick, that made two Sapphires, four Emeralds, one Amber, and a Laurel, the lone achromat. If chromawolves attacked, they looked well-able to defend themselves. If it was Asher, maybe they wouldn't have to.

She thought of her friend, and she would have felt more guilty for leaving him if he didn't have his new pack. He was happy with his new family, which gave her just enough peace of mind to offset the sadness at losing him. And as much as she liked to believe that their bond was special, she was replaceable. At least with Alabella, she wasn't. Where else was Sarla going to find a living person who'd shattered their theolith? They needed her as much as she needed them.

One of the new companions, a man with unnaturally bronzed skin characteristic of the people of Kulai, rose and greeted them. "You must be the Zeda girl."

Alabella stepped forward before Laurel had a chance to respond. "She is from Zedalum but has not been to the Fairenwild in some time now. Her goal today is the same as ours: to see what lies beneath the coreseal. There is much to do and little time to do it if we wish to be out of the Fairen-wild before dark."

It was the first time Laurel had heard Alabella call it the *coreseal*, and she wondered how the grounder woman knew that name.

They traveled quickly, following the path of the yellow roses. Surprisingly, Laurel didn't have to guide them. It was as if they walked a familiar path. The ominous feeling inside her resonated with greater boldness. Barrick carried his large sack, and the rest ripped out photospore reeds and held them high overhead to light their way. Laurel looked up into the canopy and was confused that she had yet to see a drove of skyflies. They were usually everywhere, fluttering near the entangled feytree branches.

As they continued on, she was able to spot three treelurks and a few patches of hugweed before the others stumbled into them. Barrick was particularly grateful when he nearly stepped into a stretch of writhing vines. Laurel pulled him out of the way just before he took the final step.

Hours had passed, and Laurel knew that they would soon approach the entrance to Zedalum. In the distance, where the wonderstone would be, it looked as if they were about to come out the other end of the Fairenwild. Daylight poured through the darkness.

"That's not right," she whispered.

Alabella turned to her. "What was that?"

"That light ahead," Laurel said. "It shouldn't be there."

"Rumors in Alchea said that there was a great fire in the Fairenwild the night you were hurt. Perhaps it is related. A little extra light could be useful to us if that is our destination."

Barrick, who had been eavesdropping, stepped closer. "Heard the same thing. Your people live anywhere near here?"

Oh, no.

Laurel sprinted forward without answering. If there was a fire near the wonderstone, it could have wreaked havoc on

Zedalum. The moss on the feytrees was flammable, and the photospores were quite nearly explosive.

She ran and she ran until the field came into view. What greeted her sent a shiver up her spine.

Carnage.

Destruction.

Fallen trees and bloodied bodies left for dead. Many among the corpses were Zeda people, but not all, and some were not whole.

She looked up, but in her heart she already knew. Whatever fire had raged here had spread to the north quickly, devouring trees and roads and homes. She saw only the edge of the city through the burnt treetop, but it was enough. She didn't need to see it all to know that the devastation had overcome the treetop metropolis.

She dropped to her knees, buried her face, and let tears pour down her pale cheeks. The dark of her mind filled with images of shredded corpses lying in a field of colorful roses. The tranquil memory of a quiet wonderstone was shattered and replaced by the raw noise of death and destruction.

It hurt—all of it. The truth most of all. That she should have been there.

What happened? Where had they gone? Surely, not everyone was dead. Something, or someone, had driven them away...

Alabella.

She knew about the coreseal. She knew about the yellow flowers. She already knew how long it would take for them to reach the wonderstone. She had been there before. And —gale take her—she had done this to Laurel's people.

Just then, a soft hand reached out and found rest on her tense shoulder. Her body jerked awake from its furious dream. The hand, so gentle, so caring, pressed on her with the weight of a thousand deaths. Her heart pounded. The stitches ached. Her addict hands trembled with rage. She wanted to turn around and throw herself at Alabella. Run cold steel through her heart until *her* theolith cracked. She would make Alabella suffer. She would make her taste the pains of an entire people.

But not yet.

She needed to be smart. If Alabella was responsible, this could be a test, and Laurel wasn't strong enough to fight back. She couldn't let Alabella know that she knew. She had to play along like the young, ignorant, sheltered girl they believed her to be.

Lie.

She had to lie. And if there is anything Laurel knew how to do, it was that.

The rage and fury coursing through her thread-dead veins bubbled up until her eyes filled with tears. It didn't all have to be a lie.

Laurel turned to face her demon. "They're gone," she cried.

Alabella's eyes were ice as she brushed the back of her hand against Laurel's cheek, wiping away the tears. "Laurel, these are your people? What darkness has fallen upon this place?"

It took all of Laurel's self-restraint not to charge the lying old hag.

Alabella continued, "I bet it was Great Lord Malachus. Retribution for the priest, and your friends invading his home. It is terrible, Laurel. I am so sorry you had to see this. If I'd known..."

Laurel's jaw clenched, and she spoke through grinding teeth. "My brother and my grandfather were there."

"Take that anger," Alabella said, her voice growing stronger. "Do not forget it. Anger is the great fuel of life. Take it and let it burn inside your veins until we can replace it with threadlight once again. These Alcheans believe they can kill without consequence. They think they are more righteous than you. Stronger than you. But we will heal you, Laurel. And then we will make them pay."

Laurel's heart was a skyfly's wings, fluttering with terrible speed. What ripped deepest into her heart was the ease with which Alabella weaved her lies. Her reality was malleable. Her truth was clothing donned for the occasion. She was a treelurk, shifting its hues to snare its prey, and Laurel was the passerby.

When she didn't respond, Alabella removed her hand. "Take your time. We will be at the coreseal when you are ready."

A minute later, after Alabella's footsteps faded to silence, Laurel took in a deep breath. The scent of roses laced with death danced in the swirling breeze, but none of that mattered. On top of it all, the wonderstone had broken in two, and the Emerald threadweavers were pulling the pieces apart. How had she not seen it? The wonderstone *was* the coreseal.

The warnings of the elders echoed in Laurel's mind. Something was down there. Something dangerous enough to compel an entire people for hundreds of years to protect it. Laurel's feet moved with quiet apprehension, curiosity overcoming the voice that urged her to run. What if there was nothing? What if her people had damned themselves to protect a bunch of infused gemstones? Surely, they wouldn't have considered *that* to be dangerous.

"Toss down some of those spores," Barrick directed. One

of the men stepped over and threw a dozen photospores in the darkness below the broken wonderstone.

"You seeing that?" one of the others asked.

Whispers of "damn" and "Heralds" and "gods" rode the wind. Laurel reached the wonderstone and looked down. "Gale take me," she added.

"This is good news," Alabella said, nodding her head as if to convince herself.

Below them were the partial remains of people long dead. Bits of cloth, and jewelry and bone lay strewn throughout the cavern, with teeth littered across the floor like pebbles. "These must be the heretics. Barrick, would you like to do the honors? Keep an eye out and threadlight in your veins at all times."

The large man nodded and stepped forward. He held his broad shoulders high, and his bearded chin even higher. Blue veins came to life just before he jumped, and Laurel found herself suddenly longing for her old power again. His feet landed without a sound. He picked up one of the photospores and looked around. To the east, he disappeared down some kind of corridor, just for a moment, before reappearing.

He shouted from below, "There's a path down here, but it's caved in."

"Probably the earthquakes," one of the others said.

One by one, they each dropped into the cavern—Barrick *pushed* himself back up and offered to help Laurel descend safely. When she landed, she waved away a cloud of dust drifting in the air. It was so quiet that every step, every breath, and every shuffle of clothing clung to the air like a screaming child.

She drew up close to the pile of rubble blocking the pathway and paused. "Do you hear that?" she asked.

Barrick, who'd stayed close beside her, leaned closer to the rocks. "I don't hear anything."

"I thought I heard something," Laurel said.

He shrugged his shoulders.

Alabella rose from inspecting a bracelet on the ground and smiled. "We're close. Let's *pull* these stones out of the way. Everyone, keep threadlight in your veins. Who knows what lies on the other."

A pale, alchean man with short brown hair and eyes the color of spring leaves stepped forward. Laurel and the others moved out of the way. He dug his boots into the ground, veins coming to life with Emerald threadlight, and *pulled*. Stones and rocks and pebbles exploded away from the path. The pile tumbled down as higher rocks replaced lower rocks. He repeated the process in a series of quick *pulls* until, finally, the gap in the path was wide enough for a person to pass.

Part of Laurel expected a moment of awe and wonder, as if a golden chest or mountain of bright gemstones would shine its glory through the opening. But there was nothing to greet them but silence.

"Stay vigilant," Alabella said.

The group filtered through the opening deeper into the cavern. Laurel stayed in the back with Barrick. She cringed as they passed a pile of teeth. Photospores held high overhead continued to light their path forward. As they rounded a bend, Laurel felt the hairs on her arms stand. There was an energy there. Something that pulsed with power. Even as an achromat she could feel it.

Not far away, the tunnel opened up to a large cavern, but the photospore light was too dim to see beyond the opening.

"Do you smell that?" Barrick asked.

The others all paused, lifting their noses high and taking in deep breaths.

"The hell?" one of the others responded. "Smells like a rose garden."

He was right. It *did* smell like roses, but that didn't make any sense.

Suddenly, a soft patting sound echoed from the end of the tunnel. They all looked at each other until Barrick, eyes shining with Sapphire threadlight, shouted. "Good gods."

Laurel followed his gaze but saw nothing, until she noticed the slight compression of dirt ahead of them. Footsteps, but no feet.

"Threadlight!" Barrick shouted.

Those who had ignored Alabella's instructions let threadlight pour through their veins. They cursed as it flooded into their vision. Laurel knew they could see something she could not, something invisible to weak, useless achromats like herself.

Then, as if to answer the many questions budding in her mind, the creature screeched and attacked. The pale Emerald man fell first, grabbing at his ankle and hacking down with a dagger. Three of the others surrounded him, attacking a creature Laurel could only imagine. But their efforts failed, and one by one they cried out in agony as the creature ripped them apart.

"Run!" Barrick screamed, grabbing Laurel's arm and pulling her up the tunnel.

Chaos erupted with the remaining group as they cursed and scrambled and fought their way back toward the entrance. Laurel's heart raced as she ran.

Another scream.

Then another.

Alabella, Barrick, and Laurel made it to the cavern

beneath the wonderstone. Barrick prepared to *push* off the ground toward the surface, his arm wrapped Alabella. Laurel met the woman's eyes. Not the Amber eyes of an altruistic leader, but the cruel, piss-colored eyes of a woman who would sacrifice Laurel with no remorse. The two Bloodthieves stood in the pillar of light descending from the opening, and just before Barrick kicked off the ground, Alabella's veins blazed to life.

"Wait!" Alabella shouted at Barrick while she stared into toward the tunnel. "I got you."

Her eyes were twin suns glowing in the shadows.

"Are you alone?" Alabella asked the invisible creature.

"Quick, Laurel, come with me!" Barrick shouted.

"Laurel," Alabella commanded. "I assume you brought a transfuser?"

She had, even though the transfusers were never supposed to leave her room. She reached into her pocket, removed the lid on the vial, and drank threadweaver blood. It took only a moment. She closed her eyes and the thick fluid drained down her throat, energy diffusing through her body.

When she opened her eyes, threadlight burst into view all around her, brilliant hues of pulsing light connecting her to the world. And there in front of her, thrashing against dozens of brilliant Amber threads, stood the creature. It stood on four limbs that cut out like blades into the ground. Every inch of its body, where skin or fur should have been, swirled with radiant threadlight, both captivating and terrifying as she stared. Its mouth, open wide as it screeched its defiance, was nothing more than a black hole in the center of a blazing fire.

Alabella walked forward, withdrawing the obsidian dagger that once belonged to Chrys Valerian, and stabbed the blade through the creature's skull. As soon as the blade struck, the creature exploded in a violent surge of thread-light. Then it faded away as though it had never existed.

"Stones," Barrick cursed, his blue eyes nervously watching the tunnel. "What *was* that?"

"We should leave," Alabella responded. "It'll be dark soon, and your mother may have warned you about being out at night when the corespawn are near."

CHAPTER 7

THE IDEA of a woman summoning Alverax to her room had always seemed exciting but, when the woman turned out to be a staunch-faced Zeda elder, his excitement shriveled like an old grape.

He had an ominous feeling about the request; Elder Rowan wasn't the friendliest of callers. His mind assumed the worst—that the Felians had discovered his connection to the Bloodthieves, or that Princess Jisenna had told her sister about the Sun Bath.

It was altogether possible that he was overreacting. Perhaps the negotiations had concluded, and they were free to live in Felia peacefully.

He'd rather bet on Jelium being an herbivore.

Slipping into a pair of dark trousers, Alverax glanced at the map in his room. He'd never spent much time looking at maps, but seeing all of Felia laid out so carefully held a sense of peace and clarity that he deeply needed.

He shoved the door open and there, standing in front of him, hand raised ready to knock, was an unquestionably beautiful Felian princess. Her curls moved like the fronds of a fern as she smiled. Against the brilliant white of her summer dress, Jisenna's skin burned a radiant shade of dark walnut.

"Alverax," she said with a smile. "What propitious timing."

"Jisenna, what brings you here?" He coughed, realizing for the first time that she was flanked by two familiar, well-built guards in black.

"I had a curious dream last night," she whispered with a sparkle in her eye. "In it, I had the most delightful conversation with a handsome young man that had a rather distinct scar on his back. As you can imagine, I've spent all morning going door to door throughout all of Felia asking men to disrobe in hopes that I might find him, but, alas, he eludes me yet. I hoped that, perhaps, with your *vast* connections in these lands, you might know where I could find such a man."

"Such a man," Alverax repeated, holding back a laugh, "would be wise to stay far away from a woman such as yourself."

Her brows rose in surprise. "A woman such as myself?"

"A woman such as yourself," he taunted.

"And what precisely would you know of a woman such as myself?"

"Don't you know?" he teased. "The smart younger sibling of the powerful monarch always ends up being the evil villain."

She sighed and laughed. "Is that so?"

"Oh, yes," he grinned. "After spending her life in the shadow of her sister, the once beloved princess turns from the light and embraces a dark path."

"Let me guess. Only one man has the power to stop her?"

"No, no, no," Alverax waved his hands. "She cannot be stopped! She is a storm. She is the sun itself. A force of unbridled power. However, the day she is to unleash pure darkness upon the world, damning it to utter oblivion, a yellow-bellied starling perched itself on a nearby tree branch. In a tiny voice, the bird asked, 'Are you certain?'"

Her eyebrows rose.

"Then the bird turned into a handsome prince and they kissed and did other less wholesome recreations and, before they knew it, the day had passed, and the world was saved."

Jisenna gave a light clap of her hands, fingers to palm. "A strong beginning. A gripping climax. And a devastatingly awful conclusion."

"A villain *would* hate the happy ending."

"It's the bird," she explained. "If an evil villain were about to destroy the world, no sane person would flutter over to them and ask, 'Are you certain?'"

Alverax lifted his palms. "Who said anything about sane?"

"You are a curious boy, Alverax Blightwood."

"More than you know," he smiled. "You really shouldn't be seen with someone like *me*."

"I suppose that's true," she agreed. "After all, you are the last of the Obsidian threadweavers. Heir to the Watchlords. Blessed of the Heralds. The boy with the black soul. We wouldn't want people thinking you've corrupted me."

Alverax smirked. "To be fair, my irises are black, not my soul."

"Eyes are the windows to the soul, are they not?"

"Not mine. My lips are my windows." He winced at the insinuation, stealing an awkward glance at the guards standing watch. "That is because of...food! What I meant to say is that I am very hungry, and my little starling stomach

58

could really use some of that fresh Felian fish I keep hearing about."

"Ah, so you *are* the starling in the story," she laughed. "Down at the pier, one of the vendors sells a zesty tuna bowl that'll make your lips sizzle. If you're not busy, I could take you."

Alverax couldn't suppress his smile. "I assume you're paying? I'm a little short on shines."

Princess Jisenna rolled her eyes as she covered her head with a shawl and started down the hall. "Come on, little birdie."

Alverax moved awkwardly past the black-clad guards trailing behind her.

As they made their way to the pier, they spoke of many things, finding great surprise with how much they had in common. Jisenna's mother too had passed not long after she'd been born, and both had a special relationship with their grandfather. They spoke of the ocean, the calm of the crashing waves against the shore, the prickle of cold as you step into the water that sends shivers of excitement up the rest of your body, and the peaceful feeling of weightlessness below the surface.

She told him about her father, glancing up to the sky and explaining which star she'd chosen for him. He noted the reverence she carried when she spoke of him, and wished he held the same for his own father.

When the Terecean sea came into view, Alverax felt once again like he'd seen threadlight for the first time. A delicate warmth swelled in his breast. Countless rows of ships drifted back and forth with the waves, anchored along a labyrinth of wooden docks. Sailors hauled crates, farmers sold their fares, children scuttled along the boardwalks like grasshoppers, and street performers entertained crowds of cheerful onlookers. The energy poured through his soul. And the water called to him.

"Heralds," he muttered to himself.

The warmth in Jisenna's eyes as she looked out over the pier said more than any words she could have spoken.

"I don't think I could ever tire of this view," Alverax said.

"My first tutor—" Jisenna smiled, remembering. "I would make him read the same book to me over and over again, a short story about a bee with no wings. Every day he would ask me if I wanted to read something new, and every day I told him to read *The Song of the Flightless*. After we finished, he would tell me, 'Every wave is wont to break'."

She brushed a curly strand of hair from her eyes. "I never liked him. In fact, him saying that fueled my stubbornness. I asked for that book every day for months until he finally quit. Point is that I disagree with him. Not all waves are wont to break. Some waves, like the awe that fills me when I look out over the Terecean sea, those waves forever remain at their crest."

Alverax nodded, a serious look in his eyes. "Hmm, yes. Much like my hunger."

She rolled her eyes and led him down a long staircase toward the lower pier. The shop owner, a short woman with a dozen thick braids, bowed to the princess and offered her their bowls for free. Jisenna kissed her fingertips and placed them on the woman's forehead. They sat at the base of a grassy hill and ate while they watched street performers. Alverax took a large bite filled with rice, tuna, and a savory green fruit, all topped with the slightest drizzle of a zesty cream that sizzled on his tongue. After finishing every last grain of rice, he laid back and enjoyed the performances.

He was surprised to find that nearly all of the performers were threadweavers. Their acrobatics seemed an unconventional use of threadlight, but it made for the most amazing stunts. Flips that soared high into the air. Levitating human pyramids. Sapphires juggling with no hands. Emeralds juggling upside down.

One of the threadweavers asked for a volunteer, and Alverax quickly raised his hand. The performers applauded him as he approached. "What's your name, friend?" the lead asked.

One of the threadweaver acrobats, a small woman with dreadlocks and a pierced nose, spoke something indiscernible as she dropped to a knee.

Within moments, the crowd was whispering, and dozens more were pointing and dropping to a knee. There were many who looked genuinely confused at what was happening, but some followed their peers' response. Alverax looked behind him, searching for Jisenna. But as he turned, he found himself face to face with an empty green hill. Behind him, he finally heard the words being whispered.

Heralds.

Watchlord.

Obsidian.

Fear became panic, and panic became paralysis as Alverax faced the reverent throng of Felians. Jisenna stood quietly near the wide stairs with her head still wrapped in her shawl. She watched on, waiting to see how Alverax would handle the situation.

An elderly woman, with cracked skin and hair down to her hips, stepped forward. As she approached, she lifted her hand forward and pressed it to Alverax's cheek. "Heralds, save me. It is true." A single tear rolled down her cheek and fell across her lips.

"I'm sorry," Alverax whispered. "I'm not who you think I am."

"My cousin told me there was an Obsidian in the palace!" another shouted.

"Impossible!"

"A sign of the Restoration!"

"The Heralds are returning!" cheered another.

Alverax stood in awe as nearly a hundred fisherman, farmers, sailors, and others gathered around him. They spoke in hushed tones, questioning, debating, some giving looks of disapproval and scorn. Part of him wanted to stand tall and spin a beautiful lie and become what they believed him to be, but that was something his father would have done. He had to be better. He had to be honest. He had to be good.

A hand touched his arm. He turned in time to see Jisenna pulling the shawl off to reveal her face to the crowd. Those who were not already prostrate fell to their knees. The older woman's soft eyes smiled as she bowed her head. "Blessed Sun Daughter."

"All of you, please rise," she commanded. Her shoulders seemed to pull back. Her chin rose a little higher. "Since we were children, we were taught of the great prosperity during the time of the Heralds, and the Watchlords have since taught that one day the Heralds would return. The first Watchlord was the man closest to the Heralds, their chosen, blessed to become an Obsidian threadweaver. The man beside me is Alverax Blightwood. It is true that he is an Obsidian threadweaver, but there has been no sign that the Heralds have returned. If his arrival *is* a sign, if the Heralds *are* to return, the best way we can prepare is to humble ourselves and to work hard so that, should they come, we can welcome them with great abundance.

"The two of us are needed back at the palace. Please,

friends, return to your work, and may the Heralds bless you all." She leaned in to Alverax and whispered. "Time to go."

Alverax followed Princess Jisenna back up the long staircase, stealing glances back toward the pier. While most of the crowd had dispersed, returning to their work, there was still a small crowd, huddled together, watching Alverax climb the steps toward the Palace of the Sun. He wasn't sure how he was supposed to react to what had happened. Was it a good thing? Or would they think he was trying to amass some kind of cult following? The Elders would probably hate that he'd drawn any attention to himself.

Heralds...the Elders. He was supposed to meet Rowan ages ago.

"Jisenna," he called to her. She paused on the stairs and looked down at him. "I'm so sorry. I didn't know that would happen."

She cocked her head to the side and stared at him for a moment. "Were it not my idea to go to the pier in the first place, I might have thought you staged the whole event."

"I swear that's not the case."

"I believe you," she replied. "Unfortunately, apologies do not absolve the impact. Word of your arrival will spread. Stories will emerge. My sister needs to know about this so that we can control the spread."

He ran a hand through his short hair. "I have to go meet with one of the elders, but...thank you. The food was amazing, and the company was tolerable."

She sighed and shook her head with a smile. "Take care of yourself, little birdie. And you might want to avoid the pier for a while."

He nodded and she took off in another direction with the two guards following closely behind. His feet moved with surprising speed in hopes of keeping his mind occupied. He reentered the palace, then wandered through a series of corridors looking for Elder Rowan's room. He'd gained a decent mental map of the palace, but the rooms themselves all looked the same.

What he couldn't decide was whether or not he should tell Elder Rowan what had happened. On the one hand, she'd be furious if he told her and, on the other hand, she'd be furious if she found out he hadn't.

Eventually, he found the room and gave a knock.

As the thick door slid open, Elder Rowan offered him the only look she knew how to give. In the diffused morning light, her green eyes seemed even more bothered. Many of the Zeda people had slowly begun to adopt fashion of the region, abandoning their monotone outerwear for the more colorful and revealing picks of the season. Unsurprisingly, Elder Rowan clung to her Zeda browns. "You've taken your time."

Alverax stepped into the room. It was smaller than his— there was something oddly satisfying about that. He took a seat on a wooden chair that was less comfortable than it looked, which seemed to match many of the Felian styles. Beauty over utility. Even some of the dresses were so tight and awkwardly cut that the women had a hard time walking. Not that he was complaining.

"We've important business to discuss," she said curtly. "It appears there are fundamental differences between our histories and those of the Felian people. Their texts claim that Amber threadweavers are the enemies of the Heralds. Our people are descendants of Amber threadweavers. You see the predicament?" Elder Rowan remained standing as she spoke, her arms now crossed over her chest.

Alverax let out a sigh of relief. "That doesn't sound good."

"How astute," she said. "Additionally, our texts speak of the dangers of Obsidian threadweavers, while their texts celebrate Obsidian threadweavers as the Herald's greatest allies. Apparently, the first Watchlord was an Obsidian threadweaver."

Alverax paled. That would have been nice to know before he'd gone to the pier. "But that's a good thing, right?"

"Perhaps. Perhaps not." She took a seat across from him. "I know that I have been harsh in my judgments of you, and I hope that you understand my reasons were not insubstantial. However, it is time for me to put aside my bias. The livelihood of the entire Zeda people is at risk, and you may be the key to it all. Rosemary has kept the Empress away from you during the negotiations, to protect you, but also to protect us.

"It is time for that to change. We need you to immerse yourself in their society. You already look like them. We'd like you to become one of them. A neighbor. A friend. Because of your powers, the Empress will trust you. If you can convince her that we are allies worth investing in, then perhaps we can still save our community."

A weight poured over him, dragging him down into the stone beneath his feet. His heart beat faster as her request sunk in.

Alverax, can you please fix all our problems?

Alverax, turns out we're all going to die unless you can make friends with people that will kill you if they find out that you were a Bloodthief.

Alverax, don't do anything stupid.

Too late.

He didn't understand their culture. He didn't understand their politics or their religion. They were smarter, stronger, richer. Who was he to become one of them? He was nothing. The failed son of a thief that refused to die when he ought to. The last good thing he did may have doomed the world.

"Trust me, boy, I would prefer not to bet my coffin on you either. We will continue to work the angle of cultural histories and current events, but it would be foolish of us not to use every tool available."

"I'm not a tool," Alverax mumbled.

"You are today," she said flatly.

"And what happens when they find out I was a Blood-thief?" he nearly shouted. "It's not like we've been *transparent*. My eyes aren't going to save me."

"And what is the alternative? You wish to sit back and smell the roses while our people are smeared and slandered? You wish to lay by the sea and taste the salt while my people are killed for your people's actions? That is unacceptable. Iriel thinks you are a good man, but I've seen plenty of good men turn sour when the sun sets. Tell me, Alverax Blightwood, what manner of man will you be?"

Ah! She was infuriating. Obviously, he didn't want to sit back and watch them be killed. Frankly, he'd be killed with them, so the point was moot. But the question. That damned question burned inside him. What kind of man *was* he? He'd spent his whole life answering the opposite question. He knew he didn't want to be like his father, but that was an evasion of the more important question. Who *did* he hope to be?

He thought of his grandfather. Strong. Resolute. Merciful. Good to the core. That's what he wanted to be. A light. A giver. He wanted to be who Iriel saw—a man willing to sacrifice himself to save people in danger. The Zeda were fighting an ever-growing onslaught of dangers. Like Iriel and Aydin on the coreseal, more and more dangers were enveloping the Zeda each day, and they too needed him.

"I don't know," he said softly. "I want to bring hope to people."

"Hmm," she huffed. "If nothing else, this day, in this city, you have the chance to do just that."

He sat up a little taller, the weight beginning to dissipate as his resolve grew stronger. "Okay then. What do you need me to do?"

The old woman stood up and walked over to an enormous armoire. She opened the double doors half-way and paused. "Tell me, boy. Do you know how to dance?"

CHAPTER 8

MUCH TO HIS SURPRISE, Chrys Valerian awoke on a bed of leaves, feeling much like the death he thought he had embraced. But he *was* alive, despite the throbbing in his skull and the pain in his...

Pain.

He could *feel*, which meant...he was in control.

Chrys pushed himself to a sitting position and waited for his burning eyes to adjust to the sunlight. He rubbed his neck and smiled at how good it felt for his hands to do what he asked. When Relek was in control, it had felt like he was paralyzed, but worse, because he could watch as his body obeyed another.

When he looked around, he found himself in a small hut. He stood, carefully, and took the few steps required to reach the opening. It was clear that he was still in the Waste-lands, which made what he saw even more curious.

Humans.

Four of them.

Beside them, a thriving population of purple and yellow

flowers sprouted from long stems growing out of the swamp water. Thousands of red and white bees darted back and forth between the flowers and a collection of buzzing hives in the trees. Surrounding the scene was a wall built of tall spikes bound together with green ropes. In the trees above the wall, Chrys counted eight wastelander guards perched on platforms, their inhuman faces keeping careful watch.

He was in a prison.

Chrys let threadlight pour through his veins—at least, he tried. When he did, he felt his chest expand as though he were taking a breath, but no threadlight came through. Instead, a sharp pain surged from his heart. He clutched at his breast and groaned, fighting off his instincts to release more of the healing threadlight.

One of the humans spotted Chrys, a woman with ratty blonde hair and a hooked nose. "Aye, Roshaw. Bad news, buddy."

"What?" The dark-skinned man, Roshaw, turned and saw Chrys sitting up, and frowned beneath a shaggy beard.

"Did we settle on five shifts, or six?"

"Everyone gets lucky," Roshaw said. "And you know it was three." He turned to the other female prisoner. "I swear if I get stung on one of Esme's shifts, I'm gonna throw her down the Well."

Esme burst into laughter.

The other woman, thin as a reed with a jagged cut to her auburn hair, rose to her feet and looked to Chrys. "Ignore them. Just a friendly wager. We thought you were dead."

Chrys raised a brow. "You wagered on whether or not I was alive?"

"As long as you're not an ass, it was a win-win," Roshaw said. "Either you wake up and we have a new member of the crew, or you don't, and I get to skip out on harvesting for a few weeks."

"Harvesting what?" Chrys asked.

"We'll get to that," the thin woman said. "I'm Agatha. That's Roshaw and Esme. And the last one is Seven." The latter waved and Chrys caught a glimpse of his hand. It was clear where he'd acquired the name.

"Real question is who are you?" Roshaw said.

Esme rose to her knees. "And what the hell was a thread-weaver doing east of Everstone?"

"Stones," Seven whispered, rising to his feet as the others turned to him. "Lightfather be damned. Chrys?"

Chrys looked again at Seven. Past his thick beard and gnarled hair, there was something familiar about the man. Something in his eyes. Not the achromic brown, but the shape and intelligence. *Stones.* Chrys recognized him. He'd been one of his soldiers during the War of the Wastelands.

"Pieter," Chrys whispered.

"Aye," he replied. "But Seven has grown on me. It's good to see you, sir."

"Wait a minute," Esme said, waving her arms. "You two know each other?"

Seven nodded. "That's Chrys Valerian. He led my battalion. Damn fine soldier."

"How did you end up here?" Chrys asked.

"Captured during the war."

"No," Chrys said in disbelief.

"Everyone but him," Esme added, pointing to Roshaw. "He doesn't get to be an official member of the crew until he hits five years."

Five years.

Captured during the war and caged like cattle ever since. The reality of it loomed over Chrys like a storm cloud, threatening a deluge, and darkening the moment of light-heartedness. The fact that these people had not escaped, or died, or killed themselves, seemed impossible, but no one was laughing.

When Chrys failed to respond, Agatha sighed. "It's not all bad here. They feed us well, and it's generally safe. The company is good—"

"Debatable," Esme said.

"—what I'm saying, is that it could be worse."

"Sure," Esme said. "When we first arrived, they would beat us and such, but they mostly ignore us now."

Chrys looked at each of the people now standing in front of him. Four prisoners left alone for five years in the middle of the Wasteland swamps. "I don't understand. You've been here for five years? Why keep you alive for so long?"

Agatha's face grew somber. "There were sixteen of us when we first arrived. Two died shortly after from infection. Three have died over the years from the et'hovon—the bees. A few escape attempts killed five others. And there were two friends that couldn't take it anymore and threw themselves into the Well. We're the only ones left. We've all picked up a bit of their language—Roshaw more than most. From what we can tell, they kept us around as a gift for their god. But he never showed up, so they started using us to harvest the honeycrystals."

"That's—" Chrys started.

"Horrible?" Esme cut in. "Depressing? Hell yeah, it is. But at least we're alive. And we have each other...for now."

"We've tried everything," Seven said. "We made weapons and tried to fight our way out. We dug a tunnel under the hut. Someone tried playing dead once, and they stabbed him in the heart to make sure he wasn't faking it."

"This is our life now," Agatha said quietly.

71

Roshaw rubbed his palms and a small grin carved its way onto his lips. "There is one difference—"

The others turned to him.

"Now we have a threadweaver."

CHAPTER 9

A SINGULAR SCREAM drifted through the dreary streets of Alchea, weaving its way through the stormy, night air, and climbing through Laurel's window. She sat up, cold and sweaty, with an army of goosebumps covering her arms beneath a wool blanket. They'd barely just returned from the Fairenwild, and her mind still raced with fears and questions. She'd tried to sleep, but every flicker of a shadow had threatened her peace.

Beside her bed, the chest that held her transfusers beckoned her.

Sounds from the midnight streets. Voices. Laurel wasn't sure if they were even real. Losing her threadlight was affecting her mind, and that scared her even more.

Once again, screams echoed in from her window.

She rushed over, scratching her arm as she investigated the noise.

A light rain misted over the moon-lit city, puddles forming in haphazard pockets across the cobblestone. A pair of elderly women clutched large bags and sprinted as fast as their brittle bones would take them. A unit of

Alchean guards stomped through in the other direction, each carrying a steel blade.

A tree branch rustled in the wind and its shadows wavered.

Then the empty street came alive. Small puddles at first, splashing in chaotic bursts. Rain falling in impossible ways. A subtle stirring of the ground beneath her. Then it grew. More puddles displaced. More rain struck nothing, then dripped down the same nothingness. It took her only a moment, memories of the dark beneath the coreseal fresh in her mind.

Gale take me.

Laurel reached into the chest beside her bed and pulled out a transfuser, swallowing the contents with haste. Blood ran down her throat like sugar water, threadlight seeping its way into her veins. It filled her with a vile warmth that pressed her goosebumps back into their homes.

When she looked back out the window, her heart skipped a beat. Hundreds of creatures of various shapes and sizes trampled through the street, spectral monsters born of brilliant, prismatic light. Some as small as a skittering rat, others like alien horses trampling hard against the stone. It was a disturbing beauty, celestial and captivating.

Slamming her curtains shut, Laurel moved to the hallway. If there was one thing she knew about the corespawn, it was that Alabella could kill them. The safest place she could be right then was with her.

Luther Mandrin, friend to the missing High General, Chrys Valerian, had just finished a drink at the Black Eye when a guard came through shouting about an attack on the city. Luther tossed some shines on the table near Laz and was out the door before the guard could finish his words.

After losing his youngest son to the Order of Alchaeus, and watching a false priest die at the hands of a traitor, Luther had taken to drinking more than he knew he ought to. He stayed out later and later and spoke harsher and harsher to those he loved, but it was all he could do to ignore the building pressure that threatened to consume him.

None of that mattered now. If there was danger, he had to get to his family.

Screams in the distance passed through his ears with disregard. He had one purpose, and nothing would distract.

He turned a corner with beads of rain dripping down his bald head and entered Beryl Boulevard. He nearly tripped as he came to an abrupt halt. In the center of the thorough-fare, half a dozen caravans lay toppled over, their contents spread throughout the street like blood splatter. Men and women lay dead in the street, bleeding, bite marks and scratches painted across their corpses. But one woman was alive, crawling along the road. For a moment, Luther thought of rushing to her to help, but, instead, he chose his family.

Just then, as if the world was mocking his decision, the woman's torso was torn in half, one side vanishing into nothingness, while the other sprayed blood in a horrific display of death.

"Stones," Luther cursed aloud.

He let threadlight pour through his veins. The dark stage surrounding him dropped its curtains. Multicolored threadlight danced through the streets like actors in a demonic play. Where once there had been nothing, creatures hewn of pure threadlight prowled the streets. Small beasts nibbled on corpses. Massive creatures on two legs circled the caravans, searching for prey.

One of the smaller creatures jerked its head away from its meal and lifted itself to all fours, following Luther's movement across the road. It screeched, and Luther watched a dozen more of similar size turn their heads in unison.

He set his jaw and ran as fast as he could, threadlight and adrenaline coalescing in his veins like rivers of oil-filled water. His heart raced in his chest. Drops of rain slapped across his face. He finished crossing the street and turned to find a small battalion of beasts gaining on him.

As he turned the corner, he crashed into a younger man, knocking him to the ground. Luther didn't hesitate, he *pulled* himself against the closest building and scaled the side of the wall as if the world had turned on its side. He reached the top and looked down just in time to see the creatures overwhelm the young man.

Luther took off across the rooftop and *pulled* himself toward the next building, extending his arc, then landed hard against the rooftop. He scanned the streets below for the invisible creatures, but found none, so he dropped to the ground and continued toward his home.

By the time he arrived at his house, his lungs felt ready to burst and his heart was a beating war drum. He rushed inside and found his wife, Emory, sitting with their younger daughter on her lap, the other child clutching her arm with a feral grip.

"We heard the screams," she whispered. "What is it?"

Luther slammed the door shut behind him and pushed their dinner table in front of the door. He stepped toward the kitchen window and shut the drapes, peeking through a gap in the middle. "Shhhhh."

"What is it?"

His lip snarled as he stared out the window. "Hide the kids and stay quiet. They're coming."

LAUREL RAN down the hallway and into the warehouse where clothing and equipment lay sprawled out across long tables. From the front wall, screams rose in terrific harmony. Laurel rushed over and slammed open the door to find Alabella and Sarla surrounded by a dozen corespawn, different in shape than the one they'd found beneath the coreseal—these were wider, with tall ears that stood erect— but still seemingly shaped by threadlight itself.

Threads stretched forth from the ground, grasping the corespawn and binding them in place. They thrashed back and forth while Alabella groaned, spreading her mind thin as she bound them all.

Sarla cried, clutching a fresh wound on her left arm. In her hand, she held the obsidian blade.

"Hurry!" Alabella roared. "I can't hold them forever!"

"They're invisible!" Sarla shouted angrily.

"Give it to me!" Laurel shouted over the pouring rain.

When Sarla saw who it was, she tossed the blade clumsily through the air. Laurel reached forward and snatched it, then lunged ahead, driving the blade hard into the nearest creature. She could feel the blade connect, its edge connecting with light-wrought flesh, but, as soon as it pierced through, the creature's body exploded like a pin to a bubble, thousands of beads of threadlight erupting in a cloud of radiant color.

Laurel flipped the blade in her hand and smiled.

The next closest corespawn was only a few paces away, its radiant light seemingly dimmer than the previous. She ran toward it and slammed the blade through its neck. Again, the creature burst apart in an explosion of threadlight.

"Is it working?" Sarla shouted over the sound of the growing rainfall.

Laurel ignored her and continued her rampage, water pouring down her blonde hair as, one by one, she drove the obsidian blade through each beast. Every time one of the corespawn burst apart, there was a certain feeling of catharsis that accompanied it, a similar pride she'd felt flicking spiders off of their webs in the Fairenwild.

Suddenly, all signs of threadlight vanished.

She swept her eyes in a full circle, searching for the remaining corespawn, but, in her rage, she thought that, perhaps, she'd already killed them.

Alabella looked troubled as she glanced to the other side Sarla. "What are you doing, Laurel? Finish them off. I don't know how much longer I can hold this."

Laurel looked again and saw nothing, then realized the truth: the blood from the transfuser had worn off. She cursed under her breath and moved to where Alabella was looking. She urged threadlight to pour through her veins as she had done so many times before, but none came. Only the cold emptiness she'd learned to live with.

As she approached the location, she swung the blade wildly out in front of her like a machete sifting through undergrowth. She breathed in deep, glancing toward Sarla who watched her with curious eyes. Then, quite suddenly, the dagger struck true and she felt the familiar feeling of connection and release as a corespawn burst apart beneath the blade.

"Point me to the last one," she said. But when she turned, she saw Alabella collapsing to the rain-soaked stone.

Gale take me, Laurel cursed.

There was still one corespawn left, she had no more threadlight, and it was no longer bound.

LUTHER'S FAMILY huddled into a closet in their younger daughter's room while Luther kept a lookout in the kitchen. A creature the size of a large horse circled the building, walking on two legs as it sniffed at the doors and scratched at the walls. Luther hoped the beast would become bored or disheartened and leave their home alone, but it seemed content to wait out its quarry.

As it disappeared around the back side of the house once again, Luther rushed into his room and lifted a long bundle out from beneath a floorboard. Swords were uncommon among threadweavers in Alchea, seeing as how dangerous they were to use against another threadweaver. But many in Felia maintained the warrior art, including Luther's grandfather who had gifted him this sword when he was young.

Luther slid the long blade out of its sheath. It was heavier than he remembered, but with such a large creature outside his home, he needed a heavier weapon.

A roar, like the rumble of a quaking mountain, filled their home, and Luther heard his children cry from the other room. He ran out of his room and was nearly blasted off of his feet as the front door shot from its hinges in an explosion of splintered wood. Luther dove out of the way of the table he'd propped up behind the door that came hurtling through the air like a stick.

Threadlight poured through the doorway as the creature stepped in.

Luther snarled and set his feet, gripping the blade as he'd been taught. Like holding a woman's hand. Tight enough for conviction; loose enough for trust.

It launched toward him, but Luther rolled out of the way before its long arm struck. The creature was fast for its size, but Luther *pulled* against the wall behind it, doubling his speed, and came crashing down atop its head with fury. He drove the blade down into its skull. It was an odd feeling as it entered, as if the blade were digging through molasses. He yanked it out, leaving a gaping crevice where the blade had pierced it, then dropped back to the floor.

He moved himself out of the way as the creature teetered, then watched as threadlight pooled around the wound like blood, coagulating, then resealing. In moments, it was as if his blade had never struck its skull.

The creature turned to him, leaned forward, and let out a roar that caused the walls to shake in terror.

Luther cursed. If that didn't kill it, he didn't know what would. He needed to get his family to safety or distract the beast long enough for them to get away. He had to do something, because it was only a matter of time before the building and everyone inside would be crushed by its fury.

As his mind raced, calculating his next move, Luther saw movement in the shattered doorway. Just outside, eyes and veins blazing brightly with threadlight, stood Lazarus Barlow and the Alirian Spider, Reina Talfar.

"Is too much light," Laz said, smiling his toothy grin. "Time to put out."

LAUREL TURNED IN A PANICKED CIRCLE, searching for the final corespawn. With Alabella unconscious, there was no one to stop it from attacking. In the shadow of a moment, she'd gone from predator to prey.

From the corner of her vision, she saw invisible footsteps in the puddles between the cobblestone, and they came right for her. She set her feet and waited for her moment. As the footsteps approached, Laurel dove out of the way, slashing the dagger down as she moved. But she missed, and the creature bit down on her forearm.

Laurel screamed out in pain, dropping the obsidian blade. The weight of the invisible foe came over her, knocking her to her back. She closed her eyes and felt the air shift. Her arms extended and caught the corespawn around the neck as it thrashed back and forth near her face. She kept her eyes closed, knowing that sight would only confuse her senses. Her arms burned as they struggled to keep the creature at bay long enough to—to what?

She needed the obsidian blade.

In that moment, the smell of roses overwhelmed her senses. It brought her back to the Fairenwild, home to the various varieties, each unique in their own way. But now, smelling the scent so powerfully, in the midst of stone and death, the joy it should have brought to smell such a lovely creation was ripped away from her, replaced with a new truth: death smelled of roses.

Laurel let out a guttural cry as she curled her legs in beneath her and kicked with every bit of strength within her. She felt the skin of her forearm scrape away as the corespawn was flung from atop her. She opened her eyes in time to see a puddle, not far from her head, splash where the corespawn hit the ground.

With her own battle cry, Sarla rushed the puddle and drove the obsidian blade down where the invisible creature must be. Then she backed up, swinging the dagger back and forth, watching the puddles in the street for movement. Laurel lifted herself to her feet and fixed her eyes on a single point in the cobblestone, letting her peripherals scan for movement.

After a minute of peace, she relaxed.

Sarla rushed to Alabella, checking her pulse and lifting her eyelids. "Excessive use of threadlight, but she should recover."

Laurel clutched at the gash in her arm. "She better."

LAZ LOOKED DOWN at Luther's sword and raised a brow. "Nice pointy stick."

"Not now, Laz."

The creature stalked toward them. Its entire body was nothing but a writhing mass of undulating threadlight. It had to have a weakness, but Luther didn't have time to figure it out.

"We need to get it out back," Luther said.

Reina nodded. "Easy."

She picked up a chunk of splintered wood and hurled it at the creature. It struck true and the creature roared in return.

"Come get me, ya big *hole*!" she shouted.

Laz gave her a nod of approval.

Luther clenched his teeth and the beast launched forward with terrifying speed. Luther, Laz, and Reina sprinted out of the house with threadlight burning in their veins and cut back around the side toward the backyard. As they turned the corner, a stable and a large shed came into view, along with a well-maintained garden of flowers.

"Laz, there's rope in the shed," Luther said, gesturing for him to go. "Still know how to lasso a bull?"

As he ran toward the shed, Laz understood the request. "Ha! I can do this thing!"

Luther and Reina had to distract the creature long enough for Laz to get into position. If they could tie it down and bind it, they could figure out how to kill it later.

"Be careful," Luther said to Reina.

"Worry about yourself," she said with a smirk. "Your bald head reflects more light than the moon. That thing's coming for you first."

She was right.

As it rounded the corner of the house, the creature doubled its pace and rushed directly at Luther. He held the longsword in both hands, preparing for the next attack, but the beast grew smarter and paused as it approached. It lunged in, testing the boundary, and Luther swung in a wide arc, narrowly missing the creature's face. It lunged again, but retracted when he swung, and, when the blade had passed, it swiped furiously with both hands in quick succession. Luther heaved the hilt of the blade toward the creature's head, but it was too fast. Its head cracked into his ribs and knocked him over.

"Hey, big boy!" Reina yelled to distract it. "Over here!"

It gave no heed to her and, instead, leapt toward Luther on the ground. But as it soared through the air toward him, its entire body was yanked back. Luther lifted himself up and saw Laz's rope wrapped around its neck. The hulking Emerald reeled it in like a fisherman, then leapt atop its back, wrestling it to the ground as he gathered three of its legs. He looped the remaining rope around the legs and tied it off faster than Luther could have imagined possible.

"Ha!" Laz bellowed as he jumped away from the writhing creature. "Is easy!"

"Will it hold?" Luther asked.

"Yes, probably. Most likely."

Reina stepped forward. "What do we do with it?"

Luther swung the blade around in his hand. "Now we figure out how to kill it."

CHAPTER 10

ALVERAX FELT SIMULTANEOUSLY a great king and a greater fool. He wore a single-breasted black tuxedo with a dozen golden buttons down each lapel and chains that ran from the back of each button up to the shoulder. It was slightly altered from the current Felian fashion to emphasize his shoulders by pulling the seams under his arm up higher. It made it very difficult to move his arms but, according to the seamstress, his shoulders were "delectable'" and she had "no choice but to make the alteration". He'd have nightmares about that conversation for years.

The more interesting piece of his attire was the mask. Once a month, the nobility held a masquerade ball to "diverge from their transparent culture". The mask would be removed upon entrance to ensure only the invited guests would attend but, once inside, the mask was reapplied, and all were considered "equal". It wasn't exactly true, most people were still recognizable, and some tried little to hide themselves, but, in spirit, they were equal. Elder Rowan claimed it would be a good time to immerse himself in their culture and customs. Alverax thought it was a terrible idea.

Fortunately, he wasn't alone; Iriel Valerian walked beside him.

It was, perhaps, the first time Alverax had ever seen her without Aydin. The fit of her dress accentuated her toned arms and slender waist. It seemed like every day since they'd met, she'd grown more fit. When they'd traveled through the countryside west of the Fairenwild, she'd told him stories about her martial training in Alchea. And now, the veins in her forearms served a suitable testament.

"How are you feeling?" she asked as they approached the ballroom.

"Honestly?" he grimaced as he adjusted the feathers on his mask. "If I lift my arms, I lose feeling. And if I turn my head just right, it feels like a feather duster is giving my nose a very thorough cleaning."

He could see her smile beneath her mask. "Oh, mine is dreadful. I'm pretty sure they glued it to my forehead. But it's honestly a welcome distraction."

It was easy to forget that she'd lost her husband, literally. No one knew where he was, or if he was alive. And her son was a short step from being labeled a demon by the Felian aristocracy. The mask over her face hid much, but it failed to hide the hint of loneliness in her eyes.

"I think we could all use a little distraction," he said, though he knew she could use it more than most. "Any news of your mother-in-law?"

"If she'd come west, she would have arrived days ago," Iriel said with a sigh. "No one's heard anything."

"Well," Alverax said, lifting his head high. "Tonight, you and I are going to forget it all! I will be Alexander Grant, purveyor of fine wines from a vineyard just north of the Malachite Mountains. And you will be Jacquelyn Joy, heiress to the largest collection of goats east of the Fairenwild."

Iriel let out a clipped laugh. "Here and I thought the purpose of us going was to make a *good* impression."

"You drive a hard bargain," Alverax said with a straight face. "I'll drop the name, but I'm keeping the vineyard."

She shook her head.

Finally, they entered the ballroom. Alverax was astounded by the grandiosity. Hundreds of windows covered the circular, vaulted ceiling. Starlight trickled in alongside a full moon, combining with a host of sconces lit with tiny flames along the periphery of the room. Theatrical costumes. Elegant live music. And the flowers. If the palace entryway was a bed of flowers, the ballroom was a field. Roses—white, red, and violet—filled every inch of the space not meant for socializing. The scent filled his soul.

They walked the room, filled with attendees, and found their way across the dance floor to a collection of long tables filled with food and drink. Alverax took a sip of wine, then picked up a small, triangular pastry and took a bite. A burst of apple with a pinch of honey exploded in his mouth. His eyes opened wide as he ate the rest in a single bite.

With his mouth still full, he turned to Iriel. "I heard the secret ingredient is goat milk from the Jacquelyn Joy estate."

She rolled her eyes and led him away, but not before he grabbed one more and shoved it in his mouth. As they moved, his eyes drifted to the corner of the room where something curious caught his eye. It was as though a small section of the wall, from waist high and below, blurred in his vision. But as soon as it appeared, it was gone. The wine in Felia was clearly stronger than what he was used to.

A man and woman linking arms approached them. The

man wore a white suit with a sharp, red mask with the antlers of a deer. The cut of the woman's dress crept up her leg to just below her hip, with a neckline to give any man pause. Her taupe mask shot up on one side and curved into the shape of a crescent moon. She wore a dark violet lipstick.

The woman spoke as they neared. "Merikai, is that you?"

"No, no, no," the man said. "The hair is too short, and that is certainly not Zoelle."

Alverax removed his mask. It was uncommon—or so he had been told—but it was also the elders' instruction. *Let them see your face and make them like you.* The first part was easy. He smiled wide and extended his hand. "Alverax Blightwood. It's a pleasure to meet you. Unless, of course, this Merikai character is horribly unattractive, then a Herald's curse to you both."

"Ha!" the man laughed, shaking Alverax's hand. "Always an unexpected treat to meet the new couple."

"Oh, no," Iriel nearly shouted. "I'm married. Alverax is a friend. I am called Iriel."

The woman gave a small curtsy. "Santara Farrow. And this is my eternal partner, Rastalin Farrow, first in line to the post of Watchlord."

"It is a pleasure to meet you both." Alverax placed his mask back on. A bit of feather fell off and fell to the floor. "I'm embarrassed I have to ask, but can you explain to me what exactly a Watchlord is? We're both new to Felia."

Santara gave a knowing smile. "It is not often that those new to our city are invited to occasions such as these. But men like you are an occasion until yourself."

Rastalin laughed. "A warning, my young friend. The women of Felia are teases. Trust what they say, but beware what they do not. The Watchlord is, as you asked, the guardian of truth, and the chosen of the Heralds. It is his duty, first and foremost, to prepare the people for the Heraldic Restoration. In the meantime, they serve as head of the Felian army and counselor to Empress Chailani."

Alverax's grandfather had never taught him much of his religion, but he knew the basics. Once upon a time, the Heralds walked the earth. After establishing peace, they disappeared to never be seen again. Someday, they would return and heal the hearts of men.

"And you are first in line? Meaning if the current Watchlord—Osinan, was it?—was to fall ill and pass away, you would take his place?" Alverax pursed his lips. "That is a terrifying amount of responsibility."

Rastalin's smile was egregious. "Faith conquers fear, my young friend."

Just then, the music stopped.

All heads turned to the entrance.

A woman stepped forward, her pure white dress so large, the train so long, that several attendants had to carry it as she moved. Somehow, the dressmaker had woven in dozens of white roses into the dress itself. Then he saw her. Just beyond the Empress, another woman entered. Her mask did little to hide her identity. Alverax would recognize that flowing black silhouette anywhere.

The Farrows took the distraction as an opportunity to leave, and Iriel leaned in to whisper. "If all of the Felian nobility are that arrogant, I swear I'll jump out one of those windows before this night is over."

"They're not *all* that arrogant," Alverax replied.

They talked to a dozen other people, including a young man wearing a horned mask that he claimed gave him supernatural strength. Alverax was quite sure the young man was mad. Finally, no longer able to resist, he left Iriel and approached Princess Jisenna. She was surrounded by a dozen women, laughing and trying their best to impress. She looked genuinely happy, despite the social politicking.

She looked up and, when their eyes met, his heart pounded. He steeled his nerves and advanced.

Princess Jisenna stared at him as he approached, the dozen women surrounding her turned and did the same. He immediately regretted his decision. What did he expect? That they would all leave so he could talk with her?

A woman with a reddish tint to her long dark hair spoke first. "Who do we have here?"

"I don't recognize him."

"Is he new?"

"What is your name, my lord?"

"He has a very strong jaw."

"Dark eyes. Must be rich."

"Are you from out of town?"

"That tuxedo is a quite fetching fit."

"It is certainly a flattering cut."

"Ladies," Jisenna said, coming to his defense. "Please, do not scare him away. He is one of our special guests this evening. This is Alverax Blightwood, the last Obsidian threadweaver."

Alverax smiled awkwardly as the introduction settled. Two of the women gasped aloud. Several whispered to each other, and Alverax was certain he saw one squeeze the hand of another.

A woman with a thick strand of white in her long black hair took a step toward him just as a new song began. "An honor, my lord. Please pardon our manners. These masquerades are so often filled with the same people that a little novelty is quite exciting, especially when the novelty is —if I may be so bold—a singularly handsome man."

"It was just a bit of fun. No harm done," Alverax replied, trying to hide his discomfort.

"If you're not spoken for," the woman continued, "I would be honored if you would join me for the next dance."

Heralds, save me.

"Actually," Princess Jisenna cut in, "Alverax promised me the first dance of the evening."

He turned to her.

She gave not the slightest hint of deception.

"It would be a shame to break a promise," he said with a smirk. "Perhaps another time?"

He held out his hand and Jisenna took it. Together they left the group behind and walked to the dance floor. He looked at the dozens of others already dancing and was relieved to find them moving in a style similar to what he'd practiced. He stretched out his hands, palms up, and she placed hers with the palms up atop his own. Couples who had promised themselves would dance with their palms together and, even though theirs were not, the brush of the back of her hand on his lit a flame inside of him.

For the briefest moment, despite all rationale, he let himself believe that she liked him more than she surely did. The Princess and the Obsidian. The Sun Daughter and...the Bloodthief. Who was he fooling? They would find out sooner or later.

"Is something wrong?" she asked as their feet carried them in a circle. "You've the face of a man who's made a mistake. I'd hate to think that was on my behalf."

Alverax gave her his most convincing smile. "No, no. It's just...I'm not used to all of this. Especially the attention."

"You will get used to it. In truth, you will likely tire of it," she laughed to herself. "That is assuming, of course, that you plan to stay."

"I don't think there would be a warm welcome for me where I'm from. Although, I would love to see my grandfather again before he passes away."

"Is he ill?" she asked.

"Oh, no," Alverax said. "Us Blightwoods don't die easy. He's just old. Though being old is really just being sick of life. So, I suppose he is a bit ill."

"If being sick of life is a symptom of old age, I must be ancient," Jisenna said with a wide smile.

"Well, you look amazing for your age."

"I..." he stammered, pulling his hands back.

Elder Rowan's words echoed in his mind. *Don't do anything stupid.*

"I'm sorry!" he said, quite forcefully. "I forgot that Iriel needed me for something. Thank you for the dance! And thank you for saving me earlier!"

He left without giving her a chance to respond and cringed when he saw the confused look in her eyes. Elder Rowan had been quite clear about what he needed to accomplish during the masquerade, and a poor attempt at flirting with the princess was *not* one of them. He still needed to talk to Empress Chailani and the Watchlord.

Near the food tables, he saw Iriel engaged in what seemed to be an enjoyable conversation, so he looked for the empress. She stood near the front of the ballroom, flanked by two guards and a serving woman who held the train of her dress. The man she was conversing with gave a bow and started to leave. Alverax let a bit of threadlight run through his veins to steady his nerves.

Perfect, he thought.

Hoping to step in before another had the chance, Alverax moved toward the empress. But just as he arrived, a blurry shift in the air flickered in his vision. For a moment, he thought it a mirage—no one else seemed to see it. He opened his eyes to threadlight, and a swirling maze of radiance blazed to life. It stood on two legs, like a person, but a thin tail arced up over its head. The end of the tail, spiked like a scorpion's stinger, stretched back to strike.

No.

Alverax dove forward to stop it, but it was too fast. Its stinger pierced into the empress' chest. Its arms threw Alverax atop Chailani's body as she gasped in pain. The prismatic light swirling across the creature's body called to him and, so, Alverax reached out to it with his mind and *broke* it. In a split second, the creature exploded into a million beads of light and vanished.

Screams erupted in the ballroom. The music stopped. Heads turned. The guards were on top of Alverax before he could breathe, blades ready to bare down.

It all happened so quickly.

"No!" Princess Jisenna shouted. She ran across the room, ripping off her mask, and fell at her sister's side. "Heralds, please, no!"

The world blurred in front of him. Time, like a wave against the bluff, crashed to a halt. The white roses from the empress' train seemed to fill the entirety of the room; red specks of blood stained them like drops of rain down a wet canvas.

And Jisenna, hands clutching her sister tight, tears flowing down her perfect cheeks, turned to Alverax with rage in her eyes. "What have you done?"

CHAPTER 11

THOSE FOUR WORDS, Jisenna's words, broke him.

What have you done?

Alverax may be many things—a fool, a poor judge of character, a fraud—but he was no killer. Unfortunately, the people of Felia didn't know that.

"Something attacked her," he shouted into the marble floor. "It wasn't me!"

Jisenna screamed in pain as she clutched her sister's corpse. The entire ballroom seemed to pause in time. The dancing ceased. The blaring shock faded to a silent fright, leaving only the sound of Jisenna. She was a meteor falling to the ground, and the people stood, bewildered, watching as the devastation unfolded.

The empress was dead.

"I swear it wasn't me!" Alverax shouted. "The creature! There was a creature! Someone had to have seen it!"

"Save your lies!" Watchlord Osinan shouted, appearing from the crowd.

The guards shoved his face down into the floor. Their knees dug into his back, taking the air out of his lungs. A young guard with Emerald threadlight glowing in the veins of his neck stood nervously at the edge of the crowd. For a moment, Alverax thought the guard would come to his rescue, verify that there had been a creature. But instead, he closed his mouth and said nothing, and Alverax felt his hope slipping.

Watchlord Osinan looked to Alverax, bound by thick guards, his face smashed against the floor. "We never should have trusted you. Your people lied. I want every last one of the Zeda imprisoned. They will pay for what they've done."

"You know me!" Alverax shouted to Jisenna. "I would never do this!"

She said nothing, but, when her eyes met his, he could feel her response more strongly than any spoken word could have conveyed. The quiver in her lip. The twitch of her eye. All of it said, *I don't believe you.*

The guards lifted Alverax to his feet and tied his wrists behind his back. But then, just as they were about to take him away, he saw her in the corner of his eye. Iriel Valerian stalked through the crowd like a viper, slithering between masked onlookers, fists clenched ready to strike. With deadly speed, she leapt forward, *pulling* against the far wall and ripping her way through the air toward the guards. She crashed into both, knocking them over, then grabbed Alverax's shoulders.

"Break your corethread!" she shouted, shoving him toward the window. "Now!"

His corethread *broke* with urgency, and he felt gravity dissipate. In the same moment, Iriel *pulled* again on the wall and, together, they shot through the air toward the window. The glass shattered as metal ripped out of the sill, shards drifting through the air like beads of rain, cutting at his cheeks and hands.

And then...freedom.

He *broke* Iriel's corethread as they burst out of the window into the night sky. High above the palace grounds, drifting horizontally like carefree gulls toward the Terecean Sea, he looked back behind them and nearly screamed as a spear shot passed his head. Several guards stood at the shattered window, shouting words that Alverax couldn't hear—he wasn't sure he needed to.

"We shouldn't have run," he said to himself. "Heralds, we shouldn't have run!"

"There was no other choice," Iriel said confidently. "Someone set you up."

"No one *set me up.* There was some kind of invisible creature!"

Iriel scowled but said nothing.

"The Zeda," Alverax remembered. "The Zeda! We have to do something! We have to warn them!"

"We need to get Aydin," Iriel said. "Stones, we need to get *down.*"

As soon as their corethreads reappeared, they began to fall back toward the ground and, as soon as they did, Alverax *broke* their corethreads once more, sending them down at a comfortable speed for landing. Fortunately, they were far enough from the palace that there was no way the guards could follow them. That meant that they had a little time before the Felian armies would surround the Zeda encampment. On the other hand, the elders staying in the palace were trapped already.

Their feet hit the ground on a field of jade, thin grass swaying in the coastal breeze. Neither said a word as they took off running as fast as they could toward the Zeda encampment near the southern wall. In no time at all, they left the field and entered the cobblestone streets of Felia.

Tents and pavilions and small stone shops lined the labyrinth. With the sun set low beyond the western sea, they tried their best to keep course.

When they arrived, a battalion of Felian soldiers surrounded the tents. The encampment, nestled against the high city wall, was an agitated beehive. Scared Zeda ran around, gathering their children and shouting at guards. A swarm of raging women roared at a man surrounded by a dozen guards.

"Stones," Iriel whispered under her breath. "We're too late."

Alverax stood quietly, catching his breath. This was his fault. If he hadn't left Cynosure, he wouldn't have been caught by Alabella. And if she didn't have him, she wouldn't have attacked Zedalum. They would still be safe and content living alone in the Fairenwild. Now, they were being rounded up like fish in a net.

He had to do something.

He had to help.

He turned to Iriel. "I have an idea, but you're not going to like it."

ALVERAX APPROACHED as close to the Felian guards as he dared, hiding behind a half-full wagon, and waited for Iriel to get into position. From his new vantage point, he watched one of the guards reach out and slap a sobbing Zeda woman. The blow knocked her to her knees.

Iriel arrived in position and gave him a nod. He wasn't sure if it was going to work, but he knew he had to try. The thought reminded him of his grandfather as they sat along the steep cliff at Mercy's Bluff overlooking the Altapecean

Sea. His grandfather had looked down at the water far below and asked, "Do you think there are any sharks down there?" Alverax had shaken his head in doubt. His grandfather smiled and said, "Perhaps not. But we can't know for certain up here. The only sure way to know what's below the waves is to take the dive."

He took a deep breath and let threadlight pour through his veins. Thousands of strands of brilliant luminescence burst into his vision, pulsing in chaotic harmony. Before he could doubt himself, he took the dive. One by one, with a focus like never before, he *broke* the corethread of every soldier within sight. Pressure built in his veins, pressing against his skin. Still, he continued, systematically hacking his way through corethreads like a farmer sifting wheat. But, before he could finish, a sharp pain erupted in his chest and he dropped to his hands and knees. His heart burned within him. Throbbing. Squeezing. Stabbing. He struggled to breathe.

He clenched his jaw and opened his eyes to survey the effects of his work. Dozens of soldiers screamed, and Alverax gasped. The entire squad of soldiers floated away on the westerly wind like the seeds of a dandelion to a child's breath. Watchlord Osinan was one of them, tumbling head over heel and flailing with terror stricken across his face.

The remaining soldiers struggled to hold back the fleeing Zeda people as they scattered in every direction. Other soldiers fled and tried to help their drifting comrades. But one soldier, a short man with a wide frame, shoved down a young Zeda girl. Alverax recognized her. The soldier walked forward and kicked her in the stomach, shouting for her to stay put.

Alverax lifted himself up, breathed like a raging beast, and rushed the man. With every ounce of his remaining strength, he leapt, both feet forward, and just before his feet struck, he *broke* the soldier's corethread. The collision sent the soldier blasting into the air and over the tents.

"Poppy?" Alverax asked the girl, grunting as he rose to his knees. "Are you okay?"

The girl looked up and noticed the man was gone. Her mid-length hair fell in just the right way that it looked like the droopy ears of a Felian bloodhound. "I'll be alright," she managed.

"You have to run. The soldiers will be back any minute."

She nodded and ran.

Just then, another wave of soldiers arrived, bolstered by their allies who had returned to the surface. They swarmed forward through cobblestone streets like millions of desert scarabs.

As he stared, paralyzed with fear and exhaustion, a hand grabbed his shoulder. He startled, then turned to see Iriel holding Aydin.

"Let's go!" she shouted, pulling him away from the incoming soldiers.

Alverax nodded and stumbled after her toward the wall on the other side of the Zeda tents. When they reached it, Alverax steeled his gut, and *broke* his corethread one last time while kicking off the ground. His chest seized as he floated up over the wall. No matter how hard he tried to breathe, the air refused to comply. An odd sensation blossomed near the top of his spine, like a wound breaking open. He grabbed hold of a stone crevice along the peak of the wall and flipped over flat on his stomach.

Iriel screamed.

He looked down with blurry eyes, and saw an arrow jutting out of her calf. She was falling. Aydin was in her arms, screeching, and she—Heralds, save the woman—was falling to the ground.

Alverax, knowing his body couldn't handle it, opened himself to threadlight one final time and *broke* her corethread. He couldn't stop her fall, but he could lessen the impact.

Soldiers swarmed her and the child as soon as they hit the ground.

Time slowed to a crawl. Below him on one side of the wall was chaos, and on the other side, the intoxicating lull of peace, a calm river that ran parallel to the wall. He knew he should run—only then would he have any semblance of hope in helping the others—but a potent instinct grabbed hold of him from the inside. For all Iriel had believed in him, for the trust she'd offered him, he owed her more than a lonely prison cell.

With blurry eyes and a mind on the edge of blackness, he was in no state to save her, but he couldn't let her go alone.

As his mind faded to darkness, he tried to lean toward her, to go with her. But instead of falling toward his friend, his mind blurred and he slipped. His body drifted off the far edge of the wall. The world moved slowly, trees drifting in the wind, rays of light bouncing off the water. It all seemed to slow more and more the further he fell, and then, just before he hit the surface of the river, his vision grew black.

CHAPTER 12

CHRYS FELT a wave of fear as he approached the multi-layered hive of the wasteland bees. Thousands of red and white insects, each nearly as large as a man's thumb, buzzed around the central trees of the prison enclosure, moving in and out of a conglomerate of nests. Tunnels, like man-made corridors, linked each nest together into a catacomb of terrifying proportions.

Every instinct told Chrys to open himself to threadlight, but, same as they had every day, the wastelanders had fed him a drink that blocked his source. For now, he would have to go without.

Roshaw led him forward, carefully watching each step so as not to accidentally step on one of the insects. The buzzing sound intensified as they approached the center, and dozens of bees brushed up against their bare arms. One sting, the crew said, was enough to kill a man, though it would also kill the bee. The crew claimed that no one had been stung without previously disturbing the bees—like stepping on one of their family.

"Almost there," Roshaw whispered, careful to keep his mouth mostly closed.

Then Chrys saw it. In the center of the closest nest, protruding from the bottom like a dripping stalactite, was the solidified purple material they called honeycrystal—Esme called it "bee snot". Once a week, one of them would enter the hive and extract however many honeycrystals had grown. The result was then brought to the chief of the ataçan.

Roshaw reached his hand up toward the crystallized material. Bees landed on his slow-moving hand and darted away when they decided he was no threat. Chrys watched in awe, terrified that at any moment one of the bees would fly into his eye or sting his hand. He wanted to fight back. If he was going to die, it wouldn't be while he was standing still in a tornado of wasteland bees.

Finally, Roshaw's hand reached the base of the honeycrystal and grabbed hold. He twisted and the shard broke free of the nest. Slowly, he pulled down. A hundred bees, like bats exiting a cave, rushed out of the newly formed hole at the base of the nest. Roshaw stood frozen while bees swarmed around him, prodding, testing, measuring the danger. Chrys hated watching and feeling so helpless. The memory of Iriel and Aydin on the wonderstone flashed in his mind as they were overwhelmed by dozens of tentacles of threadlight. In that moment, he'd been completely powerless.

Roshaw's hand began to lower, still holding the honeycrystal. "Back up."

Chrys obliged, and, after an eternity of slow movements, they were finally free from the spread of the hive. A great relief washed over him.

"Not so bad, right?" Roshaw said with a triumphant grin.

"Stones," Chrys cursed. "If the bees don't kill me, the stress will."

"The stress is more likely to kill you than the bees. Apparently, they don't care about humans. Now, if you were a wastelander, the whole hive would come down on you. Agatha is convinced it's their smell."

"Their smell?" Chrys repeated.

"The wastelanders have a very distinct smell. Somewhere between the sweet smell of magnolia and a man's sweaty ass." Roshaw smiled at his own joke. "You can wait here or go join the others. I need to go check for more honeycrystals."

Chrys eyed the hive with reservation.

"I'll be fine," Roshaw said, pulling on his earlobes. "One-hundred percent human."

With a nod, Chrys joined the others sitting in a bunch at the doorway to the hut. Seven was massaging Esme's feet while they watched Roshaw perform his duty. They had seen the honeycrystal extraction hundreds of times over the five years they'd spent trapped. They no longer saw danger in the act. Only duty. That, Chrys could understand.

"Well?" Esme said, her mouth open while Seven rubbed her feet. "Pretty crazy, right?"

"I would be happy to never experience that again."

"You'll get used to it," Seven said. He patted Esme's foot and stood up. "If you step on one, you'll get stung. But otherwise, you'll be fine."

"I don't plan on getting used to it," Chrys said. "I plan on showing the savages what happens when you imprison Chrys Valerian."

Agatha rose to her feet, a hint of excitement in her eyes. "The wastelanders are *not* savages. In fact, they are quite fascinating."

"Oh, no," Esme said. "You've activated the professor."

"Hush, hush," Agatha said, swatting the other woman in the shoulder. "Though they are inhuman, their culture is still quite rich. One of the more interesting aspects is their reverence for both the en'tovon—the bees—and the ataçan —the gorillas. They see the relationship between the two the same way they see their own relationship with their gods. The wastelanders are a hive. Each individual is willing to sacrifice themself to protect the greater whole. In fact, their leaders are often selected from those who have willingly sacrificed themselves yet survived. The other great purpose of the hive is to provide food for the ataçan with the honeycrystals. For the wastelanders, this means giving themselves in service to their gods."

"*Dead* gods," Esme corrected.

"Possibly," Agatha said. "From what we can gather, something happened just before we arrived. Their god, whom they call *Relek*, vanished. "

Stones, Chrys thought. *He is their god. And now he's returned.*

What would that mean to the wastelanders? Would they gather forces and finally head over the mountains? It would explain why they'd been so passive in their defense during the war. They'd never pushed a victory. Never come further than the valley. His mind raced. The wastelanders knew of Relek's ability to inhabit other bodies. That was the real reason they'd kept the prisoners alive. A gift for their god when he returned. Honeycrystal for their ataçan.

He wasn't sure what it all meant. Were they in danger? Did the wastelanders no longer need them?

Before he could respond, Roshaw returned holding a third honeycrystal, each shard a varying shade of violet, but all shaped like a thick icicle. "Aye, you ready to make a delivery?"

Chrys had so many questions for Agatha and the others, but there would be time for that. He was just as interested in the next step of the harvest, when they would deliver the honeycrystals to the chief of the ataçan, whom they called Xuçan.

The two of them left the others and walked to the large gate. Roshaw showed Chrys how to present himself so that four wastelander guards could bind their wrists together with a rope at the end that they held like a leash.

The guards accompanied them out of the enclosure, and they began their journey to the Endless Well. When he'd asked about the location, the crew had all laughed and said that he just had to see if for himself.

Chrys hated that he couldn't understand the wastelanders as they spoke to each other, especially given all of the smirking and laughing they did on Chrys and Roshaw's behalf. It felt very much like they were being led to a trap, and the guards couldn't help but revel in the inevitability. But Roshaw knew the path, and made no comment, so Chrys disregarded his instinct.

On their way, he spotted the edge of the village, which appeared much larger than Chrys had originally thought. Small wooden buildings hung suspended between trees with shaky wooden bridges between them, ladders dangling haphazardly amongst the chaos. Young wastelanders leapt from one platform to another while others swung from vines between buildings. What surprised him most was the mass of wastelanders lying on their backs in the swamp water, seemingly asleep.

They continued on and the edge of Kai'Melend faded behind mossy trees. They passed a small body of water where dozens of wastelanders knelt quietly. The still water shimmered a pale golden color as if reflecting a hidden sunset. The wastelanders approached one by one and drank from it reverently.

"What is that?" Chrys asked.

"They call it *oka'thal*, which means *life water*." Roshaw rubbed at his beard. "It's sacred. From what I understand, every wastelander comes here each week and drinks from it."

"So, they worship the bees, the apes, *and* the water?"

"Yeah, and our people revere shiny rocks," Roshaw said with a laugh. "You have to get out of that mindset. Their world is different; that doesn't make ours better. In some ways, they're more evolved than we are. Did you know their eyes see better in the dark? Or that they're partially amphibious?"

"I—" Chrys started.

Roshaw cut in. "I'm not trying to make you feel guilty. I'm just saying that there is good among them. And we're not all that different. As for the ataçan, the wastelanders don't worship Xuçan. They fear him."

Chrys turned and looked at the four guards, and felt a new sense of respect for them. They were soldiers just as much as he was, serving their commander to the best of their ability. Could he fault them for taking prisoners? Alchea had done the same. The only difference was that Alchean prisoners never would have survived for five years.

Eventually, they crested a small hill, following a well-worn path through thick vines. When they stepped out of the jungle, Chrys' heart skipped a beat. Before him lay a sprawling panorama lit by a cloudless sky, a large lake feeding a collection of majestic waterfalls that sent their waters cascading down into the Endless Well.

Chrys had expected it to be small—how large could a "well" be? But the opening in the earth was so wide that an entire battalion could step off the ledge at once without breaking rank. To his left, atop a sheer cliff overlooking the lake, a troop of ataçan stretched out over the rocks. Sitting on the highest boulder, like an emperor overlooking his kingdom, sat an ataçan nearly twice the size as the others with four thick arms. Even at such a distance, Chrys felt the power and pride of the chief of the ataçan.

"I assume you don't need me to tell you which one is Xuçan?" Roshaw slapped Chrys on the back and smiled. "The trick to the next part is to not make eye contact."

"Has he killed anyone?"

"None of the crew, but a few years back he ripped a wastelander in half that tried to bond him."

Chrys paused, not at the brutality, but at the penultimate word. "Tried to *bond* him?"

"Ah," Roshaw said. "The bond is fascinating. Some few of the ataçan choose a companion amongst the wastelanders, and a bond is formed. Honestly, I don't know much about it, except that the wastelander becomes a little more like the ataçan, and the ataçan a little more like the wastelander. There are only a handful of wastelanders bonded, and it is an instant elevation in status. Kind of like if your kid became a threadweaver suddenly. Good for the kid, but also good for the family."

The wartime reality of having an ataçan on your side was terrifying. As far as Chrys knew, no ataçan had shown up in the battles in the mountains. But if the Alcheans ever came further east, thinking the wastelanders would be easy to conquer, a single ataçan would kill dozens, if not more.

Roshaw continued. "Lots of young wastelanders attempt the bond. Even if they fail, it's a well-regarded sacrifice for their family. Generally, the ataçan kill them. Since I've been here, only one wastelander has formed a bond, and it was a young one. Xuçan exiled the ataçan who formed the bond. Supposedly, he's hundreds of years old and has never accepted one himself."

"Not even from their god, Relek?"

"Hmm," Roshaw said thoughtfully. "I guess not."

They both grew quiet as the terrain grew steeper. Their guards slowed, slackening the leash and giving more space between them. The urge to run, to escape, to fight now that they had the advantage of the high ground and a little space to work with, wiggled its way into Chrys' mind, but he pushed it away. Maybe if he had access to threadlight.

The time would come, and it wouldn't be when they were sandwiched between warriors and ataçan.

As they grew closer, Chrys got a better look at the beasts, and at their leader, Xuçan. He'd seen sketches of the apes of western Alir, tucked away in the jungles of a secluded island, but those were roughly the size of a man. The ataçan were twice that size, mostly gray with varying shades of blue. Short, yellow spikes ran down the length of their spine, and tusks cut out from their jaws, curling upward. Their arms were so thick that Chrys had no doubt about the stories of ripping a wastelander in half.

If the ataçan were a beating rain, Xuçan was a thunder-storm. Larger than the rest, he was the only ataçan with four arms, each as thick as the last. One of his tusks was broken mid-way, with the jagged edges even more threatening than the whole. He sat upon a flat boulder with brows set so deep his eyes were bathed in shadow.

Xuçan and the others noted their arrival and fixed their gaze upon Chrys and Roshaw. The wastelander guards dropped the leash and stayed behind, keeping their eyes fixed to the ground. As they approached, Roshaw lifted the lavender-colored honeycrystals, following the example of the guards and keeping his eyes down. When he was close enough, he dropped down to a knee.

Never in his life would Chrys have expected to see a man bowing before a beast, bringing him a gift as though he were the true emperor of the land.

The closest of the ataçan, a large beast with a blue streak across its face, beat at its chest with massive fists, each hit resounding like a war drum. Chrys clenched his teeth and met its gaze. It let out a series of deep-throated grunts and slammed its fists against the ground.

Then Xuçan roared. The sound seemed to come from every direction, bellowing in Chrys' ears, threatening to break his mind. Chrys turned his gaze to the ataçan chief.

A voice like thunder echoed in Chrys' mind. *You disrespect us.*

A cold shiver traveled up his spine. The beat of his heart quickened. Somehow, the words echoing in his mind belonged to Xuçan. A sense of preservation urged Chrys to fall to his knees like Roshaw beside him, to express his respect to the ataçan, but he refused. He would not bow to Relek. He would not bow to Alabella. And he would never bow to an oversized wasteland gorilla.

The great chief stepped down from his perch, passing the other ataçan as he knuckle-walked down the sloping cliffside. Chrys watched in silence, never averting his gaze from the powerful, deep-set eyes of the chief.

"Heralds, save us," Roshaw said under his breath. His eyes bore into the ground, his arms shaking as he held up the honeycrystals.

Xuçan stopped in front of Chrys, his face impassive save

for the constant downward curl of his lips. *Tell me, he-who-does-not-cower, who are you?*

The words, simple as they were, seeped into Chrys' soul. A creature like Xuçan was not asking for his name, nor his history. He was asking who he was at his core. What truths laid his foundation? Chrys was a husband, a father, a threadweaver, a warrior, but in each of these things he had fallen short. He was a failure, and his legacy was a trail of broken glass. He was a man who had given everything and received nothing in return.

Speak! the great Xuçan roared in Chrys' mind.

"I am he-who-sacrifices-all," Chrys said aloud, adopting the ataçan's style of speech.

Xuçan placed all four fists down on the ground surrounding Chrys, leaning in and letting his breath mist over Chrys' cheeks. *You are like* him, *but different. Do you serve he-who-perverts-the-bond?*

"I—," Chrys started. "I don't know who that is."

He-who-steals-life, Xuçan said. *The creature of many faces.*

Chrys furrowed his brow, then relaxed as understanding washed over him. "Relek."

Xuçan rose high onto his broad legs and roared a guttural cry that filled the entire world around them. *DO NOT SPEAK THAT NAME HERE!*

"Heralds," Roshaw said, quivering. He peeked to the side, still prostrated, but confused at the one-sided conversation. "You're gonna get us killed!"

Chrys ignored him. "He-who-steals-life has taken everything from me."

Xuçan settled down, his breath still heavy. *That name is forbidden here. He-who-perverts-the-bond is forbidden here. You will leave now.*

Chrys nodded and gave a small bow. "Thank you."

He grabbed Roshaw's arm and instructed him to drop the honeycrystals at Xuçan's feet before dragging him to safety.

"What the hell just happened?" Roshaw asked, glancing back over his shoulder toward the massive ataçan chief.

"I'm not sure," Chrys said. "But it gave me an idea."

CHAPTER 13

EACH MORNING WHEN CHRYS AROSE, the wastelander guards forced him to drink a murky liquid that suppressed his threadlight. After a few days, he'd realized that it was an inherent flaw in their stewardship. Any plan of escape was far from complete but being able to identify an area of weakness would give them a leg up when the day arrived.

Several days passed, and Chrys was surprised that the wastelanders did, in fact, leave them alone almost entirely. He was also surprised that the crew had built a functioning game board for a traditional Alchean game called Scion, a triangular board with a series of holes. Each player had ten pegs that they used to capture those of the other players. The last remaining player won.

They used the time around the board to badger him with questions, and Chrys told them everything. If they were going to escape, he needed them to trust him. So, he held nothing back. Agatha, who was so enraptured by his story that she refused to take a turn playing, asked the most questions, and gasped when he told her what happened when they'd arrived in Kai'Melend. Chrys shared that Xuçan referred to Relek as the "creature of many faces", and it seemed to haunt them all. They wondered if the fear the wastelanders held toward the ataçan was related to the apes' disdain for their god.

The wastelanders had been wary of Chrys ever since the encounter with Xuçan. None of the other members of the crew had ever spoken to the ataçan, and the occurrence seemed to affect them as much as it did the wastelanders who'd seen it from a distance. When the guards looked at him, instead of looking on with disregard as they had before, they now showed him open hostility. One slammed his spear into Chrys' stomach when he had failed to swallow the murky drink fast enough, which ended with them having to leave and come back with more.

But beyond all of the questions and answers, one vital conversation occurred: how to escape.

The crew had come together and created a plan for how they could all escape the enclosure, and, more importantly, get back over the mountains. Rather than traveling west, as they'd done before and as the wastelanders would expect, their plan took them south. Roshaw knew of a path around the southern border of the Everstone Mountains that would take them safely to the west.

But their plan hinged on two key, unresolved contributions. First, they would need Xuçan to let them pass over the ridge without allowing the ataçan to murder them all. Chrys felt confident that with one more conversation, he could arrange that. The other piece required a test.

Chrys fell to his knees and clutched his stomach, doubling over and groaning in pain.

"Aye!" Esme shouted much too loudly. "Are you okay?"

He groaned dramatically, falling to his back and

writhing against the muddy ground. All four members of the crew ran to him, surrounding him in a circle.

"Help!" Seven shouted, turning to the wastelander guards. "He needs help!"

Roshaw called out for help in the wastelander tongue, but the guards watched on impassively. They were happy to let Chrys die—especially given the conversation with Xuçan —which was exactly what they were counting on.

Chrys rolled over onto his stomach and reached his finger down his throat, shoving it as far as he could before the heaving began. His stomach seized up, and his throat tightened. Again, he inserted his fingers, triggering a series of painful heaves until, finally, he vomited into the swamp water. He smiled and did it again, unloading all of his food and water onto the floor of the enclosure. Then, he rolled over and let the others lift him up, carrying him to the hut in the center, and laying him down.

They waited for the wastelanders to realize what they'd done, but the guards stayed put in their perches above the wall and happily remained wrapped in the warmth of their apathy.

After a few minutes of quiet, Chrys signaled for the others to surround him. Chrys relaxed his mind and let threadlight pour through his veins. His body braced itself for pain, knowing that the murky liquid they fed him could very well still be in his system. Instead, the warmth of threadlight flowed from his chest down to the ends of his toes, sizzling beneath his skin. The heat engrossed him like the warm embrace of an old friend, squeezing, and promising that, no matter what, he would always be there.

The others looked at his glowing veins and tried not to smile, but Roshaw's smile was wider than them all. "This is really gonna work. I'm gonna see my kid again."

"He probably doesn't even love you anymore," Esme said.
Roshaw's smile faded.

"Psh." Esme rolled her eyes. "Don't be a baby."

Seven stared at the radiant, Sapphire hue running along Chrys' arms. "Either this is going to work, or we're all going to die."

Chrys flicked a rock across, giving it an extra *push*. "This is going to work."

CHAPTER 14

THERE WAS a certain biting chill to the morning wind that blew throughout the streets of Alchea, a fitting complement to the destruction left in the wake of the corespawn. Laurel, like many others, had spent the remainder of the night bunkered down, listening to the dissident melodies of devastation that filled the night air.

Runners from Endin Keep had announced throughout the city that the attacks had ended with the rising sun, and Great Lord Malachus called for all citizens to assemble in the sprawling courtyards outside the keep. Laurel had traveled with a company of the Bloodthieves that included Alabella, Sarla, and Barrick, the large man who'd accompanied them to the Fairenwild. They said little as they traveled to the keep, none daring to speak the truth. In the Fairenwild, beneath the coreseal, it was *them* that had released the corespawn.

When Alabella removed her Felian lightshades to wipe off the lens, Laurel caught a glimpse of her eyes. The woman had always seemed so confident, so strong. But something had changed. A shadow of fear. What they had done cracked the façade, and now, a pinch of doubt spread its roots within the woman.

When they arrived at the gates of Endin Keep, Laurel winced at the reunion. She'd only been there once, and the result had been devastating. She feared what conclusion this day would bring.

Already, thousands began to form in the courtyard of the keep, huddled below a raised platform on the far side of the great central fountain. Laurel looked at the faces of the grounders that surrounded her. Eyes sunken with fatigue. Shoulders slumped. Heads bowed. In a single night, these people had been broken. And for those who were not threadweavers, who could not even see the enemy, how could they not?

Laurel and the others approached the platform. Hundreds of soldiers lined the periphery, creating a wall of protection between the people and the dais from which the Great Lord would address them. Atop the platform, dozens of threadweavers, men and women, stood at attention, their eyes and veins still tinted from the extended use of thread-light. Laurel had a transfuser in the inside breast pocket of her jacket, but she hated herself for needing it. She clasped her shaking hands and tried to calm her fluttering heart with steady breaths.

A trumpet rang out, announcing the commencement of the assemblage. The threadweavers on the platform stood at attention and, from a ramp on the far side, a familiar woman stepped forward. High General Henna wiped the white hair from her eyes, then stood with her hands inter-locked behind her back. She scanned the crowd for danger.

Behind her, the Great Lord himself arose. There were no cheers, no chants of acclamation, the city stood on edge to hear how their leader would respond to the tragedy that had decimated their world. He approached the front of the platform, head held high, and the last remaining whispers of the crowd gave way to an eerie silence.

"We are under attack," Great Lord Malachus exclaimed. "I will not insult your intelligence by claiming it to be anything less than what it is. You have seen the devastation. You have walked the broken streets. You have mourned your fallen friends and family. It is the obligation of a responsible leader to acknowledge such reality. Only then can we move forward.

"A leader must—above all else—see to the safety of their stewardship. Today, we assemble because a new danger has arisen, something the likes of which this world has not seen in centuries. But we are Alchea! We are stone! We will stand united! We will fight! The streets of Alchea belong to *us*! Tonight, we will be prepared. And when the enemy comes, Alchea will prevail!"

The crowd let out a boisterous applause, a choir of cheers bellowing out over the sprawling courtyard. Laurel could feel their enthusiasm. She saw it in their eyes and in the curves of their lips. Great Lord Malachus wasn't just a ruler, he was *their* ruler. The powerful, bichromic Great Lord.

"To prepare for the return of the beasts, we will hereby institute the following measures effective immediately. Listen close, as these three measures will affect all of us.

"First, a mandatory curfew from sundown to sunset. Just before the sun rose over the Everstone mountains, the creatures fled to the west. To the cover of the Fairenwild. We believe a second attack is most likely to happen under cover of darkness. Luther Mandrin, one of our most decorated soldiers, was able to catch one of the creatures. Our people are studying it as we speak. With the limited knowledge we have, a quarantine is the most effective strategy to ensure the safety of our people.

"Second, all windows are to be boarded up, in both homes and stores. The majority of the creatures are small enough that they cannot break down your walls, and those that are we hope will ignore homes that are dark and quiet. Tyberius and Mirimar Di'Fier have offered to provide all of the lumber necessary, which you will find available at their mill in the upper west side. If you are unable to board up your home before the sun sets tonight, find a neighbor who has and join them for the evening.

"Lastly, as the head of the Stone Council and the Order of Alchaeus, it is my solemn duty to protect those who have dedicated their lives to the Lightfather. Until the threat is gone, the Temple of Alchaeus will be closed and all its occupants moved into Endin Keep. There is nothing I hold with more gravity than the safety of this people. Be vigilant. Be responsible. And, above all else, be strong. Together, we *will* prevail."

Again, the crowd broke out in raucous applause. But this time, to Laurel's surprise, pockets of men and women cursed their ruler. A young man standing not far from Laurel shouted up at the Great Lord. "We want to fight, not hide!"

"Aye!" the group surrounding him exclaimed.

"Give us swords!"

"Let us fight!"

"Cowards!"

The crowd turned course like a shifting wind. One by one their enthusiasm and doubt began to spread like a plague, until Malachus pointed to the young man who started it all and gestured for him to join him on the platform.

"Tell me," Malachus said to the young man with a booming voice, "have you seen one of these beasts?"

The young man shook his head.

"Have you?!" Malachus shouted, pointing to an angry man in the crowd. "You? Or you?" He continued to single out individuals closest to the platform. "You may have heard the rumor, but I tell you now that it is true. These creatures cannot be seen by achromats. If I handed you a blade, you would die to an enemy that you could not even see.

"We have a plan, but you must trust us. Stay in your homes. Board up your doors and windows. Keep your lanterns dark. And under no circumstance should you attempt to fight these creatures. Bravery and stupidity are ever at odds, and, in this case, to fight is to prove your own ignorance.

"Now, gather your supplies and go home. Tonight, stay safe. The time to fight will come."

A somber chill covered the crowd as they cowered beneath their chastisement. Laurel watched as parents clutched their children a little more tightly. Slowly, the courtyard emptied and the guards atop the platform guided the Great Lord toward his keep.

Laurel turned to Alabella and found the woman staring off into the distance. She nearly asked what was on her mind, but she knew. Their trip to the Fairenwild. The shattered coreseal. Opening the tunnel. Alabella had caused this with her reckless goals and ambitions. She'd wanted equality for all, and she'd found it. All are equal in death.

Alabella turned to Laurel and the others. "I have an idea. Come with me. We need to have a conversation with the Great Lord."

A GROUP of Alchean guards ushered them to the Great Lord's study high in the keep tower. Laurel felt a tightness in her chest as she walked the halls, the painful echo of a memory. She felt at her breast pocket to make sure her transfuser was still there. Her nerves urged her to take it and drink, but she refused. Sarla had only given her enough for one in the morning and one in the evening. She needed to save it.

Finally, the door opened, and the guards led them inside. Alabella, Sarla, and Laurel were led in gracefully, and Barrick was searched before they allowed him to enter. Inside the room, Great Lord Malachus Endin stood behind a large table, flanked by a wide window that overlooked the city. Surrounding the table were a host of other men and women, two of whom Laurel recognized: High General Henna and Luther. When they saw her, they gave each other a confused look.

"Great Lord," one of the guards said. "This is the woman I told you about."

Malachus took a deep breath and looked up from the city map sprawled across his table. "I was told you have a means of making the creatures visible. You have two minutes to explain."

Alabella placed two fingers to the rim of her Felian light-shades. "I only need one."

When she took off her lightshades, Amber threadlight blazed from her irises. One of the older generals gasped, but they all seemed to distance themselves at the revelation. But Luther knew—Laurel could see it in the fire of his eyes. He'd known of the Amber-eyed leader of the Bloodthieves, and now he saw her. His teeth crushed together as he fought to maintain his composure.

Alabella did not smile or taunt—she gave no undue

provocation. Instead, she stood tall and eyed the Great Lord with confidence. "I will be honest, if you will be patient. In this time of unexpected darkness, we must all be willing to ally ourselves with unexpected associates."

Malachus eyed her warily. "I've heard of you, and now that I see you, I do believe we've met before."

"To the future," she replied, pretending to lift a glass.

"Ah, yes. I believe we toasted to those words." Malachus lifted his hands to address the others in the room. "Friends, allow me to introduce the leader of the Bloodthieves."

Every eye bore down on her, as though she were a snake, waiting to strike. But that was not why she'd come. As much as Laurel loathed the woman, she respected her decision to offer aid to the Alchean people.

"Sheath your egos," Alabella said, calmly. "We are all here to save lives, and I come to offer a donation. Your men do not stand a chance against the corespawn, because they cannot see them. I have a supply of threadweaver blood that will give your men the ability to see threadlight, and thus see the enemy. I understand that you see the consumption of threadweaver blood as immoral. However, in desperate times, men must choose between morality and victory. You must ask yourselves if your conscience is worth more than the lives of your people."

"This is absurd!" A man in his late forties with an ill-placed scar on his lower lip and Emerald eyes, spoke with a gruff voice. "We can't—"

"Rynan," Malachus cut in. "I know for a fact that you would kill a thousand men to save one of your own. Would you not take one drug to save a nation?"

"It's not a drug!" Rynan said. "It's a blasphemy! You would be feeding *blood* to our soldiers. Blood that once ran in the body of another man."

Malachus hardened his gaze. "The smallest speck of dust can change the fate of a duel. You know this. We are not talking about a speck of dust in the eye; we are talking about an entire battle without sight."

High General Henna stood with her chin high. "The Order of Alchaeus would never support this. The Stone Council—"

"I *am* the Stone Council," Malachus cut in.

"Respectfully, sir, you are the Great Lord," Henna said. "They may call you the head of the Stone Council, but, in reality, you know that is not true."

"Whether they believe it or not, it is what it is. The Order of Alchaeus is living under my roof at this very moment. I control their future. They are in no position to question my decisions."

"What do you want, Malachus? Do you want our opinion?" Rynan asked. "Or do you want us to sit down like good little boys and do what we're told?"

"You go too far, Rynan," Malachus said, eying the man. "We've been discussing ideas for hours and we have no plan. We would be fools not to entertain an idea that could offer an advantage. I am not agreeing to it outright, but I am not foolish enough to discard the idea on the basis of some variable definition of morality. Remind me your name," Malachus added.

"Alabella Rune."

The Great Lord met her gaze, her Amber connecting with his Emerald and Sapphire. "Lady Alabella, bring your blood to the keep. We need to be prepared to use it should we find no other alternative."

Alabella nodded. "To the future."

CHAPTER 15

WHEN HE CAME TO, Alverax was lying on the rocky floor of a river, completely submerged. His body groaned as he ripped himself out of the water and drank in the air above. The skin over his upper spine stung as if he'd gashed it on a rock.

He took off his tuxedo jacket, which had rips along the seams of both armpits, and tattered edges along the chest. He tossed it aside and unbuttoned his shirt. When he examined the white dress shirt, he found only the slightest remnants of blood along the back, so he figured he would be okay.

The sun rose over the eastern horizon, illuminating the white walls of Felia across the river.

He must have been unconscious for hours.

Heralds.

Iriel and Aydin had been captured. The Elders were prisoners. If they were lucky, some few of the Zeda had managed to escape. But the more he remembered the swarm of incoming soldiers, the less likely that seemed. They were all apprehended. And they were going to be executed.

124

For what? A crime he didn't even commit. What *was* that creature? Was it even real? Was he losing his sanity? He felt okay, but perhaps madness only felt like madness to those not fully mad. No, he was fairly certain he was sane. He'd seen the creature. He'd watched it kill the empress. Then he'd watched it explode.

What worried him more than anything was wondering if there were more of them.

He picked himself up, took a step toward Felia, and paused. If he went back, they would kill him. He could head east and find a nice quiet town. Or maybe join a caravan headed south, jump on a boat, and spend the rest of his life on the beaches of Kulai. That didn't sound half bad. But that damned question—the question posed by Elder Rowan simply to torment his brittle mind—had taken a firm grip on his soul. He could hear her voice. *What manner of man will you be?*

I don't know. I want to bring hope to people.

With the great walls of Felia looming in the distance, Alverax knew what he had to do.

He made his way to the main road and met a small group of traders that let him join their caravan. One kindly old man offered him clothing to wear in exchange for his wet clothing, a deal that Alverax was certain would benefit the old man in the long run.

It didn't take long to reach the main gates of Felia. An army of soldiers crowded the entrance, but they were more focused on people attempting to leave, and the leader of the caravan knew one of the guards who let them in. After they'd passed through the gates, Alverax thanked his companions and headed north toward the palace.

He traveled down quiet paths, away from the main thoroughfare, and several times he nearly walked into patrolling guards. With the numbers he'd seen, he assumed that they hadn't been able to round up all of the Zeda, and still searched them out. Their pale skin set them apart, and the tattoo on their back was an easy identifier. Their people were not prepared for assimilation, especially in Felia.

As he grew closer to the palace, he grew more and more worried about his plan. It was audacious and required a little more bravado than he'd normally presume, but if he could pull it off, he might just be able to do something truly good. There were plenty of ways it could go wrong, but, at the end of the day, Jisenna was the Mistress of Mercy, and he hoped that would be enough.

By the time he reached the palace, he was as cold as he was tired. The pain along his spine had faded only the slightest, even when he let a bit of threadlight into his veins. He looked out over the palace grounds and found even more guards than he'd expected. They were like weeds, infesting every inch of the walls, with large groups covering every entrance. He followed the wall from a distance, looking for any area that might have less eyes watching— maybe he'd be able to float over without being seen—but the guards were efficient in their duty. By the end, he stood near the large canal that fed the palace with fresh water from the river upstream.

Which gave him an idea.

He dove into the water, letting himself sink far below the surface, and followed the current toward the palace. Soon, the canal ended with a series of large pipes, each closed off with a grate. He tried pulling on one, but it wouldn't budge. He spent a full minute underwater thrashing against the grate before he realized that there was a latch. After he released it, the grate opened with ease.

He carefully ascended for a gulp of air, then paused to prepare himself. If he went through the pipe, he'd end up somewhere in the palace. He wasn't sure where, or if he could hold his breath long enough, or even if he could find an exit large enough to fit through. But it was the best chance he had to get inside, and if anyone could hold their breath long enough, it was the breath-holding champion of Cynosure.

He filled his lungs with air and dove down, filled with renewed purpose. The tunnel grew pitch black, and he worried for a moment that he would lose his sense of direction. His hand trailed along the edge of the tunnel as he kicked his legs behind him.

After several minutes in darkness, taking twists and forks that he hoped would keep him centered, he stopped to feel the surroundings. He hadn't seen even a glimpse of light, and it was quite possible that he had missed whatever path he should have taken. He'd known it was a foolish plan, but it wasn't until that moment, surrounded in darkness and entombed by frigid water, that he realized just how foolish he had been. He'd only wanted to help, to force their hand somehow, but now he was going to die somewhere where no one would ever find him.

It was too late to turn around. He knew he wouldn't be able to hold his breath long enough to return back the way he'd come, not to mention he'd be swimming against the gentle current. So, instead, he continued on. Swimming for his life. Swimming for the life of his friends. Swimming because he was the only hope the Zeda people had, and he'd be damned if he let them die without giving everything he had to save them.

And, fortunate for him, Blightwoods don't die easy.

With renewed hope, Alverax pressed on. His hand brushed along the side of the tunnel, and he steadily kicked his feet back and forth. He *would* find an exit. He had to. But the further he went, he still found nothing. He let the last of his air out, releasing pressure from his lungs, and knew he only had one more minute to find air.

He swam as fast as his legs could propel him, but the faster he swam the more he needed to breathe. His lungs screamed in silent protest, begging for just the smallest bit of food to fill their emptiness. A rhythmic beating echoed in his skull, and he knew that consciousness was only moments away from fading.

He'd tried. It was the most he could do. He knew he was close; he could sense a shift in the water. Warmer, perhaps? But it was too late. His feet refused to kick. His body floated down to the bottom of the tunnel, scraping against the rounded walls and tearing at the wound on his back. As his mind wrestled with consciousness, he thought he saw a light in the distance. If he could only make it.

Just as he opened his mouth to breathe in his defeat, air seemed to pour into his lungs, rejuvenating him just enough to push off the ground toward the light. His body moved through the water like he was a creature of the sea itself. The light grew along with his hope. Before he knew it, he was crashing face-first into another grate. He opened the latch, pushed it open, and shot out into the open air above.

His lungs took it in like a father returning from war and squeezing his children with all his might. Never again would he depreciate the value of a single breath. Never again would he be dumb enough to swim into an endless tunnel of water without knowing what was on the other end...

He looked around and found dim lamplight illuminating a large room filled with two pools and shameful memories. Of all the places, it seemed the Heralds were playing a cruel joke.

He was in the Sun Bath.

Alverax lifted himself out of the pool and remembered his first encounter with Jisenna just days before. A mountain of curls piled atop her head. The way she'd winked at him as he left. He could wait for her there, but he needed something a little more dramatic. A little more nefarious.

Unfortunately, his clothes were soaked and there was no spare clothing in the Sun Bath. He took off his shirt and trousers, wrung them until they no longer dripped, and put them back on, pressing down with his palms to straighten the wrinkles. It would have to do.

He wasted no time, briskly hiking through the grand hallways. Servants scuttled past him, eyeing his wet clothes, but ignoring him in favor of their own tasks. As he drew closer to his destination, Alverax slowed his pace and stole a man's jacket hanging from the bottom of a sconce. He put it on and made his way forward with the fine gait of noble arrogance.

A pair of sturdy guards flanked a pair of sturdy doors chiseled to depict the two Heralds and their blessing. They eyed Alverax as he approached.

"My apologies, gentleman," Alverax said with a clipped tone.

Both guards moved in unison to intercept him but found themselves unexpectedly freed from the confines of gravity. They each tumbled forward with eyes as large as the fish their movements resembled.

Alverax strode forward and heaved both doors open, Obsidian threadlight now coursing through his veins. The heavy oak slammed against the walls and he strode into the room. His eyes moved to a large throne, occupied by a woman who seemed both too little and too great for the seat.

A dozen fastidious guards, all threadweavers, shifted in their boots. When they realized who it was, they rushed him as one, their training so well-instilled that their very footsteps fell in unison. In a wave of threadlight, Alverax *broke* their corethreads, sending the entire group tumbling through the air, screaming for others to come. His veins burned, and his chest flared like a smith's forge, but the scale was nothing compared to what he'd done at the Zeda encampment.

One of the guards hurled a spear, but it went wide, and the man tumbled backward in the air.

Empress Jisenna rose from her throne, white fabric falling from her like feathers. The elder man, Watchlord Osinan, stood beside her with fire in his eyes.

"How dare you," Watchlord Osinan said, his lips trembling as he spoke.

"I'm here to make a deal," Alverax said calmly.

"We will not make a deal with a murderer!"

"I AM THE HERALD'S CHOSEN!" Alverax screamed. He needed them to fear him. He needed them to believe that he was dangerous, even if it tore away at the part of his soul that cared for Jisenna. "Look around you. Your people are nothing to me."

Watchlord Osinan took a step forward, clutching the hilt of the sword at his side.

"I don't think so." Alverax *broke* the older man's corethread and he rose into the air. "I will not repeat myself, and there will be no negotiations. Your people honor the truth, so if you agree and go back on your word, I swear that the Heralds themselves will smite you down."

Jisenna stood alone, tears welling up in her dark eyes as she watched all those around her tumble through the air like specs of dust in the wind. "I...don't understand. What do you want?"

"I want all of the Zeda people released. They will not be harmed, and they will never return."

"Absolutely not!" Osinan shouted, still hovering in the air.

"In return," Alverax strode forward, ignoring the Watchlord and looking at Jisenna, "I will take their place. They are not to blame, however much you'd like to lay it at their feet. You have my word that I will make no attempt to escape. I will pay the price of your sister's death."

Jisenna's chest rose up and down and her bottom lip quivered, but his words had gripped her. He knew that they were grieving—Jisenna most of all. They were angry and confused. And if the Mistress of Mercy could save the lives of innocent people while still finding justice for the one responsible, he hoped she would take it.

Alverax stood in silence, waiting for her to respond. His own emotions welled up within him. He still cared for Jisenna and hated that he was deceiving her. But it was for the best. *A man would be wise to stay far away from a woman such as yourself,* he'd said to her. Oh, how right he'd been.

Jisenna glanced up at the guards still tumbling through the air and over to Osinan floating beside her. Her jaw clenched so hard Alverax was sure she would shatter a tooth, but at last her muscles relaxed and she closed her eyes. "I accept your offer."

"I want everyone in this room to hear you say it."

She opened her eyes and gazed into his own. "In

exchange for Alverax Blightwood, the Zeda people will be released and banished from Felia."

"And none will be harmed," he added.

"And none will be harmed."

Alverax dropped to his knees as the guards returned to the ground. "Heralds, save me."

CHAPTER 16

ONCE AGAIN, Alverax found himself in shackles; it was what the son of a thief deserved. He sat on cold stone with his eyes covered, thinking about his journey. Life had taught him brutal lessons, but one lesson most of all. Hope is a sham. A trick of the mind. Hope is opening your eyes at dusk and believing it is dawn. His life—he'd decided—was a setting sun.

There was a phrase his grandfather used to use in prayers: my life for yours. In the days of the Heralds, the people would speak the words when pledging themselves to a lifetime of service. His grandfather would speak them in prayer offering his own form of commitment. Alverax felt the words deep in his core, and he knew that, despite the impending reality, he was giving his life for a righteous cause.

The hardest truth was knowing just how much his death would simplify the world for everyone. The Zeda would be released. Jisenna would feel justice for the death of her sister. The Bloodthieves would have one less loose end. And Jelium would have one less fly to swat.

Watchlord Osinan had arranged his execution for the following day. The Zeda people remained in captivity awaiting the execution before they would be released. They allowed no visitors—there was no one who would have visited anyway—so, instead, he stared at the stone, imagining the ocean, knowing that a great wave would soon take him away.

He *had* had one good idea while sitting there. If they cut off his head, he could use his last moment of consciousness to *break* the head's corethread, making it float in a horrifically creepy display. He probably couldn't *actually* do it, but the thought was stupid enough to bring him some semblance of joy.

He had to give it to the Felians; they had treated him well despite his imprisonment. No one had beaten him. No one had spat at him. Most curiously, no one had even talked to him. They had simply thrown him in a prison cell and left him. The only food they'd brought was a single apple. He laughed out loud to himself about that one. He'd always wanted to try an apple. He never expected it to taste like execution.

That night, as he lay hungry and sore, guards approached his cell, a few by the sound of it. They stopped outside the door. It should have been intimidating, but Alverax didn't care. He was an exotic animal, and they had come to study him. Part of him wanted to growl at them but, in the end, he stayed quiet.

If he looked down just right, he could catch glimpses from beneath his blindfold. There was a small crack on the ground that looked like a scar. Apparently, Felia had also felt the earthquakes. He wondered if the crack had already been there, or if it had surfaced the night the coreseal was broken.

Maybe the whole prison would just collapse on him and save him the embarrassment of a public execution.

"Aye, rip," one of the guards said. "On your feet."

Alverax dismissed the command. What were they going to do? Kill him?

"I said, on your feet."

A wave of freezing cold water poured over him. The cold was bad, but the worst part was knowing that his clothes would stay wet for some time, and the cold would continue. But then he remembered that he was an idiot, and he let threadlight run through his veins. He couldn't threadweave anything unless he could see it, but he could still let thread-light warm his veins.

"Hands behind your back," the same guard demanded. "I see your veins. Threadweave, and you'll regret it."

They turned him around, bound his hands behind his back, and adjusted the blindfold over his eyes. Once his hands were tied, they sat him on his cot and tied him to the frame. The thoroughness gave Alverax a pinch of pride knowing that they truly believed he was dangerous. Apparently, he was a better liar than he'd thought.

He sat quietly as their footsteps left him alone once again. It was better this way—being alone. Would anyone even miss him when he was dead? His grandfather would, but not any more than he already did. None of the Zeda would. None of the Felians would. None of the Bloodthieves would. Was there any point in living if no one cared if he was alive?

He heard the slightest stirring near the entrance to his cell and looked up as if he could see through his blindfold. The cold of his wet clothes was beginning to awaken again, so he let a little more threadlight into his veins.

A woman's voice broke the silence. "Why did you not kill me in the Sun Bath?"

He knew that soft, delicate voice, though it was now stained with a pinch of malice.

Princess Jisenna.

No, Empress Jisenna.

"You were obviously waiting for me. And you could have incapacitated my guards easily enough. So, what was it? Were you waiting for my sister? Was I simply the wrong visitor?"

She wanted something from him. Another confession?

"She never trusted you," she said, her voice quivering. "She sent me to keep an eye on you. Did you know that?"

"I just want to be left alone," he said.

She never replied.

As much as he was already hurting, her words wounded him. He thought, even now, that their friendship had been real, something genuine in the field of lies.

He felt a slight breeze near his face and flinched. He hadn't even heard her move. She lifted the blindfold off his eyes, and then he saw her. Dark eyes filled with tears. Black smears dripping down her cheeks. She looked so angry. So tired. So desperate.

Guilt flooded over him.

"I'm sorry," he said without thinking. She had just lost her sister. All she wanted was closure.

She slapped him. "Stop it! Don't you dare be kind to me! Don't you dare! I liked you, Alverax, and you ripped out a piece of my soul. My sister was my everything. She was a light shining on the reefs not just for me but for this entire nation. Is that what you wanted? Ships crashing in shallow waters? You want this nation to fall? I will not let that happen. Her death will *not* be in vain."

She stopped.

His heart beat faster. He wanted to shout. He wanted to defend himself, to tell her the truth. He wanted to comfort her. His mind was a blur of emotions and it took all of his willpower to hold himself back.

He looked down.

One. Two. Three. Four. Heralds calm a troubled core.

When he looked back up, Empress Jisenna was staring at him with confusion in her eyes. "I don't understand you. Yesterday I was so frightened by you, but today you seem so...different. Something is wrong with you. You are broken. I see now that the world will be truly safer without you in it."

He wanted to scream out his innocence, to explain that one of those men wasn't real. But it wouldn't matter. They'd preconceived his guilt, and their justice would either be his singular death or the death of the entire Zeda people. He had to be strong...for them. For Iriel. For Aydin. For once in his Heralds-forsaken life.

Empress Jisenna stood, gave him one last look, and walked away without a word. The guards came in, covered his eyes, and removed his bindings. Once again, he was alone in his cell, lying down on a cot staring at the darkness of a blindfold. For a moment, he wondered if his father could have escaped the cell. He pushed the thought aside. He wasn't like him. He wouldn't run from his promises. He would do what was right simply because it was right.

CHAPTER 17

THE GRASSY FIELDS within the walls of Endin Keep were filled with soldiers. The only clouds in the sky had retreated earlier in the day, leaving a lasting warmth even as the sun fell below the western horizon. Laurel stood beside the doctor, Sarla, handing out small vials quarter-filled with blood. She stole three vials and, though she hated herself for doing it, the constant tremble in her hands left her no other choice.

Sarla was certain the small dosage would grant the recipient at least a short access to threadlight, but the minuscule amount compared to what Laurel had been taking seemed fit only for the smallest child. Malachus had directed the soldiers to stagger their consumption, so as not to leave their unit vulnerable. It was as good a plan as any and, still, Laurel felt a rotten feeling in the pit of her stomach.

Once the last of the transfusers was distributed, Henna confirmed her plans with the lieutenants and commanded them to take their units and assume their positions. Boots stomped in unison over the wide fields until each unit disappeared past the walls of the keep.

Alabella arrived shortly after with dark bags peeking out from beneath her eyes. "Sarla," she called out. "How did we do?"

The odd woman cracked each of her knuckles one by one as she spoke. "Given the circumstances, we were able to ration the blood quite effectively. Some units will have a little more than others, and some soldiers will never taste it, but there should be enough to last through the night."

"Good."

"I should note that the Great Lord had me double the quantity for the units with the most direct path from the Fairenwild."

"A wise move."

"He also wanted to make sure that the soldiers were unaware of the order."

Alabella smirked. "He needs them all to feel equally prepared if they are to fight with the kind of loyalty he needs."

Sarla, with an eager look in her eyes, leaned forward. "Were you able to procure a few moments for me to study the captive corespawn?"

"Unfortunately, no," Alabella said. "They were eventually able to kill it. I was told its threadlight expired."

"Fascinating," Sarla whispered. "If it expires then there must be a way for its threadlight to be renewed. An energy source, like food."

"A mystery for another day," Alabella said, turning to Laurel. "What do you think? Do we have a chance?"

Laurel shrugged her shoulders. "If the rest die as easily as the ones I killed, I think we'll be fine."

"We can hope. That reminds me," Alabella said. She pulled out the obsidian dagger and handed it to Laurel. "I believe this belonged to you. I want you to have it. A token of my trust. You've saved me with it once before; I pray you won't have to again."

Laurel took the dagger in her hands and, as she looked down its shaft, she remembered Chrys. But she also remembered that, in the keep the night she'd killed Jurius, there had been two identical blades. Something about that seemed significant.

"Thank you," she managed.

Alabella gestured to one of the towers. "It's time."

———

HIGH OVER THE ANXIOUS CITY, clouds obscured the only light the moon intended to provide. Quiet ruled the Alchean streets like a tyrannical scourge, infecting the hearts of the people, and instilling a profound dread in the minds of those who gathered to protect them. The wind itself seemed afraid to show itself.

The entire Alchean army was spread out along the western border, spanning from the north to the south, covering as much of the land between Alchea and the Fairenwild as possible without stretching their numbers.

Laurel sat along the windowsill in one of the tower rooms overlooking the motionless city far below. A map lay sprawled out on the wide table, dozens of markers scattered in a wide arc around the Alchean border designating key locations of troops. Soldiers at each position would light a bonfire as soon as they were in position, and, if the corespawn arrived, they would toss in a bag of borax salt to turn the flames green.

No flames had yet to shift their hue.

"So," Alabella said without shifting her gaze, "when do you plan to do it?"

"Do what?" Laurel asked.

The woman turned to face Laurel and met her eyes. "When we first met, I promised you that I would never lie to you. We could debate the technicalities, but the truth is: I deceived you, Laurel. I know that you know what happened in the Fairenwild."

Laurel's heart skipped a beat. Her hand had been tracing the outline of the vials in her pocket but shifted to the blade now hooked to her belt.

"If you want to kill me, you would be justified. I've even given you the perfect weapon for the job." Alabella glanced down at the obsidian blade. "This path we walk is not toward an unworthy destination. When we restore your threadlight, you will be living proof of the world we could have. A world without achromacy. A world without inequality. No fortune of birth. Imagine it, every single person able to experience the joy of threadlight. That is the future we're fighting for."

Laurel ground her teeth. Angry. Frustrated. Bothered by the fact that she agreed with Alabella. Why did some deserve threadlight over others? That which Laurel loved more than anything, why did she deserve it more than her brother? And still, unjust or not, how many deserved to die to bring that dream to life?

"I do want to kill you," Laurel said, unable to make eye contact. "For my family. For my people. And for myself. Did you know that your people kidnapped me? If not for a bit of luck, it would be my blood out there in the soldiers' hands."

A weary sadness played itself in Alabella's eyes. "I've been so overcome with the destination that I've forgotten that there are many ways to arrive. I see that now, and I want to find a better way."

Laurel raised the obsidian blade. "Do you want me to kill you? Is that why you gave this to me? You think dying will make up for all the shit you've caused?"

"I gave it to you, because I need you—"

Time dragged to a halt. Every beat of Laurel's heart was a raucous pounding that shook her to the core. The obsidian blade reflected a bit of lamplight, glistening, taunting. Memory overlaid atop reality. Jurius' blood dripped from the edge of the blade. Revenge, like the sweet nuzzle of a chromawolf, brushed against her mind. It would take only the simplest of movements to slide the dagger forward into Alabella's chest. A single choice to change everything.

"—and you need me."

"I don't need you," Laurel snapped. "But these people do. At least for now."

Alabella nodded grimly and turned to look back over the city. "The night is young. Let's pray the Heralds are with us."

THE NIGHT PASSED in eerie silence, and the enemy never arrived.

CHAPTER 18

EACH MORNING, Chrys awoke with a growing hollowness within himself. It wasn't about being a prisoner; it was about his family. Even if he and his friends were able to escape, he was afraid of what life would be like when he returned. It had been his own choice—made with clarity—that had given control to Relek and sent him trekking to the wastelands, abandoning his wife and son. The battle in the Fairenwild wasn't over when they'd left. If anything had happened to Iriel and Aydin while he was away, he would never forgive himself. And even if they were okay, he feared that they would never be able to forgive him.

More than anything, he longed to hear Iriel's sweet voice tell him that she understood, that it was the right decision, like she had the night Aydin was born. If there was anyone capable of forgiving him, it was her. Yet still he feared.

While Roshaw was paying his debt to Esme and harvesting that week's growth of honeycrystals, Chrys would be the one to deliver them to Xuçan. Their plan hinged on that conversation. If the great ataçan refused to aid them, they would be forced to take a more dangerous path through the jungle, where the wastelanders would have the advantage. But Chrys hoped that their disdain for the "creature of many faces" would be enough to make them agree.

After they ate the fruit and meat that the guards provided them for the day, and after Chrys consumed the murky threadlight-blocking substance, Roshaw steeled himself to enter the et'hovon hive. But before he did, the entrance to the enclosure swung open, revealing an entire host of wastelanders; Chrys counted more than twenty. Agatha rose swiftly to her feet and the others followed suit.

"What's going on?" Chrys asked.

Roshaw, who still stood beside him, looked to the waste-landers with reservation. "No idea."

The mob of guards split, and the god siblings stepped forward. Relek, the "creature of many faces", and his sister, Lylax, had transformed from the Alchean guards Chrys had last seen. True, they still wore the skin of Velan and Autelle, but their hair and clothing had adopted an entirely new look. Lylax wore a long, flowing gown that dragged care-lessly behind her in the swamp water. Her hair was done up with pins, and Chrys was surprised with how regal the once-guard had become.

And their eyes. No longer were their eyes the brown of an achromat. Instead, they sparkled with the entire spec-trum of colors, like prisms refracting the sun's rays. Chrys had never seen anything like it.

Relek smiled with cleanly shaven cheeks and strode forward with his sister. "Chrys Valerian...the Apogee...it is good to see you, friend."

Chrys clenched his jaw and said nothing. Somehow, Relek's voice still sounded the same as it had in his mind, and each word sent a shiver of bad memories crawling up his spine.

"I want to thank you," Relek continued, his prismatic eyes bearing down on Chrys. "Not only did you give me freedom, but your actions freed my sister as well. When we've risen to our former glory, it will be because of you."

Chrys spat at their feet. "Go to hell."

Relek frowned and turned to his sister. The goddess, Lylax, spoke in the wastelander tongue, and the host of guards gathered and surrounded Chrys, Roshaw, Esme, Seven, and Agatha. They were pushed, shoved, and shepherded forward like cattle through the swamp.

They needed to escape...now.

They could no longer wait for the end of a guard shift during the night. Nor could they wait to speak with Xuçan. Whatever they were going to do, they needed to figure it out fast. Chrys' eyes darted back and forth through the swamp, looking for anything that would give him an idea.

The procession stopped at the edge of the jungle, where the crew was ushered forward to a ledge that led down to a sunken, muddy pit, wide as a field. The far side of the pit ended at one edge of the Endless Well.

The wastelanders shoved the crew over the ledge and down into the pit. Chrys and Seven landed on their feet, but the other three stumbled forward and crashed into the mud on their hands and knees. Chrys helped Agatha to stand. When he turned, he saw an army of wastelanders—young and old—surrounding the edge of the pit with fire in their eyes.

Relek approached the ledge above them. "The people of Kai'Melend believe in the power of sacrifice," he said. "Today, your choice is *how*. There are those among these people who would be leaders in the coming war. You will fight them, and they will prove to me their valor. Those of you who wish to die fighting, you will step forward. For those who will not fight, the Well awaits you."

"What the hell is he talking about?" Esme whispered to the others.

Roshaw clenched his jaw and spoke through his teeth. "He's saying we can let the wastelanders kill us, or we can kill ourselves."

Suicide. The word crawled out from a dark cave beneath Chrys' skin. He'd always been so focused on the next step, the next goal, that he'd never considered what he would do when there were no more steps to take. Looking out over the mass of wastelanders, it was clear that there would be no escape.

In a way, death would be such a relief. To forget about his failures. To forget about that look in Iriel's eyes as he walked away. To forget the child he'd abandoned. To them he was already nothing more than a rotten ghost. A bad dream better left forgotten. The only person he had was his mother, but he would never see her again. And if he did, she would see no more than the disappointment he'd become.

He walked forward and stared into the latter option. The Endless Well extended into infinite darkness. One simple step and he could fall into nothingness. One simple step and he could end the guilt. He could end the suffering. One step...

Chrys looked down into the pit, into the void that welcomed him. There was a certain serenity deep in the abyss. A calm in the shadow. It beckoned to him, calling out, *come and be still.*

Serenity.

Tranquility.

An end to the pain.

An end.

The end.

"No," he said forcefully, shaking his head.

That was not how he would end his life.

I am He-who-does-not-cower.

If all the enemies in the world—be they wastelander or ataçan or worse—came to claim him, he would stand and fight. He would resist with every last breath within him, and, when he was at the edge of death, he would spit fire with his final breath. If they wanted a fight, he would make them pay.

For Iriel.

For Aydin.

For the men and women who died at the hands of the Apogee.

Chrys dropped to his knees and leaned over the edge, staring down into the infinite void of darkness. He reached his hand into his mouth, shoved his fingers down his throat, and vomited into the abyss.

CHAPTER 19

A STREAM of liquid came flooding out of Chrys' stomach, a waterfall crashing down into the infinite darkness below. He gripped the edge of the Well, breathed in the putrid stench of swamp water, and vomited again. His throat burned, and his stomach riled, but, if he was going to fight the waste-landers, he had to get the fluid out of his system. He needed threadlight.

The other members of the crew stared as he turned to face them. His eyes burned with purpose. When he looked at them, he felt a strong yearning to protect them. These people were in no state to fight. Even Seven, who had once been a strong soldier, was little more than skin and bone. If they fought, they would last no longer than a few seconds.

Chrys turned around, trudged back toward the wall of the pit, and looked up at the throng of wastelanders. He stepped as near as he dared and met Relek's gaze. "If you want to prove your champions, then give them a challenge! Killing these prisoners will prove nothing. If you really want to test them, let them fight me. Alone."

Relek grumbled, weighing the challenge. "You think I would extend mercy to these people?"

"To hell with mercy," Chrys said, choosing his words carefully. "I want your warriors all to myself."

"Mmmm."

"When I fall, you have your champion. But until then, for every one of your warriors that I kill, you will release one of the prisoners."

The tall god looked down on him, seeing the remains of vomit in Chrys' beard. He turned his eyes to the rest of the human prisoners. "You are a fool, Chrys Valerian. Have you forgotten that I spent years inside your mind? I know you better than you know yourself. You think you can win, but you *will* die. And I will watch with glee as each wastelander warrior cuts away at your life until you are nothing but a rotten stump of flesh." He paused, leaving enough of a break for a bead of sweat to slide down Chrys' forehead. "It is agreed."

Chrys nodded and turned to the others. "Find my wife," he said. "And tell her that I did everything I could."

The four of them, with shock and sorrow twisted over their dirty faces, gathered together and moved away from Chrys. Roshaw gave him a nod of gratitude.

Lylax spoke in the wastelander tongue and the crowd consumed her every word, cheering with each throaty sylla- ble. A thick, fierce looking wastelander stepped forward. He stood taller than the others—though still shorter than Chrys—with the noon sun shadowing the curves of his arms and bare chest. He'd pierced his pointed lobes, and his face was covered with white paint and dark lines to mimic an empty skull. Blue and red feathers fanned out at his hair- line down to his neck. When he jumped down, Chrys saw that the warrior wore gloves with sharpened bones for nails.

Chrys took one final look at those he would be fighting for, then set his jaw and widened his stance.

The wastelander champion stepped forward, and the horde of onlookers rose up in chants, screaming and shouting into the open air.

In a burst of speed, the champion dove toward Chrys. His bone claws lashed out, swiping again and again as Chrys barely managed to dodge each attack. He stepped into the champion's reach and drove a fist into his ribs. The wastelander groaned and retreated, screeching something foul in his otherworldly tongue.

Again, the wastelander attacked, this time in horrific harmony with his bone claws. Each jab grew in ferocity, each growl rising in a barbaric crescendo. The warrior let loose a flurry of kicks to throw Chrys off balance.

But Chrys was the Apogee, even without a god in his mind.

He leaned into the wastelander, grasping his wrist and driving an elbow up into his neck. Sharp pain burst in his side as bone claws cut into him. But it didn't matter. Up close, the bone claws were mosquitos nipping at his skin. Chrys' fists were lead hammers slamming into the wastelander's ribs.

Planting his forearm into the warrior's neck, Chrys tripped him and sent them both toppling over onto the murky floor. With rage fueling his every movement, Chrys pummeled the wastelander's face. Brittle bones shattered beneath his fists while claws scratched at his back. Finally, Chrys ripped out a handful of feathers from the champion's headdress and drove the sharp shafts deep into the wastelander's neck. The bundle of feathers snapped in half, still embedded in the skin. Blood pulsed out of the hollow shafts, dripping into the water.

Chrys rolled the body over face-first in the mud, then pulled off the bone claws and lifted himself to his feet. He took in heavy breaths and watched a strange crevice along the wastelander's spine open and close before its lungs ceased their rhythm.

The crowd of wastelanders grew quiet.

Chrys placed the bone claws over his own hands and looked up to the crowd. "Who's next?" he shouted.

The crew, as stunned as the wastelanders, deliberated, and sent Agatha up the steps of the ledge. The wastelanders accepted her above but did not let her pass. She turned, and Chrys saw the worry and fear in her eyes. She was frail, and surrounded by the enemy, with no belief that they would truly let her go.

Relek raised his head up high. "Ah, yes. The *power of appearance*. I remember how important you believed that to be. But I know you. I see you growing tired already. How much longer can you last, old friend?"

Lylax shouted more words Chrys couldn't understand and pointed at the crowd. She stepped forward, her voice rising and falling with vigor. While the language seemed a fitting companion to Velan's harshness, it seemed unnatural coming from Autelle's body. Chrys knew that somewhere, locked away in her mind, there was a scared woman still alive.

Two wastelanders jumped down off the ledge into the pit. They matched in nearly every way. Long, white hair, pale grey skin, each holding a weapon that looked like a bone-colored meat cleaver. The crowd burst out in raucous applause, screaming at the top of their lungs, their voices ringing out like wild beasts.

Stones. The only deal they'd made was one kill for one release, they'd made no deal about the numbers of combatants at any given time. But he still had a trick up his sleeve: the threadlight running in his veins.

Chrys sprinted forward with speckled blood trailing from his open wounds. He focused on the slightly smaller of the two and dove in fast to get out of range of the cleaver. Up close, he would have the advantage.

The other wastelander chopped down hard with their cleaver and nearly cut Chrys' hand off, but he *pushed*, his eyes blazing to life with radiant Sapphire energy, and the cleaver swung wide, slicing off the ends of several of the bone claws. Chrys jabbed forward with his other hand and claws pierced through the wastelander's shoulder. Both of his opponents backed away, muttering incomprehensible words to each other.

Chrys stepped back, panting. The layer of swamp water on the floor made it more difficult to move, and he found himself fatiguing faster than he'd hoped. He let more threadlight into his veins.

Both leapt forward in unison, combining hard overhead swipes of their cleavers with short punches from their offhand. Chrys *pushed* hard against both cleavers, sending one tumbling through the air far away. The other cleaver was tossed to the ground by the warrior to avoid giving Chrys any more advantage.

With both hands free, the warriors grew more ferocious, quicker and more daring. When one kicked low, Chrys *pushed* off the ground, and soared over them both, putting them between him and the Endless Well. He needed to do something. They were fast, and well-trained. If he did nothing, it would only be a matter of time before they overcame him.

They rushed him once more, and Chrys kicked swamp water up into the air. It wasn't much, but it was enough.

Chrys used the distraction to launch his own offense. He let loose a series of swipes with the bone claws and connected with one of the warriors' chest. Chrys smiled just in time for the other wastelander to lift the cleaver from the floor and swing it upward at Chrys' outstretched hand. It connected with terrible momentum, slashing through three of Chrys' fingers.

Chrys' eyes bulged.

Pain blossomed at the end of his hand.

But there was no time. Chrys tripped the first and pounced atop the second. His bone claws tore into the wounded wastelander's chest like a swarm of bees, stinging and stinging again and again until the wastelander no longer could breathe, and he fell back, limp. Chrys rolled to the side, narrowly dodging another strike from the other. He *pushed* on the cleaver and it flew from the wastelander's grip, launching into the Endless Well.

Lifting himself up, Chrys set his footing and eyed his final opponent. There was fear in the wastelander's eyes, hidden behind a façade of rage.

"Give up," Chrys spat.

The wastelander, unable to understand, rushed him. Chrys brushed aside his blow, stabbing bone claws into the pit of his arm, and spinning. His elbow cracked the side of the wastelander's head. While his opponent was dazed, Chrys stepped forward, spun, and kicked the wastelander in the middle of his chest. The force lifted his small frame off the ground and sent him crashing over the edge of the chasm, screaming into the endless darkness.

Chrys looked down at his hands. The right hand was missing three fingers, and blood was drooling from the frayed edges of each appendage. With his other hand, he walked over and retrieved the fallen cleaver. When he looked up to the crowd and saw Relek snarling, he thought that, just for a moment, his plan might actually work.

"Two more!" he spat.

Roshaw gestured to Esme and Seven. They gave him a sad look but took the offering and ascended the stairs to join Agatha. Chrys felt the thrill of victory. If he could only kill one more, then he could die knowing that he'd protected those who could not protect themselves.

Relek and Lylax stepped to the ledge of the pit. The beating sun seemed to distort the air around them. Then, as if the world had decided to play a sadistic joke, a floral scent drifted in the wind. Chrys' eyes darted about, searching for the source, but he found nothing. The wastelander goddess spoke and the mass of spectators gasped at her words.

The crowd split in two and a distortion in the air darted through them. Chrys opened his eyes to threadlight and beheld a lithe creature, born of light itself, leaping from the ledge and into the pit, landing with a splash. It stood on two legs, with long arms that ended in sword-like points. The wastelanders whispered amongst themselves as Lylax's full lips curled into a perverse grin.

A memory, long forgotten, swept over him in a wave.

———

"Tell me a story, mother," little Chrys asked.

Willow shook her head and smiled. "It is late. Perhaps a short one."

"Do the scary one!"

"Only because you are so brave, little flower." She tucked him in and began the story. "There was once a girl who was not loved by her family. She was the only one in the whole town who could see threadlight, and none of the others believed her."

"That's silly," little Chrys cut in.

"Perhaps, but it is hard to believe what you cannot see. Still, she was happy, finding her joy in other pastimes. One day, an older boy from her village was killed by an invisible creature, a corespawn from the dark parts beneath the earth. When a group of men went to kill the beast, they never returned. The village elder brought everyone together behind the walls of her home. After two days, the little girl missed her family's garden, and so, when she smelled roses on the wind, she snuck outside and made her way home."

Little Chrys squeezed his mother's hand. "She shouldn't do that."

"No," Willow said, smiling. "As she walked, she opened her eyes to threadlight, and saw the corespawn circling the walls of the elder's home. She stood still as an oak tree, raised her bow, and let loose her arrow. It struck true, and the creature died. No one believed her until the creature never returned, and then they celebrated her as a great hero. You see, Chrys. Sometimes our greatest gifts are those that others do not understand."

He settled down onto his pillow and asked, "Are the corespawn real?"

"Of course not, little flower."

BUT WILLOW WAS WRONG.

Standing before him, with flesh born of pure thread-light, was a creature of myth. The light-shrouded silhouette of overgrown fangs jutted out from its maw. It prowled forward and snarled.

Chrys, who had already accepted his end, snarled back.

It dashed toward him in a blur. Chrys set his feet and sprinted forward in response. The beast leapt and Chrys dropped a shoulder, covering it with the flat end of the cleaver. They collided in an explosion of power. Chrys was knocked to his back, the beast atop him, and it clamped down on his shoulder with its overgrown fangs. He screamed, hacking into the creature's torso with the cleaver until it rolled away from him.

But, as he scrambled again to his feet, Chrys watched a swirling mist of light coagulate over the wounds in the creature's side. In moments, the corespawn was healed completely.

His mother had forgotten to mention that part...

Chrys cringed as he watched the creature's wounds heal. His own had not. Chrys' shoulder was torn apart, fingers left behind like fallen soldiers, and his lungs were near ready to collapse. Threadlight crawled beneath his skin, but it was a salve not meant for serious injury.

As the creature dashed toward him once again, Chrys raised the cleaver high overhead and extended his right arm. He had one more idea, and it took the bait, clamping down its massive fangs on his forearm. Pain shot up through his tendons, up through his shoulders, and blossomed in painful agony. With his other hand, he brought the cleaver down with every ounce of his strength, fueled by rage and the promise of redemption, and cut halfway through the corespawn's neck. He yanked it out and brought it back down again. And again. And again. Until, finally, the cleaver passed through the brilliant, sinewy flesh of the corespawn.

Its jaws released his shredded arm as the severed head fell to the murky floor with a splash. Alone, it looked like a massive photospore, glowing haphazardly in the mud. Chrys kicked the headless body away from himself and fell to his knees, clutching at his shoulder and hand. Despite the pain echoing throughout every inch of his bloody body, he grinned.

One more freed, he thought to himself. He'd done it.

Then, as though time itself were playing back, the creature's head turned to ooze and slid across the water like oil until it reattached itself to the fallen body. The ooze reformed itself, slowly, into the same fanged maw of the creature he'd thought dead. Its newly formed head shivered back and forth, then settled, returning its radiant gaze to Chrys.

Stones.

He was going to die.

At least he'd saved three of them. *Sorry, Roshaw.*

His eyes locked with the corespawn. It stood still, watching his movement, waiting for some unspoken command to finish him off. Pain crept into his vision. He shook his head, clearing his sight.

He should stand. He should fight. He was the Apogee! But his mind was growing hazy. The adrenaline was fading, and pain was slithering through his veins.

Chrys turned and saw Roshaw standing alone, trembling as his only chance at survival faded away.

Screams echoed out in the open air.

Chrys looked to the west as a dozen spears slammed forward in unison, cutting down Agatha, Esme, and Seven. Time slowed as he watched his friends accept their fate, terror stricken across their faces. Slowly, with spears still embedded in their flesh, they sagged to the floor.

"NO!" he screamed, reaching out with his dismembered hand. He sprinted toward them, knowing well that there was nothing he could do.

He heard the splash of footsteps behind him and turned just in time to *push* off the ground and avoid the leaping corespawn. It slid along the wet floor and spun back toward him as he fell back to the earth.

He'd failed. He never should have trusted Relek, and their lives were the payment for his stupidity. Like every other person in his life, he had failed to protect them. As he stared back at the corespawn before him, he knew that he couldn't even protect himself. These were creatures and beings far beyond his own power. Gods and mythical creatures? Who was he to pretend that he could fight back?

In that moment, he wondered if he should have leapt into the Endless Well.

But then he heard it.

A voice.

A familiar pitch.

A timbre that sent a shiver down his spine and awakened a powerful force within him. When he looked to the sound, he saw a woman soaring through the air, eyes and veins blazing with Sapphire threadlight, wielding a blade as black as Relek's soul.

An indominable hero. A fearless protector. A herald of hope.

It was his mother.

Willow's feet hit the ground in an explosion, water erupting in a spray of droplets.

"My son is mine!"

All of the fear, the hate, the sorrow, and the pain came bursting out of Chrys' lungs in a single breath, replaced by the only emotion capable of displacing such feelings.

From his earliest memories, Chrys thought he knew how much his mother loved him. She'd provided for him, mentored him, supported him. But it wasn't until his own son was born that he'd realized the true power of paternal love. Chrys had given up everything to protect Aydin. He would do it all again. And now, standing in front of him with ratty hair and clothes painted with dirt, Willow Valerian had done the same.

Chrys smiled so wide it nearly broke his jaw.

The corespawn leapt at Willow and she threw herself forward into it. Chrys, overwhelmed by her arrival, became suddenly aware of the danger she was in. But as the creature opened wide its arms in a deathly embrace, launching toward Willow, she roared and slammed her dagger up into its gut.

As soon as the blade pierced its hide, a hideous screech cut through the dull of the enraptured crowd. The corespawn burst apart in an explosion of threadlight, thousands of specs of multi-colored sand erupting in a thunderous blast.

Willow turned to Chrys and his eyes drifted to the dagger in her hand. He knew it well; it was once his. The thread-dead obsidian blade.

He had so many questions, but there was no time. The corespawn was dead, and it was clear the wastelanders would not let them live. They had to move.

Chrys scanned the throng of wastelanders lining the wall of the pit. The entire crescent was filled. There was only one other way to go.

"Roshaw!" Chrys yelled. "To the Well!"

The lone man reacted decisively, sprinting at full speed toward the Endless Well, while Chrys and Willow did the same.

A hoard of wastelanders leapt into the pit, sloshing through the puddled ground, and rolled toward them like an avalanche. With each second, the sound roared louder. Screaming. Howling. Chrys peeked back and saw one of the

159

wastelanders riding a bonded ataçan, its massive limbs thumping against the earth with each step.

As they approached the edge of the chasm, Chrys came to a halt. He turned just as Willow reached him. "I can't believe you came for me," he said.

"There is nothing in this world that could have stopped me," she said with a smile.

Stones, but he'd missed that woman. He looked down into the void, grabbing hold of her hand with his good one. "If this kills us, I'm glad I saw you one last time."

She smiled with a twinkle in her eye. "If this kills us, it would still be worth it."

"Heralds, save me," Roshaw whispered as he arrived.

Chrys smiled, and, together, all three leapt into the infinite darkness.

CHAPTER 20

THE REMAINDER of the Alchean night passed in a timeless blur, waiting, fearing, then rejoicing when the sun rose. Every man and woman in the city had dark eyes and hearts that sagged in their chests, but when not a single corespawn arrived, it was as though a fog had lifted.

"Laurel, grab your things. We need to leave, now."

Laurel shot up in the chair where she'd nearly fallen asleep. She rubbed at her eye and gazed out of the large window that looked out over the city. Alabella moved throughout the room, gathering papers and shoving things into a bag.

"What is it?"

Alabella listened at the door. "Our safety is predicated on the presence of the corespawn. If they do not return—even if the people believe they will not—then you and I are no longer safe. If they don't need us, then we will be imprisoned or killed. If we leave quickly, we can be gone before they come for us. A caravan can take us somewhere safe."

"What? No," Laurel said. "We can't leave."

"You have to understand. Every moment they allow us to

stand beside them is a moment of disrespect. It doesn't matter that we were trying to do the right thing. We are their ally only when there is a greater enemy and, if that enemy is gone, then their eyes again turn to us."

"Even if the corespawn never came, your transfusers prevented a widespread panic. They had no plan to protect their people."

"No single action can scrub clean a mountain," Alabella said, as she continued to gather her belongings.

Laurel's hand rubbed at the transfusers in her pocket. It was a new day—she'd waited long enough—so, she kept one eye on Alabella to make sure her back was still turned and pulled one out. She brought the vial with trembling hands to her lips. Iron slid down her throat, and warmth suffused throughout her body. The quaking of her hands faded away.

Still, that didn't fix the larger problem. They had to leave Alchea. Maybe... "If they're going to pursue us, we should go west. There's nothing to the north, and it's too flat to the south. It would be too easy to track us. Plenty of hills to the west and, if we can make it all the way to Felia, they won't be able to follow."

Alabella thought it over for a moment. "I'd prefer we go south, but you are right about the visibility. It would be dangerous. If we keep the group small, we could ride horseback to Feldspar, then pick up a carriage to continue west through the night. We'll need to move quickly, and we'll need Sarla."

Laurel nodded.

They moved to the door and Alabella knocked. In a few moments, the door opened, and a group of uniformed guards glared at them. One, a shorter man with a mustache, put a hand on the door. "What is it?"

Alabella's veins blazed to life with Amber threadlight. "I *am* sorry." Her eyes glowed a brilliant yellow just before the guards all clutched at their legs and sunk to the ground, overcome by a tangle of invisible threads. In seconds, they were sprawled out across the floor in a writhing mass of blue and white uniform. The door drifted open.

When Laurel stepped out, a single guard remained standing, just beyond the others. He looked ready to soil himself and, when Alabella met his eyes, he dropped to the floor. But Laurel was quite sure that it was of his own accord, rather than Alabella's threads.

It was just before dawn and the night sky still flooded the hallways of the keep with an eerie darkness. They ran down the hallway with their shadows wavering in front of them like spirits, beckoning them to follow. They moved swiftly, but cautiously, taking care to not rouse suspicion from the servants that worked quietly.

They turned a corner near a staircase and came face-to-face with three people Laurel would never have expected to see.

Luther, holding a small crate, paused beside Laz and Reina. When they saw her, Laz's cheeks flushed, and she knew that the three of them were doing something they ought not to. Alabella's veins began to glow, and Laurel put a hand on her arm.

"What are you *doing* here?" Laurel asked.

"We could ask you the same," Luther replied, eyes narrow as he clutched the box. Laurel thought she heard the sounds of movement coming from within the box.

"We *could*," Reina added with a nudge. "Or we could all pretend like no one saw anything, and continue on about our business... "

Despite how badly Laurel wanted to know what was in

the package, she knew that her and Alabella also needed to move quickly. "If you didn't see us, then we didn't see you."

"Is good," Laz said with a thumbs up.

When Laurel and Alabella moved to descend the staircase, so did Luther, Laz, and Reina. They looked at each other uncomfortably for a moment before continuing down. Each step of the spiraling stairs echoed loudly as they made their way to the bottom floor.

As soon as the stairs ended, Laz gave her a final nod. A small cooing sound came from the box just as they moved to go. Luther looked to Laurel. His cheekbones cut tightly against his skin as he clenched his teeth. Before she could ask, he nodded and took off. Laz and Reina followed closely behind.

Alabella had a curious look in her eyes but let them go. They each tossed their hoods on and walked quietly past the guards posted outside the keep. Laurel spotted a tint of Emerald in the veins of one of the guards. His tired eyes scanned the courtyard while the others stood still. With the threat of a corespawn invasion, their priority was making sure nothing came in.

Once outside of the keep walls, Alabella cut south and they made their way to the warehouse where they'd been staying. Laurel still had a hard time keeping the direction, but she thought she was finally starting to recognize some of the grounder streets and landmarks.

However, it all felt different now. Windows were boarded up. Doors barricaded. Carts and stalls were left abandoned in the streets. Holed up inside each home were children sleeping and parents with red eyes that stressed over the future of their families. Laurel hadn't thought about it, but, in a way, she was glad that the Zeda people had been forced west. Perhaps, the world was safer away from Alchea and the corespawn.

They reached the warehouse and, after knocking and waiting for the barricade to be shoved aside, they entered. Laurel was surprised with how many people were there. There must have been hundreds, young and old, spread out across the warehouse floor like cocoons. She recognized some as the seamstresses and tailors that worked the floor for Alabella's legitimate business.

Alabella smiled as they entered.

"What is this?" Laurel asked.

"Many of our workers have homes on the outer rim of the city, or out in the countryside. I asked Sarla to offer them a safer home for now."

Laurel stared at the woman. She couldn't understand her. In some ways, she would sacrifice everything to move toward her grand vision of the world. But then this? An outpouring of empathy.

Alabella continued through the quiet warehouse, waving at a few of those who remained awake. When they entered Sarla's quarters, they found the strange woman sleeping on her back, cradling a stack of parchment with her odd glasses placed atop. Alabella strode forward and woke up Sarla with a gentle hand to the shoulder.

When her eyes opened and she saw who it was, Sarla shot upright and shoved her glasses on. "I am quite certain that I did not fall asleep. There is far too much to do, and too little time to do it all."

"Pack your things," Alabella said. "Whatever you can carry on a horse. We need to leave the city."

"Humans or corespawn?" Sarla asked.

Alabella smirked. "Humans. The corespawn never came."

"An unlikely outcome," the odd woman said, jumping to her feet. "Then the Alcheans will have no further need of our product or our alliance. I'll gather my things." She paused. "There is something you should know."

Alabella cocked her head to the side.

"Jelium knows about the boy."

"Heralds be damned," she cursed. "It was only a matter of time. We'll need to get our shipment out before he finds it. I've no idea what he'd do with it, but he would destroy it for nothing more than to molest us. Send one of our people back. I want it out of Cynosure and out to Felia as soon as possible."

They found Barrick awake in his room and asked him to fetch some horses. While they waited, Alabella gave instructions to a short, blonde woman on how to continue running the warehouse. When Barrick returned, the four of them saddled up and never looked back.

CHAPTER 21

WHEN THE HOOD lifted and his eyes adjusted to the bright sunlight, Alverax nearly peed himself. Ten of thousands of Felians solemnly assembled throughout the colossal hippodrome, staring with broken hearts at a broken young man while a choir of circling birds sang his death march. They gathered to witness the death of the last Obsidian threadweaver, and to watch their hopes of a Heraldic return die with him.

The strength he'd shown while trading his life for the Zeda people had all but vanished. Now, he stood upon frail bones and hunched with the posture of a man resigned to his fate. He turned his eyes from the people; it was more than he could bear. He could weather the storm raging in his own mind—a story of failure and ill-fate wrought by his father's curse—but each time he locked eyes with one of the Felian people and saw the tragedy in their gaze, it broke another piece of him.

He felt more alone than any man should in a sea of souls.

Somewhere, the Zeda were still imprisoned, forced to

wait until after his execution before they were exiled. He wished he could have seen even one of them again, a single nod of approval for the only selfless choice he'd ever made.

As he stared at the circular stone floor beneath him in the center of the hippodrome, he was taken aback by the familiarity of the runes carved upon its surface. It reminded him of what the Zeda called "the coreseal". This platform was much larger, but its shape and style were certainly comparable. His eyes followed the chain wrapped around his ankles that ended at a point fixed to the ground.

"It is typically our custom," Watchlord Osinan said quietly, his chin raised high as he inspected the chains, "to allow the condemned an opportunity to address the people. However, we have decided that you are not deserving of such a platform. So, you will be given no such opportunity."

The slightest commotion broke through the crowd, like leaves rustling in the wind. Alverax turned his head to see Empress Jisenna summiting the platform, dressed in a flowing black dress with dozens of thin, golden tassels draping from her sleeves. In another life, the bright sun and the singing birds would have been a fitting accompaniment to her arrival, but, today, Alverax looked away and cursed the birds to silence.

As the empress approached the center of the platform, she kissed her fingertips and placed them in the air in front of her.

"Today, we grieve the loss of our beloved empress." She spoke with power, letting her voice travel through the acoustics of the hippodrome. "While her ship may now sail the infinite sea, her spirit and her ideals remain with us. The truth is that we have been deceived. A ship, flying a false flag, entered our harbors and stole a piece of our soul."

Stole.

The word seared itself into Alverax's mind. Was that how he would be remembered? The man who stole a life? For years, he'd fought to distance himself from the tainted heritage his father had left, and now, history would etch his name beside the very man. The thought broke what was left of his brittle pride. Tears swelled up in his Obsidian eyes. His lungs quaked within his chest. His lips quivered. He'd sworn to never be like his father, and, whether he was or not, the world believed he was.

The world spun around him in a blurry mass of prismatic color. He closed his eyes and tried to hold back the tears from streaming down his cheeks, but the cracks in his heart were too wide, and his mind was too feeble.

"I have been called the Mistress of Mercy," Jisenna continued. "But there can be no mercy without justice. It is true that this man is an Obsidian threadweaver. We welcomed him in the name of the Heralds, and now we enact justice in their name. My sister's death will not be in vain if its redress serves to protect the world from further pain."

Watchlord Osinan stepped beside the empress. "It is our custom to allow the accused a chance to provide evidence of their innocence. There are times, however, when we must break custom. This man has pleaded guilty, and both Empress Jisenna and I have agreed that he will not be given a final address. We will not let his tear-filled fabrications sully this moment of restitution."

Alverax had been holding out hope that Jisenna still believed in him, but her words shattered that hope. It was inevitable now, and yet, he felt a strange sense of relief. As odd as it was, he felt at peace knowing that he was sacrificing himself for others. He'd been worried that, given a platform to defend himself, he would break down and plead his own innocence. Now, with no platform to speak, he could continue in silence, following through with his decision with the smallest semblance of grace.

Two dark men in bright white garb lifted the massive wooden beam and walked it over to Alverax. In the center of the beam, a space had been carved out for a man's neck and, at the ends, metal rods arched upward like twin scythes. Together, the men heaved it high and placed it over Alverax's shoulders, then clasped both sides together around his neck.

The weight of the wood alone was staggering. No one had explained the process to him in the prison cell, but the metaphor seemed obvious to him now; he would bear the weight of their grief.

A familiar face from the masquerade, the prideful man, Rastalin Farrow, approached the platform first. "Two stones for the people of Felia."

The men in white grabbed two circular slabs of stone with holes in their center, lifted them high, and placed them over the metal rods on the end of Alverax's cross. The wood near the base of his neck dug hard into his skin, the weight of the stones compounding with the weight of the beam.

As Rastalin returned to his position, Watchlord Osinan approached the front. "Two stones for the Heralds, who look down with disgrace."

Again, the men lifted two slabs of stone and placed them over the metal rods. The pain seemed to multiply exponentially. His legs could barely carry the weight, but, if he collapsed, the beam would crush him. He groaned in agony as he fought to remain standing. Then, he realized that he could, at any moment, break the threads of the stones and lighten his load. The pain would stop. The suffering would cease, but he would taint his own sacrifice.

Empress Jisenna returned to the front of the stands and paused, raw eyes lifting to meet Alverax's own. On her cheeks, he saw the remnants of a morning filled with tears and sorrow. The next stones would crush him—he could feel that truth in the grinding of his vertebrae—and, though she may be the Mistress of Mercy, she had accepted his fate as much as her own. "Two stones for the Lady of Light, the Sun Queen, the Empress of Felia, my sister and my dearest friend."

The circling birds chirped louder, taunting him as he awaited the placement of the final stones. He wanted to scream, to fight, to survive, but this moment would define him.

The men approached with the final circular stone slabs, larger than the rest. They lifted the stones with concerted effort.

"My life for yours!" a desperate voice screamed from the crowd.

Alverax lifted his eyes, barely able to keep his knees from buckling, and looked to the source of the voice.

An old woman with green eyes and a scowl shouted from the crowd. Alverax knew her. Elder Rowan, red-faced and filled with passion, screamed once more. "My life for yours!"

Alverax choked on his breath. Beside the elder, he saw a group of the other Zeda people, piled together and bound in chains, forced to watch the death of their companion.

The Felians would execute her for what she'd just done.

He wanted to scream at her to run, to take his sacrifice and go, but he could do nothing with the stones weighing him down.

"Enough!" Osinan screamed, "There will be no surrogacy!"

A second voice, a man's voice with a certain gruffness to it, repeated the phrase. "My life for yours!"

Alverax looked and saw Dogwood standing tall in the crowd, raising a fist high overhead.

Before Osinan could respond, yet another voice shouted, "My life for yours!"

Elder Rosemary.

The rest of the Zeda elders, speckled throughout the crowd, joined in the chorus, repeating the same words.

Then, a child's voice called out, "My life for yours!"

When he looked, he saw the young girl, Poppy, whom he'd protected from the Felian soldier.

Something about the little girl's offering snapped the last remaining cord in his mind. He fell to his knees, the weight of the stone slabs bearing down on his body while the words of his friends bore down on his soul. Tears flowed down his cheeks, and he heard one final voice.

Iriel Valerian, her child nowhere to be seen, stood firm in a storm of uncertainty, and said the one phrase that Alverax would never wish her to speak. "My life for yours!"

"Enough!" Osinan shouted. His eyes alternated between Alverax and the increasingly agitated crowd.

Alverax glanced at Jisenna and thought he saw a shimmer of doubt in her eyes, but then she turned to the men in white. "Two stones for my sister!"

Just then, one of the circling birds fluttered down to the platform and landed near Alverax's head on the wooden beam. It stayed for only a brief moment, then took off into the sky.

The world faded around him, and Alverax fell into a story, a memory of his own construction. He saw Jisenna standing atop a green hill overlooking an endless sea. An evil princess set to destroy the world. A small, yellow-bellied starling rested on her shoulder. As she looked out over the tumultuous waves, the little bird spoke to her and said, "*Are you certain?*"

When the words were spoken, the vision fled, and Alverax returned to a painful reality. The weight of four stone slabs tore into his shoulders, blood trailed down his torso where the wood cut into his skin. The entire crowd of men and women stared, awaiting his death. And the empress, the woman who'd once shown him such wonderful kindness, stood in silence, a single tear drifting down her cheek.

Only a few moments passed before the little bird flew away, but, sometimes, a few moments change everything. Her eyes softened. Her shoulders fell. The quiver in her lips faded away as they parted. "Wait," she whispered through the commotion.

The white-garbed men lifted the stone slabs and placed them over the metal rods of Alverax's cross.

"Stop!" the empress screamed as the weight of the final slabs settled.

The addition of the final two slabs would have crushed Alverax had he not heard Jisenna's plea. He opened himself to threadlight and *broke* the threads of all six of the stone slabs. The overwhelming weight of the beam and stones lifted from his shoulders, and he rose once again to his feet.

"Do not touch him!" Jisenna said as the men in white reached for the swords at their waist.

Watchlord Osinan stepped forward, fire in his eyes. "Sun Daughter! What is the meaning of this?"

"Sun *Queen*," Empress Jisenna corrected with a powerful resolve in her gaze. "This man did not kill my sister."

CHAPTER 22

FALLING TO HIS DEATH, Chrys had never felt so alive. The light from above was fading fast, and he was beginning to fear that the Endless Well would live up to its name. In the split moment he'd made the decision to jump, based on the assumption that there *would* be a bottom, he'd not taken into account the real possibility that by the time they reached the bottom, there would be no light. If they couldn't see, they couldn't threadweave. And if they couldn't thread-weave, their landing would be much less graceful than he'd hoped.

He looked to his mother, and his eyes swelled with pride. The dirt in her hair, the scum caked on her clothing, she was a mess...for him. The damn woman had crossed mountains. She'd trekked through uncharted jungles. And she'd found him. She was to him, what he hoped to be to his family. Come what may, he *would* find them again.

So long as they didn't die at the bottom of the Endless Well.

They fell for what seemed an eternity with no end in sight, until, quite suddenly, hundreds of orbs of dim light faded into view below them, spread out in tightly coupled bunches. The orbs illuminated a lake of clear water with an island of barren stone at its center. Water, fed from the waterfall on the other side of the Endless Well, crashed in foamy bouts into the lake.

"NOW!" Chrys shouted over the rush of the wind.

Willow understood, and both of their veins blazed to life with Sapphire threadlight. Chrys grabbed hold of Roshaw and *pushed* against the ground. Their descent came to an abrupt halt as their feet landed hard atop mossy rock.

Roshaw collapsed to his back, hands atop his head, and caught his breath. Despite the massive width of the opening, the light coming down from high overhead was nothing but a spec in the darkness, like a single star in the night sky. Chrys spun in a circle and dozens of patches of photospores shined their bioluminescence in the sprawling cavern. Below one patch, the broken body of a wastelander floated face up in the water. He saw other bones scattered throughout the cave, with bits of broken spear and shredded clothing.

"Well," Willow said, rubbing at her chest. "I love what you've done with the place. A little dark, and the size is a bit pretentious. But you know me, I've always liked cozy cottages more than subterranean chateaus."

Chrys let out a clipped laugh.

"On the other hand," she continued, "I'm sure there was a discount for the gaping hole in the roof."

Chrys shook his head. "Would you believe they charged me extra for it? The corpse cost me eighty shines."

"Unbelievable," Willow said, laughing. Then, without another word, she lunged forward and embraced him, squeezing him with a ferocity that only a mother could know, and held it until her arms were shaking. Chrys shuddered at the pain in his shoulder where the corespawn had left its mark.

Despite his myriad wounds, Chrys' heart filled with joy. "I thought I would never see you again. How did you find me?"

"When I saw what happened in the Fairenwild, I turned around. Luther let me hide out at their home for a few days until a raving soldier from the mountains claimed that the Apogee had slaughtered his camp. No one believed him, but it was all I had to go on. Then...I found this." She reached into a pocket and pulled out a pocket watch. The same one that Relek had discarded in the mountains. She handed it to him, and he held it carefully, surprised to still hear the ticking sound still played.

Chrys couldn't help but smile. "Let's hope it wasn't for nothing."

"I found you," she said. "That's enough for me. Now let's get you back to your *your* son."

Roshaw had lifted himself to his feet with tears in his eyes. In the days Chrys had known him, Roshaw had always been so lighthearted, the first to gamble and the first to laugh. But now, at the bottom of the Endless Well, his eyes burned with fury. And Chrys understood him. The waste-landers had lied. Relek had lied. They'd promised freedom, but instead they offered death. Chrys could still see the spears piercing their skin. Agatha, so frail and delicate, crying out in agony, while Seven, eyes filled with betrayal, looked to the ever-smiling Esme. Five years they'd searched for freedom, patiently biding their time, only to die to the whims of a god.

Roshaw's lip twitched. "He killed them."

"Don't focus on that right now," Chrys said. "Focus on getting out of here."

"It should have been me." Roshaw looked back up to the spec of light high above. "They were good people. If anyone deserved to die, it should have been me."

Chrys nodded to Willow as he left her to stand beside Roshaw. "You don't deserve to die."

"Neither did they!" he shouted, his words echoing in the vast cavern. "Agatha, Esme, Seven, they were good people. Better than me. I'm a piece of shit."

"You know," Chrys said. "My mentor once told me, after a battle where the wastelanders wiped out half of my men, that the only difference between the living and the dead is that the dead are done changing. The moment you die, your life and your legacy are fixed in stone. He told me that the best way to grieve the dead is by using the gift of life to make yourself a better man.

"I don't care if you're a piece of shit or a piece of gold. Someone or something is out there waiting for you. If you want to grieve Agatha, if you want to grieve Esme and Seven, then let's get the hell out of this cave and make ourselves into something better."

Roshaw was silent for a moment, clenching his jaw as he thought. The man's age seemed more pronounced amid the flickering lights of the photospores. There was a certain weariness in the expression of his eyes. When he finally spoke, he nodded and met Chrys' gaze. "I don't know. It's a nice thought, but it's just not that simple. The people I hurt will never forgive me for what I did."

"Who cares?" Chrys said. "Whether or not someone forgives you doesn't change anything. This is about you, and me, and my mother. We received a gift today that, as sickening as the truth is, not everyone around us received. Now, I don't know about you, but I'm not going to waste it. I'm getting out of here. I'm going to find my wife and son. And

I'm going to squeeze them so tight their eyes bulge out of their damn heads. And I'm going to do that with or without you, but I would much rather have you by my side."

Roshaw met him eye for eye in a battle of resolve. Chrys watched the older man's jaw flexing beneath his gaunt cheeks, his chest rising and falling beneath his tunic. "I just...I wish they could have made it out too."

"Me too," Chrys said.

"When we get out of here, I'm going to name a star for each of them. And if I can, I'd like to find their families and share their story."

"I think that would be very nice."

"Yeah," Roshaw said mostly to himself. His eyes wandered along with his mind, drifting off into the surrounding darkness of the cavern.

Chrys turned to Willow and she gave him a warm smile. He gestured for her to follow. They stepped carefully over wet stones, wading through knee-deep water, and made their way toward the periphery of the cavern. The small lake in the middle of the Well gave way to slick, slime-covered stone that Roshaw stumbled on, but managed to keep his footing. Eventually they found their way to the outer edge of the cavern, each pulling off a few photospores to illuminate their path. Little shadows danced along the walls and over the rocks as they searched for a path.

Willow was the first to see the tunnel, but Roshaw, filled with a new sense of determination, was the first to enter. The walls were smooth, as if the stone had been pounded flat. The smallest drips of water leaked from overhead along the edges, and stalactites grew from the ceiling. The silence was broken only by the occasional skittering of tiny footsteps in the puddles.

As Chrys walked on, he squeezed at his palm, eager for

the bleeding from his missing fingers to subside. There was a sick form of irony in the fact that, after losing three fingers, he'd taken upon himself Seven's title. It would take some getting used to, but if it was the price required for freedom and a reunion with his mother, he'd pay it a thousand times. Either way, he needed some fresh water so he could clean out his wounds. Otherwise, infection would soon take hold, and he didn't have access to any of the salves he knew of for dealing with such an affliction.

From further down in the tunnel, a subtle voice echoed across the smooth stone.

Willow had the obsidian blade out before Roshaw had even stopped walking. Chrys whispered for them to leave their photospores behind and follow him. They approached with soft steps, and soon found light emanating from further ahead. When they rounded the final bend, they saw the most curious sight.

A man wearing a wide brimmed hat sat at a table hewn of a single rose-colored stone. Haphazardly placed around the table, an array of wood chairs were filled with oddities: a translucent snake wrapped around petrified wood, a glowing fish swimming around a large crystal bowl, and a half-finished statue of a monster with the tail of a scorpion.

But odder than the rest was the man seated at the table. Beneath his hat, his eyes were closed tight, and long, dark hair fell to his naval.

"Sister?" the old man called out. When he turned his head, keeping his eyes closed, the sight reminded Chrys of the blind priests of the Order of Alchaeus.

Chrys clenched his jaw and gestured for the others to remain still. The likelihood that a blind man was alone in the caves far below Kai'Melend was nearly zero. So, they waited patiently, hoping he would think their steps were something else.

"You know I haven't bathed in years," the man said with a laugh.

When no one responded, the odd man took to his feet. He was old and wiry, and his loose fit tunic opened up at the chest, exposing a wildly undernourished body. The man took a few steps toward them, leaning in with his ears toward their direction.

"Lylax?"

Chrys and Roshaw swiftly backed around the corner at the word, and Willow followed.

"He definitely said *Lylax*, right?" Roshaw said.

Chrys nodded and turned to his mother. "Quick debrief. The voice I was hearing in my head turned out to be a wastelander god that can inhabit other people. His name is Relek. He's taken a new body, and he has a sister named Lylax who can do the same. If that man out there knows Lylax, then we can't let him know we're here. If they know we're alive, we're in danger."

Willow, after a momentary blank stare, closed her eyes and shook her head. "I...Iriel told me about the voice. A wastelander god?"

"Turns out I wasn't losing my mind, only sharing it."

"Stones," she cursed.

Roshaw cut in. "What do we do? Find another tunnel back at the Well?"

"No," Chrys said. "We need food and supplies, or we'll die down here. If that man is here, then he has to have something we can use."

"He's an old man," Willow said. "We can't kill him."

Chrys held his finger up to quiet her. "We're not going to kill anyone. We're going to steal from him." He thought he saw a smirk on Roshaw's lips at the suggestion. "But we also can't leave him here. So, we're going to tie him up and bring him with us. If we're lucky, he can help guide us out."

"He's blind..." Roshaw said.

Chrys rubbed his beard. "I have enough experience with blind people not to underestimate—"

"Hello," a voice said from behind them.

The three of them startled back, and Willow's blade swung forward, slicing Roshaw's forearm on the way up. Chrys pushed the others back and took a fighting stance between them and the bare-footed old man, then let a bit of threadlight course through his veins, lightening his stance.

"Oh, my," the odd man said, his eyes still shut tight. "I'm so sorry! I thought you were someone else. You see, I don't get many visitors. I've forgotten my manners. Please, please. Do come in and take a seat. You've a fine story, I'm certain of it. And I mean to hear every last word! If you promise me no harm, I will happily return the gesture."

The old man gestured for them to follow him, but Chrys stood in complete astonishment. Now that he was closer, something tickled at the edge of Chrys' mind. Maybe the old man *was* a priest and he'd seen him before. But why was he down there? Either way, Chrys knew there was information to be learned.

"Thank you," Chrys said. "Perhaps you could help us."

"Ah!" the old man choked on his word. He was quiet for a moment, then touched a finger under his closed eyes, wiping away a tear that fell down his cheek. "I...cannot explain how lovely it is to hear your voice. I'm so sorry. It feels almost like a dream. How many of you are there? I thought I heard others."

"There are three of us," Willow said.

"Three!" he laughed. "Three companions explore the

caves far beneath the surface. I'm afraid I know the ending of such a story. Three is a cursed number, I'm certain of it. Better if there were only two of you. It is a safer number. Please, please. Do come in."

He shuffled away and a little creature darted out from beneath the table. It looked like...Chrys let go of threadlight and the little creature vanished. He let threadlight flow through his veins, and the little creature reappeared.

"Stones. Is that—"

"He's called Chitt," the old man said. "He's quite harmless."

Chrys stared at the creature, curious about its connection to the corespawn he'd fought in the wasteland pit. "You're sure it's not dangerous?"

"Quite certain. His is one of the few friendly breeds. Though—don't tell him—not one of the most intelligent either."

As they followed, the little corespawn scuttled up the old man's leg and came to rest atop his shoulder. Chrys turned his gaze to survey the rest of the cavern. Light filled every corner of the sprawling space from dozens of photospores that grew in perfectly lined bunches along the outer edges. A dozen different tunnels led in every direction, and, on the far side, a massive pool of golden water emanated a faint glow of its own. A small waterfall fed the pool, leaving an ever-present glimmer as the water rippled at the surface.

There were no other corespawn creatures.

Out of the corner of his eye, Chrys could see Willow squeezing the obsidian blade in her hand. Everything about this felt wrong. The place. The company. The glowing fish that Chrys was certain was watching him. It almost felt like a dream, like he'd been drugged by the wastelanders and now slept while his mind delved into a deep psychosis. He looked down at his hand, and hoped that were true, but the pain he felt was real. Which made it all the stranger.

Down one of the corridors, a collection of instruments and gadgets was strewn about haphazardly across the floor and against the wall. Chrys noted the room, assuming that it was where he'd find any useful supplies for their exit.

"If I had known you were coming, I would have taken a bath," the man said. "My sister told me to jump in when she left, but...ha! I must sound mad! Of course, none of this would make sense to you. I'm so sorry! It's been so long."

"No apology needed," Willow said with a soft voice. "We are grateful for your hospitality. Though we are certainly curious what it is you are doing down here."

"Ah! Another collector of stories! And this is the grandest of them all." He paused, scratching at his over-grown beard as he pondered his response. "I suppose the summary is that we often do silly things for family."

Willow raised a brow. "Your family sent you here?"

"No, no, no. We discovered it, together," he said. "You know, I have often dreamed of sharing our story—the whole story. But my sister thinks it would be unwise."

"Your sister?" Chrys asked. "Is she here?"

The blind man turned to face Chrys and, though his eyes were closed, he seemed to take in Chrys' expression. "She should return any moment. However, I think it would be better if you were gone before she returns."

Interesting. The tone assumed that Lylax was dangerous, but Chrys had the sneaking suspicion that the old man was more than he appeared. Either way, if Lylax would return, they needed to get answers quickly, and get out even more so. "We know your sister and your brother, Relek. They slaughtered our friends."

The air in the cavern chilled as footsteps echoed down

one of the tunnels. The old man froze in his seat, his hands resting on the table. With his eyes shut, it was as though he had become a statue. But the little corespawn on his shoulder reached its neck out toward the sound and made a chirping noise.

The old man spoke in a hushed tone. "Do they know you are here?"

Chrys, Willow, and Roshaw all rose to their feet.

"Come, quick," the old man said. "You must hide!"

CHAPTER 23

LUTHER HELD his wife quietly in a farmhouse outside of Alchea. Their life would never be the same, but sometimes you have to make changes to make room for what's important.

"Try to get some sleep," he whispered to Emory, pressing his lips against her forehead.

She nodded but said nothing. She hadn't said much since they'd left, but he knew she would come around. It was the right decision, especially with the inevitable return of the corespawn. Even still, he should have warned her beforehand—he knew that—but he knew her deeply held beliefs would have clouded her judgment.

He rose from the bed and stepped to the door, pushing it open as quietly as he could. It made the slightest creak as he closed it behind him.

What he needed more than anything was a drink. It had been such a long day, and emotional, and horribly stressful. If not for threadlight to send a bit of liquid comfort throughout his body, he's not sure he could have made it through.

Fortunately, when he rounded the corner to the main room, Laz stood with a mug of ale in each hand, waiting for him. "Is time for drink."

"Please tell me that's not all there is," Luther said as he accepted the mug.

"Is whole barn full!" Laz said with a toothy grin. "Cousin is wild man."

Luther chugged half of the mug in one go, cringing at the taste. It was foul—much worse than city ale—but he knew he wouldn't sleep that night if he didn't drink more. It had been that way ever since the priests had taken his son. If he didn't drink, his mind would spin for hours while he lay awake, or he'd wake up to nightmares and fits of stress.

"You good?" Laz asked.

"I'll be okay." Luther sipped again on the ale. "It'll take some time. Our whole life was in Alchea. Family. Friends. But what the hell was I supposed to do?"

"You did right thing."

"I hope so," Luther said. "I think so. Stones, but I wish Chrys were here. He always knew what to do."

"Chrys would say, 'To be boss, must know how to count. Now, you have right count!'" Laz laughed at his own terrible impression.

The right count. It was a strangely wise way to look at it, coming from Laz especially, but he was right. Luther had been feeling incomplete, like an arch without its corner-stone, and alcohol only filled the gap with mud.

"Thanks, Laz. For everything."

"Is no problem," the thick red-headed man said as he sipped his own mug.

"I'm not drunk yet," Luther said. "So, I hope you believe me. But I'm really going to miss you, Laz. These past months have been hell, and you've been there beside me every damn day, sipping your nasty milk stout and helping me keep my demons at bay. You're a damn good friend, and I owe you more than I could ever repay."

He paused, waiting for Laz to make a joke, but, instead, the big man wrapped him in a bear hug, his massive hands squeezing against Luther's back. Laz was the only man Luther knew whose heart perfectly matched their frame. He found himself feeling unexpectedly emotional as he embraced his friend for what could be the last time.

When they pulled away, Laz had tears swelling in his eyes. "Don't tell Reina I cry. She would make more fun of me."

"Your secret is safe," Luther said.

Laz lifted a bag off the floor and tossed it over his shoulder. "Time for me to go back now. Take care of yourself, you hole."

No matter how many times he used the insult, Laz had still yet to explain what it meant. But, somehow, that felt perfectly fitting for the man.

"I still think you should stay. It might not be safe for you back there."

"Is fine," Laz said, brushing it off. "Reina will lie for me."

Luther nodded. "Okay, then this is it. Lazarus Barlow, it has been a pleasure being your teammate, your friend, and the one who can always outdrink you."

"I share secret," Laz said, smiling his doping grin. "I always can outdrink. I let you win. Ha! Goodbye, friend."

With that, the big man pushed open the door and stepped out into the starry night. Luther turned back to the hallway and stepped toward the room. Laz's cousin's farmhouse had an extra room that they weren't using, which was all they could ask for. With everything going on, Luther wanted his kids in his room with him at night. It felt safer, even though it was unlikely anyone would find them there. Still, old habits die hard, and paranoia was a healthy habit for a soldier.

When he entered the room, Luther stepped over to the bed and smiled. Two children lay quietly asleep beside Emory, unaware of the growing dangers in the world. He wished he could be like them.

He looked to the foot of the bed where a small white bassinet lay. Inside, slept a small child.

His third.

Luther reached down and rubbed the little boy's cheek, filled with an overwhelming joy that he was once again theirs, sad only that the boy would forever be blind. Every other piece of his soul felt like a missing gear had been replaced, and finally his life would run again.

To hell with the Order of Alchaeus.

No one would take his son from him ever again.

CHAPTER 24

THE OLD MAN in the caves beneath Kai'Melend led Chrys, Willow, and Roshaw to a curved, dead-end tunnel. His little corespawn, Chitt, skittered toward the far end and disappeared into the darkness where the light from the golden pool faded away.

Roshaw entered first, scrambling to follow the little creature. They passed crates filled with cloth, mounds of colorful gemstones, and a variety of carefully organized tools and items. In the far corner of the tunnel, a collection of nearly one hundred man-sized alabaster statues stood in a carefully aligned collection.

As they approached and their eyes adjusted, Chrys could see Chitt popping in and out from beyond the shadows. The statues, like stone sentinels, were carved with precision, each one depicting a different breed of terrifying beast. Some stood on two legs, others prowled on four. Spikes protruded from the shoulders of some, while others had horns or barbed tails. But each creature bore two clear quartz gems fastened to the place where the eyes would be.

They moved among them, brushing up against cold

stone, hardly able to see their own movements. Willow grabbed Chrys' good hand, and a dark feeling grew in the pit of his stomach. There was something off about the statues. Something darker than the lack of light.

They settled between them and let go of the threadlight in their veins. The Sapphire radiance faded away, and their bodies succumbed to the shadows.

Muffled voices echoed from beyond the bend. Though he could not hear the words, the tone he would never forget.

Relek.

They stood in silence, living statues among the dead, hoping that the old man would keep their secret.

"Agh," Chrys groaned. He shook his hand and brought it upright near his chest. Without threadlight in his veins, he couldn't be certain, but he had a feeling the little corespawn had licked the dried blood on his missing fingers. Chrys looked down the tunnel, and flickering shadows grew along the wall.

Relek's voice resounded along the stone. "I heard about your stonemasonry. Lylax says your collection of corespawn is quite impressive."

"It's not exactly a collection," the old man replied. "More of a taxonomy really."

With a look that said, "I don't care", Relek continued his approach. His eyes were alive with color, a turbulent swirl of spectral light. He leaned in and touched the face of one of the statues, a large creature the size of a bear, with two massive fangs that cut out to its jawline. "I must admit, I don't much like seeing these creatures without threadlight."

Relek's eyes moved over the collection of statues. Chrys, Willow, and Roshaw hid themselves behind the alabaster figures, breathing through their mouths only when they could no longer hold their breath. Relek moved to investigate further, but then the old man crouched and made a clicking noise with his tongue. Skittering feet, starting from within the collection of statues, scratched against the floor until the old man rose back to his feet, cradling an empty hand. "Like I said, brother. It was only Chitt. Don't be so paranoid. You are immortal after all."

"It's not the ones who escaped that I am afraid of. There are at least two Creators west of the mountains. A woman—powerful, but limited in her knowledge—and a child."

"You are frightened of a child?"

"Don't be a fool. It is simply that I refuse to be trapped again."

"I know a little about being trapped," the old man said, turning from the tunnel and stepping toward the larger cavern.

Relek followed. "But you could explore the endless caverns of the core. The wastelanders die if they do not drink the elixir regularly. What matters is that I will take whatever measure are necessary to never be trapped again. This time, there can be no mercy." His voice trailed off as they rounded the bend into the cavern.

Chrys, Willow, and Roshaw remained still for what seemed an eternity, not daring to assume that Relek had left.

Without threadlight in his veins, Chrys began to feel the effects of his fighting. His shoulder throbbed, and his hand pulsed with every beat of his heart. He closed his eyes, wincing at the pain. When he opened them, the quartz eyes of the corespawn statues all seemed to turn and look at him. The bruised flesh over his ribs tightened and his breathing increased.

When Willow squeezed his good hand, he startled, nearly knocking over a statue in front of him.

"Your hand is shaking," she whispered. "Are you okay?"

"No." His voice came out strained.

"You need to lie down. You've lost a lot of blood."

"I'll be fine."

Willow let go of his hand and he saw her make her way out of the collection of statues. The closer she drew to the bend, the more her silhouette grew in the rippling gold light. She stood at the edge of the tunnel, pressed up against the stone wall, and waited. Chrys found himself praying in the back of his mind, hoping that Relek would not find her. Failing to fight off his blurring vision, he grabbed hold of a large spike protruding from the back of a statue nearby, and its feet began to wobble against the stone floor.

Roshaw reached over and steadied the statue before it made more noise. "Grab my arm," he whispered.

Chrys took hold of Roshaw's upper arm with his good hand and tried to breathe, but the air amongst the statues was stale and cold, with hints of chalky dust that swirled in his lungs. He stifled a cough, but the pressure in his chest was worse. The little light remaining in the far recess of the tunnel warped into shifting shadows and blobs of taunting darkness that coalesced and split in nightmarish waves. Time passed, and Chrys felt his entire world dissolving into a chaotic dream, filled with pain and confusion. And just as he closed his eyes to flee from it all, his legs collapsed beneath him.

WILLOW FELT a wave of relief as the wastelander god, Relek, cupped the back of his brother's head, bringing their foreheads together, then left. As his footsteps faded away down a far tunnel, the blind old man waited patiently at his table, running his hand along the back of his invisible pet. They continued for another minute, Willow spying and the old man waiting, until finally he rose from his seat.

"Psss," Willow said. "Are we safe?"

The old man nodded. "They will not return for quite some time now."

Just as Willow felt a sense of relief, the sound of shattering stone exploded through the cavern. She whipped her head around and raced through the small tunnel to find the dim outline of Roshaw holding Chrys. Beneath them, one of the corespawn figures was strewn across the floor in a hundred broken pieces.

"Chrys!" Willow rushed to her son. She hadn't come this far to let him die in a cave. As much as she wanted him alive for her own self, she knew more importantly that his wife and son needed him. No matter the cost, she would reunite them. Her grandson deserved to know how good a man his father was.

She helped Roshaw lift him out of the assembly of corespawn statues, feeling at Chrys' forehead and panicking at the burning temperature. The old man was close now, and she turned to address him. "Please, my son is dying. Do you have any herbs or medicines? A bed at the least where we can lay him until his fever breaks?"

"I—" The wrinkles of his forehead creased out from his blindfold and his lips puckered. "He will die, you say?"

"He's lost a lot of blood," she said.

"He collapsed out here," Roshaw added. "Looked really dizzy before he did."

The old man frowned and nodded. "Life is more valuable than secrets," he said to himself. "Come, come. There is a way. Your son will live."

Willow *pushed* against her corethread, offsetting Chrys' weight, and carried him chest-to-chest with his arms wrapped around her neck. Despite his size, the position reminded her of the many years she'd spend carrying him this same way. Her little boy. She'd been so lonely during those years, refusing to grow too close to anyone lest they discover her secret. The intimacy she craved, she could not have, because the tattoo on her back would give too much away. And as much as she wanted her new life, she would not have it at the expense of revealing the Zeda people. So, instead, she'd only had Chrys. Her son. Her little flower. The firm root in the storm.

She'd needed him, and now he needed her.

They entered into the large cavern space, and the old man walked carefully toward the sprawling golden pool. Chiseled steps led up to the surface of the water where small ripples refracted the gold light emanating from within.

"If you want him to heal," the old man said, "place him in the pool."

Willow looked into the shimmering pool. Stalactites high overhead reflected from its surface and a strange energy seemed to draw her toward it, beckoning her to enter. For a moment, she lost herself in the beauty of the water, transfixed by each singular ripple as it extended from edge to edge. But she shook the feeling away and focused instead on Chrys.

"In the water?" she repeated. "How deep?"

"All the way," the old man said.

"He'll drown."

"You may keep his head above the water if it comforts you, but it is not necessary."

She placed Chrys along the edge of the pool. His feet slid in first—it seemed to be only as deep as a man's waist—and then she slid in the rest of his body, keeping a hand beneath his head. Once he was fully submerged, she let go of the threadlight in her veins, and slumped against the steps.

"Are their salts or herbs that we need in the water?" Willow asked. "Roshaw can fetch them for you."

"No, no," the old man said. "The truth is that this is *not* water. It is the first great secret of my family. We call it *elixir*. When we discovered it, we soon found that it contained within it a certain healing property. Your son will come out stronger and healthier than ever before."

"The wound in his shoulder?" she asked.

"Healed."

"His missing fingers?" Roshaw asked incredulously.

"Restored," the old man said with confidence. "It will reset his body to its ideal state. If he were old, it would even *heal* him of his old age."

It all seemed so...impossible. An old man in a cave claiming there was a pool that would heal any wound? Even old age? If something like that existed, it would change everything. If you could heal old age, people would be —"Immortal," she said aloud.

"The first great secret," the old man repeated.

Roshaw shook his head. "No. Come on, now. If that were true, why are you so old? Jump in the pool and soak for a few minutes and you'd be young again. It doesn't add up."

"Ah," the blind man said. "A keen observation, and a question I've discussed with my sister many a time. To me, age is not a curse, but a core part of the human experience. Choosing to ignore such a central part of humanity would be to become less and less human. I do believe my brother and sister are examples of this divergence. Where I hope to maintain my humanity across the centuries, they seek to disavow it. It is not easy to grow old, or to lose your sight, especially knowing that you could at any moment change your situation. But to me, it is better to see truth than light. It is better to hold on to the crux of the human experience."

Roshaw looked stunned. "Well, there it is. The old man is completely mad."

But Willow wasn't so sure.

If Relek and Lylax were immortal—which they had reason to believe—then their brother would be as well. And the old man *had* protected them from Relek, so Willow had no reason to disbelieve him. "Will Chrys be immortal now?" she asked.

"No, no," he said. "It does not prevent death. However, if he were to journey here every twenty years for the rest of his life, then yes. He would never die of old age."

"So Relek can die?" Roshaw asked, suddenly interested once again. "And if he doesn't come back here, he would grow older and eventually die?"

The old man clenched his teeth. "My siblings have long moved on from needing the elixir. It is the reason we parted ways so long ago. But I conceded eventually, not because I agree with them, but because they need me at their side. It is important to keep ties with those that do not believe what you do. If your beliefs are never questioned, they become sour."

"You said they've moved on," Willow pressed. "What do you mean by that?"

The old man grew quiet, taking steady breaths while he debated within himself. Willow knew there was something here. Something important. She needed him to tell them.

"Do you know that they are amassing an army?" she asked.

He pursed his lips.

"Our friends were only the beginning," she continued.

"They will kill many more. If you know anything that can help us stop them, countless lives are at risk."

"They promised me!" the old man shouted. "They swore that they would not seek revenge."

"We can stop them, if you'll help us," Willow prodded.

The old man dropped his head. "I am no fool. I knew they were lying when they told me. I just...hoped that it would be different. That somehow time had changed them for the better."

Willow wanted to press him again but held back. She could see in the way his shoulders fell forward, his hands fidgeting, that he was close to breaking. Whatever secret he held back, was standing on the precipice, ready to leap.

"It *will* be different this time." Slowly, the old man lifted his head and opened his eyes. Two prismatic irises, slightly muted by a cloudy film, swirled with every color in the spectrum. It took only a split second to realize...they were the same eyes that Relek and Lylax now had.

Willow's free hand fell to the obsidian blade at her side.

The old man turned his gaze to Willow and held his head high. "It is time for my siblings to die."

CHAPTER 25

THE SUN QUEEN, Empress Jisenna of Felia, stood quietly in the doorway. Both hands rested on her hips, separating her billowy white harem pants and an off-the-shoulder white top trimmed with gold.

Alverax tried to hide the last hint of red in his eyes and the salty tears that had dried over his cheeks, but, as soon as their eyes met—something about the way she looked at him —his façade was torn asunder, and the tears he'd hoped to hide came pouring out of his sunken eyes. He didn't want her to see him like that, but tears have a mind of their own, and no man can impede their arrival once they've chosen to surface.

Jisenna approached him and sat, gesturing for her guards to stay outside the door. But she didn't speak. She simply sat, her shoulder brushing his own, and stared at the floor. They sat in silence for a time. Her presence brought with it a feeling of peace despite everything they'd been through. Finally, after longer than he'd wished, his tears stopped, and his breathing calmed.

"Jisenna" was all he managed, but it was enough.

"I was so *angry*," she said quietly. "And you were right there. Such a convenient enemy. I knew—Heralds save me, but I knew—it was never you. But I was in shock and what had happened, and then you ran. Heralds, Alverax. If you didn't run...I don't know. I'd like to think that we would have believed you."

"I shouldn't have run," he said sheepishly. "I know that, but you should have seen how the people were looking at me. Your sister already didn't trust us. Osinan had blood in his eyes the moment it happened. And when *you* blamed me...I don't know. I was terrified."

She closed her eyes. "I wish you would have come to me, even after you ran."

"Well, technically I did," he said with a fake smile. "I hope you don't blame yourself. Heralds, if I didn't look guilty enough at the masquerade, I admitted to doing it in front of a room full of your guards."

Jisenna looked deep into his eyes. "But you *didn't* do it, and deep down I knew that. And you...you knew that confessing would end in your death, and still you gave yourself to save them."

"You make it sound so heroic, but it was just guilt. I deserved it more than they did."

She eyed him carefully. "You think you deserved it?"

"More than they did."

"Why?" she asked.

Alverax ran his fingertips over his eyes. "I don't know."

"Come now," she prodded. "Why do you think that you deserved to die?"

"I said I don't know."

She scowled. "I cannot understand you. In one moment,

you're full of wit and charm, and, in the next, you believe yourself deserving of death. So, which is it? Who are you? And don't you dare say you don't know."

He felt his pulse quicken, a rising tide of frustration and anger billowing beneath his skin. "You want to know the truth?" he asked, nearly shouting. "I am nothing. I'm the son of a thief. I hurt people. I break promises. I make stupid choices. I'm not a hero. I'm just a dumb kid that thought that maybe, just once, he could finally do something good with his life."

She moved to speak but paused. Her eyes pierced deep into his soul. "I don't know what you've done in the past, but I do know this. The choices we make when no one is watching bear more weight than the choices that are forced upon us. You alone made the choice to give up your life to save another. I wish I saw it sooner. But when I saw you fall to your knees, on the verge of death, I finally understood what you'd done. And it had nothing to do with my sister."

"I'm not who you think I am," he said, looking down at the floor.

"Then tell me."

Her quick words stunned him. He wanted to tell her everything. He wanted to unload the burden of his secrets. But he knew he couldn't. It was hard to remember that she was the empress of all of Felia now, here she was speaking with him like they were friends. The truth was that one wrong word and he'd go right back to prison.

"It's about the Bloodthieves, isn't it?" Jisenna turned her shoulders to face him more fully. "Alverax, I swear to you as Empress of Felia, with my heart uncovered for the Heralds to see, that anything you tell me now will bring no judgment upon you. We all make mistakes. Your past only defines a single trodden path, but who you are here, and now, in this very moment, is another path filled with infinite possibility. I don't want to know who you were so that I can judge you. I want to know who you were so I can understand you."

He wanted to...he wanted to so badly.

Her lips parted, and her eyes softened. "Alverax."

The persistence that should have been infuriating was a warm invitation. "I've trusted the wrong people too many times, and I just—."

"There's nothing to be—"

"I know. I know. I'm in my own head," he said. "You're honestly one of the kindest, most good-hearted people I've ever known. When I look at you, it feels like threadlight is burning through my veins. I know that I should trust you, but Jisenna, you're the *empress*. That terrifies me."

She lifted the crown off her head and placed it beside her. "Today, I'm not the empress. Today, I'm just a girl hoping that a boy will trust her as much as she trusts him."

Her voice, calm yet absolute, felt like springtime to his wintered mind. This was the real her. Free of her crown. Free of her duties. One on one, overflowing with empathy for those she cared about. She may now be the Sun Queen, but she was still the Mistress of Mercy.

They locked eyes and he spoke. "I do trust you."

"Then let's start from the beginning," she suggested.

Alverax nodded to himself and took a deep, steadying breath. "I guess the first thing you should know is that I've never met my mother. Back then, my father used to leave home for months at a time and come back with stories that no one fully believed. But he always brought trinkets and treasures that lent some bit of credibility. Once, he left for a whole year, and, when he returned, he returned with me.

Met a woman in a small village, fell in love, and a short time later I was born. But she died in childbirth, and he brought me home."

"That's horrible," she said.

"There have been times when I wish I'd known her. My grandfather helped raise me while my father continued on his trips. That's when he started working for Jelium."

"Who is Jelium?"

Alverax pursed his lips. "He's the ruler of Cynosure."

"Hold on," she said, waving her hands. "You are from *Cynosure*?"

He nodded.

"Watchlord Osinan will want to know all about that!" she said with excitement. "Our spies have told us all about the little commune of criminals."

"Little?" Alverax cut in. "I wouldn't call twenty thousand *little*."

Jisenna's brows perked. "Twenty thousand? We were told two thousand at most. They said it was 'nothing to worry about.'"

"Twenty thousand, at least. You might want to check the back pocket of your *spies*."

She paused, thoughtfully. "I'm sorry I diverted us. You were saying...about your father?"

"He started working for Jelium, one of the Amber threadweavers that rules Cynosure."

"An Amber threadweaver?" she said with a pinch of fear in her tone. "Is he dangerous?"

"Only if you're a slab of meat," he said with a smirk. "The man's a human sandhog. Mean, tough, and fat."

She paused, opened her mouth as if to respond, then furrowed her brow. "You're better than that."

"What?"

"Mocking others' appearance is the lowest form of humor. If a man is cruel, speak of his cruelty. If a man is vain, speak of his vanity. Physicality plays no part in the morality of men."

"Oh, come on," he replied. "He is a horrible person. Heralds, he killed my father! I'm not allowed to mock him?"

"I've seen your wit, Alverax Blightwood. If you're going to mock him, pay full price. You debase yourself with such discounted humor."

"Where I come from people think it's funny."

"I don't doubt that," she said flatly. "But you and I walk a different path than most, and it will require us to change in uncomfortable ways."

Her words stung, because they were true. If he wanted to make a difference in the world, he had to become something more than what he was in Cynosure. Something more than what he was in that very moment. And with Jisenna there next to him, he thought that he just might be able to do it.

"You're right," he replied.

"What was that?" she said with a smile. "I'm not certain I heard you."

"Let me try again," he said, rolling his eyes. "O great Lady of Light, your words are brilliant rays, illuminating the shadowed recesses of my soul. And now I, a humble sinner, humbly come before you to shower your feet with humble tears. The humblest of tears. So humble. Humbleness of the like this world has never seen. Such humility that the ocean of my tears will cause your toes to wrinkle in their humble tide. A humility of such grandeur that—"

"Okay, okay," she said laughing.

Before he could continue, a knock came at the door

followed by the entry of one of her black-clothed guards. "Empress," he said with urgency.

She rose to her feet. "What is it?"

"Smoke signals are rising from the watchtowers," he said, glancing at Alverax. "Empress, we are under attack."

CHAPTER 26

ALVERAX FOLLOWED Jisenna to a balcony overlooking the whole of Felia. The sweeping landscape nearly filled the view from horizon to horizon, the high walls of the city proper looming over the tiny homes along the perimeter. To the east, smoke plumed up in billowy clouds from a signal fire in the guard tower.

"What is happening?" Jisenna asked.

Watchlord Osinan, hand on the hilt of his sword, scowled when he saw Alverax. "There is an enemy at our walls."

Jisenna lifted her chin. "Are we prepared for something like this? Surely, they can't get past our defenses."

"The walls are sturdy, Empress," Osinan said, "but they are not impenetrable. Our nation has not seen war for many years, and time is an erosive substance. For now, we must wait for messengers to bring us word. I've sent the generals to lead on the front lines."

As they looked out over the city, two more towers lit their warning fires.

The doors pushed open and the first messenger arrived, panting and sweaty from his journey. "Watchlord," the messenger said gruffly. "Empress."

"Quickly, now," Osinan said. "What is happening?"

"We're not sure, sir."

"What the hell does that mean? You came all the way here to tell us that you're not sure?" Osinan's eyes were bright as the warning flames.

"Sir, the enemy is invisible."

"What?"

"If I had not been there myself, I would not believe it. An entire army of invisible beasts. Well, not entirely invisible, sir. Our threadweavers can see them in threadlight. And some are as large as a house."

Osinan's lip quivered. "Heralds, save us. It cannot be."

Jisenna stepped forward. "What is it, Osinan?"

"If it is true..."

"Osinan," Jisenna commanded. "Tell us what you know."

The elderly Watchlord looked worried. His thumb rubbed at the hilt of his blade. "Within the Hallowed Library, the Anathema contains our oldest texts. Many are deemed heretical, but it is a duty of the Watchlords to know even the darkest parts of our religion. These texts speak of times long past, when the Heralds still walked the earth.

"There are records from this time of a scourge covering the land, beasts that destroyed everything in their wake. But the Heralds protected the people, casting the creatures back to their dark home. These beasts could only be seen in threadlight, and some could not be killed by mortal blade. Were it not for the Heralds, the creatures would have ended mankind.

"They were called corespawn, and, if the creatures at our

walls are the same creatures from the texts, then we are in grave danger."

The words bounced around in Alverax's skull like razors, cutting away at his memories and butchering his understanding. Invisible creatures only able to be seen in threadlight. It had to be...

Jisenna shook her head. "How have I never heard of these corespawn?"

"They are heretical texts, locked away in our vaults," Osinan replied. "Most of them have little or no evidence to their truthfulness, or they contain information that we know to be false, but we keep them for the preservation of our people."

"Jisenna," Alverax cut in. "Your sister...I think it was a corespawn."

She turned to Osinan, her eyes growing wide. "Didn't one of your guards say they saw an anomaly of threadlight?"

"It is possible," Osinan said, his eyes growing thin. "But none of the other threadweavers saw the creature."

Alverax recalled the moment. Graceful dancers spun in unison through his mind, sweeping over the marble floor. Empress Chailani conversed with a group of Felian nobles, and Alverax watched as he approached. He'd been nervous to speak to her, but knew he needed to if he wanted to help the Zeda people settle into Felia. He'd let threadlight enter his veins to calm him. And that's when he'd seen the creature. A spindly monster of pure light, blazing in a dark room, reaching toward the empress, and thrusting its tail into her chest. Alverax had run toward her—how could no one else see it? He reached out with his threadlight toward the creature to *break* its corethread, anything to protect her. But as soon as he'd reached it, and pressed against it with his Obsidian power, the creature had burst apart.

"I killed it," Alverax said in realization. "I tried to *break* it like a thread, and it exploded. I...I thought it vanished somehow—or maybe I was crazy and it was never there—but I remember. I reached out to it like any other thread, and it *broke*."

Watchlord Osinan eyed him suspiciously, his hand still resting on his blade. "It is possible. It would explain why the Heralds valued the Obsidians so highly."

"The Heralds are with us," Jisenna said. She turned to Alverax. "Can't you see it? The only Obsidian in the world shows up in our city just before an enemy arrives that only he can defeat. The Heralds might as well be walking our streets for how closely they are watching over us."

Osinan pulled his sword out of its sheath, the moon reflecting across the all-black blade. "This sword is called the Midnight Watcher," he said. "It has been passed down from Watchlord to Watchlord for centuries, ever since the departure of the Heralds. It is no ordinary blade. From cross-guard to point, it is hewn of a unique obsidian material that can pierce through threads. It was once used to slay corespawn alongside the Heralds. Alverax, I still do not trust you completely, but even I cannot deny that the people of Felia need you. If the corespawn are here, it is my duty—and your heritage—to end their assault." He reached out a hand. "Will you join me?"

Alverax stared for a moment, incredulous. This was it. The Heralds had saved him that day when he'd awoken in the pit of bones. They'd saved him from the death that every other failed experiment had suffered. For this. So that he could protect the people of Felia. He had never been a religious person, but, in that moment, he was certain that the Heralds had played their hand.

"I will," Alverax replied, grasping the Watchlord's hand.

Osinan sheathed the Midnight Watcher and untangled one of the golden tassels dangling near his shoulder before allowing a hint of a smile to cross his lips. "Then we fight."

As THEY EXITED the Sun Palace, a retinue of guards and horses awaited them. They rode for what seemed an eternity as the distant smoke signals continued to rise into the night sky. The closer they came, the louder the commotion at the walls. Screaming and shouting intermixed with the foul cries of their invisible enemy. Alverax felt his heart quicken and his hands tremble knowing the danger that awaited them, but, if he could save even a few, all the fear in the world would have been worth it.

They rounded the edge of a large building with a geodesic dome roof and came into view of the carnage. A Felian guard crawled along the dirt, half of his leg missing, the other half tattered and bloody. They rode past him without hesitation. High above on the wall-walk, men and women flailed their blades in chaotic strokes, swatting at an enemy they could not see.

Alverax jumped down from his horse and let threadlight pour through his veins. A warm tingle flowed from his chest out through his arms and legs, filling his body with warmth and energy, but his eyes filled with dread. As threadlight blossomed in his vision, hundreds of creatures came into view, each a different shape and size, but all formed of a brilliant, pulsing light. His eyes grew in horror as he looked up and saw more and more of the corespawn lifting themselves over the top of the wall, overwhelming what was left of the guards.

His fear faded to anger, and his anger swelled, until his

black eyes saw nothing but red. But he was too focused on the wall and didn't see the corespawn dashing at him until it was mid-flight, pouncing toward him. He pulled back, flinching at the sudden movement in his vision. Just before it reached him, the corespawn exploded into a cloud of threadlight as the Midnight Watcher cut through its spindly body.

"Careful, boy," Osinan warned, his eyes blazing with Emerald threadlight. "If you can truly kill them, it is time for you to go to work."

Alverax nodded, planted his feet firm into the dirt, and searched out the closest corespawn. A small, skittering creature darted back and forth across the field of grass, frantically searching out its next victim. Alverax focused on it, gathered his energy, and directed it toward the creature just as he would to *break* its corethread. He felt a mild resistance, like a knife cutting through bread, and then gasped as the creature screeched and burst apart, as though it had exploded from within.

Watchlord Osinan stopped in his tracks, whipping his head toward the explosion of light. He turned back to Alverax. "Was that you?"

Alverax nodded, incredulously.

"If we survive this, I owe you an apology." The elder Watchlord swung his blade in a circle. "You take the north; I'll take the south."

With that, they split paths and Alverax ran forward, filling himself with wild amounts of threadlight. One by one, he *broke* the creatures, and each time they burst asunder. One corespawn, larger than the others, with long arms that it used to stand upright as it walked, leapt down from the high wall, hitting the ground with a rumble. Alverax grabbed hold of it with his mind and squeezed. The pressure built—he could feel it intensifying—like gripping an orange and knowing that if he just squeezed hard enough the entire fruit would burst. He shouted into the battlefield, every muscle in his body tensing with the effort, until finally the corespawn exploded into misty beads of light.

Alverax dropped his hands to his knees, panting at the exertion. He knew it wasn't wise to threadweave too much—he'd made that mistake in the Fairenwild and nearly killed himself—but he also knew that he was one of the only people who could fight them. He had to. He was willing to give up his life for the Zeda people. Why would he not do the same for the people of Felia?

Suddenly, the ground trembled...then stopped. Alverax looked up just in time to watch the entire outer wall quiver as again the ground quaked. And again. And again. Men and women steadied themselves. Guards fell from the wall-walk, tumbling to their death far below, until finally, with a deafening groan, the outer wall shattered and collapsed. Stone crumbled in upon itself, tumbling down like an avalanche.

Then, between the dust and smoke and debris, Alverax saw a nightmare made manifest. A corespawn twice the height of a home, blazing like the sun itself. It stepped toward the shattered wall and threw its fist once again. Stone blasted through the night sky. A massive tail, like a scorpion's stinger, dragged over rocks and shrubbery.

Heralds save us.

Coming from the southern wall-walk, Watchlord Osinan dashed toward the monstrosity. He leapt up onto one of the crenellations and launched himself in a deathly arc toward the creature with the Midnight Watcher held high overhead.

The creature swung its massive head toward Osinan.

Alverax reached forward with all his strength and lashed out against the creature. Trying to *break* it felt like trying to move a mountain, but he had to try. If not, Osinan would die. The corespawn roared in pain, thrashing its head back and forth as it fought the stranglehold of his Obsidian threadlight. Alverax's body felt ready to burst, his veins swelling and his heart pounding against his ribs.

Watchlord Osinan fell atop the monstrosity's head and slammed the Midnight Watcher through its light-wrought skull. Its tail whipped out with terrible speed, impaling Osinan in the blink of an eye. The old man screamed in pain as the corespawn let out its own deafening roar. Its body succumbed to the combined power of the obsidian blade and Alverax's threadweaving, bursting apart and sending Osinan falling to the ground.

"NO!" Alverax screamed, sprinting forward. He was too slow; there was no way he would make it in time to catch him.

But he didn't have to.

Alverax reached out as he ran, grabbing hold of Osinan's corethread. Then, he *broke* it. Gravity let go of the man, but still his momentum carried him down until he crashed into the ground. Alverax reached him shortly after and held him down until gravity took back hold.

He was still breathing, but blood drooled out from his side where the corespawn's stinger had pierced him.

"They're running away!" someone shouted behind him.

"Heralds be praised!"

Threadweavers cheered while achromats cowered in disbelief, unable to trust what they could not see for themselves.

Alverax looked up from Osinan, and surveyed the battle-field, taking in the destruction to the wall and the hundreds dead along its perimeter. They were right...the enemy was retreating. Alverax assumed it was because they'd killed the largest of the corespawn, or perhaps they retreated to regather their numbers. But, either way, he had a feeling they would be back.

CHAPTER 27

THE SUN, barely over the Everstone mountains, cast long shadows as Laurel traveled west. After sneaking out of Endin Keep, they'd rode in silence for the entirety of the day, looking over their shoulders, worried about who may be pursuing them. When they reached the small town of Feldspar, the only trouble they'd had was Laurel's ass burning like a bonfire. She decided, quite handily, that horses were less fun to ride than she'd been made to believe.

In Feldspar, they purchased two carriages to take them on the journey west. The sun had long fallen, and they sat in silence, heads bobbing as the carriage raced away from the grounder capital. Part of Laurel wanted to stay, to fight, but what could she do? And she hoped that their final destination was where her family would be.

The second carriage was occupied by Sarla and Barrick, whose snoring could be heard from the moon. Across from Laurel in their own, Alabella sat upright, her elbow leaning against a small armrest. She scratched at her forearm as she stared out of the open window. The lush Alchean country-side, filled with sprawling viridian plains and fruit trees in all their variety, seemed to roll by more slowly than it should have.

Pity, though try as she might to deny it, crept its pearly tendrils into Laurel's heart. In no way was Alabella an innocent woman—her crimes were as plentiful as the stars in the sky—but the weight of it burdened her. When she looked closely, she thought she saw a hint of Amber in the veins on the back of Alabella's hand. Laurel imagined the soothing effects of threadlight and yearned for it herself. But they'd given all their supply to the Alcheans—except for a single remaining vial that Laurel kept hidden in her pocket.

Alabella closed the window, then turned her head slowly until she was fully facing Laurel. "All I ever wanted was to make the world better," she said, mostly to herself. "And we were so close. Just a few more days and we could have returned to the coreseal. We'd have an endless supply of infused gemstones. We could have offered threadlight to everyone." She paused. "Did I ever tell you about how I became a threadweaver?"

Laurel shook her head, and, though she had hoped to keep quiet, she *was* curious.

"I was born in Felia. My mother had too many men to name a father, so we lived alone. She beat me from the time I was very young. Four, maybe? She said our misfortune was my fault. If I had been born a threadweaver, we wouldn't have to suffer like we did. If I had been born a threadweaver, the empress would provide for us. If only I had been a threadweaver...When I was twelve, she died of an infection, and I was all alone. I fell in with some people who saw the value of an unexceptional girl, one that no one would give a second glance to.

"Our little group thrived. Once we even conned the Farrows—a powerful Felian family—out of ten thousand shines. Our leader, a boy called Pai, found out about a section of the Hallowed Library called the Anathema, filled with treasures. We planned it all out—Pai and I would be the ones to break in—but the place was much different than what we'd been told.

"It wasn't filled with treasure, but old books. Not a single shine in sight. I opened a few of the books—we thought they might be worth something—and since Pai couldn't read, it was up to me to decide which books we should take. One of them had an image of a man lying on a table with one of the Heralds standing over him, placing a stone near his heart. A girl walked in the room, blonde like yourself. After her shock at seeing us there, she pushed Pai aside and stabbed me in the chest.

"I woke up in a prison cell, surprised to be alive, and even more surprised to find threadlight in my veins. Somehow, I'd become an Amber threadweaver. It wasn't hard to break out from there. But I couldn't stop thinking about that image, especially with what happened to me. So eventually, I made my way back to the Anathema and stole a few of the books. That's where I learned about theoliths and the coreseal. And that's when I made it my mission to bring threadlight to everyone."

Laurel was completely entranced by the woman's words. "How did you end up in Cynosure?"

Alabella laughed. "My friends...well, that's a story for another time. The point is...my dream is dying, and watching a dream die is the cruelest form of torture."

The carriage slammed to a halt, nearly knocking them out of their seats. Laurel grabbed onto the windowsill for balance. Once they'd settled, Alabella opened the door but it slammed back shut.

"Stay inside and keep quiet," the driver whispered with

urgency. "Stones, but I thought they'd be gone by now. They killed a whole caravan just the other day."

"We are in a hurry," Alabella said as she kicked the door open. "Come, Laurel. Let's teach these thugs a lesson in civility."

Laurel nodded and followed her out of the carriage. The bright sun warmed her skin as she surveyed her surroundings, but there were no bandits in sight. To the south, fields of endless grass. To the west, open road as far as the eye could see. And to the north, nothing but a field of pear trees. She thought, if she caught the right angle between trees, she could see the edge of the Fairenwild in the distant northern horizon.

"I don't see anything," she said.

"You shouldn't be out here," the driver said.

Alabella ignored him. "Where are they?"

The carriage driver pointed toward the pear trees. "I seen 'em hiding behind the trees up ahead. No idea how many. Blend into the grass, they do."

Laurel rubbed at her arm with a shaky hand. She felt jittery, like a child who refused to stay still. It didn't help that there was a slight wind that chilled her arms. She looked back down the road from where they'd come, expecting an army to appear at any moment. They needed to keep moving, and if some thugs thought they could slow them down, then the Gale could take them all.

Alabella and the driver turned to her just as she pulled out the obsidian blade and took off at a sprint toward the field of trees. Behind her, the driver shout something, but she ignored it. When she reached the orchard, she hid behind the closest pear tree, which was plenty wide to hide her thin frame. Adrenaline pumped through her veins, a weak substitute for threadlight.

Laurel crept forward, tree by tree, staying low in the overgrown grass. A light breeze danced between the leaves, causing branches to quiver and dandelions to take flight. She peeked around the thick trunk of a pear tree and thought she saw movement up ahead, hidden beneath the grass. She'd expected to find the bandits partially obscured behind the trees, but they were smarter, hiding on their stomachs in the underbrush.

She mimicked their stealth and dropped to her hands and knees. Dirt slid beneath her fingernails. Long strands of green grass swept across her pale skin. She held the obsidian blade as she bear-crawled through the brush, the tips of her toes pressing deep into the soil.

There was a rustling up ahead.

Something deep inside her flared to life, and she rolled to the side just before a massive body came barreling through the grass, pouncing where she had just been. Her heart pounded and adrenaline raged. As she rolled back to a steady position, she turned to see a massive creature. Green fur blurred into the surrounding grass, white strands blew in the breeze, and, far behind it, two tails danced back and forth with fervor.

Fear began to sink its teeth into her racing mind as the chromawolf turned to bare its yellow fangs. Step by step, she moved back, keeping her eye on the chromawolf's movement. Her offhand reached up toward the transfuser in her breast pocket. She was going to die, and she knew the drug wouldn't help.

Behind the chromawolf, green-furred heads rose through the grass as the rest of the pack joined their brother. Laurel's heart pounded against her ribs. There were so many, a dozen at least. She needed Alabella.

From the back, a final head rose through the grass.

Green fur with a strand of white running near its left ear. Twin tails danced up over its head. As it saw her, its eyes lit up like two crescent moons grown full.

"Asher!" Laurel said with a smile as wide as a feytree.

Asher stepped forward, barking and howling as he passed the others, then launched himself toward her in a burst of joyous energy. They tumbled over dirt and grass, wrestling like children, growling at each other and swiping with playful paws. When they finally came to rest, Laurel on her back with Asher standing over her, the tone shifted. Asher whipped his head to the side and snarled.

"Laurel," Alabella's calm voice spoke, dragging out each syllable. "There is at least a dozen more behind you. Roll to the side, I can *yolk* it, then you run. On my count."

Laurel lifted her head to see Alabella standing a short distance away with her palms outstretched.

"One—"

Asher snarled.

"Two—"

"No!" Laurel shouted. "Asher's my friend!"

Alabella stood with a wide stance, brows furrowed in confusion.

Laurel lifted herself up and rubbed Asher's fur. The other chromawolves lay spread across the orchard, some still crouched beneath the tall grass, and others standing tall, ready to defend their leader. "Asher's my friend. He won't hurt us. Will you?"

Asher nuzzled her shoulder. She was certain he'd grown even in the short time they'd been apart.

"And the others?" Alabella asked warily.

"He won't let them hurt us." Laurel reached forward and hugged the chromawolf's neck. "I've missed you, big guy." A happy growl rumbled from its chest. "I saw what happened at the Fairenwild. Then the corespawn. We both lost our home. Asher, I'm so sorry." She looked into his eyes and rubbed the top of his head. "I wish we'd never parted ways. From here on out, it's you and me, no matter what."

Asher pulled back and looked into her eyes, unblinking, knowing. He lowered himself and brought his forehead to hers. She could feel his warmth as they pressed their minds together. And then she felt something curious. A single spark burning inside her. Growing. Roaring to life until it raged like a bonfire. Asher howled and his eyes glowed white with hints of green reflecting from his fur. The pain struck, and Laurel howled too. She felt flames inside her escaping through her skin. Heat beyond reason.

The world seemed to shift around her. Distance shortened. Colors shifted. She could hear the leaves shuffling beneath Alabella's feet. She could taste the musk of the chromawolves upwind. She felt her veins expanding.

"Laurel," Alabella said, still wary of the other chromawolves. "Are you okay? What's happening?"

Her mind swirled like a whirlwind, blurring and twirling in chaotic disarray. Her eyes burned like never before until a single spot of darkness began to spread like oil over her heightened vision. The world grew darker. Trees faded away. Chromawolves vanished. And finally, as new energy charged through her body, the darkness filled the final vacancy in her mind, and she collapsed to the earth.

CHAPTER 28

WHEN CHRYS AWOKE, he felt...different.

Where once a fog clouded his mind, now there was nothing but clarity. He felt more alert than he had in years. It was as though a veil had lifted, and the storm clouds had given way to a flawless sky.

He put a hand down to push himself to a sitting position and gasped as the realization hit him. It couldn't be. It was impossible. He was dreaming. Even still, tears formed. Where once there were only seven, again there were ten. He looked down at his hand to confirm and swelled with emotion while his newly regrown fingers wriggled back and forth.

"Chrys?"

He turned and found his mother rising from the rose-colored table where the old man and Roshaw sat. She gestured for him to join them. "I'm sure you have questions," she said with a knowing smile.

"I—" he paused, lifting his hand and inspecting it. "This is a dream, right?"

"It's not," she said, smiling and nodding to the old man.

"He healed you. The golden water has kept him alive for hundreds of years, and today it kept you alive...and some."

Chrys turned his eyes to the pool, golden light shimmering across the surface and emanating out into the cavern. It called to him, *drawing him in*, beckoning him to bathe in its warmth. When Chrys turned his eyes back to the table, he saw the old man...or the man who *had* been old. His eyes swirled with colors, and his face, though still pale and wrinkled, seemed to have shaved off a dozen years.

"Why don't you have a seat, Chrysanthemum," the old man said with a grin. "Willow, would you and Roshaw go see if you can find a box in the storage room containing a collection of talismans? Each should have an engraving of four circles knotted together within a gemstone. We'll need three of them."

Willow nodded and led Roshaw away.

He turned back to Chrys. "While you were recovering, your mother shared with me your story. It is a tragedy, I must admit, but the ending is yet to be written. And that is where we must focus. Relek and Lylax have caused you to sacrifice so much already, and I worry that what comes next will bring even more. Though I tried to dissuade him, my siblings *will* take power once again. Chrys, if you are to stop them, you must understand the dark power they possess. What do you know of the source of your power as a threadweaver?"

Chrys tried to breathe steadily, but every time the old man spoke of his siblings, Chrys' heart raced within his chest. "They say it is a gift from the Lightfather."

"Perhaps, if there is a god, he does play a part in the selection, but the source is different. Chrys, embedded within your chest, in the center of your heart, is a sliver of a gemstone. This stone absorbs energy from the realm of threadlight, and, when you release it, that energy flows through your veins and gives you power. We call this gemstone a theolith, and it is the only thing that makes you a threadweaver. Without it, your eyes would fade to brown and you would be powerless.

"Over time, my siblings and I discovered this truth, and, with the aid of the healing elixir, we embedded within our hearts each of the four gemstones, giving us the power of all of them. Open yourself to threadlight and see for yourself."

Chrys let threadlight pour through his veins, feeling the warmth in his chest, and wondering at the truth of the words. The old man lifted his hand and *pushed* a cup across the table. It slid, scraping over the rose-colored stone and, just before it reached the edge, he *pulled,* and it slid back to his hand. Then, he picked it up and held it in the air. In the blink of an eye, the cup's thread *broke*, shattering into a hundred beads of light. He let go, and the cup floated gracefully in the air. He *created* four threads that latched onto the cup and sent it tumbling back to the table.

"Such a display is silly, surely. But I'm certain you can understand the implications." The old man tipped the cup over and let the water spill across the rosy surface. "What happened next, we did not expect. Once all four gemstones enter a heart, they fuse together into a singular structure, and a subtle change occurs. Not only could we see and manipulate threadlight, but we could suddenly see something else. A flickering spark of red energy in the center of a man's heart. At first, we thought it was a theolith, but we realized it was something else entirely. And so, we called it *lifelight.*"

Seeing Chrys' confusion, the old man continued. "My brother was the first to discover that we could both see *and* manipulate lifelight, though I refuse to participate in the latter. You see, my siblings and I held the secret of the pool to ourselves, but our immortality was bound to it. Relek discovered that he could create a connection between his own lifelight and the lifelight of another. His own mortality became tied to theirs. From then on, their life drained into him. He no longer aged. When he would be killed, one of the others would die in his place. And then, he discovered that he could transfer his own lifelight into the body of another, which is what you experienced. And so, his own immortality was no longer tied to the pool.

"I tried to stop them, but they would not listen. They left the cavern for good and became gods among men, with thousands of souls bound to each. They discovered that binding a threadweaver allowed them to siphon their powers, and so their threadweaving became unparalleled. They used the elixir from the pool to create more and more threadweavers, binding their lifelight and expanding their own strength. There was no end to their greed, until their own followers saw the darkness.

"A group of Amber threadweavers banded together, tricking Relek and Lylax to return to this very place. They combined their powers, using knowledge my siblings had mercifully given them, and sacrificed their own lives to create a web of threads that sealed the core of the earth from the surface world. But Relek was not beneath the surface at the time as they'd thought. He was with the wastelanders, wearing one of their own's skin so that they would bind their lifelight to him. But when the seal was created, he was stuck in the wastelander body with no way to return here.

"What you must understand is that the wastelanders have a crippling mutation. They cannot survive without the elixir. A pool above ground contains trace amounts of it and allows the wastelanders to survive, so long as they drink from it often. If they do not, they die. And so, both of my siblings were trapped. One with me. The other, with a people who cannot leave their home.

"And that, my young friend, is the crux of our story. All building to the conclusion that you cannot kill my siblings."

"We can't kill them," Chrys repeated.

"Unfortunately, no. And they came down not long ago, so their human bodies are once again hybrid threadweavers, able to manipulate lifelight."

Chrys leaned forward cross the table. "I refuse to accept that they cannot die."

"Accept it or not," the old man replied. "Truth is not dependent on your acceptance of it. But that does not mean that there is nothing we can do. The group of Amber thread-weavers bound my sister once before; we could do it again. Willow says there are two Amber threadweavers. A woman and your son. You must bring them to me. With their power we can bind my siblings beneath the earth again. Perhaps not permanently, but long enough. When a generation has passed, and the lives of all those bound to them have ended—"

The old man trailed off for a moment, his prismatic eyes drifting to the stalactites high overhead. Chrys thought he saw, hidden in the bags under the old man's eyes, a tear forming.

"—I will kill them," the old man said faintly. "Chrys, your child is the key. You must protect it. My siblings are wise, and they will not be so easily tricked a second time. If they find your child, they will not allow it to live."

A storm raged within Chrys. A storm swirling with rage and purpose. A storm that called him to action. Light-ning crackled in his veins. Thunder pounded in his chest. If the immortal gods of the wastelands conspired to take away his son, then he would be there waiting, life or death.

"That is not the only way," Chrys said. "If every person bound to them were to die, then they would be vulnerable."

"My siblings have bound every living wastelander. Would you slaughter an entire race?"

"For my family, I would consider anything."

The old man hesitated. "If that is true, then you are no better than they are."

"I said I would *consider* it," Chrys said with a fire in his eyes. "Obviously, we will move forward with your plan. Bring the Amber threadweavers and use their power to bind Relek and Lylax beneath the earth. Then you kill them."

The old man eyed Chrys warily. "Your mother and Roshaw are already in agreement, which means that we are ready for the first step in the plan."

"What is that?"

The old man held up two slivers of gemstone, one green, one black. "It is time for one to become three."

CHAPTER 29

ALVERAX STOOD IN A CRAMPED ROOM, watching as physicians and nurses attended to Watchlord Osinan. They'd stitched the wound, but the stinger had poisoned his blood. One of the physicians believed that the introduction of foreign threadlight from the corespawn had attacked the threadlight already in his veins, causing them to bulge beneath his dark skin.

There was nothing they could do...Osinan was dying.

Empress Jisenna sat on a stool beside the bed, holding the older man's hand. The two of them had a long history together, and, by the way she leaned into him, Alverax knew just how much she cared for the man. He wasn't family, but he was the closest thing she had left.

Outside the room, Alverax spotted Rastalin Farrow, whom he'd met at the masquerade. The man leaned against the wall with a self-satisfied look that made Alverax want to punch him in the face, but Rastalin was first in line to become the new Watchlord when Osinan passed, and Alverax knew not to slap a happy hog.

"Clear the room," Osinan said, coughing and wincing at the pain. "Clear the room, please."

Jisenna turned and nodded to the others. Alverax followed the physicians and nurses toward the exit.

"No," Osinan said with a growl. "Alverax, stay."

At the sound of his name, Alverax turned and raised his brows. Osinan nodded and Jisenna gestured for him to pull a stool beside her. He did.

Osinan pushed himself to a sitting position, wheezing and moaning as his stitches pulled at his side. Jisenna moved to help and he brushed her away. "The only thing that frightens me about death is that I'll no longer be able to help those in need."

"Don't say that, Osinan," Jisenna said. "We'll find a way to heal you."

"Sun Daughter," he said, smiling at her like a father smiles at his child. "It's not weakness to embrace the inevitable. What matters most is what you do next. In this case, there is little more I can do. Alverax, would you please bring me my blade?"

Alverax lifted the sheathed sword off of the ground beneath the bed and laid it across Osinan's lap. The Watchlord placed his hands atop the sheath and moved his hand down its length. The image reminded Alverax of stories he'd heard as a child of mighty warriors being buried with their blades. Seeing Osinan's reverence toward the weapon brought those stories to life just a little more.

"Do you know how long I have been Watchlord?" Osinan asked. "Twenty-eight years, before either of you were born. The previous Watchlord passed away unexpectedly, leaving me a long letter detailing the true duties of the office. I wrote a similar letter many years ago. Publicly, we preach that a Watchlord is to prepare for the return of the Heralds, guiding the people so that they might make of themselves a righteous offering to our gods. The truth is that the Heralds are not going to return. We say they left to prepare the afterlife for the righteous, but we don't truly know why they left. One day they were simply gone, and never returned."

Jisenna grew pale, her eyes wide as she shook her head back and forth. "Don't say such things, Osinan."

"Just by speaking them I feel a weight lifted." He closed his eyes for a moment and breathed. "The priests would have me slain if I spoke the truth in their presence. They only know what the Watchlords of the past have told them, which is what the people needed. Hope, Jisenna. The world needs hope, and the truth is often at odds. So, for the greater good, we lie, and we say that the world is one way when it is in fact another. But when it brings them hope and gives them reason to live a good life, we pat ourselves on the shoulder. Perhaps, over time, we even begin to believe the lies ourselves, because hope is sweet, and the truth can be quite bitter."

"Why?" Jisenna whimpered. "Why are you saying this?"

Alverax shifted on his stool, staring at the ground as he listened to the dying man. He recalled the many years sitting together with his grandfather, while his guardian taught him about the Heralds, that one day they would return and, if Alverax was a good boy, the Heralds would take him into their fold. He hadn't questioned the words until after his father was killed, something about the loss had cracked the façade. He'd spoken their name out of habit —*Heralds, save us*—but never in true prayer.

"Everyone!" Osinan shouted, a firm resolution in his voice. "Please, come back in! I have an announcement I would like to make!" He smiled and slumped back against the wall.

"Please," Jisenna said. "You cannot say these things to them. It would break our nation."

Osinan turned to her. "Felia needs hope now more than ever. Do not worry, Sun Daughter."

The physicians and nurses entered first, followed by a drove of men and women in noble regalia, including the ever-stately Santara and Rastalin Farrow. They filed in reverently, awaiting the words of the man whom they exalted above all others, their proxy for the Heralds themselves. Only Alverax and Jisenna knew the truth, that his celestial calling was drafted of men.

As they settled in, Alverax faded away to the side of the room so that he would not block the others' view. The black and gold of the Watchlord's deific robes flickered in the lamplight. The sword remained draped across his lap as he began his final sermon.

"At a young age, we speak the sacrificial oath: my life for yours. I have done my best to offer my life in service to the Heralds, in preparation for their inevitable return." His eyes moved confidently from one attendee to the next. "Our world is changing. The corespawn have returned, but the Heralds have not left us defenseless. It is no coincidence that an Obsidian threadweaver has found his way to our city in our time of need. It is a sign that the Heralds are pleased with us. It is a sign that their return draws near.

"It is with this knowledge that I share an announcement, born from the very heritage I symbolize. The first Watchlord was an Obsidian, and so shall it be again."

Eyes, like the sharpest of blades, turned on startled hinges toward Alverax. His heart raced in his chest, and his hands trembled at his side.

"Alverax Blightwood, son of Felia, I solemnly bestow upon you all of the rights and honors associated with the office of Watchlord, and declare you now the Highest Servant, He-Who-Watches-The-Sky, the Surrogate of the Heralds themselves."

His chest burned inside of him, constricting and coiling like a snake stuck in a furnace. It was a dream. It was a mistake. Alverax was the son of a thief, not the Surrogate of the Heralds.

Osinan gestured to the sword on his lap. "Take it, son. The Midnight Watcher is yours. The protection of these people rests in your hands now. You have been preserved and you have been prepared. One day you will see this."

Santara Farrow, filled with indignation, huffed at the words. "This is absurd. Tradition is clear, the office must pass to the next in line, chosen by the council."

"It *is* rather unusual," another man said.

Rastalin, unable to contain himself any longer, spat as he shouted. "The boy was nearly executed days ago and now he is to be Watchlord? It reeks of conspiracy, and the people will see that. Such an accusation, true or not, would endanger our peace in a very delicate time."

"It *does* seem rather odd," the another said.

Rastalin continued, gaining confidence with each word he spoke. "I suggest we delay the transference of power until after we have dealt with the invasion."

"For the safety of the people," his wife added.

Osinan scowled and tried to push himself to a fully upright position, but he failed, groaning and gripping at his side. "The people will trust my judgment."

"The people will see a dying man," Rastalin replied. "A man whose mind is warped by a seditious poison from our enemy. How could they trust the judgment of one under the influence of our adversary?"

"Under the influence..." Osinan began, his voice rising.

"Enough!" Jisenna said. "Rastalin, you have made your point. Could you, in good conscience, tell everyone in this room that Osinan is 'under the influence of our adversary'?"

Rastalin's eyes darted back and forth across the room, teeth grinding between pursed lips.

"Then as your empress, I expect you to relay your confidence and endorsement to any people who may express doubt of the decision made this day."

His eyes burned with fury, and Jisenna met his gaze with her own.

"Good," Jisenna concluded. "Alverax, I believe your sword awaits you."

Alverax moved forward, hesitation guiding his steps. Every eye watched his movement, judging him, weighing his worthiness, and he knew he could never live up to their expectations. But even as he doubted, he reached the edge of the bed and stared down at the sheathed blade.

Osinan spoke quietly, lifting it toward him. "People will see the clothing, they will see the sword, and then they will see your eyes. They *will* accept you, if you will accept yourself."

The room grew silent.

Alverax reached his hand forward and grasped the hilt of the Midnight Watcher.

THAT EVENING, former Watchlord Osinan passed away in his sleep, smiling while the Empress of Felia slept beside him.

CHAPTER 30

"AHHHH!" Roshaw screamed as the old man stabbed him in the heart for a third time. He writhed in pain until Chrys poured a pitcher of the healing water over the wound. As soon as it touched the broken flesh, new skin grew over and the wound closed. Roshaw dropped his head back onto a dense pillow.

Since crossing the mountains into the wastelands, there was one word that had evaded him completely: hope. Even their plan to escape had held a feeling of unlikelihood that he'd merely brushed aside. But now, everything was different.

He let threadlight pour through his veins and marveled at the change. Where once his veins had lit with a piercing blue, like the hottest flame of a smith's fire, now they swirled with blue, green, and black. Three of the four theolith variants. Unfortunately, Lylax had purged all of the Amber theoliths they'd discovered over the years, though the old man knew she kept a few somewhere; he just didn't know where.

Another sleeveless arm came up beside his own, veins

matching in their chaotic dance of multi-colored thread-light. "Hard to believe it's real," Willow said.

Chrys nodded, but his mind wandered to his son and the Amber in his veins. Somewhere, he was with Iriel. He wondered where they were, and what they were doing. Willow claimed that Zedalum had been destroyed, which meant that, if Iriel and Aydin were alive, they would have headed west toward Felia. It was on the other side of the continent. Weeks journey even were they above ground. But the old man claimed to have a way to expedite the journey. If it meant finding his wife and son sooner, he was open to anything.

Chrys turned to the old man, who inspected Roshaw lying on the ground. "Any concerns?"

"No, no," the man replied. "Without the elixir, he would have died. The two of you would likely have survived, since your theolith provides a measure of healing in and of itself. With three theoliths, the healing effects should be magnified now, as with the rest of your abilities."

"How has no one discovered this before?" Willow asked. "Surely, someone would have thought it odd when they saw a rock in someone's heart."

"Ah," the old man said with a smirk. "A theolith is no ordinary rock. When it enters a person's heart, it is bound to the lifelight of that person. If you detach it, or if the person dies, the connection is broken and the theolith crumbles to dust."

"So, you cannot remove a theolith from one person and use it in another?"

"Fortunately, no," said the old man. "If that were possible, I can't imagine the dark things men would do."

Willow shook her head as she stared at the old man. "All

these years, we believed threadlight the gift of some unknowable god, when it was simply a stone in the heart."

"It could be both," the old man said.

"*You* believe in a god?"

He shrugged his shoulders. "There is much that it would explain, and many other questions that it would create. What I do know is that we know so very little. We are nine parts ignorance and one part enlightenment, but we grab hold of that little knowledge we have and pretend that it is greater than it is. The man who is ignorant of his own ignorance holds most tightly to his perception of the truth. Unfortunately, I have lived long enough to know just how little I truly know. And, so, I do not claim to know whether there is or is not a god, only that it is certainly possible."

If the past weeks had taught Chrys nothing else, they had taught him just how little he knew of the world, its inhabitants, and its machinations. He'd once thought the wastelanders nothing more than savages, but now he knew more of their story, like their willingness to sacrifice for the greater good. There was a beauty in knowledge—a danger in ignorance—and he hated knowing just how little he knew.

Whether *he* believed in the Lightfather or not, he wasn't sure. He remembered the Zeda elders speaking of *divine providence*, and he wanted to believe it true. But he feared that, even if there was a god, he couldn't trust a being willing to let creatures like Relek and Lylax walk the earth.

Roshaw awoke with a gasp, clutching at his chest and springing to an upright position. "I'm done!" he shouted. "That was three, right? No more? Heralds, please, let that be the last one."

"Heralds—" the old man mumbled.

"I feel," Roshaw continued, "incredible! Willow, Chrys,

did you both feel this *light* after? It's almost like..." He looked down and, with multi-colored veins spiraling beneath his skin, he floated in the air just inches above the ground. "I'm flying! Ha! My father—my son—they would never believe this!"

"Careful," Willow said. "If you threadweave too much, you'll get sick."

The old man's eyes lit up. "Actually, you'll find that with three theoliths you are able to threadweave for a longer period, and with a greater intensity."

"Stones," Chrys cursed.

"Indeed," the old man laughed. "Three of them."

WHEN THEY WERE ready to leave the cavern, the old man took them to the supply room and provided them with packs and wide-brimmed hats that he'd made himself. Chrys stared at the hat he held in his hands. The color and the shape held something familiar, a memory of another life, a moment buried in his mind, scratching at the surface. Then it vanished, like a silk handkerchief slipping through his hands.

He stared at it for a moment longer, but the feeling was gone. He placed it on his head and followed the old man as they departed the cavern.

Together, they traveled through a dimly lit tunnel filled with stale air. Water dripped from the ceiling, running off of stalactites and staining the wall with dark streaks. Chrys steeled himself for a long journey, knowing that their destination would be well worth the time. The small tunnels soon grew into massive corridors that seemed more fit for giants than men.

As they progressed, the vast tunnel split into multiple paths. The old man had warned them that corespawn often roamed the same tunnels, but they saw none. Still, Chrys kept threadlight in his veins.

They followed dark paths for hours, reiterating their plan to trap Relek and Lylax below the earth, but spending most of the time in silence. Chrys, Willow, and Roshaw tested their new abilities as they walked, *breaking* threads, *pushing* and *pulling* on rocks. It was disorienting, after so many years, with such an intimate familiarity of the Sapphire ability, to suddenly be able to manipulate threads in new ways. As he practiced *pulling* against the wall and walking along it like a spider, he thought of Reina and his old crew. He wondered if Luther was still drinking away the loss of his son, or if he'd found a more sustainable way to move forward. A part of him yearned for his friends, but not in the same way that he yearned for Iriel and Aydin. His friends were a warm blanket, but his wife was the raging fire. And he was shivering.

"We are almost there," the old man said as they passed over a small bridge spanning a large crevice in the ground.

Roshaw looked down the crevice as he passed over. "Did you make this?"

The old man nodded. "I've explored every corner of this underground world. If we had time, I would show you a lake of molten lava, or gemstones so large a man could live inside if they were hollowed out. There are countless wonders here, but around this bend is one that surpasses them all."

Roshaw jogged ahead, excitedly.

As Chrys rounded the bend himself, he saw Roshaw standing perfectly still, his wide eyes radiant with multi-colored threadlight, gazing out into a sweeping cavern. Chrys stepped forward and a vast dome of prismatic light burst into view, swirling and spinning as bolts of energy broke out across its surface.

"We see the world as a collection of threads, each connecting one small piece to another." The old man settled into position beside Chrys and the others, who all stood in awe, their eyes radiant with threadlight as they took in the spectacular view. "The space between one location and another is a thread of sorts, representing the distance between them. But, like your corethread when you *push* against it, it is possible to manipulate that connection. This place," he gestured to the dome of energy, "allows you to manipulate space itself."

"Manipulate space?" Roshaw repeated.

The old man smiled, and the wrinkles of his eyes deepened. From his pocket, he pulled out a string and pinched both ends. "Pretend that this string is a road between here and your home. You could walk from here to there." He pulled his finger along the string from one end to the other. "Or you could travel from there to here." He repeated the gesture in the other direction. "But there is another option." Pinching both ends, he slowly brought them together. "Same string. Same connection. Shortened path between the two. Think of this concentration of threadlight in front of you as one end of the string."

Chrys ran a hand through his scruffy beard. "And where is the other end?"

"Ah!" the old man said, waving a finger. "That is the question indeed. It may be hard to distinguish because you are not yet acclimated to your new powers, but did you feel the change in energy as we approached? Can you feel your own threadlight being magnified? From what you have shared with me, I don't believe it is the first time you have been near a place like this. A *convergence*."

The realization shot through Chrys like a surge of lightning. He *had* felt a similar feeling as this. A place where his own threadlight had been magnified, allowing him to reach greater heights than he ever had before. The place where he'd left his wife and son.

"The coreseal," he whispered.

"Indeed."

Chrys stepped forward, connecting pieces of the puzzle. "There is a *convergence* beneath the wonderstone. The Amber threadweavers used the magnified power to create the coreseal and bind you and your sister below the earth."

"That is right," the old man said.

"Stones," Chrys cursed.

Roshaw approached the dome, and the others followed. There was something intoxicating about the warbling mass of threadlight, an invitation, a strange beckoning to enter, to stay and take root. He remembered the feeling when he'd first stepped on the wonderstone—the overwhelming desire to threadweave.

"Thank you," Willow said as she gave the old man a slight bow, "for everything. You could have turned us over to your brother, but instead you chose to help. It is a hard thing to go against your own family."

The old man's eyes seemed to grow more tired. "Yes, it is. But it's a harder thing to betray your own sense of morality."

"Do you think it will work?" she asked.

"If the Ambers can gather at a *convergence*, they should be able to combine their power to create a new binding. Just be sure Relek and Lylax are below the earth before the seal is formed."

All three nodded in unison, an unspoken acceptance of their path. Chrys was filled with purpose. It permeated every piece of his soul. He had a destination. He had a goal.

He had a plan. Slowly, he was regaining control of his life and his destiny.

Chrys lunged forward and wrapped the old man in an embrace. "Your sacrifice is going to save countless people. When this is over, the world will know your name."

Roshaw turned to face the old man, a slight blush reddening his cheeks. "I don't actually know what your name *is*."

Chrys opened his mouth to answer but realized that he too did not know the man's name. They both turned to Willow and she shrugged.

"I'm sorry," the old man said. "My manners once again elude me. I am called Alchaeus."

"Alchaeus?" Chrys repeated, emphasizing the word. "As in the Order of Alchaeus?"

"I'm certain I don't know what you mean."

"The Order of Alchaeus! Stones, you even quoted scripture before. Better to see truth than light?"

The old man scratched his head. "I...you must be mistaken. I've not left this place in many centuries."

Willow placed a hand on Chrys' shoulder. "He's not the only man ever to be named Alchaeus. It was common enough before Alchea was established."

"And the quote?" Chrys said.

"A coincidence?"

The only coincidence, Chrys thought, *was the brother of the eastern gods having the same name as the god of the west.*

"Perhaps," Alchaeus said thoughtfully. "Perhaps it is yet...no." He looked down at the string, still pinched at both ends hanging like a bridge between his hands. "You should go. You'll have a head start before my siblings head west. Find the Amber woman. Find your son. Bring them to me.

When their powers are amplified by the *convergence*, they should be able to create a seal that will endure."

They offered him a final goodbye and stepped toward the *convergence*. Its influence grew stronger with each step, a drink taunting an addict. His mother took his left hand, squeezing with maternal ferocity.

Together, they stepped into the light.

CHAPTER 31

AFTER AN EVENING of being pampered and worshipped and taught the extent of his new duties, Alverax was certain he'd never been more tired in his life. He picked at one of the tassels dangling beneath his arm that had become tangled with the others and walked toward a tent erected not far from the breached wall. He urged the priests following him to remain outside and stepped through the opening. A group of veteran generals examined him as he entered.

A younger general with a well-trimmed goatee stood. "Watchlord," he greeted with a nod of approval.

"Generals," Alverax said, cautiously.

Before the Divine Council could whisk him away, Alverax had spoken with Jisenna. She'd told him what to expect and described dozens of people he would meet—if only he could remember them now. More than anything, she'd explained how respected Osinan had been. The office of Watchlord is first and foremost a religious appointment, but he was also the head of the Felian army. Each Watchlord down the line had balanced the two responsibilities in their own way, and Osinan was renowned for his contributions to both. Alverax would be happy if he lived through the night.

"Please, continue," Alverax added. "I'd like to learn about the plans to protect the city."

"Maybe he can help answer the question we're debating," the same younger man added.

An older man, hunched over in his chair with a scowl, let out a loud harumph.

Alverax nodded. "I'd love to help however I can."

"Thallin. I'm General Thallin, and these," the younger man said, gesturing to the older generals, "are Generals Nevik, and Hish. I'll speak for all of us when I say congratulations, and we are eager to learn more about you." Each of them was a threadweaver with eyes as hard as they were bright.

Alverax wasn't sure if he should step forward and greet them but, based on their looks, he decided to stay put. "It is nice to meet you."

"The debate," Thallin continued, taking a seat, "is about the effectiveness of using tar to cover the corespawn. We're limited by the number of threadweavers we have, but if we can drench them in some kind of dark substance, they'll be visible to our achromat soldiers as well. General Nevik and I agree that it will work, but General Hish is not convinced that their invisibility is based on the laws of nature. You fought beside Osinan. You've seen them first-hand. What say you?"

All three generals shifted in their seats, curious to hear his response.

"It's a wonderful idea," Alverax said. "Their greatest advantage is their stealth. If we can take that away, then we have the numbers. The problem is that General Hish is right. It won't work."

General Hish perked up.

Alverax continued. "I saw hundreds of corespawn last night of every shape and size, and do you know what I did not see? Dirty feet. If nothing else, their feet would have been covered with dirt and mud. Not to mention the blood. I saw a corespawn bite into a man's chest, and not a drop of blood was in the air where its face would be. If dirt and blood don't stick, I wouldn't bet on tar either."

"Hmm," General Nevik said, pursing his lips. "I will admit that his logic is difficult to dispute."

General Hish nodded. "The evidence is light, but we have no reason to believe otherwise. Besides, even without spending time planning out a way to mark them, we have more preparations than time."

"What else do you have planned?" Alverax asked.

General Nevik stood. "We plan to make them pay. With fire and with alchemy and with our most valuable weapon."

"That sounds promising," Alverax said with interest. "And what is that?"

General Thallin smirked. "You."

As THE SUN FELL, Alverax rose high to the top of a quickly constructed tower near the eastern wall. It overlooked the portion of the wall that had been breached, though they'd hastily rebuilt it as well as they could in a single day. The generals were expecting the corespawn to re-enter from the same route and had built up a series of ambushes for the creatures, the last of which was their very own Obsidian threadweaver.

The young General Thallin accompanied Alverax at the top of the tower as the armies below fell into position. With the sun falling, they expected the assault would come at any moment. They only hoped their preparations would be enough to fend them off while they learned more about the enemy.

A westerly breeze was the only sound as soldiers stood their ground, wielding swords and preparing for what came next. Lines of Sapphire archers stood atop the remaining wall-walk, overlooking the surrounding countryside.

Alverax had always hated silence, but never more-so than in that moment. It pricked at his skin like a mosquito, sucking away at his confidence. He knew they'd set him upon the tower as nothing more than an emblem for the soldiers and, no matter how hard he tried to explain that as an Obsidian he could kill the creatures, they still wanted him away from the frontline. A beacon of hope amidst the eerie silence.

"Do you see something?" Thallin asked.

"Huh?" Alverax looked down and noticed that he'd begun to threadweave, his veins pulsing with a dark radiance. "Oh, no. Just keeping warm."

"I'll have the men bring you a blanket."

"No, no. It's really okay."

Thallin stared back at him. "I'm surprised you haven't soiled yourself yet."

"What?"

The young general smiled with one side of his lips. "I said that I'm surprised you haven't pee-peed down your fancy Watchlord pants yet."

Alverax started to laugh but was so taken aback that instead he simply stood with his mouth wide open.

"Come now," Thallin said. "I remember the first day I became a general a few years ago. The weight of the responsibility, the fear of not being enough, and the damn looks everyone gave me. There were a dozen others who wanted the position. I lost a lot of friends that day. I remember a sinking feeling in the pit of my stomach just certain that at any moment someone would realize I was a fraud."

Alverax nodded. "Is it that obvious?"

"Of course, but that's not a bad thing."

"What did *you* do to get over it?"

"Ah," the young general said, shaking a finger. "I dueled."

"You...dueled?"

General Thallin unsheathed his sword and brandished it in a wide arc. "It's the reason I was selected in the first place. I'm the best swordsman in all of Felia. So, when doubt started to creep in, I focused on my strength instead of my weakness. Instead of being intimidated by the other generals, or anyone else, I'd look at them and think just how easy it would be to destroy them in a duel. And that was it."

"Heralds know I could use a lesson or two on how to swing this thing." Alverax patted the hilt of the Midnight Watcher.

Thallin shoved his sword back in its sheath. "I'd be more than happy to show you sometime, but that was not the point of the story. Dueling is not your strength."

Alverax let out a small laugh. "No, it is not."

"However, it's pretty clear what is." Thallin pointed to Alverax's Obsidian eyes. "The first Obsidian threadweaver in generations! I'm honestly surprised by how humble you are. If I had eyes like yours, I'd be pride incarnate."

"Trust me, it's not humility," Alverax grumbled. "It feels like I'm swirling in a cyclone and everyone but me is holding a steel bar. I'm standing atop a tower in the middle of a war with fabled creatures as the bloody figurehead of the nation's hope. I have no idea how I ended up here, and Herald's know I don't belong."

Thallin let the words simmer as he pondered them. "Why do you think Osinan chose you?"

"He was dying. I don't know. Guilt? I don't think he liked Rastalin much either."

"Oh, come now. No one likes Rastalin, but that's not the reason. And we both know he didn't break generational tradition because he felt guilty about being mean to you."

"I don't know."

"Do you even know what people have been saying about you?"

Alverax stared out over the wall, saying nothing.

"There are rumors that you cannot die."

"Well, that's—"

"The night the Empress was killed, an entire army tried to capture you, but you escaped. Then you sacrificed yourself, and again you were saved from death. And last night, with mythical beasts rampaging our city, you fought a corespawn as tall as a building, and you came out unscathed. Where our Watchlord fell, you stood. The unkillable Surrogate of the Heralds."

"Well, that's ridiculous," Alverax said.

Thallin stepped forward and leaned over the edge of the tower. "We become what the world believes we are."

Unkillable. Technically, his grandfather had been saying it for years: *Us Blightwoods don't die easy.* But this was different. This was a child embracing a wolf, expecting it to protect him from the night. Hope standing on a tightrope while the winds surge all around. The people needed hope, and so they grasped hold of the anomaly, and eased their fear with lies.

But what is truth if not a lie that has yet to be revealed?

"I don't know if I want that," Alverax said, leaning over the edge next to him.

"It's a heavy burden to bear," Thallin said, still gazing into the night. "But you have a gift, and with it you can literally ease the burdens of those around you, including yourself."

"It's not the same."

"Perhaps not, but I've seen you give hope to an entire people without a drop of threadlight. I don't think it's the Obsidian in your eyes that is the gift. And that, Alverax, is why Osinan chose you. He saw it, and one day I expect you will too."

A spark flickered to life within him, not much, just the smallest of flames, but even a small flame can warm an empty heart.

His mind warped the world around him, and a memory swirled in the darkness. He was young, and he walked with his father along the steep path from Mercy's Bluff to the shore. They sat on the rocks they'd named the Lost Sisters with their feet swimming beneath the surface of the ocean. Cool waves splashed at their knees, and the noonday sun beat overhead. The smell of the ocean filled his lungs. His father told him he was leaving.

"Can I come with you?" little Alverax asked.

"Not this time. Someday, I'll take you with me. I'll show you the mountains, the forests, the orchards. I'll even show you where I met your mother. But it's not safe for a boy your age."

"But I'm a Blightwood!"

"You are," his father said laughing. *"But you're much more than just a Blightwood, son. One day you will see that."*

He tried to shake the memory away, but his eyes filled with emotion. That wasn't his father. His father was a thief. He was all of the parts of Alverax that he refused to be. He would not lie. He would not steal. And most of all, he would not abandon his responsibilities to another.

They spent the rest of the evening in silence, only broken on occasion when guards came to relay information to Thallin and Alverax. Throughout the night, Alverax forced himself to remain standing at the edge of the tower where the soldiers could see him. His legs shook and his eyes hung like a crescent moon, but he remained steadfast.

A beacon of hope that was never needed, because the corespawn never returned.

CHAPTER 32

WHEN CHRYS STEPPED into the *convergence*, a surge of energy washed over him. Pockets of colorful energy danced around like skyflies in the night, hovering for a moment, suspended, weightless, then streaking through the air back into the greater whole. His heart expanded in his chest, absorbing the raw power that radiated all around.

Chrys could feel his mother's hand in his own, but where she should have stood, there was only light. He held tight and searched through the chaos, looking for an exit, but the world around the *convergence* had faded away, replaced by a void of blackness. There in the distance, he thought he saw a face. And he knew those eyes—the brilliant Amber eyes of his son, Aydin. But as soon as he saw it, an overwhelming surge, like a great wave, poured over him, pushing him away. He stood his ground, reaching out to his son, screaming out into the void for him. One after another, waves of energy washed over him, filling him with such immense pressure that his veins felt ready to burst, urging him to turn back.

An odd ticking sound accelerated beneath him.

He felt his mother's grip tighten.

Finally, as the dancing colors shifted their hues once more, he succumbed and felt his body swept away in a torrent. Lights blurred around him in all directions. He tumbled head over heel, losing his mother's grip, and falling into nothingness. He tried to right himself, to stabilize, but his body simply spun in a cage of light as the world pulsed with brilliant energy.

He spun and spun in an endless cycle, until, like a bird emerging from a cloud, his body burst through the edge of the *convergence*, crashing into the hard stone. Another thud sounded beside him, and he saw his mother. Finally, Roshaw came tumbling through, landing further away. They all slowly rose to their feet, checking themselves for injury and eyeing the seemingly undisturbed dome of energy.

"Everyone okay?" Chrys asked.

"I'd be happy to never do that again," Willow said.

Roshaw nodded. "I'd be happy to never *see* that thing again."

"We'll have to see it one more time if our plan works," Chrys said.

They made their way through a dark tunnel, feeling their way along the walls and floors, stumbling at times, and cursing at others. Eventually, they found their way through the silent darkness to a large cavern with a gaping hole high overhead. A dim light shone through the hole. Chrys had never felt such relief. Part of him wanted to fall to the ground and rest, soaking in the smallest of victories. But their journey had only begun. They needed to get to Felia, find his family, and find the queen of the Bloodthieves. Only once the coreseal had been reformed would they be able to rest.

With the added strength of the *convergence* magnifying their Sapphire abilities, they each *pushed* off the ground and soared up through the opening, landing atop the broken remains of the wonderstone. Where once the feytrees had eclipsed the canopy of the Fairenwild, now the moonlight shone through an open sky. Stars sprinkled across the heavens, twinkling as a light breeze ruffled the feytree leaves. Across the fields surrounding the wonderstone, flowers lay flat across the ground, fallen beneath a stampede of footprints, or crushed by fallen feytrees. The dark intensity that had once permeated throughout the Fairenwild was gone, replaced by the quiet reverence of a ruined civilization.

Roshaw stared up at the sky. "There, beside the Broken Wheel."

"What?" Chrys said as he looked up at the stars.

"There are three stars right there at the southern edge of the Broken Wheel. It's perfect for Agatha, Esme, and Seven." He shook his head, the slightest smile on his lips. "They deserve to be remembered."

Chrys squinted and thought he saw the small cluster in the sky.

"That small one up there, beside the Siblings," Roshaw pointed to the western sky where two bright stars shone. "That's my mother's star."

Willow joined them, looking up into the heavens. "I've heard a little of that tradition from a Felian family I once knew. We don't have it in Alchea. How does it work?"

Roshaw took a breath and laughed to himself. "When my father explained it to me, he said that when people die their spirits drift up into the heavens. When you choose a star for them, it gives their spirit a home. Then, whenever you miss them, you can look up into the sky and know they're looking down on you from that very place."

"That's beautiful," she said.

"I used to think it was bollocks," Roshaw said, looking down at the swirl of colors running through his veins. "But, Heralds, if we can travel half the continent in an instant, and immortal gods are real, who's to say what is or isn't possible?"

"I'd like to name a star for my brother, if that's okay?"

Roshaw nodded with a smile.

"Something near the Siblings would be fitting," Willow said, as her wide eyes took in the sky. She closed her eyes for a brief moment, her face still directed to the heavens, then opened them with a soft smile. After a moment of quiet, she sighed. "I think he'll like it there."

They all grew quiet and gazed at the stars for a time. Looking out into the infinite expanse, Chrys felt a sense of peace wash over him. Everything was coming together.

———

FOR MANY HOURS, the three companions walked through the ominously quiet darkness of the Fairenwild. At first, Chrys had led them cautiously, wary of chromawolves or treelurks, or any number of the native dangers, but the forest was empty, not even the sounds of birds from high overhead. So, with photospores in hand, they quickened their pace, watching the ground for hugweed, and made quick progress through the forest.

Each time they came across a body of water, they rested, taking the opportunity to drink and to find whatever berries and vegetation were available. It seemed an endless hike through the darkness. At times they thought themselves lost or circling back, and each time Roshaw would run up a feytree to get a look at the sun above the woven canopy.

Finally, after days of roaming through the forest, they stepped out of the Fairenwild.

Chrys looked out over the horizon to the southwest, toward Felia, and hoped with all his soul that Iriel and Aydin were there. That they were safe. And that he could find them in time.

CHAPTER 33

"Any change?" Alabella asked, looking down over Laurel's unconscious body. The girl looked more at peace than she had the entire time Alabella had known her.

"Not yet," Sarla said.

Their carriage had continued its journey west, despite what had happened to the young Zeda girl. There was too much to do, and too many dangers if they were to pause their trip. The army of corespawn, and the subsequent disappearance of the same, had thwarted all of Alabella's original plans. Alchea was closer to the coreseal, and would have been a better central location, but Felia would still work. And there was a certain poetic justice in returning to her birthplace after so many years.

"When the supplies arrive," Alabella said, "I want her graft done immediately."

"Of course," the doctor replied. "If she survives the surgery, then we can proceed with a more typical achromat candidate. If transfusers are enough to predispose their heart to threadlight, then this could be the breakthrough we've been waiting for. But if it doesn't work on the girl, then it certainly won't work for others."

Alabella nodded. She could feel it in her bones. They were so close. Her life mission so near to a reality. "Have you had time to think about Alverax? I'm still convinced that there is something we're missing. If transfusers are the key, why did he survive?"

"The boy is an anomaly," Sarla replied. "I'd like to believe there is a reason behind his success—it would greatly simplify my work—but even in science there are deviations. I'm not convinced he's anything but lucky."

"Perhaps," Alaballa said thoughtfully.

"Do you think he'll be there?"

Alabella looked out the window at the passing country-side. "If any of the Zeda survived, they would have gone west. If the boy's alive, he'll be with them."

"And what if the corespawn are in Felia as well?"

"Enough about the corespawn! Heralds, I've already had to listen to you drone on and on about their metaphysical properties for days."

Sarla pursed her lips and adjusted her glasses. "You are the closest thing I have to a friend, Alabella. Which perhaps isn't saying much for either of us, but it is true, nevertheless. If you want to talk about it, I am here for you."

"About what?" Alabella said.

"It's our fault the corespawn are free," Sarla said, bluntly. "It's our fault they attacked Alchea. It's our fault that hundreds are now dead. Even I can see the weight you bear because of it."

"I am fine."

"Are you?"

The doctor had her use, but she was insufferable. Alabella had long ago learned to bind up all of the suffering she held and bury it deep within herself. As a little girl, she'd learned that feelings would get you killed. It was better to be strong. Smart. No one can hurt you if you can't feel.

"I am fine," she repeated more forcefully.

"Because there is no reason to feel guilty," Sarla continued. "There is no way you could have known this would happen."

"You want to know the truth?" Alabella asked. Since the beginning, she'd held onto one secret above all else, because she knew what it would mean if others knew. "I knew the corespawn were there. I knew when we broke the seal that they would come. I knew when we traveled to find the infused gemstones that they were most likely trapped behind the collapsed tunnel. But they were a necessary part of the plan. When we show the world that we can create threadweavers, just imagine how much more willing they will be to accept our cause. An enemy that only threadweavers can fight? It is the simple economic law of demand.

"The only thing I feel guilty about is underestimating their numbers. There will always be casualties in the path that leads to greatness—I know this. I only hoped that there would be less."

Sarla's eyes darted back and forth across the floor as she digested Alabella's confession.

It was a relief, finally sharing the truth with someone. Sarla would understand, in her own way, but she would also never look at Alabella quite the same. That was fine. Sarla was in too deep to back out when they were so close. Still, Alabella would have to kill her eventually, but not until they'd perfected the ventricular mineral graft. At that point, when they were creating hundreds of new threadweavers every day, the doctor would only be a liability.

Then, the world would place Alabella's name amongst

the Heralds themselves. She would give threadlight to the entire world.

And no one would sully that for her.

CHAPTER 34

THEY WERE a day away from Felia, according to a local farmer, when Chrys felt the earth begin to shake. It started small, a distant note he couldn't quite hear, but then it grew in intensity. Soon, the entire grove shook, leaves from the orange trees quaking like fearful children in the night.

"What is happening?" Roshaw groaned.

With the sound of the bellowing earth, and oranges falling from trembling trees, Chrys' mind returned to the war. The first battle in Ripshire Valley. He saw soldiers, scattered along the grass, bleeding out as their comrades ignored them to save their own lives. Thousands of wastelanders fought with bloody abandon, falling by the dozens from Alchean arrows, screaming out in the rage of battle. He saw their leader—he'd forgotten that face, those beady eyes flanked by tattoos that wrapped up from the edge of his brow to his chin like tusks. Chrys had seen the man cut down Alchean soldiers with ease. But when Chrys had attacked, the wastelander had thrown himself at Chrys with a smile. A swirling cloud of darkness. Hundreds of dead around him. And a voice that roared in his mind.

Sweat beaded down Chrys' forehead as he remembered the moment the Apogee was born.

"Stones," Willow whispered, her multi-colored eyes growing wide as she looked back the way they'd come.

Chrys shook off the memory and opened himself to threadlight. An army of glowing corespawn stampeded through the orange grove, small ones darting back and forth between the trees, large ones charging straight through, and massive corespawn, like towers of light, toppling trees beneath their feet.

He'd only seen two living corespawn before that moment, and neither prepared him for the vision before him.

"RUN!" Chrys shouted.

Their veins lit with threadlight as they *pushed* off the ground, lessening their weight just the slightest as they ran for their lives. From tree to tree, Chrys, Willow, and Roshaw sprinted over fallen leaves.

Thud, thud.

The corespawn grew closer. Chrys heard Roshaw curse as he twisted his ankle on one of the fallen fruits. But he kept going, hobbling along at a breakneck speed.

Thud, thud.

Chrys turned and saw the horde of corespawn closing on them. The massive monstrosities crushed trees like blades of wheatgrass.

Thud, thud.

The edge of the grove was close; they were almost there. If they could make it out before the corespawn caught up...then what? Chrys realized their mistake, but it was too late. They could never outrun the corespawn. The creatures were too fast, and there were too many.

If they...wait, where were the others?

Chrys turned and saw Willow hunched over Roshaw behind a tree, trying to lift him up. He ran to them, but he knew in an instant that he wouldn't reach them before the corespawn. Still, he didn't care. His mother had risked everything to protect him; he would do the same.

He ran with reckless abandon, *pushing* off trees behind him, *pulling* on trees in front, accelerating with all the speed of a rushing wind. But it wasn't enough. Corespawn rushed past them on both sides of the tree, ignoring them, or not seeing them, for now. Roshaw rose to his knees, clutching at his ankle, and Willow looked up to see Chrys. As soon as their eyes met, Chrys spotted a massive foot, wrought of pure threadlight, descending atop the tree behind which they hid.

"NO!" Chrys screamed.

The monstrosity trampled the tree, snapping it like a twig, colossal force falling down upon Willow and Roshaw. His mother screamed out, her hands lifted high overhead, her veins a raging torrent of multi-colored threadlight. Energy engulfed her like a dome, a barrier that seemed to pulse with life. When the monstrosity's foot connected with the dome, it roared out in pain as sparks of threadlight exploded at the point of collision. The monstrosity stumbled back, then continued forward, stepping on a safer section of the orchard.

Chrys fell to his side, sliding across the leaves as his momentum took him the rest of the way to his mother and Roshaw. "Your corethreads!" he yelled to them. "Break them now!"

They both looked to him and the dome of energy disappeared as their corethreads burst asunder beneath them. Then, grabbing them both by the arm, and with a surge of threadlight, Chrys *pushed* off of the ground and they shot up into the sky with such tremendous force that Chrys nearly lost his grip.

In moments, they were in the sky, looking down on the stampeding horde of corespawn. From such a height, they took in the full panoramic view of the Felian countryside. To the southwest, in the path of the corespawn army, the grand city of Felia gleamed white behind its high walls.

"Heralds, save us," Roshaw said as they floated amongst the clouds.

The stampede of corespawn looked like an army of ants that trailed for miles. There were tens of thousands of the creatures, all on their way to the city where he hoped his wife and son would be.

CHAPTER 35

"SHE'S WAKING UP," a man's voice said.

Laurel opened her eyes and felt her entire body shiver. A deep sweat glistened over her pale skin, and her muscles ached as though she'd been crushed by a tree. She lifted herself to an upright position and stabilized herself with both hands as blood rushed to her head. A sharp pain in her stomach greeted her along with a pair of familiar faces.

She tried to remember what had happened, but the only thing she could think of was the last remaining transfuser in her pocket. "Where's my coat?" she said, scrambling around the bed. "WHERE IS MY COAT?" she shouted.

"Laurel," Sarla said, grabbing her shoulder. "It's okay. You're okay."

"I NEED MY COAT!" Laurel yelled again, swatting away the woman's shoulder.

"I can get you a blanket."

Something in Laurel broke. She burst into tears—she wasn't even sure why—and buried her face in her shaking hands. Another shiver skittered up her spine. "Please," she whimpered. "I need my coat."

Sarla fiddled with her glasses in silence, before finally understanding. She moved across the room and grabbed the last remaining transfuser out of a drawer in the desk. "Is this what you wanted?"

Laurel didn't *want* it. She *needed* it. And while she poured the blood down her throat, she hated herself all the more. But it helped. In moments, warmth rushed through her veins, and she felt the bitter fog inside her burn away to clarity. That's when she finally looked around the room. She certainly wasn't in a carriage anymore, and the style of the décor seemed odd.

Sarla turned to Barrick on the other side of the room. "It appears I am correct once again."

"You said she would be better a week ago," Barrick replied. "I don't think that counts."

"No one is counting anything. Merely observing the realization of a hypothesis."

"Whatever you say."

After first flicking her hand out as if to shoo away Barrick's words, Sarla reached toward Laurel's face.

"What are you doing?" Laurel asked with a flinch.

"I wanted to get a good look at your eyes. With the other physical changes, I was curious if your iris would have been affected as well, but it seems that is not the case. Although, your pupil does seem slightly dilated."

Laurel pushed herself to the other side of her bed, distancing herself from Sarla. "What are you talking about? What happened?"

"You fell in the field, next to the chromawolf," Sarla explained. "You appeared to have some kind of episode. Do you have a history of blood issues? Any neurological problems run in your family? It could have been stress-induced.

However, I am unfamiliar with any such conditions that would cause the change in your hair."

Laurel reached up, feeling her hair, and grabbed a lock to inspect it. It was ratty, and could use a good wash, but otherwise seemed normal. "What's wrong with my hair?"

Sarla leaned forward. "May I?" When Laurel nodded, Sarla grabbed a chunk of hair toward the back of Laurel's head and brought it forward.

It was...green.

"Gale take me," Laurel cursed.

"At first, I believed it was stained from the grass, or perhaps an odd moss. But I gave it a thorough cleansing when we first arrived in Felia. The color is permanent, Laurel. It happened when you fell. Most curious symptom I've ever seen. If I can make it to the Hallowed Library, I'll see if I can find any information. It's possible your fainting spell was singular, but it is also possible that it is a symptom of an ongoing illness, in which case it would be wise for you to take it easy."

Laurel rejected the comment and rose to her feet. "Honestly, I feel better. Absolutely starving but, other than that, I feel okay."

"Hunger is expected. I had Barrick fetch an assortment of breads and fish for you. They are in the other room. Eat slowly. Your stomach will have shrunk considerably."

The comment awoke a reality within her. "How long have I been asleep? You said we're in Felia already?"

"You've been passed out for a week," Barrick said flatly. "Sarla's been feeding you like a baby."

"It is not healthy to go so long without food," Sarla said, defending herself. "I only gave you a bit of grape juice. A little energy to keep your body going. And you should know that we expect your new theolith to arrive any day now along with the supplies I need to perform the ventricular mineral graft."

"Thank you," Laurel said abruptly. A flicker in her mind brought her back to the orchard. "Asher! Where is Asher?"

"Asher?" Sarla repeated.

"The chromawolf."

"Ah," Sarla said with a laugh. "The entire pack followed us until we arrived at the walls of Felia. A singularly strange experience at first, until we realized they weren't a threat. For a moment, I thought they might try and enter the gates with us."

"Are they still out there?" Laurel asked.

"I don't know, but the alpha—I assume that's the one you call Asher—seemed particularly keen on staying near you. I expect they are still out there somewhere."

Laurel turned to Barrick.

"Don't look at me," the large man responded. "I need to run a few errands for Alabella, but just so you both know, she's in a sour mood. So, I'd suggest you steer clear."

"Why?" Laurel asked.

"So you don't get killed."

"No, why is she in a bad mood?"

"It seems an old friend of hers isn't so easy to kill." Barrick smirked. "Sarla, you'll be interested in this as well. Apparently, Alverax Blightwood is now a special advisor to the empress. He arrived with a group of Zeda. They're camped out near the eastern wall."

Laurel's chest nearly burst apart with happiness at the words. The Zeda. They were alive! And they were there. She tried to restrain her hope, in fear of what the truth may hold. She had no idea who had survived the attack in the Fairenwild. If her brother, Bay, or her grandfather, Corian, were hurt, she wasn't sure what she would do.

266

As Barrick stepped out of the room, Sarla looked as if her mind were racing in a hundred different directions all at once. Her eyes darted back and forth across the room and she whispered to herself before she left without a farewell.

Laurel smiled and tried to steady her racing heart with deep breaths, but she could neither calm the storm nor wish it departed.

She'd found her people.

CHAPTER 36

THREE NIGHTS HAD PASSED since the corespawn breached the eastern wall of Felia, and they had yet to return. Empress Jisenna and the generals found themselves suppressing their hope, fearful that the creatures would return as soon as they let their guard down. So, instead, the army maintained a healthy detail along the walls, preparing smoke signals for the day the corespawn would return.

Alverax, like many of those in Felia, had begun sleeping during the day and staying awake at night, as if the enemy would only attack when the sun had set. The Divine Council lectured him daily on theology and letters, claiming that a Watchlord required a certain level of education, regardless of the present danger. All the while, Osinan's final words resonated in his mind.

While the other generals had begun to tolerate his presence, General Thallin had become a true friend. They spent a bit of every evening together while Thallin taught Alverax Felian military history, tactics of famous Felian victories, and...Felian swordsmanship.

"Good!" Thallin shouted with a smile. A light sweat

shimmered across his bare chest. "Again."

Alverax lifted his practice blade. "Can I please take these off?" He still wore his Watchlord robes, despite the sweat dripping from his forehead.

"If you're expected to wear the robes at all times, then you'll be wearing them when you need to fight. Better to train your body to be used to it. Now, again!"

Alverax groaned, then set his feet and attacked. Dull steel clashed against dull steel. Alverax swung to the side, and Thallin parried it with an inverted blade. Again, and again, Alverax attacked, faster and harder each time, until Thallin sidestepped a wild lunge and slapped Alverax across the shoulder.

"Be patient, and never lunge without the proper footing for a hasty retreat. Lunging is a dangerous commitment. Better to move in circles as you swing. I heard you once danced with the Empress. Think of it like that! I am Jisenna, and you are the eligible bachelor dancing in circles around her."

"Mmhmm?"

Alverax and Thallin both turned in unison.

In the doorway of the practice room, Empress Jisenna stood smirking. She wore a long, black dress under a gold-patterned shawl, her tight curls pulled back into a braid. Her guards stood looming behind her.

"Empress," General Thallin said, dropping to a knee with his practice sword held behind his back. He looked down at his own bare chest and reddened. "My apologies. I was not aware you would be coming."

"Nothing to apologize for, General. I came because I had a feeling that our new Watchlord may have forgotten about his responsibilities this evening at the Sanctuary, and it appears I was correct."

Responsibilities? Alverax thought. *Heralds, save me.* He'd forgotten that it was the day of prayer, and he was to preside. At least Brother Henthum would be giving the sermon, and Alverax had only to attend. "Thallin, we're going to have to finish this tomorrow. Thank you again."

Thallin nodded and Alverax walked over to Jisenna. She smiled as he approached, and he couldn't help but return the offering.

"Watchlord."

"Empress."

She gestured for him to follow, and they left the practice room. "It's nice to see you getting along so well with one of the generals."

"Honestly, he's the closest thing I've had to a friend in a while. If you can—I don't know—give him some more land or something, he totally deserves it."

"More land? For being friendly?" Jisenna laughed. "I suppose it would set a pleasant precedent, but, as my advisors would say, friendship itself *is* the reward."

Alverax shook his head. "Not in my experience. Friendship is just the appetizer before the burnt meal."

"The more I learn of it, the more Cynosure seems like an altogether unpleasant place."

"The views are nice," he said, shrugging his shoulders. "But what can you expect from a city where all of the people are runaways, outcasts, or criminals."

"Not all of them," she corrected with a wink. "A few of them are kind and selfless and trying their best to do what is right, even if they have oddly shaped scars inside and out."

Alverax stopped walking and stared at the Empress.

She stopped beside him.

As he looked in her eyes, it was if all that was good in the world had coalesced and taken root between the various shades of brown. She'd read his story and, rather than toss them aside, she held the pages against her breast as if they were the most precious thing in the world. She held the promise of who he could become, and it made him want to be better.

The words she used to describe him—kind, selfless—these were her words to claim more than any other, but he could see it in the way she looked at him how much she believed they were his.

"Is everything okay?" she asked.

"I—" he began, fumbling his own thoughts. "Just thank you."

"Come on, we don't want you to be late to prayer."

AFTER TRAVELING FOR SOME TIME, passing maids and servants and fawning nobility, they arrived in the vestry attached to the backside of the Heraldic Sanctuary. The priests had previously explained his limited role in the services, but, as they walked, Jisenna had educated him on the history of the Sanctuary itself, where the Heralds held their annual covenant ritual, or so the Divine Council taught. The Heraldic Sanctuary was a tall structure with white stone that had become overgrown with all manner of budding greenery. The building overflowed its capacity with those who'd come to see their new Watchlord preside.

Inside, they greeted Brother Henthum of the Divine Council, who was scheduled to give the sermon. He gave Alverax a firm embrace, which made him altogether uncomfortable, but he still wasn't sure what he should, or could, refuse. Eventually, they led him through a doorway where he found himself looking out over a packed room with hundreds of attendees who all perked up when they saw him enter. Alverax kept his head high and took his seat on the dais.

"Today," Brother Henthum announced to the audience, "is a most extraordinary day. Behind me, we are presided over by Watchlord Alverax Blightwood, the first Obsidian threadweaver in all of Arasin for generations. Please, join me in welcoming him with the Sign of the Giver." Smiling faces lifted both palms to their foreheads, covering their eyes, then extended their outstretched hands to Alverax. He'd seen the gesture before and did his best to mimic the same.

While Brother Henthum continued with the sermon, Alverax found himself preoccupied with the weight of his new world. The title. The expectations. Not to mention the impending army of mythical corespawn. It had only been three days since he became Watchlord, but it felt like an eternity.

Brother Henthum concluded his sermon and, afterward, seats began to empty. Alverax could see in the way they stepped, in the way they held themselves, that they'd received an added portion of hope to accompany them. It was then that he truly understood Osinan. Despite knowing that the Heralds would never return, Osinan had dedicated his life to giving people a worthy reason to be good. He'd filled the void, and, false though it may have been, it had made the world a better place.

A small child, no more than four years old, ran through the Sanctuary, between the chairs and up the stairs of the dais until he stood smiling from ear to ear in front of Alverax. Despite having little experience with children, he'd always enjoyed their company.

Alverax crouched down and smiled. "Well, hello friend. What's your name?"

"Kyan."

"And how can I help you, Kyan?"

"Can you ask the Heralds to take care of my daddy?" The boy shuffled his feet. "The monsters killed him. But my mommy says you can protect us from them."

Alverax clenched his jaw. He knew that many had died the night of the attack, but he'd never thought about children losing parents, or men and women losing a spouse. Death was a landslide that muddied the earth for miles. "Don't worry about the monsters. I'll take care of them. Have you found your dad a star yet?"

Kyan shook his head.

"You know, my father died too. How would you like to come outside with me so we can name a star for your father?"

The little boy's eyes grew twice the size of the moon. "Really?"

"If your mother will allow it, of course."

Kyan's mother stood beneath the dais, mortified at her son's actions, but filled with pride in their conversation. She nodded her head, her eyes glistening in the flickering light.

"Follow me," Alverax said.

He took the boy by the hand and gestured for the mother to follow. They exited the Sanctuary through a side door and stepped out into the night. Out of habit, Alverax looked to the east, wondering when plumes of smoke would once again signify the return of the corespawn. But that night, only moonlight and stars filled the dark expanse.

He crouched down beside the boy. "Do you know any of the constellations?"

Kyan looked confused.

"Some of the stars look like shapes," Alverax explained, "and we give them names to help us describe where they are. Look over there." He pointed high overhead to the north. "See how some of those stars are brighter than the others? And the bright ones make a circle? We call that circle of stars the Broken Wheel."

"Broken?"

Alverax laughed. "I remember asking my grandfather the same thing. Wheels are meant to spin, and that one doesn't, so they say it's broken. Look at that one over there, the brightest star in the whole sky. They say that one is the Moon's Little Sister. The Empress told me that the small star right next to it is the one she chose for *her* father when he passed away. Maybe your father's star could be close to that one, so he can be friends with the emperor."

Kyan's grin widened. "Yeah! Daddy would like that!"

"Well then, it's settled. Now look at the star, think of your father's name, and his spirit will fly to it. And every time you miss him, or you're feeling scared or worried, you can look up into the sky, find the Moon's Little Sister, and see your dad's star watching over you."

When Alverax looked up from Kyan to his mother, he found her cheeks stained with tears. She mouthed the words *thank you* to him before ushering her son away.

He watched them walk away, then looked up into the sky. He'd avoided the tradition for so long, never feeling that his father deserved a named star. As he gazed into the infinite expanse, thousands of stars glittering in the darkness, he closed his eyes. Some day he would forgive his father for leaving them. Someday he would name a star for him. But he wasn't ready for that just yet.

When he opened his eyes, plumes of smoke from the signal fires billowed up from the eastern wall.

CHAPTER 37

ALL OF FELIA buzzed to life as men and women prepared for the attack. The sun had just fallen below the western horizon when Alverax arrived at the war tents. He leapt off the horse and entered to find the four generals hard at work, giving orders to their lieutenants, receiving scouting reports, and puzzling over the map.

"Watchlord," General Thallin said. The other generals gave him a nod of acknowledgment, which was more than Alverax had expected.

"I saw the smoke and came as fast as I could," Alverax said as he approached the table. "Are the corespawn attacking the same part of the wall? Where can I help?"

"Take a seat." General Nevik looked to him with a grim countenance. "The corespawn have yet to attack."

"They are gathering outside the wall," General Hish added, the veins in his thick neck radiated Sapphire threadlight.

"Gathering?" Alverax repeated. "That's—"

"Terrifying," Thallin finished for him. "Bloody terrifying,

because it means they are smarter than we thought. Not to mention the numbers."

"At least ten thousand," General Hish said, "and more gathering every minute. The monstrosity that broke through our wall wasn't the last of its kind either. Our lookouts have seen at least ten of them in the gathering."

"Heralds, save us," Alverax whispered.

General Nevik lifted his chin. "I wouldn't count on the Heralds showing up for this one, Watchlord. We have the tools, and our traps are in place; the fight is ours. However, General Thallin had an idea on how to improve our odds even more, and we think you could help."

"Anything, what is it?"

Thallin cocked his head to the side. "The Zeda are nearly all threadweavers. Most of them aren't soldiers, but we need eyes more than swords. If you could convince them to help, we could use their threadweavers."

Alverax looked to the three generals, each of them eyeing him warily. They were right that only a select few of the Zeda were warriors, but, if they could help coordinate the use of weapons and traps, there was a chance their help could change the tide. "I'll see what I can do."

With that, Alverax left the tent and stepped back into the brisk open air.

If they were going to use the Zeda, he needed to get to them quickly.

CHAPTER 38

LAUREL WANDERED the streets of Felia, using the fallen sun as her guide. Where she'd thought Alchea a rushing river of people, Felia was an ocean, filled with such diversity and movement that it was hard for her to keep focus. Still, nothing could distract her from finding her family. She only hoped it wasn't too late.

People rushed around the streets in a hurry, some with smiles, some with looks of terror. She heard people yelling, but she brushed them aside. She stopped a young boy who stood against a white building and asked him if he knew where the Zeda were, and he gave her directions. From there, it didn't take long to find the encampment.

In what looked like a series of large fields, a sprawling metropolis of quickly constructed tents dotted the landscape. She recognized the clothing immediately, and the hair, and the manner in which the Zeda carried themselves. Familiar faces walked the grassy paths between tents. Laurel ignored their expressions as they greeted her. There were only two people she needed to see, and she found herself hoping with all her soul for their safety. If they'd been taken from her, she wasn't sure her thread-dead heart could handle it.

She stepped forward, like a widow wandering a graveyard, each tent a headstone marking her fallen family. The tremble in her hands crept up her arms and covered her with ghostly shivers. Her hand rubbed at her empty breast pocket.

Then she saw Bay. Her sweet, sickly, do-gooder brother stepped slowly out of a tent holding a book, and Laurel felt a weight lift from her shoulders. When he saw her, he stopped in his tracks, leaned toward her, and blinked his eyes.

"Caterpillar!" Laurel shouted as she sprinted toward him.

As soon as he heard the word, his lips opened into a wide grin and he tossed his book back in through the open tent door. He braced himself for impact, and Laurel leapt up onto him, wrapping him in a tight embrace.

"Little wolf," he whimpered. "You're quite heavy."

She released him and dropped to the ground. He panted and shook his head back and forth with a smile.

"I saw what happened in the Fairenwild. I thought you were dead. I swore if anything had happened to you—"

"Me?" he asked, incredulously. "When you and the others never returned, the elders were certain that *you* were dead, or at least that we would never see you again. How did you find us?"

"It's a long story," she said. "Where's grandfather?"

Bay's face grew grim. "In the tent, but he's sick, Laurel. The physicians think he'll pass in the next few days. He'll be glad he was able to see you one last time."

Laurel's heart sunk in her chest. He was old—she knew he only had so much time left—but still the thought of him passing away squeezed at her insides. She looked to the tent, the scent of sickness wafting out from the opening.

Her pulse beat faster than a hummingbird's wings as she stepped inside. She couldn't even see her grandfather yet, and already tears were forming in her eyes. As she approached, she saw him laying on a cot in the corner, bundled up beneath a pile of wool blankets, his chest rising and falling with each breath. Laurel walked to him and stopped beside his bed. His skin seemed paler, and his hair thinner. Looking down at his frailty, tears flowed down her cheek. She wiped them away and sniffled away her running nose.

The sleeping man stirred, taking in a deep breath as his eyes began to open. Laurel tried to contain her joy as he awoke, but it came out as a curtailed giggle. He turned his head and saw her for the first time. Their eyes met and his lips quivered.

"Laurel," he whispered.

Hearing her name from his lips broke her. She collapsed into his arms, squeezing him harder than she knew she ought to, but she loved this man so dearly that no logic could prevent her from expressing it. "I thought I would never see you again."

With her head on his chest, she could hear his lips part into a smile.

"I'm so sorry," she continued. "For everything. I was reckless and stupid. I don't know what got into me. I should have stayed with you and Bay. I never should have gone with the grounders."

"No," he said with a deep weariness to his voice. It seemed scratchier and deeper than she remembered. "You know, you remind me so much of your mother—how I've missed you both."

"I missed you too."

He let out a series of coughs, each worse than the previous.

She took his hand and squeezed it gently. "Do you remember the night my parents died?"

He nodded. "How could I forget?"

"Do you remember what you told me?"

He shook his head.

Laurel sat on the edge of his cot. "You held Bay and I, one in each arm, and squeezed us like the wind would take us away as well. I still remember staining your shirt with my tears. And you just held us in silence. After a time, you let go and it felt like I could finally breathe again, but I didn't want to. You sat us on the kitchen chairs and knelt in front of us. You took our hands, and you finally spoke. 'When the dead look down on us, they don't want us to mourn. They want us to live.'"

She watched as a single tear traced down his cheek. "Your mother would be so proud of you."

Would she? If she knew the truth—that Laurel was working with the Bloodthieves, that she'd killed a man, and was addicted to drinking threadweaver blood—there was little to be proud of. But there was still time. She could still make them proud, somehow.

Curiously, the slightest scent of citrus entered the tent.

"A fallen leaf ne'er travels far from the tree."

Laurel startled at the voice, turning to see a pair of elderly women standing in the doorway of the tent, each a stark contrast to the other. Elder Rosemary's lips curled up, and Elder Rowan's curled down, but their eyes both held a similar sense of relief. Laurel wasn't sure how to respond to the old adage.

"A thorn in the hand will tomorrow be a thorn in the foot," Elder Rowan added.

"Oh, come now, Rowan," Elder Rosemary said, slapping at the older woman's shoulder. "Laurel, we are both so delighted to see you. I can't imagine your journey has been altogether pleasant."

"I...I want to apologize," Laurel replied.

Elder Rosemary rose a brow. "Whatever for?"

"For everything. You were right to take away my position as a messenger. I see that now. And I understand if you're still frustrated with me—you've every right to be. But I'm going to be better. I want to make sure my brother and my grandfather are safe. That's more important than whatever it was I was trying to prove to myself."

Elder Rowan eyed her grandfather. "She sounds more and more like Tarra every day."

"Looks like her too," Elder Rosemary added. "Except...is that a streak of green in your hair? And your eyes..." She paused. "A story for another time. Laurel, we came here for the purpose of apologizing to *you* and welcoming you home. These are dangerous times, and our people need to be more united than ever before. Darkness has come to this city, and it will come again."

Laurel perked up. "The corespawn."

The elders turned to each other in surprise. Elder Rowan spoke first. "An army of them attacked the city. They killed many and destroyed a portion of the outer wall."

"They attacked Alchea too."

"Father of All, help us," Elder Rosemary said. "I assume you know that Zedalum was attacked?"

She nodded again, biting the inside of her cheek.

"Laurel, we failed," Elder Rosemary said sternly. "The coreseal was shattered, releasing the corespawn."

A voice echoed behind them from among the tents, but Elder Rowan ignored it. "We need to find a way to fix it. We don't know how our ancestors created the seal, but we know that they were Amber threadweavers. It is no coincidence that the Father of All has brought an Amber threadweaver to Felia to help us—"

Laurel shifted in her boots. How did they know she'd come with Alabella? The woman had destroyed their home and orchestrated the shattering of the seal. Surely, they didn't believe she would help them fix it.

"—We just need to survive long enough for him to grow into his powers."

Gale take me, she thought. *They mean Aydin.*

Laurel's mind flashed with an image of Iriel carrying Aydin while Asher carried Chrys through the dark of the Fairenwild. It seemed an eternity ago. She was a different person then; she was still a threadweaver.

"Chrys and Iriel are here?" Laurel asked.

A dark pain settled over their faces. Elder Rosemary clenched her jaw before she spoke. "Iriel and the baby are here, and they are safe. We've not seen Chrys since the night we left the Fairenwild."

Suddenly, a figure appeared in the doorway behind the elders. A boy, not much older than Laurel, standing tall in clothing that seemed fit for both fighting and priestly duties.

"Elders," he said, addressing the older women.

"Alverax?" Elder Rowan said with a hint of bitterness in her tone.

His eyes slimmed. "The corespawn are here. We need your help."

CHAPTER 39

LAUREL STARED at the boy standing in the doorway of the tent. His eyes were black as the Fairenwild at midnight, and his veins pulsed with darkness. And that name...*Alverax*. It took only a moment to make the connection. He was the Obsidian threadweaver Alabella had created. He was the proof that she wasn't lying. That Laurel *could* have her threadlight back.

But there was no time for that now. If he was right, they were all in danger.

Laurel had hoped to never hear the word corespawn again, but it was like a fly that followed her from room to room, buzzing in her ear wherever she went. She felt at her side and the presence of the obsidian dagger gave her a sense of relief. With it, she could protect her family. She could protect her people after failing to be there for them before.

"The corespawn have returned?" Elder Rosemary asked with a grimace.

"Gathering outside the walls," Alverax said. "They're not attacking, but they are amassing an army ten times larger than before. But I'm not here just to warn you. We need the Zeda people. Most of the Felian soldiers are achromats. They can't even see the corespawn. We've done everything we can to prepare, but we need more thread-weavers so that soldiers know when to spring traps and when to cast arrows. If any Zeda will fight, Heralds know we could use them. But if they're not, we need lookouts even more. I know the Felians don't deserve your help, and I have no right to ask for it, but this city will fall if we do nothing."

Elder Rosemary lifted her chin and looked to him. "If anyone has a right to ask for our help, it is the man who saved us all from captivity and death. Alverax, I do not care for your new title nor your new associations, but I know you. And you would not put our people in danger if it were not necessary."

"In a way, you are to blame for the return of the cores-pawn," Elder Rosemary added with a flat tone. "It is fitting that you be the one to lead the charge to destroy them."

Laurel saw the boy redden. He was a curiosity. On the one hand, he wore immaculate robes and stood tall and strong, speaking with confidence. But on the other hand, he seemed so young.

"I'm trying," he said. "I know it's my fault. Heralds, I can hardly sleep some nights. But what's done is done. I can blame myself every day for the rest of my life, but it wouldn't make a difference. Fighting will. You both know I'm not a warrior. But if it means I can save some lives, then I'm damn well going to fight with everything I have."

"I'll fight," Laurel said.

Corian coughed from his bed and tried to rise. "Laurel."

"I fought the corespawn in Alchea. Killed a handful myself." She pulled out the obsidian dagger. "If the corespawn are coming, then sitting behind a wall won't keep us safe. It's time the Zeda did their part. I'm going to do mine."

The two elders looked to each other in silence for just a moment before they nodded. Elder Rosemary turned to Alverax. "Our people were tasked with protecting the core-seal, so that the corespawn could not return. We failed that duty. I will speak with Dogwood, and we'll gather the threadweavers. Some of us are old, but we yet have thread-light in our veins. Where would you have us?"

THE EASTERN WALL of Felia loomed high overhead with a wide crack splitting the finely joined stone. The gaping hole had been filled with wood and rocks and all manner of material, but it was haphazard and would not stand long against an attack. The scent of death still rode the wind, but no one save Laurel seemed to care. Even her brother, Bay, who stood uncomfortably close to her as they traveled through the wide dirt field, seemed unaffected by the horrible stench.

Hundreds of Zeda trailed behind, silent in their commit-ment to aid the grounders. Laurel felt an overwhelming pride for her people, though she understood their choices were limited. Dogwood, one of the true warriors of the Zeda, led a large group up the long staircase leading to the wall-walk. They spread out across the entire eastern wall, providing added coverage of the surrounding terrain.

With Zeda support, the amassed army of corespawn would have no way to sneak up on the city. And when they came, the archers would loose their arrows, fire would rain down from trebuchets, and a hidden layer of spikes at the base of the wall would be lifted. Lastly, in preparation for the enormous monstrosities, dozens of ballistae were in position to launch a volley of burning steel.

Laurel found herself beginning to believe that with all of the grounder preparations, they just might be able to win.

But then the earth shook.

Over and over, like fists pounding against the earth, ripples of energy quaking along the surface. Chaos erupted throughout the city, with lookouts shouting for everyone to stay calm. The corespawn weren't moving, but that didn't stop the people from panicking.

Bay grabbed Laurel's shoulder for support. "What is happening?"

"I don't know," she said. "I need to find Alverax. Go somewhere safe."

As Laurel rushed through the pandemonium, she lifted her head and sniffed the air. Her mind filled with faces and odd assumptions about the world around her, but one in particular stood out. She turned toward a tent not far away and ran as fast as her legs would take her. She never knew how much she loved the wind in her hair until she was dashing through the dirt with danger all around. Her heart pounded and her eyes pierced through the darkness. She felt so free.

She rounded the other end of the tent and saw Alverax standing in the doorway, talking to a man with a sharp jaw. "Alverax!" she shouted, coming to a stop. "What's happening?"

The other man turned to her with a look of confusion. "Who are you?"

"She's one of the Zeda," Alverax responded. "She helped me convince the elders. Laurel, was it? This is General Thallin."

She nodded just as another resounding thud shook the

ground. "Did this happen the last time the corespawn attacked?"

"No," Alverax said.

Again, the earth shook.

He turned to the general. "Should we send out scouts to see what they're doing?"

"They're too far away from the wall," Thallin replied. "There's nothing they can do from that distance, and I wouldn't want to send one of our threadweavers on a suicide scouting mission."

Alverax turned to Laurel. "I need you to work with Dogwood and make sure the Zeda are in position and ready. The last thing we need is for whatever this is to frighten people and ruin our preparation."

Laurel nodded. In that moment, she realized that Alverax had no idea that Alabella and Sarla were in the city. When Sarla had told her all about the Obsidian threadweaver they'd created, she told her that the boy had abandoned them and was likely dead. Whatever his reason, Alverax would certainly want to know that they were here. But not now. They had bigger problems.

The quaking of the earth grew stronger.

Screaming.

Laurel, Alverax, and Thallin turned their gaze to the screams coming from the south, where a large creature dashed through the streets at terrifying speed. Somehow, she knew, even before she saw his green fur blending in with the moonlit grass.

Asher.

The chromawolf sprinted toward her and she took a step in his direction. Thallin unsheathed his blade, and Alverax followed suit.

"No!" she shouted, pushing them aside and rushing

forward. The wind bit at her cheeks as she picked up speed. She had to get to him before the grounders hurt him. They were right to be afraid, but wrong in the most important way.

As they approached, she slid on her side, reaching out for threadlight to *drift* across the dirt, but finding none. She came to a halt and watched as an arrow cut through the night and smashed into Asher's shoulder. The chromawolf crashed to its side and Laurel howled out into the night. Pain ripped through her arm, gripping at nerves and tendons. She stumbled to her feet and lifted her other arm high into the air, waving it in the direction from which the arrow had flown.

When she looked to her own shoulder, there was no wound. Whatever pain she'd felt wasn't real. But Asher's was. She knelt beside the chromawolf, his fur now marred by blood and dirt. His breath was heavy, his chest heaving up and down as his head writhed back and forth in pain. She touched his chest with an outstretched palm, and he turned his eyes to her.

And in the middle of the chaos, with armored boots stomping over rubble and soldiers and civilians shouting hymns of terror, Laurel heard a voice in her mind.

Danger, Asher growled. *Tunnel.*

CHAPTER 40

Laurel continued to press her hand against the chroma-wolf's chest. Somehow—impossibly—he had spoken to her. But they weren't words, they were ideas, passed into her mind and translated to words with a voice that just like Asher's growl.

"Danger?" Laurel asked.

Asher shook his head. *Digging. Far.*

She couldn't believe that it was really his voice. Had he always been able to communicate with her? Could other chromawolves do the same? But wait...

Digging.

"Alverax!" Laurel screamed, looking back over her shoulder. "Alverax, come fast!"

She turned her attention back to Asher and looked at the arrow in his shoulder. She grabbed it by the shaft, and, as she gripped it, she felt a dull throb in her own arm. Gritting her teeth and taking a deep breath, she pulled the arrow out of Asher as fast as she could. Her own are throbbed as she felt the shadow of an arrow pull free.

Alverax approached, his black blade returned to its sheath. "Laurel, are you okay? Did that thing hurt you?"

"I'm fine," she said. "Asher would never hurt me."

"Asher?"

Laurel sat up, one hand gripping her shoulder, though the pain had all but vanished. "Asher is with me. If anyone so much as touches him, there will be hell to pay."

Alverax looked down at the wound in Asher's shoulder. "Is it going to be okay?"

"*He* will be fine. Alverax, the corespawn are digging a tunnel. They're going *under* the wall."

His eyes grew. "Under? All our traps would be useless. Wait, is that even possible? Thallin!" he shouted. "Ahh, never mind. Come on. Can it walk? I wouldn't leave it here or someone will do something."

In response, Asher rose to his feet, though he favored the injured one as he hobbled beside Laurel. On every side, soldiers and civilians gawked at the massive chromawolf sauntering through their homeland beside a Zeda girl and their Watchlord. Something about it made Laurel feel powerful, as if her bond with Asher was some great expression of strength.

"Thallin!" Alverax shouted as they moved. "The corespawn are digging a tunnel under the wall! I don't know how far they've gotten, but we need to get ready in case they emerge from the ground on this side."

General Thallin furrowed his brows and stared at Asher with his head held slightly back, then shifted his gaze to Alverax. "Slow down. What are you talking about?"

"The corespawn!" Alverax repeated. "The quaking is *digging*. They're making a tunnel that will go right under the outer wall."

"Heralds," Thallin cursed. "Where is the messenger? I want to know every detail."

Alverax turned to Laurel who turned to Asher. "Laurel, where's the note?"

Laurel paused. "What note?"

"The message that the wolf brought you. You said it brought you the warning."

"No, I didn't," she said. In that moment, she realized how insane it would look if she tried to explain the truth. No one would believe that Asher could speak to her. And even if they did, how could they believe information from a chromawolf? "Ohhhhh," she said, backtracking. "Sorry, yeah. The note was from a Zeda scout."

"Can I see it?" Thallin asked.

"I..." Laurel patted at her pockets. "It must have fallen out. The paper doesn't matter as much as the message. You have to turn your attention inward and rearrange the traps, you can still catch them by surprise."

Thallin stared at her with doubt in his eyes. "If we turn our attention inward and you're wrong, then the corespawn army can simply march forward and destroy our wall again, uncontested. I need more than a missing note to change all of our preparations."

Laurel clenched her jaw and turned to Alverax. "I swear it on the wind. They are digging a tunnel and, if you do nothing, people *will* die."

The ground rumbled beneath them, intensifying with each passing minute.

Alverax looked to the ground, thoughtfully, and Laurel thought that he just might believe her. But then he turned to the general. "I trust your judgment. Is there any way we can watch both?"

General Thallin shook his head. "Not without sacrificing

one or the other. One option is to turn the ballistae inward, and if we see the corespawn approaching from the outside, we can swivel them back around. But the people and the traps are too connected to the wall. Moving them could be catastrophic if we're wrong."

"Do that," Alverax said. "If they tunnel in, I can help with the smaller corespawn. The ballistae can hold off the larger ones."

"I'll have them position the ballistae immediately." With that, Thallin rushed off to the tent where a group of messengers awaited orders.

A few minutes passed while Laurel watched messengers deliver their orders to the soldiers on the wall-walk. Several large ballistae shifted their aim, rotating the huge bow-like machines inward. It wasn't much, but it was something.

As they stood side by side, Laurel looked at Alverax. If they survived this, she wanted to know his story. Especially the part where he betrayed Alabella.

Just then, she caught an odd scent on the wind.

It smelled like...roses.

The earth just inside the wall spewed forth dirt and rubble. Soldiers shouted, scrambling about. Dirt blasted out of the ground. Laurel searched for threadlight, but found her mind grasping into an empty void. For a moment, she thought she felt something, a prickle of power, but then it was gone.

She cursed and took out the obsidian dagger.

Alverax unsheathed his blade, and it gleamed in the moonlight. Laurel looked back to her own and was surprised to see the similarity.

"Nice sword," she said.

He looked at her dagger. "Nice knife."

"Mine's better," she said.

292

Alverax let out a clipped laugh and looked to the tunnel.

Laurel knew it would be difficult to fight the corespawn if she couldn't see them. But it wouldn't be impossible. If only she still had a transfuser, something to give her access to threadlight, then she could make the beasts pay.

Eyes, Asher's voice growled in her mind.

Yes, Laurel thought. *I can't see the corespawn.*

No, his voice echoed. *Eyes.*

Laurel looked at her friend, confused. "I don't understand," she said aloud.

Share. Mine. Eyes.

The scent of roses saturated the night air, and that simple fact gave Laurel pause. Ever since the incident in the orchard, something had been changing with her. The smells. The speed. The pain. The...hair. It was as if she was becoming more and more like a chromawolf. And now, she could feel Asher's pain. She could speak with him. Somehow, their souls had bonded. *Share. Mine. Eyes.*

What if...

Laurel closed her eyes and reached back into the empty space where threadlight had once lived within her. She searched for a single leaf in the howling wind...and she found it. There, like the smallest seed, a spec of threadlight that echoed with Asher's soul. She reached out to it and felt power surge through her. She could hear the crunch of fallen leaves underfoot on the other side of the field. She could hear the breath of the guards atop the wall-walk. An entire world of information came pouring into her.

And then she opened her eyes.

Threadlight burst into her vision. Tens of thousands of multi-colored threads pulsing and dancing in the moonlit air. And in the midst of the field, in the center of thousands of Felian soldiers, a horde of corespawn came crawling out of a gaping hole in the ground.

———————————

ALVERAX GRIPPED the hilt of the Midnight Watcher with white knuckles as he watched a swarm of skittering corespawn digging their way out of the growing hole. With each corespawn, the opening grew, until a massive hand plunged its way out, slapping against the ground and pulling itself out of the tunnel. It was one of the same monstrosities that had broken through the wall before, twice the height of a house and a barbed tail dragging behind it. Threadlight swirled across its massive body.

Every ballista that had been turned inward fired off a thick bolt at the monstrosity. Steel blasted into the creature, embedding deep in its glowing body. But no sooner had they hit then the beast grabbed hold and ripped the bolts back out, tossing them aside as threadlight pooled in the wounds.

The wounds healed, and the monstrosity roared.

Next to him, Laurel smiled, and Alverax was quite certain the girl was mad. But despite the fact that she seemed quite feral, she'd been right, for all the good it did them. He should have listened to her.

He was surprised to see her lips curl into a snarl as she flipped her dagger in her hand and whispered something to the chromawolf. Then, she took off toward the corespawn with Asher stumbling after her.

"Heralds, save us all," Alverax mumbled.

Then, he too rushed toward the tunnel.

Even at a dead sprint, he could pick off the smaller corespawn nearest to him. He would latch onto their thread-

light with his mind and *break* it, instantly bursting the creatures apart in a cloud of misty magic. But Laurel and Asher
were so fast that they arrived long before him. He watched
as she slashed at the corespawn with reckless abandon,
dashing in, swiping, spinning, and slamming down her
dagger into the neck of the next. She seemed to move with
inhuman speed, the corespawn falling apart at the touch of
her obsidian blade.

The chromawolf seemed interested only in protecting
Laurel as she continued in her mad rage. Each time one of
the corespawn, whether small or large, tried to attack her
from the flank, the chromawolf would lunge forward,
striking the creatures down and fending them off until
Laurel could turn around and finish them.

Alverax finally caught up. "Watch my back and I'll watch
yours!" he shouted.

Laurel barely managed a nod before diving back in to
explode the next corespawn. Alverax held his sword in a
battle stance he'd learned from Thallin but focused on using
his threadweaving. While Laurel thrashed out at the creatures, cutting them down like a child popping bubbles,
Alverax picked them apart from a distance. One along the
wall-walk about to attack an archer. *Pop.* Another climbing
the wall to kill one of the Zeda lookouts. *Pop.*

He searched through the chaos, looking for where he
could best help the people, all the while threadlight burned
beneath his skin, sizzling from his chest to the ends of his
fingertips. By the dozens, corespawn swarmed out of the
massive hole like lava, oozing out over the land, devouring
everything in their wake. Alverax wasn't fast enough. There
were too many.

Another monstrosity ripped itself out of the hole. It
swung its arms out over the field and flung soldiers through

the air, crashing against tents and towers and the stone wall. Screams filled the battlefield, and it took all of Alverax's willpower not to add his own to the chorus.

All around him, chaos reigned. Soldiers toppled from the wall-walk. Others were flattened beneath the feet of the monstrosities. And yet others lay strewn out across the grass, their corpses torn open from the smaller, feasting creatures. He spun in a circle, and, everywhere he looked, he saw death. Their defenses were broken.

Rage boiled beneath his skin. The Heralds had saved him for a reason. He couldn't just stand there and watch the corespawn destroy the entire city. He had to do something.

The largest of the monstrosities broke away from the field and marched toward the palace. Flaming arrows and balls of acid exploded across its body, and it continued as if they were nothing more than rainfall.

Alverax ran. He ran faster than he'd ever run, gripping the Midnight Watcher as if it might try to turn back. Step by step, he gained on the slow-moving monstrosity; he had to stop it before it arrived at the palace. Jisenna was inside.

He cursed his heavy robes and charged forward. With threadlight burning through his veins and his heart pounding with fury, Alverax reached out to the monstrosity and attempted to *break* it. The threadlight forming its body vibrated like a magnet repelling its twin, pushing back against Alverax's efforts. Inside, it felt as though his veins were expanding under the pressure, but Alverax ignored it and raced forward.

The corespawn monstrosity swung about face, crushing a building with its tail. When its head faced Alverax, it leaned forward and roared.

Alverax *broke* his corethread and launched himself, weightless, through the cool night air in a straight line toward the beast. He lifted the Midnight Watcher high above him and, as he crashed into the monstrosity's head, he slammed the obsidian blade into the mass of pulsing threadlight. The sword connected. Energy shocked through his arms and throughout his body, sizzling and burning beneath his skin. The monstrosity burst apart like a mountain exploding into millions of shards of rock and dust.

The force sent Alverax crashing toward the ground, his corethread reappearing just before he struck earth. The sword tumbled away from him. His breathing came in bursts while his heart beat in chaotic pulses.

The moon's little sister winked at him.

No.

He refused to give up. He pushed himself to his feet and rubbed at his chest. But when he stood, the battlefield had changed...for the worse.

The remaining monstrosities had broken through the wall while the smaller corespawn were attacking soldiers and lookouts from within. Now, they prepared to march through the city, devastating everything in their path. Alverax knew he had to fight, but he couldn't kill all of the monstrosities by himself, even with the Midnight Watcher. Still, if he didn't try, what would that mean for the people of Felia?

"Alverax!" Laurel's voice shouted in the chaos. The wild Zeda girl, bloody and clutching at her arm, ran up to him, followed by her chromawolf companion. "We can't stop those things. What do we do?"

But he didn't know. Heralds, save him. He didn't know.

General Thallin was nowhere to be seen; the other generals had been in the tent that was torn apart by one of the monstrosities. There was nothing left for them to do.

They were going to lose the city.

They'd failed.

Suddenly, two pairs of boots crashed into the ground, landing in a crouch not far from Alverax and Laurel. A regal man that seemed to glow in the sky, and a woman with a flowing dress that drifted in the wind. Their eyes, like perfect prisms, radiated the full spectrum of colors. There was something about them, a confidence, a power.

The man looked to Alverax and smiled. "Do not worry, child. The Heralds have returned."

CHAPTER 41

THE TWO BEINGS who called themselves Heralds leapt into action toward the stampeding monstrosities. In moments, they were hovering above the corespawn army, speaking to the beasts. Their words caused the creatures to howl and thrash about as they backed away. The woman flew forward and struck at the closest of the massive beast. To Laurel, it looked like a bird crashing into a feytree, but, in reality, as soon as the monstrosity was struck, it was launched backward, tumbling over dozens of the smaller corespawn prowling in the field.

The rest of the monstrosities roared in unison, then fled toward their tunnel. One by one they dropped into the gaping hole and disappeared. Thousands of smaller corespawn scuttled in after them. However impossible it seemed, the streets and wall were soon free of the enemy, populated only by the wounded Felians and Zeda who'd stood their ground and fought.

Laurel stared at the Heralds who hovered in the air overhead.

Danger, Asher growled in her mind.

"Alverax," she said. "Who are they?"

The young Watchlord was frozen in place, eyes plastered to the godlike beings who'd saved them. "Osinan was wrong."

"What?"

"The Heralds *did* come back," he said. "The bloody HERALDS!" A smile broke out across his face. He rubbed his dirty hands through his hair, his feet dancing back and forth. "Do you know what this means!?"

Laurel looked back up to find the Heralds slowly descending back to the earth, hands outstretched to the congregating soldiers and civilians. They were everything she would expect of a god, graceful and benevolent, saviors to a fallen people. But something tickled at the back of her mind.

"People of Felia!" the male Herald announced. His voice carried far in the silent aftermath of the battle. "Your Heralds have returned. Come to us and be healed."

Men and women flocked to the gods. Laurel followed Alverax as they joined the amassing throng. Asher kept his distance.

As they grew closer, Alverax led them through the crowd. When the people saw his robes, they parted. Soon, they came into view of the Heralds once again, and Laurel watched in awe as a dying man was placed in front of the gods. A bite had opened the dying man's stomach, blood pooling across his naval and down his sides. The male Herald poured a few drops of water into the open wound, then pressed his hand down gently atop the bleeding, whispering words of power. The dying man inhaled until his lungs were filled to bursting. Then, his head fell to the earth.

The crowd gasped, and the Herald lifted a hand to calm them. As he raised his other hand, he revealed the gaping wound from the man's stomach. It had been completely healed. "This man will live but must now rest."

"Come all that are wounded, and we will care for you," the female Herald said.

They continued their healings until General Thallin appeared. Laurel saw Alverax take a step forward but hesitated as his friend approached the gods. They finished healing a woman who'd had a series of scratches across her face but left without blemish. Part of Laurel wanted to offer herself to them, to have them heal her bruises, but she knew others had greater need...like her grandfather.

As soon as the thought entered her mind, she moved to go fetch him, but paused when Thallin spoke.

"Divine Heralds!" he said. "I am Thallin Haichess, swordmaster and general to the Sun Queen, Empress Jisenna Vayse. We have long awaited your return to this world."

The male Herald stepped forward. "As have we, Thallin Haichess. Tell me, where is the empress now?"

"She is in the palace, my god."

"Go. Tell her to prepare for our arrival."

Thallin nodded. "It will be done."

As the general departed, hundreds of Felians crowded the field. Laurel pushed herself through the growing crowd until she finally escaped its clutches. She ran, and Asher joined beside her. Together, they headed to the Zeda encampment. People gawked as she ran opposite the crowds, some in fear and some in awe at her enormous chromawolf companion. But she ignored them all. This was the miracle she needed to save her grandfather.

If she hadn't seen it with her own eyes, watching them hover in the air and banish the corespawn with nothing more than words, she'd think the grounders had lost their minds. But she *had* seen it. She'd watched the monsters fleeing through their dark tunnel like frightened insects, and she'd seen the gods descending from the skies, taking wounded and healing them.

If the Heralds were real, and they *had* returned, what did that mean of her own beliefs? The elders taught of the Father of All, a singular entity who created the world and all of the beauty upon it. And then, when the world was rich with life, he offered drops of his own soul to inhabit the world. People. Divinely born children of a heavenly being. And when a person died, the Father's essence would ride the winds back to the greater whole to continue in a cycle of rebirth. The elders claimed their beliefs predated the beliefs of the pagan grounders, but the age of a belief doesn't make it any more true.

If the Heralds were real, and they *had* returned, was none of it real? Was there no Father of All? Was the divinity of man a lie? What of the Gale? If there was no rebirth, and no essence to return to the Father of All, why would they sacrifice the elderly to make room for the young?

Anger swelled within her, but she pushed it away. It didn't matter, not right now at least. What mattered was that there was a way for her to help her grandfather.

She reached the Zeda encampment and was surprised to find it as empty as the rest of the city. Her people, who didn't believe in the Heralds, had gone to witness the pagan gods in person. She wandered the tents, trying to remember which one was her grandfather's. So far from the battlefield, silence seemed to linger in the air like a thick fog. She kept her bond with Asher, illuminating the threadlight around her. If there were any corespawn still around, she wanted to know. She lifted her nose to the wind and followed the putrid trail of illness.

When she found the tent, she pushed the flap back and

stepped inside. Her grandfather slept on his bed and she hoped with all her heart that the Heralds could heal him. He was a good man, and good men deserve good things. But the world had a tendency to step over good men and leave them with nothing but muddy prints to lie in.

She approached Corian and took his hand in her own. "Grandfather, I found someone who is going to heal you."

She rubbed the back of his hand with her other.

"You wouldn't believe it, but I saw them heal a grounder missing half of his stomach."

She moved her hand to his shoulder and pressed.

"I'm sure your cough will be nothing."

Her grandfather continued to sleep. He was so calm, a firm root in the soil, basking in the lamplight. She imagined herself after *bonding* with Asher, quietly sleeping for days while she recovered, her chest rising and falling as her mind sailed through the storm.

But her grandfather's chest did not rise, nor did it fall.

His body rested in the perfect measure of stillness. It was a painting, so vivid she could see the wrinkles in his cheeks and smell the odor of his skin. So lifelike that she could feel the coarseness of his fingertips. It had to be a painting—it couldn't be real—because, if it was, that would mean...

Her grandfather was dead.

No.

Please, no.

Not him.

Not now.

Father of All, I just need one more hour.

Please.

She reached up to feel for his pulse but stopped. She couldn't. She wouldn't. In her heart, she already knew, but she could not let herself truly *know*. She could feel it in the stiffness of his palm. She could see it in the tint of his lips. But she refused to accept the truth. He wasn't gone. Not him. His essence was a bird migrating for the winter, and, at any moment, it would return, and he would resume his life once again.

Tears swelled within her, a cracked dam in a raging river, but it was her brother's voice that broke her. "Laurel."

That single word slammed an axe through the wood, and she broke in two. She could no longer hold back the pain. She could no longer lie to herself. Asher nuzzled her, whimpering as he tried to comfort her.

She turned as Bay limped toward her. He ignored Asher —he ignored their grandfather—and he wrapped her up in his long arms more fiercely than a mother clutching her sickly child.

They held each other as they embraced the cold darkness swirling in the tent. Laurel felt a strange sense of deja vu as she remembered mourning the death of their parents. But, where once her grandfather had lived to comfort them, now they were alone to comfort themselves. It wasn't fair. After all they had gone through. Laurel felt a stirring inside her, a harsh pressure squeezing against her mind, burning away the pain and leaving nothing but the charred remains of anger. It wasn't *fair*.

She pulled away from Bay, an idea beginning to bud. "They can still heal him."

Lifting herself to her feet, she looked at the cot her grandfather was on.

Bay's eyes were like two red sunsets set against a pale sky. "Laurel, what are you—"

"Asher," Laurel said, stroking the chromawolf's face. "I know you don't like doing it, but I need you to carry my grandfather for me."

Asher nodded, and his gravelly voice resonated in her mind. *Carry. Good.*

"Bay, help me lift him onto Asher," Laurel said. "It's not over yet."

"Laurel!" her brother shouted. "What are you talking about!?"

"The grounder gods are here. They're at the battlefield healing the wounded. They can save grandfather."

He furrowed his brows. "Laurel, I want him back as much as you do, but he's gone."

"No, he's not."

"Laurel..."

"He's not gone yet!" she shouted. "Help me get him on Asher. I can still save him."

Bay hesitated but complied. Together, they lifted Corian face-down onto Asher's thick green fur, draped over like an old rug.

It was going to work.

It had to.

Otherwise, she didn't know what she'd do.

CHAPTER 42

ALVERAX STARED in awe as the event for which he was sworn to prepare came to pass. He wanted to believe—hell, they'd saved the city and healed nearly a hundred people—but, even with such astounding evidence, he found himself doubting. If only Osinan could have seen it, he could have died knowing that the words he'd preached for so many years weren't just hollow hope; they were true.

The Heralds has literally saved them!

His grandfather had told him that the Heralds watched men from their divine realm, only transcending to ours in the world's hour of greatest need. Which, in a way, meant that the Felian resistance had failed. The corespawn would have destroyed them all. But, in a more important way, it meant that they were safe now.

"Watchlord!" a voice called out. A young woman with hair pulled back in tight braids against her scalp pointed at Alverax in the midst of the crowd.

He hesitated as the people around him suddenly became aware of his presence. They backed away, eyeing his robes.

Both Heralds turned to him.

His heart raced in his chest, threadlight beckoning him for release. Their prismatic eyes bore into his soul, weighing him, judging his worth and questioning his loyalty. He wanted to run, and keep running, until he was back in Cynosure where he could hide in the shed out back behind his grandfather's home. Somewhere far away from responsibility and expectation.

"Who is this?" the female Herald asked, approaching him as she finished healing a minor scrape.

The male Herald eyed the sword still dangling from Alverax's limp wrist. "It cannot be." He approached Alverax and stretched out his hand. "May I?"

"Of course," Alverax said, handing the Midnight Watcher to the Herald.

A pale hand caressed the length of the blade as the Herald smiled at the sword. In that moment, Alverax realized that both of the Heralds looked more Alchean than Felian. He'd always imagined them with darker skin, similar to his own.

"Where did you get this?" the male Herald asked.

Alverax tried—and failed—to keep the gaze of the Herald, but the prismatic eyes were too much. Instead, he alternated his gaze between the ground and the Herald's eyes. "It was given to me when I became Watchlord. They told me that it's been handed down from generation to generation. A gift from you to the first Watchlord."

"Mmmm," the Herald said. "Tell me, what is a Watchlord? I do not..." He trailed off and smiled. "You are a Destroyer."

"I—what?" Alverax said, his heart quickening.

"Ah, yes. You would call them Obsidian threadweavers. I

can see it in your eyes. You have the power to destroy, do you not?"

Alverax nodded.

"And what of the Amber threadweavers? Are there any here?"

The question caught him off guard and, at first, it angered him. He thought of Alabella. He imagined her becoming the right hand of the Heralds, and the idea boiled his blood. But then he thought of Aydin, the little Valerian child, he was an Amber threadweaver too. Maybe, he—

"All Amber threadweavers," the Herald announced, opening himself to the rest of the crowd, "are to be brought to us at once. We will need them for the days to come. Anyone with information about the whereabouts of such people will be rewarded."

"I know where to find one!" a familiar voice called out. The crowd parted in chaotic fashion as Laurel and her chromawolf stepped through the throng. A man was draped over the back of the massive chromawolf. As she approached, her voice grew quieter. "If you heal my grandfather, I can bring one of the Amber threadweavers to you."

"You..." the male Herald said, pausing to contemplate the request. "You are bold to make such a demand. But I am feeling generous. Bring him to me."

Asher growled, and Laurel reprimanded him. Alverax thought he saw her whisper something to the chromawolf as if it could understand her. The animal strode forward and rolled its shoulder so that the Herald could lift the man off its back. Alverax was close enough to see that it was the same old man that had been lying on a cot in the Zeda tent. His skin was pale and stiff.

The Herald turned his head to Laurel. "This man is dead."

"You're a god," Laurel said flatly. "Bring him back."

"Death can be prevented, but it cannot be undone."

Laurel stood tall, staring into the Herald's prismatic eyes, a slight quiver in her lip.

"Mmmm," the male Herald said, tilting his head slightly. "You say you know the location of one of the Amber thread-weavers? Bring them to me, and I will help this man."

"You can bring him back?"

"Yes," the Herald said. "If you bring the Amber thread-weaver to me."

A deep growl emanated from the massive chromawolf beside Laurel. She snapped her head to him and furrowed her brows. She shook her head, then whispered something.

"I'll be back," Laurel said. She turned to Alverax and her eyes released their tension. "Can you help me lift him?"

He nodded, and they lifted her grandfather, setting him atop the chromawolf.

Surprisingly, Laurel leaned in for an embrace. Alverax softly returned the gesture as Laurel whispered so only he could hear. "Don't trust them. Meet me at the clocktower in two hours. Alabella is here."

Laurel let go of the embrace and led Asher back the way they'd come.

CHAPTER 43

CHRYS GESTURED for Willow and Roshaw to follow as he crouched behind a large rock formation. Not far beyond, the army of corespawn had amassed, but, instead of battering against the massive Felian wall, they'd dug a hole. A gaping hole wide as a large house, that extended deep into the earth. The massive corespawn monstrosities slid their hands through the ground like dough, kneading and discarding it in colossal chunks.

"If we head further south, we can sneak around them," Chrys said to the others. "We need to find a way in."

"Are you being serious, Chrys?" Roshaw asked. "There are corespawn around the *entire* city. We're not going to sneak around them."

Chrys clenched his jaw. "So, what? We go through the tunnel? You want to fight your way through thousands of corespawn in the dark?"

Roshaw raised his brows. "Chrys, I love you, but you're an idiot."

Chrys scowled.

"We're basically the most powerful people in the world now." Roshaw raised his hands, showing off his multi-colored veins. "We don't have to go through...or under. We can just go over."

"Stones," Chrys said. He'd spent his entire life becoming the pinnacle of a Sapphire threadweaver, but he was so much more now. "Let's stick together, make sure we don't drift apart, and try to stay low. We should still wrap around to the south where there are less gathered, ideally where there are none of the big ones. I don't want anyone getting swiped out of the sky, or any boulders flying our way."

"Sounds good to me." Roshaw nodded. "But first, I want to know how Willow stopped that thing's foot from coming down."

Willow, lifting her chin with a bit of pride, gave him the smallest smirk. "Sapphires can *surge* their threadlight, *pushing* out with an unfocused burst, but it does little good. There's not enough energy to stop the incoming force of any projectiles. Unless you surge both Sapphire and Obsidian at the same time. The Obsidian *breaks* the projectile's acceleration, and the Sapphire *pushes* it away. "

"Heralds, but that's clever."

"I always knew my overwhelming wit would one day save lives," she said with a grin.

Chrys looked out over the field. "We should go. It's only a matter of time before—"

Chaos and clamor bellowed out from beyond the Felian wall.

"Stones," Chrys cursed. "Their tunnel must have breached the city already. We need to go, now!"

The three companions snuck around to the south, finding a section surrounded by relatively few of the corespawn horde, and none of the giants. They *broke* their corethreads and *pushed* off toward the top of the city wall, drifting in an unnaturally straight line. A howling wind blew them slightly off course, but they linked arms and stayed together. As they drifted over the top, they *pulled* on threads connecting them to the wall, and landed back on solid footing.

A pair of guards and a young boy stood paralyzed a short distance away. The guards held swords, but their stance told Chrys enough about their experience.

"It's okay," Chrys said, his own eyes glowing with multicolored threadlight. "We're here to help."

The young boy, Emerald eyes aglow, took a step back.

Chrys raised his hands to calm their fear. "We're going to continue on. Keep an eye out for the corespawn. Do not let them over this wall."

The guards seemed to accept that, relaxing their guard, but still eyeing the three with caution. Chrys waved for the others to follow him and they leapt from atop the wall-walk, *pushing* off the ground for a graceful landing on the dirt far below.

They moved eastward, toward the site of the breached tunnel. Surprisingly, the sound of warfare had ceased. There was no screaming. No battering of metal and wood. No trembling of movement across the ground. Only eerie stillness, sweeping through empty streets.

The cobblestone felt good beneath his feet, a familiar feeling he'd never have expected to miss, and, as they searched the streets for people—for his wife and son—the sense of familiarity soothed the rising tension in his shoulders.

As they walked, Chrys caught Roshaw filling his pocket with a handful of nuts from an abandoned stall.

Suddenly, a green blur came barreling through a side street, accompanied by a young blonde girl. It took Chrys only a moment to recognize *the one that got away.*

"Laurel?"

He took off after her and the others followed.

CHAPTER 44

As Laurel walked through the Zeda camp, the stillness took on the calm serenity of a haunted field, people wandering like unsettled ghosts. Bay helped Laurel place Corian back in his cot, and she took off to the north to find Alabella.

Each Felian city-street brought with it a life of its own. As Laurel wandered through them, trying to find her way back to Alabella's safehouse, she saw some streets bustling with festivities, and other streets so still and quiet that they might have been nothing but a mirage.

She reflected on her experience with the Heralds. The man had told her exactly what she'd wanted to hear, but only after she'd promised them Alabella. Something about that bothered Asher as much as it did her. Either way, her grandfather was now back in the Zeda camp with Bay.

Asher's words, as she'd spoken with the Heralds, chipped away at her hope, but she ignored him. What else could she do? If she didn't try to save her grandfather, she would never forgive herself.

They passed a cart filled with smashed elletberries, a

delicious striped yellow and red fruit that turned the color of dung when mashed together and had a very distinct scent.

Disgust, Asher said beside her.

She picked one from the abandoned cart and ate it—they'd been a favorite of hers growing up—but now, as the flavor touched her tongue, she spit it out. Somehow, it tasted the same but also disgusting at the same time.

"Disgust is right," she said to Asher, wiping her fingers on her pants.

"They're better in jam," a man's voice said.

Laurel turned to see a large man with his massive hand outstretched in greeting.

"Barrick!" she shouted with excitement.

"Heard a girl and a chromawolf were wandering the streets."

"I'm lost," Laurel said. "I'm glad to see you. I need to find Alabella."

"Of course, of course. The house is just around the corner," he said, gesturing for her to follow.

She did and in no time they were entering the small safehouse. Barrick gestured for Asher to stay outside, but the chromawolf refused, and Laurel assured Barrick it would be fine. The large man seemed to doubt her, but also seemed uninterested in fighting them on the matter. The door swung open with a loud, creaky groan. And when they entered, she found Alabella and Sarla sitting beside a small table in the corner of the kitchen.

"Laurel!" Sarla said with excitement. She'd changed her clothes, now wearing a bright red dress that matched the color of her two-toned hair. "We have news!"

Alabella waved her over. "Come, come. It's not safe out there, and there is much to discuss. Like why Asher is with you, and why you smell so terrible." She paused. "Wait, you were there, weren't you?"

"Where?" Laurel asked as she approached the table.

"The battle," Alabella said. "Barrick heard rumors on the streets, people saying the Heralds have returned. Do you know anything about this?"

"It's true," she said. "I saw them with my own eyes."

"Heralds—" Alabella began, but she caught herself and laughed. "Guess I'll need a new curse."

Sarla's eyes grew wide beneath her odd glasses. "I *must* speak with them. Think of all the knowledge they must possess! The questions that we can answer! Infinite possibilities. Imagine the inventions, the progress! Everything could change."

"We did this," Alabella said. "They are here because of the corespawn. I knew there was a connection! We brought back the bloody Heralds!"

"At what cost?" Laurel said.

"Cost be damned!" Alabella said with a laugh. "The loss of a few forgettable lives in exchange for the return of the Heralds? It makes it all worth it. Everything we've done."

"They can tell us why the previous grafts have failed," Sarla said. "They can show us the proper way. Laurel, you can receive a theolith from the Heralds themselves!"

"Speaking of," Alabella said, pushing her chair into place beneath the table and looking to Laurel. "The ship arrived with your new theolith."

Laurel's eyes grew wide, her breath catching in her chest. Threadlight. The gift she longed for more than anything else. The gift she still reached for out of habit, though its influence had long left her behind. If they had a theolith, the warmth of threadlight could once again run from her chest out through her veins, heating her from within, and healing her. A slight tremble returned to her hand, or perhaps it had always been there, and she only now remembered it.

"There is nothing more for us to do but take a trip to the docks." Alabella continued. "I had not expected it so soon, but it is time. Laurel, you are going to be a threadweaver again."

"I..." Laurel trailed off.

What had once seemed impossible was now within her reach. One trip to the docks and she could be a threadweaver again. Then she'd be done with...

Alabella.

The woman the Heralds wanted.

But the Heralds were not what they seemed. As soon as the man had told her he could save her grandfather, Asher had growled into her mind: *lies, evil, run.* No matter how much she wanted to believe the Herald, he'd said it himself. Death cannot be undone.

Laurel wandered in her mind, grasping at truths that shifted like shadows in the night. But still Alabella's words echoed throughout her.

"Laurel?" Alabella said, tilting her head to the side, still waiting for her answer.

But Laurel didn't respond, instead she stood in silence with a single word sizzling on her tongue: why? Why did she want to be a threadweaver? Because it made her feel powerful? The part of her that craved threadlight was a crutch. Her weakness was not that she wasn't a threadweaver, but that she needed it to feel whole.

The truth fueled her, burning energy within her. She didn't need threadlight to be whole. Look at her! Without threadweaving, she'd stood in a sea of mythical creatures and slaughtered them like livestock. She was already strong.

317

She was already enough.

So, she made a decision.

In the blink of an eye, Laurel slipped out the obsidian dagger and thrust it into Alabella's chest. The woman's eyes and veins blazed with Amber threadlight, but it was too late, and the thread-dead blade could not be stopped.

Sarla gasped, her hands springing up to cover her mouth.

"No!" Barrick shouted. He rushed forward with fire in his eyes, but Asher leapt between him and Laurel. The large man attacked the chromawolf, fighting to get through to Alabella, kicking and attempting to wrestle the massive wolf. But Asher was strong and smart. And though he tried not to kill him, Barrick wouldn't stop. He landed a massive fist across Asher's face, and the chromawolf responded with teeth bearing down on the flesh of his neck. Barrick slumped to the floor.

Laurel leaned into Alabella and used the leverage of the knife to shove her up against the wall. Blood drooled from the dying woman's mouth. Laurel stared into her Amber eyes, twisting the knife into her chest. "May the winds guide you."

The door of the safehouse creaked behind her and a familiar—but unexpected—voice screamed, "NO!"

CHAPTER 45

CHRYS RUSHED FORWARD AND, when Asher growled and tried to stop him, he *broke* the chromawolf's corethread and floated helplessly. He rushed to Alabella, shoving Laurel out of the way and ripping the knife out of her chest. He pressed against the open wound with his palm. Blood streamed from the gash, running over his hands like an overflowing kettle. She coughed blood onto his face.

He couldn't let her die. Their plan would fail without her. Aydin was the only other Amber threadweaver, and they couldn't put the fate of the world in the hands of a child.

"Come on! Breathe!" he shouted.

He pushed harder against the wound, but it made no difference. The woman's eyes went cold, and her body sagged to the floor. He watched as the life faded from her Amber eyes.

She was dead.

Chrys turned to Laurel, his lips quivering with rage. "What have you done?"

Laurel took a step back, her brows furrowed, and her

cheeks flushed. "She destroyed Zedalum. She killed my people. She...she tried to kill your family!"

"Child," Willow said from the doorway, standing beside Roshaw. "You have no idea what you've done."

"I'm not a child," Laurel snarled.

"No," Chrys spat. "You're the little woman that damned us all."

"What is your problem?" Laurel said angrily. "We all wanted her dead. You. Me. All of the Zeda wanted revenge. Even the Felians want the Bloodthieves dead! You should be thanking me!"

"I should rip your damn heart out!" Chrys shouted.

"Chrys Valerian!" Willow said sharply. "Laurel had no way of knowing. She did what she thought was right with the information she had. Calm yourself."

Ahhh! Chrys wanted to throw his fists against the wall. Bash them until they were bloody pulps. This was their chance! She was the crux of the plan. Not Aydin. He wasn't strong enough, and they couldn't wait however many years it took. He strangled the hilt of the obsidian blade, barely holding himself back from hurling it across the room.

"No way of knowing what?" Laurel said.

Willow stepped into the room, eyeing the dead man on the floor and the odd woman that both stood quietly in the corner. "The corespawn are only the beginning. There is something much worse coming."

"Worse than the corespawn?" Laurel asked.

Willow nodded. "We came from the Wastelands. Their gods are planning a slaughter. We came to stop them, but we needed her." She gestured to the dead woman.

Laurel clenched her jaw and pursed her lips, looking to Asher for a brief moment. "Why does it have to be Alabella?"

Willow sighed. "We need Amber threadweavers."

"So, take her theolith and put it in someone else," Laurel said. "It doesn't have to be her."

Chrys paused.

"It doesn't work like that," he said.

Laurel kept his gaze, challenging him. "You still have Aydin."

"You know where he is?"

"They're both here," she said. "In the palace."

Tension flowed out of Chrys like a smith's bellows releasing its air. They were alive! He felt the winds of rage within him shift their course, homing in on a greater purpose. He needed to find his family, and he needed to get them to safety.

A light seemed to flicker in Laurel's eyes. "Wait," she said. "We don't need an Amber threadweaver! We have something better."

All eyes in the room turned to her.

"The Heralds!"

"What are you talking about?" Willow asked with a sense of reservation.

"The Heralds have returned! I was there. They fought off the corespawn and won the battle. They've been healing the wounded ever since."

"The Heralds," Chrys said, wincing as he tried to make sense of it all.

"Stones," Willow cursed.

Chrys looked to her. "What?"

"No, no, no, no," Willow repeated, running her hands through her hair. "We were so wrong."

"What?" Roshaw repeated.

Willow looked to Laurel. "Those are not the Heralds."

321

CHAPTER 46

THE HERALDS HAD SPOKEN LITTLE on the journey from the battlefield to the palace, but there was something about the look on their face that disturbed Alverax. A certain sense of displeasure or disdain that seemed uncharacteristic of a god. But still, he'd seen the miracles, and witnessed their victory over the corespawn. He never would have expected such an event possible had he not seen it with his own eyes.

When they entered the throne room, he felt a chill in the air, the shadow of a fear not yet realized. Jisenna stood beside the throne, not daring to claim such nobility in the face of gods. Even her clothing seemed less extravagant. Where she normally wore white and gold, she'd changed to wear black and silver. He found himself smiling when he saw her, the face of peace in a turbulent time.

She dropped to a knee and bowed. "My Heralds," she said. "There are not words to express our joy at your arrival. Not only because of the war at our walls, but because of our long-held belief that you would one day return to reclaim your people."

The male Herald strode forward, head held high. He

looked around the room at the swarm of guards lining each side of the dais. "We will speak to the empress alone," he said.

The guards, hesitating despite the order from their god, bowed and filed out. Alverax moved to join them, but the Herald gestured for him to stay.

"It is my understanding that the two of you are representatives of the people, and, in a small way, you are also meant to represent the two of us." He and the female Herald approached the dais, eyeing Jisenna's clothing that draped along the floor where she knelt. "In the coming days, your loyalty will be tested. We will protect Felia. We will protect its people. But the corespawn are not the only enemy. Other nations are plotting your destruction. With our aid, you will bring all other nations to heel, and Felia will be the greatest empire this world has ever seen."

Jisenna, biting her lip, lifted her head to meet the Heralds' eyes. "We are at peace with the other countries. If you help us stop the corespawn army, surely there is no need for further bloodshed."

"You think you know more than your gods?" the female Herald asked with a hint of spite. "You are a pebble advising the mountain on how to stand firm. Do not question our words."

Jisenna bowed her head. "Of course, my gods."

A knock sounded at the door, and the female Herald moved to open it. A guard spoke to her then retreated into the hallway.

She turned to the male Herald and smiled. "They found the child."

"Good," he said. "Take care of it."

She nodded and exited the throne room, leaving only Alverax, Jisenna, and the male Herald.

"You," he said, turning and gesturing to Alverax. "Do you also question us?"

Alverax bowed his head, suddenly feeling that being in the presence of gods was more dangerous than he'd expected. "No, my Herald. And I don't think that Jisenna would ever question you either. There is a reason the people call her the Mistress of Mercy. She will serve you well."

Jisenna peeked up from her kneeling position and gave him the slightest smile. It was then, with that smallest of gestures, that Alverax realized how much he cared for her. Jisenna was all that was good in the world. She'd made him a better man. She'd made the world a better place with her words and deeds.

The Herald scowled. "What did you say?"

"She will serve you well," Alverax repeated, feeling a sudden tightness in his chest.

"No," the Herald said. "What did you call her?"

Alverax felt a sense of relief. "The Mistress of Mercy. She's built a reputation for being kind and merciful to the people of Felia."

"Mercy," the Herald said, lifting his chin and eyeing Jisenna from narrow eyes. "There can be no mercy."

He raised the Midnight Watcher and the world slowed.

Alverax's chest swelled.

Every bit of breath vanished from his lungs.

A fire raged in his soul.

And he froze as the obsidian blade struck down Jisenna.

A cloud of darkness swirled in his vision, dizzying, burning, pulling at the warmth he felt for her. But it was too late. Still kneeling, the blade struck her neck. It lay embedded in her like she was just another log for the fire.

The Herald yanked it out of her bloody corpse, and she collapsed to the floor with her brown eyes wide open.

He turned to Alverax with a face free of all emotion. "The empress gave her life to strengthen the Heralds. It was a heroic offering, and she is to be remembered for her sacrifice. You understand?"

Alverax nodded, but he barely grasped the words.

She was gone.

Jisenna, the woman who'd saved him.

The woman who'd changed him for the better.

Dead.

"Good," the Herald said, wiping the blade and handing the hilt of the Midnight Watcher to Alverax. "The sword is yours, Destroyer. I have no need of it. So long as you are loyal, I will make you a god among men. Now, go. Tell the people of their empress' sacrifice. They will love her for it."

CHAPTER 47

Chrys felt a shiver crawl up his spine. As soon as the words left her mouth, he knew Willow was right. Two Heralds, showing up to save the city from the corespawn? It had to be Relek and Lylax.

"What do you mean they're *not* the Heralds?" Laurel asked.

Willow's gaze intensified. "Let me guess. One of the Heralds is a tall, light-skinned man, mid-thirties, red hair. The other is a woman, maybe forty, dark hair? They both have eyes that shine like prisms?"

"I don't..." A light turned on in Laurel's eyes. "Gale take me. They're the wastelander gods."

"It doesn't make sense," Roshaw said. "They were coming to destroy the city, not become their gods. Why would they...oh, shit."

"What?" Chrys said.

Roshaw massaged his temples. "What if they *are* the Heralds? The stories say the Heralds just disappeared one day at the height of their power."

"The coreseal," Willow said.

"Exactly," Roshaw said, pointing his finger at her. "The Amber threadweavers bound them far away from here, and now they're back for revenge."

Chrys took in every word, feeling the weight of it pulling on him like a thousand Amber threads. Relek and Lylax were not just the gods of the east, they were the gods of the west as well. But Alchaeus claimed they were coming to exact revenge for their centuries of imprisonment. Why would they become the Heralds again?

There was too much at stake to let the details go undiscovered.

Laurel paled. "They said they needed the Amber threadweavers for their plans, but really they wanted them out of their way."

"Only the Amber threadweavers can create the binding to stop them," Chrys said.

"Gale take me," Laurel whispered to herself. "I did exactly what they wanted."

"You had no way of knowing," Willow said. "We'll find another way."

"We need to find Iriel and Aydin," Chrys added.

"There..." Roshaw hesitated. "There is another option. In Cynosure, there is another Amber threadweaver. A man called Jelium. I would have mentioned it before, but we didn't need him. And I doubt he would be willing to help us."

Chrys scowled. "The lives of hundreds of thousands of people are at stake. If there is someone who *can* help us, I will not take no for an answer."

"You really don't know Jelium," Roshaw said.

"No," Chrys said with fire in his eyes. "And he doesn't know me. If he's the last chance we have at protecting the world, then that's too damn bad. When the world is at stake, you don't get to be a selfish asshole."

"The ship!" Laurel chimed in. "There is a ship at the docks that came from Cynosure. The crew will know how to get back."

"Good," Chrys said with a nod. "Laurel, take the others and prepare the ship."

"Alverax!" she nearly shouted. "I'm supposed to meet him at the clocktower. He's *from* Cynosure. If I can convince him to come, he can guide us when we're there!"

"Fine," Chrys said, tossing her the obsidian blade. "But be at the docks as soon as you can. Roshaw, see if you can figure out which ship it is." He turned to the odd woman in the corner. "What do we do with her?"

Laurel responded as she walked toward the door. "She's harmless."

"Okay." Chrys nodded, looking to the woman. "You are free to leave."

She did, quietly.

Chrys turned back to Roshaw. "At the docks, don't hide that you're a hybrid threadweaver. The crew may need a little convincing. My mother and I will go find Iriel and Aydin in the palace. I want the ship ready to depart as soon as we arrive. There's a chance we'll have an army, or worse, chasing after us."

Laurel rushed out the door with Asher, followed by Roshaw.

Willow looked to Chrys and smiled. "Let's get your family back."

ENTERING the palace was surprisingly easy, as most of the guards were posted around the outer wall, and those still guarding the palace held no fear of human enemy. Willow asked a servant shuffling down one of the hallways where they could find the Zeda guests, and they quickly made their way up two flights of stairs and down a series of winding pathways.

Anxiety prickled away at Chrys' mind. From the proximity to Relek and Lylax, to the search for his wife and son, to the scent of roses filling the palace that now reminded him of the deadly corespawn. Ominous feelings surrounded him like a midnight mist.

As they walked through a particularly wide corridor, Chrys heard a voice, and it set his heart aflame. He ran to the end of the hallway, and, when he glanced around the corner, he saw Iriel, holding Aydin, encircled by a squad of Felian soldiers in black.

He left behind all sense of caution, and ran at them head on, letting a river of threadlight pour through his veins. One by one, he grabbed hold of the corethread of every guard and *broke* it, then, with as much force as he could muster, he *pushed* off the wall behind him, launching forward like a ballista bolt. He crashed into one side of the guards, and his momentum transferred to their weightless bodies, sending them flying down the hallway, crashing off the walls and each other.

Chrys rushed in close to the remaining guards, using a mixture of hand-to-hand combat techniques. With their corethreads *broken*, every blow—even those that were blocked—knocked the guards off balance, tumbling in awkward, weightless flips. He brought his foot up and kicked the final guard, launching him down the hallway in an impossibly straight line.

When he turned and saw her, his heart burst into flame

Iriel.

His heart and soul.

His purpose.

His uncut diamond.

He tried to smile, but his quivering lips refused to form the arch. It seemed a dream to see her again, a trick of the eye. Her eyes swelled with tears, and, when she said his name—no more than a breath slipping from her lips—Chrys shattered. He rushed to her, and she to him, and they embraced with such ferocity that he thought their souls would meld together.

He looked down and saw Aydin, eyes open, cooing in her arms. Such innocence caught up in such chaos. But his father was there now. He would protect him. And someday soon, Aydin would aid in protecting the entire world.

"I knew you would come back," Iriel said.

Chrys smiled, remembering his mother's words. "There is nothing in this world that could have stopped me."

Willow, only a few paces away, smiled. "Chrys, we need to go."

He nodded and took Iriel's hand. "We're getting far away from here. I'll explain everything later."

She lifted his hand, kissed it, and let go.

They took off down the hallway, threadlight in their veins, but just as they rounded the first bend, they stopped in their tracks. In the center of the walkway, accompanied by an older man with a sword, stood Lylax, goddess of the Wastelands, immortal Herald of the west.

And she was smiling.

CHAPTER 48

"You," the goddess said with a smirk. "I thought you were dead."

Chrys' lip twitched. "Iriel, get Aydin to safety. Mother, you know where to go."

As soon as he said the words, he felt a wrenching in his gut. He'd traveled hundreds of miles, through the wastelands, through the core of the earth itself, to reunite with his family, and now he sent them away. But he had no other choice. They couldn't kill Lylax—she was immortal. More people only meant more danger for everyone, especially Aydin.

No, this was Chrys' fight.

He-who-does-not-cower.

The Apogee.

"Chrys," Iriel said. "I can help."

"Not this time," he said, fighting off the pain of their shortened reunion. "I'll be right behind you."

Willow hesitated, then nodded. He knew it would tear her apart to leave him behind after giving so much to get him there, but she understood, and he loved her for it all the more. She tossed the obsidian dagger to Chrys, and they headed down a different hallway, Iriel leading the way.

Chrys spun the dagger in his hand and looked to Lylax. "I heard you can't die. We'll see about that."

The guard standing beside Lylax stepped away, carrying his sword with trepidation.

Chrys rushed her, and her lips curled into a sadistic grin.

Lylax's veins swirled with prismatic color, and threads, like ghostly hands, stretched forth from the ground, grasping at Chrys' legs. His own Obsidian threadlight surged and the artificial threads burst apart beneath him. He continued forward, his voice growing to a crescendo with each step. She tried once more to bind him with threads, and once again he *broke* them without breaking stride.

Finally, she snarled, set her feet, and took off toward him. As they collided, Chrys found an opening and slid the obsidian blade up through her sternum. With both hands free, and one of his still clutching the hilt of the dagger, she set to work pounding into his skull and scraping her raw nails against his skin. He rolled to the side, kicking her away and yanking the dagger back.

He looked to the place where he'd struck with the blade and saw less blood than he would have expected. Instead, threadlight pooled in the wound, swirling as if a gust of wind were drawn into her body. Somewhere far in the east, a wastelander was collapsing into the swamp water as their lifelight was drained by the goddess.

He couldn't kill her—he already knew that—but it had still felt damn good to run her through with the blade. The truth was that he didn't need to win; he just needed to keep her occupied long enough for his wife and mother to escape.

The man who'd accompanied her was standing off to the

side, closer to Chrys now than Lylax. He stood quietly marveling at the immortality of one of the Heralds—this fight would cement her godhood in his eyes. But that didn't matter...Chrys had an idea.

He took off toward the man, *pushing* off the wall behind him and *pulling* on the wall in front, blasting through the air faster than he'd ever moved. He crashed with such force that he was sure the man was dead on impact. Chrys felt a pain surge up through his legs as he hit, but threadlight coursed through his veins in record amounts, providing strength and a small trace of immediate healing like never before.

When he looked up, Lylax was walking toward him, frowning with Autelle's lips and scowling with her eyes. Chrys reached down and lifted the man's longsword off the ground. It had a good length, though it was lighter than he'd have preferred. He had to be careful. As a prismatic thread-weaver, Lylax could *push* and *pull* the blade just as easily as he could. It would make the fight more dangerous. He hoped that her inability to do the same to the obsidian dagger would be enough to confuse her attention.

Suddenly, he felt a sense of vertigo wash over him, and the walls seemed to close aroud him. Something reached into his soul, grasping at his lifelight. It was her. She was trying to do what Relek had done in the mountains to the soldiers. Chrys threw his will against it, just as he had done to Relek in his own mind, and he felt the attack retreat.

"You're out of practice," Chrys said, feeling a sense of relief.

She glanced at the sword in his hand. "Perhaps, but you are only delaying the inevitable. You cannot kill me, and you will make a mistake soon enough."

"You lost once. You can lose again."

At the final word, Chrys pounced at her, slashing down

hard with the longsword. She *pushed* on the blade, sending it wide, so he thrust in with the obsidian dagger in his offhand. She *pushed* again, but the blade continued forward, cutting at her side. Her dress slit and the skin cut open for a moment before resealing.

Chrys reached out to her corethread and *broke* it. She responded with the same, while simultaneously creating a new corethread for herself from artificial threads. Chrys *broke* those as well, and soon they both hovered above the air, weightless. This was the moment his idea would succeed or fail, and, if it failed, he would have no choice but to run.

He pointed the longsword at her, letting threadlight build up within him until his veins were ready to burst, then released it all in a surge of energy, *pushing* the longsword in a straight line. He then reached out to the blade with his mind, and—thanks to Willow—created a dome of energy around it. The sword shot forward in a blur of light and, when Lylax tried to *push* it out of the way, the dome rejected her. The longsword shot through her chest, impaling her, and sending her weightless body blasting backward into the nearest wall. The force of the momentum embedded the blade in the wall through Lylax's stomach to the hilt. The goddess choked, hanging on the wall like a tortured painting.

As soon as his corethread reappeared, Chrys walked over to Lylax. Her own gravity had also returned, and her body sagged against the longsword, coughing and choking, though no blood came out.

"You will pay for this!" she spat.

Chrys calmly cut off a piece of his tunic, tied it over her eyes and tossed the sword back to the dead man. "This isn't over."

Then, he ran.

CHAPTER 49

ALVERAX RAN OUTSIDE, gasping for air, and dropped the sword as he collapsed to the ground. His heart throbbed in his chest, pounding with such fervor it threatened to burst. He tried to breathe, but each breath was a war that he wasn't sure he wanted to win. Nothing mattered anymore. He didn't *care* anymore. Jisenna, the woman who'd cut her way into the deepest part of his soul, was gone.

He looked up into the night sky. The sea of stars blurred and shimmered, distorted by the layer of tears that poured from his eyes.

It wasn't fair. Not her. Anyone but her. She was too *good* to deserve such an end.

The Moon's Little Sister sparkled in the darkness. Beside it, the star that Jisenna had chosen for her sister. He scoured the sky for the brightest star he could find, it was what Jisenna deserved, but none shone as bright as the Moon's Little Sister. And in that moment he realized, that *was* Jisenna's star. It had been all along. Her father was the sun, Chailani was the moon, and she was the little sister that outshone them all.

A small spec shimmered beside the cluster, and Alverax recognized it as the star that little Kyan had chosen for his father. A simple gesture, meaningless in the grand scheme of life, but significant for the little boy to move on—something Alverax had yet to do. In that moment, he decided it was time. Not for his father. For himself, and because he knew that it was what Jisenna would have wanted. She had once said that their path would require them to change in uncomfortable ways. And as uncomfortable as it felt, he knew it was time.

The endless sky of stars grew in clarity as his resolve overcame his sadness. He searched for a star for his father. Something small, discreet, perhaps easy to forget. The thought gave him pause, and he realized that he didn't want to forget his father. He may not have been around much, but, when he was, he'd been good to him. There were no bad memories of his presence, only sad memories of his absence.

There, to the east of the Broken Wheel, three stars clustered together. He chose the smaller of the three and committed it to memory. That would be his father's star. Each time he looked into the sky in the dead of night, no matter where he was, his father would be with him now. He felt an odd comfort in the statement, but also found himself missing the man more than he would have ever expected.

Alverax picked up the Midnight Watcher, though it sickened him to do so, and promised himself that, come what may, he would avenge Jisenna. Gods or not, the Heralds would pay for what they'd done.

He ran from the palace, remembering Laurel's words. He couldn't avenge Jisenna alone—he knew that. A dark hollowness permeated through him as he traveled through the streets of Felia. To his mind, there were no shops. There were no people. There was only the cobblestone beneath his feet that carried him forward.

Soon enough, he arrived at the clocktower. The wide plaza was empty, though bits of food and fabric dotted the stone from where tents had sold their goods earlier in the day. He stared at the slow turning of the long arm of the clocktower, wishing that he had the power to turn it back. But instead, as if taunting him, it spun forward with disregard—a cruel reminder that some deeds cannot be undone.

By the time Laurel arrived, side-by-side with her chromawolf companion, Alverax wasn't sure how long he'd been staring at the clocktower. A chilling numbness prickled at his skin, and, where he should have felt some measure of curiosity, or danger, or even hope, he felt only emptiness.

"Alverax!" Laurel shouted, running the rest of the way. She came up beside him, but he didn't move. He simply stood, continuing to stare at the large, ticking hands overlooking the empty plaza. "You okay? You don't look so good."

"I'm fine," he said.

Laurel looked up at the clocktower to see what he was staring at. "I need you to listen, and I know it might sound crazy, but the Heralds...they aren't what you think they are."

His mind seized at the mention. He turned his eyes to her, feeling a bit of heat return to his chest.

"Gods or not, they are evil. Chrys knows more, but whatever good they're doing here, it's a lie. Something bad is going to happen, unless we stop them." She paused, letting the words sink in. "Alverax, we need your help."

Alverax nodded to her, accepting the offer, despite not knowing the details. He knew her words were true before she spoke them. There was something *wrong* about the Heralds. They weren't deities come to save the people like the Felians believed, and Alverax no longer cared about his

337

duty or his responsibilities. He glanced down at the Midnight Watcher at his side and wanted only revenge. "What do you need me to do?"

A gleam flickered in her eye. "How would you feel about taking a trip to Cynosure?"

CHAPTER 50

WHEN CHRYS ARRIVED at the docks, it didn't take long to find their ship. He went directly to Iriel and embraced her again, this time kissing her with the enthusiasm of a man half his age.

He caught up with Roshaw and met the crew, who seemed at awe of their multi-colored eyes. They spent their time waiting for Laurel and finishing last minute preparations of the ship. The captain and crew were six others. When one refused to work for Roshaw, he'd *broken* the man's corethread and kicked him off the ship, flying out into the ocean. From that point forward, the crew seemed eager to serve.

More importantly, Chrys learned about Jelium, the Amber threadweaver they would recruit to their cause. Although Cynosure had no formal government, Chrys could tell from Roshaw's words that Jelium was the closest the city had to a king. How a single man could have one hundred brides, Chrys could not understand, but it did tell something of the man's disposition.

Roshaw went below deck, but not before Chrys saw him

sneaking a glance to the heavens and smiling at the stars he'd named for Agatha, Esme, and Seven.

Finally, as the moon hit its highest point, Chrys spotted two figures and a chromawolf striding forward from beyond a distant building. As they approached, he noticed the fine clothing of her new companion, a young Felian man with a sheathed sword at his side. Laurel had a pension for rash choices, and Chrys hoped that her new companion was not one such decision.

Willow joined Chrys at the starboard railing.

As Iriel did the same, her eyes lit up as she saw the two approaching. "Alverax!" she said excitedly. "Chrys, that's the young man that saved Aydin and I in the Fairenwild."

Surprised, Chrys took another glance at the young man. He was tall, handsome in a morose sort of way, with strong shoulders. "Then I owe him everything," Chrys said quietly.

The captain and crew, even having been warned, backed away from Asher as the final three travelers boarded the ship called the Pale Urchin. The crew began to settle, and the ship groaned as it pushed away from the Felian harbor. The sun was beginning to rise in the east, and the winds were strong for sailing. Chrys felt a sense of accomplishment as the ship departed. They had a goal, and they had a plan. It was all coming together.

When Roshaw surfaced from below deck, he was smiling and waving his hands. "Finally got the damn thing to fit. Didn't expect—"

He stopped himself mid-sentence and his face paled.

The young man, Alverax, leaned forward. "Dad?"

EPILOGUE

FAR BELOW THE SURFACE, in a dark cave lit only by a few haphazardly placed photospores, an old man stared into a dome of threadlight. There were so many truths Alchaeus had learned over the centuries, truths few could have learned without immortality to guide them. But the *convergence* was still a mystery. A congealed mound of threadlight that sparked with the light of the world. Had it always been there? Or had it grown over time? Were the convergences the source of the world's threadlight? Or was there yet another source?

He'd traveled through the portal countless times over the years during his many explorations, but as Chrys and the others stepped through, a new question beckoned him. A question born from Chrys' words. A question far beyond his own understanding. But it was close. A brilliant fruit ripe to be plucked if he could only reach it.

The string in his hand dangled from his fingertips, taunting him. Teasing him. His own words mocked his understanding. It was possible. It had to be. But there would be consequences. There always were. He took the string between his thumb and index finger on each hand and held it up. His eyes traced it from end to end.

It would explain the answer to another riddle. He replayed his trips through the *convergence*, visualizing each step, each feeling. There was something there.

Alchaeus took a deep breath, feeling the youthfulness of his younger body. If he was right, perhaps he could stop his siblings. If not, then he would need to enter the waters. He would need to be stronger for the coming events, both physically and mentally. An air of sorrow washed over him at the thought of what he would have to do.

He stepped toward the *convergence*, taking in the massive, warbling mass of threadlight. It beckoned to him, pulsing with otherworldly energy, calling him to bathe in its transcendence.

He put the string in his pocket and stepped in.

End of Book Two

IF YOU ENJOYED THE STORY, please take a moment to leave a review and tell your friends!

ACKNOWLEDGMENTS

When I published Voice of War in 2020, I had no idea what the future had in store for me as an author, or the series as a whole. I have been blown away at the support of all of the authors I've met, the bloggers and readers that have given me a chance, and the kind reviews that have given me so much inspiration to forge forward.

Speaking of forge (nailed it), I couldn't have an acknowledgements without expressing gratitude for The Fantasy Forge, the writing group I belong to. They have helped me in so many ways, including constantly pointing out my weird first-draft metaphors that make absolutely no sense. Thank you all!

Once again, I have to thank my incredibly patient wife for listening to an endless stream of weird ideas as I work through these books. I could not ask for someone more supportive or helpful to have by my side.

Thank you to my beta readers: Brandon Williams, Sean McQuay, Alma Madsen, Jason Nugent, and a special thanks to Kerri McBookNerd, who helped review some key areas of sensitivity in this book. Some of you are returning beta readers, and some of you are new, but you all had crucial insights that helped fix some of the core issues in the early drafts.

And to my readers. THANK YOU. Every time you leave a review, post to Instagram, tweet, or reach out directly, it gives me an added portion of tenacity to continue onward. I hope above all else that I can create a story that entertains and inspires you.

To the rest of you who I may have missed, thank you. I'm in awe at your support and hope that you've enjoyed part two of this journey!

ABOUT THE AUTHOR

Website www.zackargyle.com
Twitter www.twitter.com/SFFAuthor
Facebook www.facebook.com/ZackArgyleAuthor/
Instagram www.instagram.com/ZackArgyleAuthor

CPSIA information can be obtained
at www.ICGtesting.com
Printed in the USA
LVHW020057230321
682109LV00011B/345